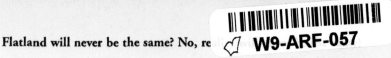

"Rudy Rucker's *Spaceland* is a homage to Abbott that challenges readers to imagine what life might be like in a world with four spatial dimensions. . . . It is Rucker's determination to one-up the dimensional explorations of *Flatland* that gives *Spaceland* [its] appeal."
— *The New York Times*

"The current crop of SF humorists . . . don't seem to pack the same intellectual punch as their forebears. With one exception that is: the astonishing Rudy Rucker. . . . Like the mutant offspring of Jonathan Swift and Philip José Farmer, Rudy Rucker finds mankind a species whose glorious buffoonery is matched only by its capacity to laugh at itself."
— *The Washington Post*

"*Spaceland* puts the hyper into hyperspace and the high into higher dimensions. A fast-paced tribute to the classic *Flatland* that challenges all of our comfortable assumptions about the world we inhabit."
—Ian Stewart, author of *Flatterland* and *The Annotated Flatland*

"Filled with nicely drawn characters, a good story line and an engaging look at the inhabitants of a weird space-time continuum, Silicon Valley, *Spaceland* is a must read for geeks of all dimensions."
—SFRevu.com

"As always, Rucker laces his hard science with ample doses of humor to create an SF adventure for the dot-com generation."
—*Library Journal*

"Books on higher dimensions with such beauty, breadth, and insight are rare. Dr. Rucker's *Spaceland* is chock-full of mind-boggling images and ideas. The eclectic Rucker is both a mathematician and science-fiction guru, and with the cold logic of the one and the inspired vision of the other, he covers an array of topics sure to stimulate your imagination and sense of wonder at the incredible vastness of our mathematical universe."
—Clifford Pickover, author of *Surfing Through Hyperspace*

Books by Rudy Rucker

Novels

As Above, So Below: A Novel of Pieter Bruegel
(forthcoming from Tor)
Spaceland (from Tor)
Realware
Freeware
The Hacker and the Ants
The Hollow Earth
Wetware
The Secret of Life
Master of Space and Time
The Sex Sphere
Software
White Light
Spacetime Donuts

Nonfiction

Saucer Wisdom (from Tor)
All the Visions
Mind Tools
The Fourth Dimension
Infinity and the Mind
Geometry, Relativity and the Fourth Dimension

Collections

Gnarl!
Seek!
Transreal!
The Fifty-Seventh Franz Kafka

SPACELAND

Rudy Rucker

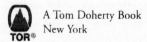

A Tom Doherty Book
New York

SPACELAND

Copyright © 2002 by Rudy Rucker

http://www.mathcs.sjsu.edu/faculty/rucker/spaceland.htm

Edited by David G. Hartwell

Illustrations by Taral Wayne

Book design by Jane Adele Regina

A Tor Book
Published by Tom Doherty Associates, LLC
175 Fifth Avenue
New York, NY 10010

www.tor.com

Tor® is a registered trademark of Tom Doherty Associates, LLC.

Library of Congress Cataloging-in-Publication Data

Rucker, Rudy v. B. (Rudy von Bitter).
  Spaceland / Rudy Rucker.
    p. cm.
  "A Tom Doherty Associates book."
  ISBN 0-765-30366-3 (hc)
  ISBN 0-765-30367-1 (pbk)
  1. Computer industry—Employees—Fiction. 2. Fourth dimension—Fiction. I. Title.

PS3568.U298 S73 2002
813'.54—dc21   2001059661

Printed in the United States of America

D 10 9 8 7 6 5 4

For Tom Banchoff, Kee Dewdney,
Martin Gardner, and John Walker

CONTENTS

It was the last day of the 1999th year of our era. The pattering of the rain had long ago announced nightfall; and I was sitting in the company of my wife, musing on the events of the past and the prospects of the coming year, the coming century, the coming Millennium.

—Edwin A. Abbott, *Flatland*

New Year's Eve

My idea for handling December 31, 1999, was that Jena and I should fix a nice meal, drink champagne, watch TV, and stay clear of the Y2K bug. I bulldozered over Jena's gently voiced objections. I figured that at midnight the power would go out and the rioting would start. We'd lock the door and light some candles, and Jena would smile at me and kiss me and say I'd been right to make us stay home. In my mind, that's what was going to happen. And, hey, even if I was wrong about the rioting, we'd miss a Millennial traffic jam.

My secret hope was to get Jena in bed *before* midnight so we could be in each other's arms right at the moment of the Big Flip, all those nines rolling over to zeroes and the two of us close as close could be. That was the right way to usher in a new Millennium! Yes! Not that I came out and told this to Jena, as I knew very well that she would have preferred to go somewhere complicated and expensive.

Jena liked sex even more than I did, but she didn't like for me to make assumptions about when we'd do it. It was always supposed to be some kind of surprise. A spontaneously occurring romantic impulse. A force of Nature, unpredictable as an earthquake or a hurricane. When in fact it was inevitably every one to four days. One of the ways I passed my time at work was to update an Excel spreadsheet tracking our sex frequency. I had a formula in one of the cells to compute what I called the DBS index. A rolling average of the days between sex acts. When the DBS rose above three, it was time to turn on the charm. Buy flowers, talk about Jena's problems, do like that. Not that I always did. To tell the truth, a high DBS was my fault as often as it was Jena's. Even though I talk a good game, I'm not the most highly sexed guy around.

Thanks to a stressful Christmas visit with Jena's mother and stepfather back in Prescott, Arizona, the DBS was up to 4.1. I should have at least planned to take Jena out for dinner on New Year's Eve. Put us both in a romantic mood. But by the time the facts hit my radar, every place was booked and full, as things always were in California. Not that I really and truly looked that hard for someplace to go. I was fixated on my game plan. Hit the sack before midnight and the romance would take care of itself!

Late in the afternoon of New Year's Eve I drove over to the Kencom campus in San Jose to bag this experimental TV set from our lab. In my pinheaded ignorance of what women actually care about, I had the notion that if I brought home some really cool electronics, then Jena would be down with staying home on New Year's Eve. As if.

Spazz Crotty was there in the lab, busy at his giant flat-screen monitor as usual. A tall, skinny guy, late twenties, a few years younger than me. I'm thirty-one. Spazz was wearing baggy, long skater pants, black leather sneakers, and a T-shirt with The Finger on it. He had short, bleached-blonde hair, with the sides of his head shaved. He had a ring in his nose and a big silver stud up on the top of his ear. I kind of admired him. Spazz was cool. He had tattoos. Jena had always wanted me to get a tattoo.

"Yo, Spazz."

He did a voice recognition thing, answering me without looking up. "Hi boss. Want to watch me write some TRACE statements? Nasty bug in the serialization code." Even though Ken Wong had hired me on as the product manager for the 3Set development team, I knew next to nothing about programming, and Spazz never let me forget it.

"You shouldn't be working, Spazz. Today's a holiday. The Big Flip."

"So what're you doing here?" Spazz broke into coughing, having trouble getting his voice started up. He coughed a lot.

"I want to take the 3Set home and test it out. You haven't broken it, have you?"

"It's working," said Spazz. He had a hoarse, wheezy voice, and he talked very slowly. Every time Spazz spoke, he made it sound like he was letting you in on a big secret. "I was watching the Teletubbies this morning. I was getting really good depth. But then when I went to save and reload the image I got a power-switch crash."

I felt a surge of annoyance. "We don't need the freaking save and reload. We took it outta the beta spec last week. It's developer gold plating. You were at the meeting. Why are we even talking about this? It's New Year's Eve, dude."

Spazz turned and stared at me for a minute, fingering the hoop in the side of his nose. And then he smiled, suddenly happy as a kid let out of school. "Thanks for reminding me. What time is it? I'm supposed to meet Tulip at home." He glanced back at his screen. "Jesus, it's almost six. I'll ifdef out the serialization code, do a rebuild, and close it down." He hit a few keys and the build messages began scrolling down the bottom of his screen. No warnings, no errors. We were almost ready for production. "You're taking the 3Set?" said Spazz. "Does Ken know?"

"I might have mentioned it to him," I said. Though of course I hadn't. No way would Ken want the 3Set leaving the lab. It was so secret that even his venture capitalists didn't really know what it was. Not to mention the fact that the 3Set was, theoretically at least, dangerous enough to be a liability risk.

Spazz grinned. "You're the boss, Joe." He copied the fresh build of the 3Set driver software to a Zip disk for me, shut down his computer, put on his leather jacket, and held the doors for me while I carried the 3Set out to my leased silver Explorer SUV, a premium model with the full Eddie Bauer trim package. The 3Set was a heavy mofo, with a thing like a fish tank instead of a picture tube. A true 3D display. The chips in it had a way of combining successive TV images to build up a 3D image inside the tank. It was pretty neat, when it was working. The risk aspect had to do with the fact that there was a hard vacuum inside the tank, and it could conceivably implode. But I was cool with that. I set it onto my back seat and fastened the seat belt around it.

Spazz's red Japanese motorcycle was next to my car; he took out his keys and unfastened his helmet from it. "We're outta here, huh Joe?" said Spazz. It was getting dark. There was a Wells Fargo bank right across the lot, with people lined up to get money out of the cash machine. I'd already gotten mine.

"What are you doing tonight, man?" I asked Spazz.

"Riding up to San Francisco with Tulip."

"Was it hard to get reservations?"

Spazz gave me a pitying look. "The taquerias on Mission Street don't take reservations. You're so uptight, Joe. It's like you're middle-aged. I bet you're planning to stay home and watch TV. On the 3Set, right?"

"You're gonna wish you were with me when all the lights go out," I said. "The roads'll be gridlocked. It'll be straight outta *Mad Max.*"

"I have to admit I'm just a little bit worried, too," said Spazz earnestly, using his slowest, hoarsest voice. "I have this mental image of the Earth as being like one of those chocolate oranges, pre-cut into time-zone-sized segments. And when the Millennium hits, the segment with Tonga works its way free and tumbles off alone into black space, the sun glinting on the curved sector of its rind, with Tonga's part of the South Pacific all sloshing off the segment's edges. It's probably already happened, dude, but they're covering it up. And presumably the rest of the South Pacific is pouring down into the huge, wedge-shaped gap that Tonga's segment left, it's a thousands-of-mile-high waterfall that vaporizes into steam or even into plasma when it hits the molten nickel of the Earth's exposed core. It's gonna drain the Pacific dry. And more and more of the segments are falling out, needless to say. I wonder how soon the drop in the water level will be noticeable in the San Francisco Bay." Spazz broke off in a fit of coughing, bending nearly double.

I looked at him for a minute. He was putting me on. "Freak."

"I'm articulating the basic fear," said Spazz, straightening up and fingering the stud in his ear. "It's atavistic. The Y2K bug is a psychological displacement mechanism. People are terrified of the Millennium, and, ashamed of their fear, they project it onto this specific little computer problem. A niggling factoid to talk about instead of facing their inner Void. Hell, I know some of the hackers who helped hype the bug. It's a hoax on managers, man. A way to take down the industry for a few billion bucks."

"I hope you're right," I said, though really I hoped he was wrong. "Look, why don't you and Tulip stop by my place on your way up to the City. We're on your way." Spazz and Tulip rented a crappy shack in the Santa Cruz mountains even though Tulip was a very well paid process engineer at a chip fab.

"You're really staying home with Jena?" asked Spazz. "Where do you live, anyway?"

He looked slightly interested. Spazz had met Jena at the Christmas party and they'd hit it off. Jena was a real live wire in social situations. As a marketing manager for a web tool company called MetaTool, face-to-face interactions were her thing.

"In Los Perros," I answered. "We bought a townhouse next to Route 85. It's at 1234 Silva View Crescent. Just a starter place till Kencom goes IPO."

Ah, the IPO, more eagerly awaited than the second coming. Until Kencom went public, our shares of founder's stock were toilet paper. The thing was, Kencom still hadn't come up with the killer product that would galvanize the market. For a dot-commer, Ken Wong was kind of old school. We knew we wanted something to do with communication, fine, but Ken had this obsession with making our new product from wires and plastic and chips—instead of from Java and press releases. Frankly, the 3Set looked like a bit of a dog. I mean, a full-grown man could barely even carry the thing. Where was that at, in this day and age?

I wrote my home address on the back of a Kencom business card and handed it to Spazz. "Stop by around nine."

"Maybe I will," said Spazz with a wheezy laugh. "Jena's hot." What a thing to say. Sometimes it was like techs didn't realize that I actually had a mind. Like I was an ape, or a robot.

On the way home I picked up a fresh loaf of sourdough, a couple of Dungeness crabs, a bottle of Dom Perignon, and some roses.

Jena was just getting out of the shower, wet and gorgeous. She was half Yavapi, and she had that classic Native American face with a strong, perfect nose and high cheekbones. Her eyes were narrow, as if designed for seeing across great distances, their color a clear shade of hazel. On her mother's side Jena was Norwegian. She had a good figure, pink skin and hair light colored enough to dye to regulation-issue California blonde. Did I mention that she had cutely bowed lips? She was the kind of woman that guys turned around to stare after in the street.

Jena was happy with the roses I'd brought; she laid them on the built-in dressing table while she started drying her hair in front of the mirror, standing there naked. I sat on the bed watching her, drinking her in, the curves and colors of her body. Jena always enjoyed being the focus of my attention.

"I got champagne and two Dungeness crabs," I told her.

"That sounds festive." She gave me a warm smile in the mirror. I walked over and kissed her. Held her in my arms. She made a soft noise and leaned back against me. I should have put a move on her right then and there, but I was kind of into getting the 3Set installed. And it seemed better to save the sex for midnight.

So I went out in the living room and got to work. I had to plug the 3Set into the wall, hook it to the cable TV line, run a USB cable from the 3Set to my computer, plug a Zip drive with the 3Set software into my computer's parallel port, and jack a Playstation controller into the game port for changing the viewpoint on the 3Set. The more tech we get, the more wires we need. It's like a law of nature. N times N or something. I had to get down on all fours under my composition board OfficeMax desk to figure out the wires, which is something I hate. Rooting around in the dust bunnies knowing you're probably getting it wrong.

"What are you doing?"

"Jena!" I scraped the side of my head getting back out. Jena was wearing a party outfit, a shiny little red dress. She had her makeup thing happening, and her dyed blonde hair was piled up in this slutty heap with plastic clips holding it in place. I loved it when she did her hair like that. "You look so sexy. I'm lucky you married me." We'd lived together for three years before tying the knot. We were working day jobs and taking night courses at University of

Colorado in Boulder. Right at the end of our courtship Jena had actually been close to leaving me. Marriage had seemed like the best way to solve our problems.

"You'll do," said Jena, laughing a little. She liked it when I flattered her. "What's that tank thing on your desk? Another video game?"

"That's the 3Set I'm always talking about. From Kencom. It takes network TV and makes it look three-dimensional. I brought it home for watching the Millennium shows. Let me shower off real quick and put on a clean shirt. You want a glass of wine? Or should we start with the champagne?"

"I'm not going to drink that much, so let's have the good stuff first. We can wait till you're done with your shower." She started looking through the CDs. "I'll put some music on."

I showered, shaved and put on some clean khakis, a tight white T-shirt and a dark brown silk shirt. Jena had her techno house music on the speakers and was doing a little dance. We'd made it to a few raves and she liked them a lot—not the drugs so much, but the scene itself. The dancing and the way people looked. The house music was really filling the place up. Party time! I danced with her for a little while.

Our living-dining room isn't very big, just a white drywall box with white carpeting and white mini-blinds over windows that don't really open. We hadn't gotten around to doing anything yet in the way of decorating it. Since we knew we'd be moving up soon, we'd gotten really inexpensive furniture. Our dining table and chairs were that shiny, molded, one-piece-of-plastic patio stuff: a round white table and a couple of chairs. Cost about seven bucks. Our only good furniture was our king bed and our beige leather couch.

Jena had put the roses in a souvenir beer mug and had prettied up the table with a tablecloth and some bright orange candles. We'd never done dinner at home with candles or a tablecloth before;

usually we ate something at work and just grazed on junk when we got home. I turned the music down a notch, sliced the bread, and set out the crabs. They'd looked forbidding in the market: big, red, and impregnable. But the guy behind the fish counter had taken them apart and cracked their shells all over with a hammer. I had a jar of cocktail sauce to go with the crabs, and Jena had put together a fancy salad from the supermarket salad bar. While I'd been out, she'd gone to the store, too.

We sat down at our little table and I opened the champagne, with Jena telling me to be careful. The cork bounced off the low ceiling and just missed her. I caught the first big spurt of foam in her glass, then filled mine.

"Here's to the end of a great year!" I said.

"It's been rather momentous," said Jena, smiling and clinking her glass with mine.

"We got married in June, moved to Silicon Valley in August, and bought a house in September," I said. "Heavy duty. Instant respectability."

"Maybe we're a little too respectable," giggled Jena. "Can you believe we're managers in Silicon Valley computer companies? Here's my business card." She peeled a piece of crab shell off one of the legs and handed it to me.

"Nice texture," I said pretending to read the piece of shell. "You must be a player. Let's network. We'll do more than talk the talk . . ."

"We'll walk the walk," completed Jena. It was one of my favorite phrases. She tapped my wrist with the sharp end of the crab leg. "How do you eat these things?"

"The man at Whole Foods said to just keep picking out the meat with your fingers," I said. "He says that most of it's in this big middle part. The body. You should have seen these puppies with their shells on. Like aliens or giant insects."

"How appetizing. Tonight's special is Venusian cockroach." Jena pulled a piece of meat out of her crab leg and dipped it in the cocktail sauce. "Mmm. It's *succulent*. Firm and fresh. Not like those frozen King crab things back in Colorado. Did you ever have those? Buck Sawyer was always taking me to the Red Lobster and ordering King crab. It tastes like cardboard." Buck Sawyer had been one of the guys Jena almost left me for. An old boyfriend, never quite fully out of the picture. A car salesman, a real lowlife. Jena gave me an innocent look and fished a big lump of crabmeat out of the crab's body. "Succulent," she repeated. Jena liked words, they were pets that she played with.

"I think this is the first time I've ever eaten crab in my life," I said. "I was scared it might be fishy. But it's not. The sauce helps. Horseradish. More champers?"

"Right on," said Jena. "Is the salad all right?"

"Sure! I like all the stuff you put in it. It's great with the crab."

We ate and drank for a couple of minutes, the house music pooting and tweeting along in the background. So far so good.

"Three and a half hours to go," said Jena presently. "That's a long time. Do you really think the power will fail?" She pursed her lips the way she did when she was thinking.

"We're ready," I said, not wanting to get into a debate on this. "We've already got our candles happening. We got that candle holder for our wedding, huh?"

"Candelabrum," said Jena. "My Aunt Sue gave it to us. She said it's sterling silver. And she gave us this tablecloth, too. 'For your little celebrations,' she said. Aunt Sue is such the romance hound. She almost caught my bouquet herself. I didn't want *orange* candles, but they were the last thing left on the shelves. You're not the only one who's freaking out. Oops." She hopped to her feet. "I forgot to turn out the lights. Glamour. Not to mention disguising the fact that we're in a four-hundred-thousand-dollar white cardboard packing crate next to a freeway."

"Aw, come on, Jena. Hey, it looks good with the lights out. Did you get a lot of candles?"

"A whole box. Happy Halloween! The orange glow is nice, isn't it? You look pretty, Joe. Remember how back in college you'd light a candle when I spent the night in your room? You had it stuck into a Ruffino wine bottle." We'd dated for a couple of years before moving in together.

"The only way to go," I said. Actually, the candle had been my roommate's. I glanced at my watch. "It's almost nine. I'll fire up the 3Set and see how the Millennium comes down on the East Coast."

"Oh great," said Jena. "We spend the next three hours watching TV. Do they still do Dick Clark? Or is he finally dead? I hope so."

"Did I mention that this guy from work might stop by?" I offered.

"Visiting the shut-ins," said Jena. "Who?"

"Spazz Crotty. You met him at the Christmas party. Skinny guy with bleached blonde hair and a nose ring?"

"Oh, I remember him all right," said Jena. "He kept staring at my butt. I was like 'Take a picture, it lasts longer.' "

"You said that to him?"

"You know how I get when I have margaritas. He laughed it off. He was embarrassed. I said it in front of his girlfriend. This tall girl with really nice smooth brown skin—though she did have some acne scars—she had some kind of flower name, but I was so wasted I don't—"

"Tulip," I said. "Yeah, I told Spazz and Tulip to come by around nine."

"Well good," said Jena. "We can share our dessert. I bought this decadent tiramisu cake."

I got the 3Set going and we watched the Millennium roll over in Time Square. I thought it was kind of cool that we were the only people in the world watching it on a 3Set, but Jena wasn't impressed. The 3Set image was pale and grainy and didn't look all that three-dimensional; it only fattened up when the camera was on one person who was moving a lot. Jena said it was like watching a motel TV, which was, she added, appropriate for the kind of place we were living in. The champagne wasn't doing my cause a lot of good.

The ball dropped and the lights in Times Square kept right on shining. Everyone was laughing and yelling and partying their asses off. I was sort of surprised there was no disaster.

"We should be out with other people," said Jena, slitting her eyes. "I can't believe we're sitting in this crappy little townhouse watching your weird television. I feel like such a *loser*." She'd poured out the last bit of the champagne. "Where's Spazz and Tulip?" she continued. "When did you say they'd come?"

"Um, I'll call him."

So I got Spazz on his cell phone, and, naw, man, he's not gonna make it over, him and Tulip came straight up to San Francisco, with the bike it wasn't all that hard, and now they're down near the waterfront dancing and waiting for the fireworks. It's great. I should've come, too. Maybe I'll see him and Tulip on TV. Spazz telling me all this like it's something really worth hearing, and stopping every few sentences to cough. I said good-bye and hung up.

"He's not gonna make it," I told Jena, not looking directly at her. I stared into the tank of our 3Set like I was seeing something interesting. There were a lot of chips with micro mirrors on the bottom, the mirrors vibrating like crazy and painting virtual images up into the empty space of the tank. Like those saucer-shaped novelty items that make it look as if there's a quarter floating up above them? That's kind of the way the 3Set worked. There was no air in the tank, because if there were air, the supersonic vibrations of the mirrors would hit you and it would be bad. Poach your brain like an egg. As it was, the thing gave off a pretty loud hum—more like a whine than a hum. And in there I could see Dick Clark and some girl singers; they were about six inches high, and they looked pretty much like flat cut-outs, except that whenever they moved, the chips managed to fatten them up to look 3D. For being so expensive and complicated and dangerous, the 3Set was kind of a cheesy product. We were probably never going to ship it, and Kencom was never going to go IPO. I was wasting my time working there. I was a loser and my wife was mad at me.

"How about some margaritas?" said Jena.

"Um . . ."

"I'll make them," she said.

If Jena got into the margaritas we were doomed. "Look," I said. "Maybe we should go out."

"*Right* on. Where?"

"Hell, we'll go bar-hopping in Los Perros. We can be there in ten minutes."

"Fun." Jena smiled and looked relaxed for the first time that evening. I realized how stupid I'd been acting. If Jena was happy, so was I. When it came down to it, making Jena happy was what I cared about the most. Even my geeky little DBS index—it wasn't really about the numbers. It was just my idiotic way of measuring our relationship. If only I could ever remember for more than fifteen seconds that it all came down to the relationship, and not to my getting my own way.

"Be sure to bring some walking shoes and a warm coat," I heard myself saying. "In case we have to hike home."

"We can always take a cab."

"If the axe comes down there might not be cabs."

"Poor Joe," said Jena with a little smile. "He worries so much that he acts middle-aged. We'll take him out and cheer him up. Just a sec while I fix my makeup. You can get our leather coats. Don't even think of wearing a tie."

Ten minutes later I'd parked my SUV on a side street and we were out on Santa Ynez Avenue, the Los Perros main drag. It was a two-lane street lined by single-story shops. Los Perros was a yuppie enclave embedded in the southern lobe of San Jose's suburban sprawl; its charm stemmed from the fact that it felt like a village. The stores' lit-up windows didn't cover the fact that the buildings themselves were cheap and rickety, as makeshift and cobbled together as what you'd see in a Colorado mining town.

I liked this flat little village under the big night sky. It was human-scale, homey, and—as long as you didn't hear the people talking, or compare their clothes—not so different from rural Matthewsboro, the town I'd grown up in. It seemed like a good place to raise children, not that we were planning that for any time soon. Jena and I were both hell-bent on moving up in our companies. Even so, I couldn't help thinking sometimes that it would be nice to have a kid.

There were a fair number of people out and about, though maybe less than on a normal Friday night. I wasn't the only one worried about the Y2K bug. The Christmas decorations were still up on the lampposts, wobbling in the gusty breeze. It was a damp night with a chill in the air. Some highschoolers rolled past on skateboards; three guys and a wiry girl in an orange watch cap. A pickup full of kids slowed to whoop at them, the skater girl raised her arm to pump the heavy metal, devil's-horns salute, and the kids in the truck whooped some more and pulled over to hang out. Up on the corner ahead of us was a middle-aged married couple frowning at each other. Bickering. Like my parents before they'd gotten divorced. Ah yes, my parents.

With my parents it had gone further than bickering. Ed and

Mary Cube. They were country people who'd come into town to work, my mother as an accountant at a WalMart, my Dad as a clerk in a store selling ranching supplies. Dad would have liked to have been a rancher himself, but he didn't have any land. Being a high-school graduate, he felt he was too educated to be a mere cowhand, though he looked and talked like one. The only concrete sign of Dad's education that I ever noticed was that he read and collected Western comic books.

Mom and Dad were always kind of raw and yokel, even for Matthewsboro, Colorado. They did some incredible things. The worst was this: My father was a terrible womanizer, a real Casanova, and my mother ended up stabbing him in the stomach with a carving knife. It was the worst thing I ever saw. It happened right before dinner one evening; I was twelve and my sister Sue was fourteen. Sis told Mom she'd just seen Dad on top of a girl in the woods by the lake, and all at once Mom's patience was gone and she stabbed him.

Dad recovered—and settled for an easy divorce instead of pressing charges. I'd expected it to be a relief to have lanky, ne'er-do-well Dad out of the house and all the fighting over. But it turned out I never felt safe around Mom again. The stabbing wasn't the kind of thing I could forget. In high school I joined every activity I could to stay out of Mom's way, and once I left for college, I never went home to Matthewsboro for more than a day or two at a time.

Eventually Mom died from a series of increasingly debilitating strokes. I used to go see her twice a year in this little nursing home at Centerville, a slightly bigger town near Matthewsboro. Even when Mom was in her wheelchair with half her face paralyzed, I was still a little scared of her pulling a knife, my fear mixed in with heartbreaking pity.

Mom had hated it in the home, the food especially. Raised on a farm as she'd been, she was very particular about the purity of what she ate. Mom's final stroke came while she was eating. She died choking on a mouthful of canned, over-salted, cut-rate chicken soup. Terrible. It had been five years now.

As for Dad, he drifted down to Denver, where he worked for a ranch supply wholesaler. He still kept up his interest in collecting comics, branching out from Westerns to include Batman and Donald Duck. He lived alone in a rooming house. He had a series of woman friends—some of whom he met at comic book conventions. Women were always interested to meet a cowboy type like Dad. But he never married again, or even moved in with a woman.

In high school, every now and then I'd go down to Denver and spend a couple of nights with Dad, reading his comics and following him to work to listen to the ranchers and cowboys wrangling about feed, horse troughs and barbed wire. In college and after, we'd get together a few times a year to "tie on the feedbag" at some roughneck Denver watering hole near the tracks. He wasn't a bad guy, even though he talked like a dumb cowhand. Part of that was just an act.

It had only been a year now since I'd found out Dad had lung cancer—the news had come on Christmas Day, 1998. He'd gone down fast. I'd only been to see him the one time in the Denver VA hospital before he died. I'd thought he would last longer; I missed my chance to get any last words or final blessings out of him.

"Let's never get old, Joe," said Jena, who'd been looking at the middle-aged couple, too.

"We won't," I said, glancing over at her. When Jena was worrying about things, like she was now, her nose got sort of a pointed look to it. Her cheeks a little drawn in. You could see the unhappy young girl right there under her beauty. She worried more than most people realized. I put my arm around her and kissed her. She kissed me back, and for a few seconds it was just us inside the kiss, the way it's supposed to be. But then I broke the kiss, wanting to start on the task of figuring out which bar to go to.

The middle-aged couple had crossed the street to head for D. T. Finnegan's, the yuppie pub I'd been planning to steer us to. But, hell with that, if Finnegan's was where the bickering geezers were going, it wasn't for Jena and me. We walked on down the block to a dive bar named the Night Watch. It was jammin' inside, with Nirvana blasting on the speakers, colored little Christmas lights tacked to the black plywood walls, loads of happily drunk people our age, and not a suit or a necktie in the bunch. Lots of the women were decked out in sparkly little dresses. Jena and I looked just right. We found a spot to stand in, and I pushed my way to the bar and got us two glasses and a shaker full of margaritas. Let it come down.

When I got back to Jena, there were a couple of people talking to her, a tall, slim-waisted woman and a handsome guy with short bleached-blonde hair, the sides of his head shaved, a T-shirt with a picture of The Finger, and a silver stud in the top of his ear. It took me a second to believe my eyes.

"Spazz? Didn't you just tell me you were in San Francisco?"

Spazz gave me his hoarse laugh. "Sorry, boss, I couldn't resist rattling your chain. Turns out Tulip's like you. She didn't want to chance going into the City. You remember Joe from the Christmas party, don't you, Tulip? He's Jena's husband. Joe Cube."

"Cube?" said Tulip, laughing a little. She had nice teeth and a merry smile. Three heavy gold hoops in each ear. Her skin was smooth, with a few pimples. A hank of her black hair hung down on one side. "That's not your true name, is it?"

"Yes it is," said Jena protectively. "And my last name's Bonk, so go ahead and mock that too. Joe and I have odd, short names. We're Americans of Humorous Descent. What's *your* last name, Tulip?" Jena narrowed her eyes, waiting to pounce on the answer.

"Patel."

"How nice. Does it mean something?" Jena took a quick sip of
her margarita. She could definitely get into being bitchy.

Tulip shrugged. I noticed that her skin was unusually dark underneath her eyes. "You'd have to ask my father. It's a common
Indian name. Don't worry, be happy. I'm sorry I laughed. I can
never tell when Spazz is joking. He has a humorous name too. Let's
drink to the new year! To Spazz, Cube, and Bonk! From sea to
shining sea!" She had a standard California accent. An intriguing
woman and, according to Spazz, one of the best custom-chip de-
signers in the valley. She worked for ExaChip, the company that
made our 3Set's ASIC chips.

"Long live Tulip," I chimed in, and she smiled regally down at
me. There was a seriousness around the corners of her mouth. With
her heels she had an inch or two on me, though not on Spazz.

The rest of the evening was your typical bar scene. Not really
my favorite thing. The music gets louder and people yell *whooo* and
there's a line for the bathroom and everyone flirts like mad—except
for the guys like me, who usually end up talking to each other about
sports or cars or computers or the stock market. Talking about
freaking numbers. It's what I do.

I was leaning close into Spazz, going over the performance specs
of the 3Set and trying to figure why the display basically looked so
crappy. But then Jena got me to start dancing with her. That was
good. Jena's fun to dance with, and it made me proud to be shakin'
it with a woman that everyone was staring at. Tulip and Spazz were
dancing too, and we switched partners for a while, and then
switched back again. Tulip smelled exotic, like spices. It was almost
like the four of us were friends.

And then, boom, it was countdown time and Jena and I were
kissing and we all sang "Auld Lang Syne." Like all the other New
Year's Eves. Even though it was the 21st Century now, it was still

ordinary human people wanting to love and be loved, hoping for the best for themselves and their families, shooting for the same old goals like a place to live, enough to eat, and decent work. I got a little misty there for a minute.

The bar had a computer-driven laser up near the ceiling, with the vibrating green beam writing HAPPY 2000 on the wall. Spazz pointed at the computer and bugged his eyes. "Behold, O Cube," he said to me in his most portentous tones. "Our Lord and Master liveth!" Whatever.

Jena was wasted by now, out on her feet. Me, I'd switched to no-alcohol beer around ten so I could drive home. "We're gonna bail," I told Spazz.

"We'll leave too," he said.

On the street, Spazz gave the lamppost a kick and reeled back a little. "Still real," he said. "Deep down, I thought there'd be like this instant decay of matter. All the electrons spiraling into their nuclear suns. The advent of the End Times." He broke into a long, deep fit of coughing.

"I'll drive," said Tulip, twisting the ropy hank of her hair that hung down across her cheek.

"Okay," croaked Spazz. He got on the back of his motorcycle and Tulip took the seat up front. She had a helmet and a leather jacket too. With a wave and a roar they were off.

Jena and I passed a gaggle of three blonde girls talking on cell phones. I was glad to see the phones still working. Two of the girls were talking a lot, but the third looked like she was just pretending, trying to be like her friends, trying to blend in.

The girls giggled after Jena and I walked by. I was pretty much holding Jena up; her feet kept turning at the wrong angles. And when we got to our car she puked on the street. I drove slowly and took the back way home.

The 3Set was still on, though the display looked kind of screwy. I helped Jena into bed before going to power it down. There was no way we were going to have sex. Oh well. We'd made a night of it, one way or another. Bottom line? New Year's Eve sucks.

A Visitor From the Fourth Dimension

Jena was asleep in seconds. I sighed and walked into the living-dining room. There were little pinkish blobs in the 3Set display, jiggly looking things about an inch across, like balls or cocktail sausages. Some kind of glitch, nothing new for the 3Set. The main image showed a newscaster's talking head doing a rundown on the lack of any Y2K bug worldwide. Nothing had happened even in the Third World countries that hadn't done jack about the bug. No airplanes falling out of the sky in Burundi. Spazz was going to be riding me about this all week. At least I knew he hadn't gone to San Francisco either. That Tulip, she seemed like a terrific woman. Attractive, but not so overwhelmingly beautiful that you couldn't talk to her. Approachable. I liked the way her long waist had felt in my hands when we danced. And her exotic, spicy smell.

I turned off the 3Set's power and the announcer went away. But the blobs were still in the tank, lit up by the lamp on my desk. A screen saver Spazz hadn't told me about? I leaned under the desk and pulled the 3Set's power plug out of the wall. The blobs remained, eight or nine or ten of them, bouncing around together, sometimes merging, sometimes changing their size, their colors drifting from light to dark pink. It was almost like a lava lamp.

"Greetings." The voice was a woman's low, thrilling whisper, very close by. Jena? I looked behind me, but there was nobody there. Turning back, I saw a quick motion beside the tank.

"Joe," said the voice again. "Joe Cube." And now I saw the thing floating in the air outside the 3Set. An irregular little trumpet shape, like a soft, empty ice cream cone, just hanging there, flexing a bit as if thinking things over, a fleshy thing of skin and muscle. Dark pink along one edge. Like a lip? I felt sick to my stomach. Could Spazz have dosed me? My heart was going a mile a minute. And then, to make things worse, half the blobs came floating out of the 3Set tank, moving right through the tank's walls. Had the chips poached my brain?

The trumpet shape was talking to me some more, but I was too freaked to listen to it. I reached over to the tank and, yes, the walls were still in place; thick, smooth glass. The rest of the blobs drifted through the tank wall too. They did some odd little jiggly-doo, briefly winking out of visibility right where they would have touched the barrier. And then they came over and nudged my hand. A peremptory touch, firm and insistent. The first bunch of blobs tapped me on the side of my cheek.

"God help me," I groaned. I could hardly breathe. I was having a heart attack. A stroke. I had to get to the hospital. It wasn't far. I could walk there if I had to. No, better to drive. I looked around the room for my keys. The little blobs kept being near my face. Oh man, this was bad.

My keys, my keys, my keys—I'd left them in my jacket. I walked over to the couch where I'd thrown it. The fleshy globs got there first. They pinched in on my jacket and lifted it into the air. Held it up by the ceiling, waggling it at me. I jumped for the coat; it darted to one side. There was a low laugh.

"You must listen to me." The crooked little trumpet right in front of me. It was a kind of mouth, a mouth with no face. I saw a white flash of crooked teeth down inside it. My stomach clenched hard and then I was puking into the waste basket by my desk. The crab, the salad, the champagne, the margaritas, the Kaliber no-alcohol beer.

The globs floated down to poke at my vomit. The mouth thing drifted into view, pointing attentively up at me, flexing and smacking like someone chewing gum. I noticed that the skin beside the lip had a faint fuzz of blonde hair on it. The hairs kept coming and going, sprouting out and disappearing.

"I'm from the fourth dimension," said the mouth in a gentle tone. "My name is Momo. Fear me not."

The fourth dimension meant nothing to me. Math, science fiction. Less than nothing.

"Momo," I murmured, my voice cracking. There was sour puke in my throat. "Wait a minute." I walked across to the sink and rinsed my mouth out with water. Gargled. Rinsed again. Drank a sip. Splashed my face. The blobs and the trumpet-shaped mouth were right with me. I noticed that some of the blobs had fine ridges on one side, and crescent-shaped patches of hard stuff on the other side. They were clustered together in two groups of five. Fingertips. I reached out and touched some of them. They pushed back against me, unyielding as stone, then jiggled up and down. I was shaking hands with Momo. Was this how it felt to be crazy?

"I'm Joe," I muttered.

"I know this," said the trumpet in a low, womanly voice. "Fear not, Joe."

I dried my face and went to the bedroom door to peek in on Jena. Fast asleep. I threw myself down on the couch. I took a couple of long, deep breaths. Finally my heart rate was slowing down.

"Momo from the fourth dimension," I said to the trumpet. "Right." I didn't know what to think. I reached out and touched the fingerballs again. They felt warm, hard, very firmly anchored in the air. "This is part of you? The rest's invisible?"

"Not invisible," said Momo's mouth. "Outside of your Spaceland. Do you wish to see more of me?"

"No. Leave me alone. I'm going to bed." This wasn't happening. I was imagining things. It was time to be safe in the dark bed with Jena. I got to my feet.

Five of the skin-covered balls grew longer, bunched themselves together, and formed a palm-sized blob at their base. A hand. The hand pushed me and I flew back onto the couch.

"Observe," said the trumpet-mouth. It changed shape and ballooned out to one side. Something like cheeks and a nose and chin appeared. A cloud of hair on one side, partly brown, partly blonde. The blank skin near the top of the face puckered and two eyes popped up, not quite the same size, the eyes shifting about in the face like yolks in eggs. At the same time, a neck had appeared beneath Momo's head, a neck and a lumpy body with arms connecting it to the two hands. She was wearing yellow tight silky material on top, like a fancy T-shirt. Her lower parts were wrapped in something like blue jeans. She was hideously deformed. And she was moving towards me.

I decided then that Momo was a criminal of some kind. She'd broken into our house. She'd been hiding here when we got home, and now she was going to get me. I scooted up over the back of the couch, putting the furniture between us. In the next instant, without even seeming to move, Momo was behind the couch with me, jiggling and shifting, her arms bending at crazy wrong angles, her head an irregular balloon, her eyes rolling and changing size.

"Help!" I shouted. "Wake up, Jena! Help me! Call the police!"

Momo enfolded me, her arms wrapping around me like padded iron bands. Her terrible face was right up against me. I shrieked at the top of my lungs. If Jena wouldn't wake up, there were always the neighbors. We shared walls with other townhouses on both sides.

"This must not be," said Momo and lifted me up as easily as a feather. I felt an uncanny pressure on every part of my body,

Momo carried me towards our outside wall, and then, just as we would have hit the wall—something happened. There was a feeling of rotating in some unknown direction. And now my view of our living-dining room was very odd; I was seeing it as if I were looking at a floor plan: the thick lines of the walls, the blob of the couch, a rectangle for the counter. My point of view moved past our outer wall, and I glimpsed what was inside it: the crumbling white of drywall, the yellow fluff of insulation.

We turned and sailed along outside my house, heading towards the park nearby. As we moved, my cross-sectional view of things wobbled up and down. For an instant I thought I glimpsed Jena lying in our bed. It was a very disturbing sight indeed. I could see her insides, her bones and muscles and blood. Oh my God. Had Momo butchered her? I was squeezed too tight to speak.

I saw some wooden circles move by: the cross sections of trees. I craned back towards our condos, but the blueprint-like outline was now too far away to read. I felt another rotation and then a feeling of release. I was standing in a field in the park. Momo had killed Jena and now she'd kidnapped me. I drew in a breath to scream.

"Silence!" said Momo, giving me a rough shake.

"Did you hurt Jena?" I demanded. "I'll kill you if—"

"Calm yourself, fool. I have no business with your wife. She sleeps."

"I saw her blood!"

"Your Spaceland forms lie quite open to the fourth dimension. I've done nothing to your wife, nor do I mean you any harm. But if you scream again—"

"All right," I said, drawing a deep, shaky breath. Momo was still holding my shoulder.

Being with Momo was better in the dark; it was better not to see her. She had a smell to her, but it was nothing I could pin down. It seemed to change with every breath I took. Shoe polish, pine trees, women's underwear, roses, ham, horses, candle wax, the beach— pleasant odors. I was beginning to accept that Momo was real. "If you cry for help, I'll take you into the fourth dimension never to return," she continued. "Am I understood? I release you now so that we may comfortably converse. Entertain no plans of fleeing me."

She moved back from me a bit. My clothes were all twisted and crooked; I had to wriggle around to get my pants resettled on me before I could reach the pocket. And then I took out my wallet.

"I have six hundred dollars on me," I said. I'd loaded up in case the cash machines went down. "You can have it all. Here." I pulled out the money, but Momo didn't take it.

"I'm not here to rob you," said Momo. "I come to bring you knowledge of the fourth dimension."

I could hear the cars on Route 85 driving by the same as ever. Nothing was happening over at my townhouse complex. Jena and the rest of them were out cold. I was alone here with—what?

"What are you?" I asked.

"I'm a woman from a higher order of reality," said Momo. "I come from four-dimensional space. We call our world the All."

"I don't know anything about the fourth dimension," I said. "I majored in History and I got an MBA. I don't read science fiction. I don't want to hear about any freaking fourth dimension. How did we get out in the park?"

"We traveled through the fourth dimension. I pressed in upon your sides lest you be torn asunder."

I sighed and put my money away. "What do you want from me, Momo?"

"You must help me change your world," she said. "You'll speak to your fellows of the fourth dimension, Joe, and with my guidance, you and your adherents will develop a miraculous technology. You will prosper. My mission is to help you change your world—which we call Spaceland. I want to do something very special to inaugurate the onset of your new Millennium. I plan to augment you: to give you four-dimensional skin and a third eye."

"I heard the Millennium doesn't really start till next year," I said uneasily. "You're too early."

"Your planet is most favorably located relative to my city just now," said Momo. "It's convenient for me to approach you." She paused for a moment, then took a different tack. "You haven't had sex for many days. If I augment you, it would enhance your abilities to read your wife's moods—and thereby become a better lover."

"You've been hovering over me all week?"

"Not at all. The first I saw of you was when you returned to your home, although I admit I used my subtle vision to read through your personal papers while I was waiting. If I know that your reproductive reservoirs are rather full, it's because I can see inside your body."

This was a definite turn-off. It was nasty to think of Momo peering into the crannies of my private parts. Was she maybe talking about dissecting me? I cocked my head, looking for the glint of a knife.

"Your increased heartbeat indicates fear," said Momo. "Calm yourself. Ratiocinate. I'm trying to tell you about subtle vision. My retina is a solid ball, rather than a flat disk as is yours. In observing you, I form an exact model of your full body inside my retina. An actively working mimicry. I can very easily read your physical signs, although I confess that it lies beyond my abilities to decipher your thoughts from the flickers of your brain."

"I don't understand how you see inside me," I said finally.

"You have no skin facing towards the fourth dimension," said Momo. "I can touch your insides. Behold."

There was a sudden wriggle in my mouth. Something smooth, the size of a beetle. I tried to spit it out, but I couldn't. In the dim light I noticed that one of Momo's arms was pointing towards my head, but the arm ended in a rounded-off stub. The forearm and hand were invisible, with one of the fingers somehow materializing at just the right spot to touch my tongue.

"Stop or I'll scream again," I said thickly. The finger went away. I took a step back from Momo. Her lumpy yellow top shone dully, reflecting the lights of Route 85. Her face was still puffed and crooked. But I was slowly getting used to her.

"Have you ever augmented anyone before?" I asked.

"Indeed we have," said Momo. "Though I confess that it's not always led to happy results. Your fellows are savage, fearful brutes, implacably against the new. But this time will be different. Joe Cube shall triumph! We'll not speak of religion or magic. Business and technology will be our path. You will spread the word of the fourth dimension, gather a coterie of followers, and build a wondrous device. I have every confidence that you are the one for our Great Work. That clever machine of yours; it's what attracted me."

"The 3Set? I didn't build it. Spazz Crotty did. He's the one you should be talking with."

"But you're the project manager. The dog that wags the tail. The spoon that stirs the coffee. The brains behind the brawn. The engineer in the locomotive. The quarterback."

I recognized the empty, parroted phrases; they were expressions I'd used in a self-evaluation I'd been working on for Ken Wong. Sheer horse manure. Momo must have read the copy in my briefcase. It was ironic to have my words come back at me this way.

"Spazz is the guy you want," I repeated. "I don't even know what the fourth dimension is. And I don't want to know, either. I think we're done here." I turned to walk away.

A sharp pain down inside my stomach brought me up short.

"Stop it," I said. Momo was standing right behind me, one arm pointing at me, with the end tapering off to nothing as it had before when she'd put her finger into my mouth.

"I will augment you now," she said.

"I don't want to get augmented! Whatever the hell that means. If you augment me I'll die."

"Fear not. As far as Spaceland goes, you'll be the same as before—but stronger and able to see through walls. The augmenting occurs outside of Spaceland. I'll stimulate your body to a four-dimensional burst of growth. Your pineal gland will send an eye-tipped stalk vout into the All, while your muscles and skin will grow to cover your vinner and vouter sides. My family passed down the secrets for initiating the process. I've studied well, and I'm confident of our success. You'll be a complete four-dimensional being, albeit of very modest hyperthickness along your vinn/vout axis. Ready to help with the Great Work."

"Vinn and vout?" I challenged blindly. "Those aren't words."

"If you were a two-dimensional gingerbread man and your planet a flat disk upon whose rim you walked, you'd know of only two dimensions. You'd have an up and down, and you'd have a left and right," said Momo calmly. "You wouldn't be aware that your body had a front side and a back side. There would be a whole other direction beyond your imagining. The third dimension. The fourth dimension is like that for you, Joe Cube of Spaceland. You know about up and down, left and right, front and back. But there's another direction of your body that you can't imagine. The fourth dimension. Your vinn and vout. As I said, I'm going to give you skin to cover your vinner and vouter sides."

I wanted to run away, but I could feel Momo's hand like a rock inside my stomach. I had the feeling that if I took another step she'd tear a hole in me.

"Show me vout," I said. If nothing else, this might get her hand out from inside me.

The pain in my stomach went away. Momo held out her arm with a wobbly hand pointing at me. And then she moved her shoulder and her arm disappeared, first the hand, then the forearm, and then the rest of it. "This is vout," she said. "Now I'll point vinn." Her arm grew back: biceps, elbow, wrist and fingers, and then it disappeared again, much as it had before. I shivered. I never had managed to get my jacket, and I was getting cold.

"All you did was make your arm invisible," I said. "Two times." I could hear the whizz of the cars on the highway. The wind had risen a little and was tossing around the trees. I shivered again. I wanted to think this was a bad dream. But there were too many details for a dream. How long was it going to continue?

"How do you imagine that I carried you through the wall of your dwelling?" asked Momo.

"You dematerialized the wall. Used a force field or something." Suddenly a thought hit me. "You're an alien, aren't you? From a UFO. You've got a dematerializing ray." I glanced up, almost expecting to see a saucer hovering there. I saw low clouds, a little pink from the lights of San Jose. No saucer, but yes, I was standing out here talking to an alien. The grass damp and springy underfoot. Everything so very real.

"I am indeed a kind of alien," said Momo. "Your legends do not entirely miss the mark. We do have ray guns and flying saucers. But my homeland is not one of your space's planets. I'm from the All, Joe Cube. A world of four dimensions. I climbed down through a tunnel to get to Spaceland—to your world. Spaceland lies in an endless cavern like a strange, subterranean sea. Spaceland very nearly lacks a fourth dimension; it extends less than a nanometer in the direction of your vinn and vout—which actually point in the direction of our up and down. Spaceland appears to us as something like a rug—but unlike a rug, Spaceland is cunningly filled with motion and life. It seems the Creator put Spaceland in place to separate the All in two. My people, the Kluppers, live up above it, and another folk called the Dronners live down below. They are our enemies, hidden below Spaceland." Momo paused, as if agitated by the thought of the Dronners. "You'll turn the tide against them, Joe."

She had her hand back inside my stomach again. I had no choice but to stand and listen.

"You're bewildered," said Momo. "Try to understand that I didn't dematerialize your wall. I lifted you over it—lifted you in your voutwards direction, that is. More precisely, I rotated you, lifted you, and carried you to the park, all the while pressing in upon your sides lest your innards should spill out. And then I rotated you back and laid you down again in Spaceland. Didn't things look odd to you while we were in progress?"

"Like outlines," I said grudgingly.

"You were seeing a cross section of your world," said Momo. "As would the flat gingerbread man looking at his plane from outside it. You must revolve these matters in your intellect until you understand them. Analogies are most useful. Four is to three as three is to two. A flat man would have a small, line-like retina at the back of his eye. If you lifted him up from his plane and turned him to look down upon his world, he would see only along the line where the extended plane of his body crosses the plane of his world. A cross section."

"I have no idea what you're talking about."

"For the flat man to see properly in three dimensions, he must grow a three-dimensional eye, an eye with a disk-like retina. For you to see properly in the four-dimensional All, you need a four-dimensional eye with a ball-like retina. A third eye! You'll have subtle vision. It's part of the augmentation, Joe. A third eye and higher skin."

She released her hand from my stomach then. I seized the moment and took off running across the field in the direction of my house. I didn't hear or see Momo following me, and for a moment I thought I was free. But then something hit me—a great gush of liquid coming at me from every side. It filled my mouth and nose and lungs, warm and tasting of bitter salt.

At the same time I felt a staggering pain in the center of my head, something like an electrical shock, powerful enough to knock me flat on the ground. The electrical energy kept on coursing through the salty liquid all around me, spreading out from my head to the rest of my body.

I lay there twitching, desperate for air. The liquid in my lungs was drowning me. With a supreme effort, I coughed it out and began to breathe.

As I gasped down air, the electrical tingling continued. My brain felt like there was something writhing around inside it. An uncoiling snake. It was a terrible sensation. I forced myself up onto all fours, trying to find my voice for a scream.

A second wave of pain hit me, this time all over my body, spreading into my skin, my muscles, my organs, my joints and my bones. A crawling sensation in every part of me, as if I'd been infested by a billion flesh-eating worms. The crawling reached a fever pitch and then diminished, replaced by a faint itch.

And then something poked me in the side, sharp as a commandant's jackboot kicking a prisoner of war. Momo? I thought I saw her hovering somewhere nearby. I felt in control of my muscles again. Full of adrenaline, I jumped to my feet and ran for home, the night air cold on my wet hair. I was running faster than I'd

ever run before in my life, yet I didn't feel out of control. My arms
and legs were wonderfully powerful.

I cut between two blocks of houses to get to Silva View Crescent.
My footsteps pounded across the asphalt. I grabbed the doorknob
of our townhouse and rattled the flimsy metal. Locked. I pounded
on the door so hard that I made a dent in it. Take it easy, Joe. I
looked behind me. It was strange—in one way I thought I could
see a ghost of Momo, yet in another way it looked as if our street
was empty. I knocked again, not quite as hard as before.

"Come on, Jena," I murmured. "Please let me in."

And now, as I stared at the door and thought about Jena, I
realized I could *see* the inside of my house. I had a third eye sticking
up into the fourth dimension.

This is hard to describe. I knew our little townhouse really well,
of course. We'd been in there for almost four months. I carried a
full mental image of it in my head. The difference was that now all
of a sudden I was seeing the image in real time. I could see Jena
stirring in our bed.

Let me back up and try to explain this better. You can always
visualize the place where you live—the rooms, the furniture, the
stuff in the drawers. You know where everything is and you know
what everything looks like. You don't normally visualize your house
from any particular point of view. It's not like imagining a picture
or even like imagining a whole bunch of pictures. You know where
everything is in relationship to everything else and you know what
everything looks like from every side. You know your house from
the inside out. If you want to imagine it from any particular direction you can immediately do that. You know your house like your
own body.

And now, staring at our door and wondering if Jena had heard
me, I was seeing a total image of our house—and not just as some

stored-memory mental database, no, I was seeing the real thing. The total contents of my house with real-time updates, everything at once, seen from any angle or viewpoint I liked. This was what Momo meant by subtle vision. I saw Jena sit up and feel around and say something, and then, as I knocked again, I saw her stand up and rub her face and walk to the door.

"It's me, Jena," I said. "Let me in." My voice sounded the same as before. I used my regular eyes to glance all around the front stoop and sidewalk. A puddle of liquid had dripped off me. I didn't see any Momo in the real world, but somehow my third eye could see her watching me from hyperspace. She was sitting on a little metal dish, a miniature flying saucer. Hopefully she was done with me for now. I'd definitely been augmented.

"What are you doing, Joe?" slurred Jena, her narrow eyes squinting in the light. "You're all wet." My subtle vision made her look funny. It was like I could see the flesh and blood beneath her skin. But it wasn't horrific, it was more like I was experiencing her body from the inside. A deeper form of reading someone's mood from the expression on their face. I could sense Jena's headache, her need to pee and brush her teeth.

I didn't know where to begin to explain. "I locked myself out," was all I said. "I'm sorry. Let's get in bed." My number one priority was to fall asleep and wake up and have all of this crazy stuff be gone like some weird dream.

I threw my soaked clothes in the washer and dried myself with a towel. Jena used the bathroom, and when she came back out, she snuggled tight against me. With my subtle vision, our bodies felt at one, the way they did when we made love. But even though I could feel every bit of Jena's body, I couldn't read her mind.

She reached around and touched me. "I love you, Joe," she murmured.

It didn't take telepathy to know that it was time to make love.

But I wasn't up for it. I ached all over and Jena was still drunk. She caressed me a bit more, but nothing happened.

"Are you mad at me?" whispered Jena.

"I don't feel right," I said, rolling away from her.

"Jerk."

I put my head under my pillow and fell asleep.

Momo's Cross Sections

Jena approached me again in the morning, but again I put her off. I don't know why. I guess I felt I needed some quiet time to process what had happened to me. In any case, Jena got really huffy. She thought I was freezing her out, as I sometimes did.

While Jena was in the shower I took stock of myself. My third eye was on a slender stalk about four inches long, sticking vout of the center of my head. If I turned my third eye vinn towards our world, I could look at where my eyestalk met my higher skin—a sheet of skin and muscle that closed my innards off from the fourth dimension. It was really true.

Though my third eye could see its stalk, it couldn't see itself, so I couldn't judge how big the eye was. Maybe quite small, like a lobster's eye. Jena couldn't see the third eye and it wouldn't show up in any normal mirror either, because the stalk to my third eye led vout of our Spaceland into the fourth dimension.

I used my new eye's subtle vision to take in my surroundings. As I moved my mental viewpoint around within the image, I could see Jena soaping herself, see the dishes in our sink, see the yellow grass outside and even the cars droning past on Route 85. A Volvo, a Ford, a Toyota, a Lexus, a VW, another Volvo . . . I snapped out of watching traffic and thought some more about how I was seeing all this. It was like my third eye held a copy of the world that I could study from any side I chose.

I went into the kitchen and started the coffee. Jena liked her morning coffee; this was a special grind from the Los Perros Coffee Roasting coffee shop. Maybe it would help get us back into a friendly mood.

My arms had an extra powerful feel to them. Presumably that sheet of muscle under my higher skin was helping me. I went over to my barbells in the corner and hefted them. And, yes, I was a little stronger than before.

I was still playing with looking at things in different ways with my third eye. When I turned it vinn towards our world it formed a complete view of everything, inside and out. I could contemplate my third eye's image from any location or direction I chose, and by controlling my viewpoint in some ill-defined way I could even see inside things.

I could see the sand inside the plastic disks of my barbells. I could see the bottom of the chair I was sitting on. But, again, when I turned my third eye upon my own body, I didn't see inside it at all. Instead I saw my higher skin.

I heard a noise behind me and, without turning around, I used my third eye to see Jena walking across the room towards me. She looked pale, tense and unhappy. She was wearing her robe with nothing under it. I adjusted my third eye's viewpoint so that I was seeing her skin but not her internal organs.

"So how's your big Y2K bug, Joe?" said Jena.

I hadn't thought about it yet today. "Why don't you turn on the TV," I suggested.

"I can't," said Jena. "Not with your stupid fish-tank thing attached to the cable."

The 3Set. Momo had said that's what had gotten her attention in the first place. "I'll unhook it," I said. "I'll take it back to Kencom."

"Oh great. And leave me alone on New Year's Day?" Jena sighed and rubbed her temples.

"You can come, too," I suggested. "We'll drop off the 3Set and get brunch somewhere. There's a good sports bar near Kencom. We could watch the Rose Bowl."

"I'm hungry right now," said Jena. "Starving for food and for love."

"Aw, Jena." I hugged her and kissed her on the cheek. She felt warm and soft in my arms. "I'm not myself today. Something weird happened last night."

"Are you mad because I puked?" A penetrating look from her narrow, hazel eyes.

"That's not it at all. The bar was fine. We had a good time. But last night, after you fell asleep I saw this, this—"

"Porno site on the Web?" She shoved me away and glared at me, her eyes squeezing down to slits. "Are you doing that again? Is that why you're giving me the cold shoulder? Just you and your little mousie and no real women needed?"

"Jesus, Jena, are you out of your mind? I saw an alien last night. That's what happened. Momo from the fourth dimension. She augmented me and now I can see through walls. I have a third eye."

Jena regarded me for a minute, then shook her head. Input rejected. "What were you doing outside last night, anyway? Was it raining?"

"Momo took me there. She carried me through the wall."

"Did she give you sex?" said Jena, beginning to be amused. She got a wallop out of science fiction. "That's what aliens usually do. Gathering the seed of Planet Earth."

"She augmented me," I said. "Not up and down but some other

way. She made me grow a new eye on a stalk into the fourth dimension. And now I can see past walls. I have subtle vision."

"Did you watch me in the shower?" Jena cheeks were shading back up to their normal shade of pink.

"Yes. A little. And then I started looking at the cars on 85."

"Typical. I don't know why I married you. Looking at cars. You should have been watching what I did at the end of my shower." Jena walked past me to the kitchen counter and got some coffee.

"You think I'm kidding, but subtle vision is real," I said, getting a coffee too. "I need your help with this, Jena." I glanced over at the fridge. "I can see inside the freezer," I told her. "There's a pack of Lender's raisin bagels right beside the door."

"Whoo-hoo," said Jena. "I subtly see a can of orange juice in there, too. You want some?"

"Sure. Wait a minute while I think about how to convince you."

Jena opened the freezer, got out the juice, handed me the bagels. "Toast me one," she said. "You think Spazz will be at Kencom?"

"Probably. He's there all the time." I glanced over at Jena's purse on the counter. A full image of it formed inside my mind. It was more like knowing than it was like seeing. Knowing exactly where everything was. "There's two quarters and a penny inside your wallet's change purse."

"I wonder if the ATMs will be working today," said Jena, scooping the frozen juice into a pitcher.

"Look in your wallet, Jena. See that I'm right."

"How do I know you didn't already look at it?" said Jena, turning playful. "Let's try something harder." She added water to the pitcher, mixed up the juice, drank off a glass of it, wiped her hands on a dishtowel. She walked over to the other end of the counter. "Turn your back, Joe."

I obliged, but of course I could see her just as well as before. She picked up a pencil and a pad of paper, wrote on the top piece of paper, tore it off, folded it in four and dropped it into the pocket of her robe.

"Okay, Joe, you can turn back around. What did I just do?" She cocked her head and smiled, waiting for my answer.

"You wrote 'Love Me' on that piece of paper in your left pocket."

Her jaw dropped. And then finally we had sex. It should have been great—our first love-making of the Millennium—but it was only so-so. I was only just beginning to learn how to control my subtle vision. I kept getting distracted by all the things I saw around me, such as the neighbors and Jena's wet, red innards. I wasn't at all sure that subtle vision was really going to make me a better lover. And I still had the feeling of being stronger and more massive than before. I was almost worried that I'd hurt Jena, and it made me a little tentative. But she seemed to think I felt the same as ever. The equipment worked. We finished.

"When I wrote on the paper in the kitchen, you saw me reflected in the window, didn't you?" said Jena, smiling up at me with her hazel eyes wide open. "Subtle vision indeed."

"I'm telling you, Jena, it's really true. I can see right into your womb."

"Oh no! I forgot! I haven't been able to take my pill all week. People were stockpiling them because of Y2K and the drugstore ran out."

"What if we did have a baby?" I said idly, still lying on top of her.

She pushed me off. "If you knock me up, I'll kill you, Joe. I'm not ready to turn breeder for a long, *loong* time." Jena ran into the bathroom to take precautions. I turned my attention elsewhere. The neighbor's kitchen was right on the other side of the wall by the head of our bed. A fat guy called Dixon. He was sitting at the table peacefully studying the inner pages of his newspaper. It wasn't much effort for me to read his front page.

"No Y2K problems at all," I called to Jena.

"How do you know?" she said, stepping out of the bathroom. She was nibbling on one of her fingernails while she talked to me. The thought of getting pregnant always made her uptight.

"I'm reading Dixon's paper." I hooked my thumb at the wall.

Jena got a sudden gleam in her eye. "Cards!" she said. "Can you read cards, Joe? Wait." She rooted around in one of the suitcases she used for a dresser and came up with a deck of cards.

We sat there cross-legged on the bed, naked and facing each other. One by one I told Jena the top card on the deck and she flipped it over. I was always right.

Jena began whooping and laughing. "Subtle vision! Let's drive to Tahoe, Joe! You can break the bank at blackjack. We'll take down Nero's Empire. That particular casino's on my hit list. They lobby like hell against Indian Gaming. We'll make a million and then we'll go skiing."

"I've never played blackjack. I don't know the rules. The gangsters will beat me up." And then I saw the look on her face, and I caught myself, realizing what a fuddy-duddy I sounded like. Sure I could do it. If Jena believed in me, I could do anything. "Reset. Actually, Tahoe sounds like a pretty good idea. Can you teach me about blackjack?"

We had a little more breakfast in our robes, and then Jena gave me a blackjack lesson. She was interested in gambling. During her summers in high school and college, she'd worked as a bingo caller at the Yavapi-run Chucky's Casino near her home town of Prescott. Thanks to Jena's father having been a Yavapi Indian, Jena had plenty of contacts at Chucky's, not that Jena had had all that much to do with Native American culture growing up. Her mother and stepfather tried to raise her Norwegian. There were a lot of Norwegians around Prescott.

Jena's mother Jean was this very buttoned-up country woman

who'd inherited the family ranch outside of Prescott from her Norwegian widower father. Jena's mother was an only child, and she'd never seen life as any kind of laughing matter at all. I always thought of old Jean when I heard Garrison Keillor talking about Lake Woebegone. According to Jena, Jean had been a virgin till she turned thirty, at which point she'd had a brief fling with a cowboy who worked on her ranch. This had been Jena's father Sonny. Sonny had died in a motorcycle crash before Jena was born, but thanks to Sonny, mother Jean had finally gotten the hang of being with men, and she married a Norwegian insurance salesman named Oley. Jena's stepfather. He looked like a long, slimy piece of white fish— like this one particular kind of preserved fish that Norwegians ate. Yeah, Oley was six feet of *lutefisk*. And a drunk as well.

It was thanks to Oley that Jena was as screwed up as she was. Oley didn't like to admit that Jena was part Indian, so right off the bat she'd been told to deny half of what she was. He ragged on Indians every chance he got. And when Jena started blossoming out, the real trouble started. Oley had been totally unable to deal with the notion of Jena going out with boys. He'd even made some half-assed attempts at sexual abuse, and when Jena told her mother, her mother had taken Oley's side. Jena had needed to stay away from Jean and Oley as much as she could. Chucky's was a haven for her.

Chucky's was a slots, poker, keno and bingo place, with a big native crafts giftshop. The didn't actually have blackjack there, but Jena had thoroughly researched the whole topic of gambling as her senior project as a Communications major at University of Arizona. She'd drawn up a draft for a pitch the Yavapis could make to the State of Arizona for a full range of games in their casinos, but thanks to a bunch of out-of-state lobbyists from the Vegas casinos, nothing had ever come of it.

After half an hour of lessons from Jena, I was drawing each of my hands up to the maximum total possible without busting. With my subtle vision, I knew what the dealer had in the hole card, and I knew which cards were next on the deck. I was winning maybe three-fifths of the time. A nice edge for an even-money game.

"How long did that alien say your power would last?" asked Jena. "Let's hurry up before it goes away. Let's get dressed and pack. I figure we'll stay up at Tahoe for a couple of days."

"She didn't say how long," I said, following Jena into the bedroom. "It might be forever."

"Did the alien want something back from you? In return?"

"It wasn't that clear. It's like she wants me to start a company. Build some kind of machine for the fourth dimension."

Jena guffawed. "What would you tell the investors?"

"I could do it," I said defensively. "I'm a good presenter."

"About the fourth dimension?" said Jena. "What is the fourth dimension, anyway?"

"I have no idea," I admitted.

I was ready way before Jena, so I used the extra time to disconnect the 3Set and carry it out to the car. With the added strength of my higher muscles it was easy. When I got back into the apartment, it occurred to me to check my weight, but it was the same as before. Even though I had some extra body parts in hyperspace, the new mass didn't seem to count towards my weight down here. Good deal.

"Why's that stupid machine in there?" asked Jena when we went out to the car.

"I want to drop it off at Kencom before we do anything else. Ken Wong would fire me if he found out I brought it home."

"You're not going to need a job once we get through playing blackjack," said Jena. Her cheeks were pink with excitement. "We'll retire!" She burst into song. "Take this job and shove it! . . ."

"Even so, I don't want to get into trouble," I said. "Kencom's right on our way. It's Saturday. Nobody will be there but Spazz."

Driving wasn't as hard as I'd thought it might be. I was getting better and better at filtering out the subtle vision of things I didn't need to see—things like the engine under my hood, the rocks under the road, and the insides of the other cars.

The only vehicle in the Kencom lot was Spazz's red motorcycle. I got Jena to help me get the 3Set inside the building; she held the doors for me so I wouldn't have to set the thing down.

Spazz was there at his screen as usual, tapping his nose ring and occasionally typing. I could see into his body and sense how it felt. Hungry, lungs congested, a bit of a backache. But I couldn't read his thoughts any more than I could Jena's.

"Too late," said Spazz, looking over at me. "Ken already called the cops."

"Oh no!" I cried.

Spazz was seized by rhythmic spasms, making a noise that was a mixture of laughs and coughs. "Joke, boss-man, joke," he finally got out. He was wearing a different T-shirt today, a cartoon of a man with his head up his butt and a label saying YOUR2CHEEK BUG.

Now Spazz noticed Jena. "Hi, Jena!" he said. "Ready for that motorcycle ride to Big Sur?"

"I have no idea what we said to each other last night," said Jena, smiling prettily. "Don't hold me to it. It was another century, my dear." Thanks to my subtle vision, I could sense her heart beating a little faster. She was actually interested in Spazz. I hadn't realized that before.

"You'd dig it on my bike," Spazz was slowly murmuring, his body buzzing as much as Jena's. "It's like flying. But maybe today's a little too chilly. Especially with your husband in here." He turned his attention back to me. I was screwing with the cables, getting the 3Set hooked back up, not looking directly at him.

"So the 3Set didn't work so good, huh?" said Spazz from behind me, his expression a mixture of pity and contempt. "I've been thinking about some things to try. I'm glad you brought it back. I'm gonna see what happens if I trade off some of the frame rate for increased resolution. You mentioned that you left it running while we were at the bar. Did it look any different when you got home?"

"Uh—no," I said. Jena and I had agreed that we'd keep my subtle vision a secret for now. "It looked the same."

"Let's have a look," said Spazz, turning it on. The Rose Bowl parade appeared, little floats moving across the bottom of the 3Set tank.

"Jena and I better get rolling," I said. "We're driving up to Tahoe for the day."

"Snowboarding?" said Spazz, mildly interested.

"We're gonna hit the casinos," said Jena, pursing her lips. She didn't say more than that. I knew it was killing her not to talk about our plan. Jena hated to keep secrets.

Spazz let out a sudden bark of a cough, staring at something over my shoulder. "Who's your friend?" he asked. I'd been so busy watching Spazz and Jena look at each other that I hadn't stayed aware of the door behind me. But now I put some of my attention back there, and, oh God, it was Momo.

I turned around and looked at her with my regular eyes. She was presenting herself differently from yesterday. She didn't look all jiggly and deformed. She looked, in fact, almost like a regular woman. A blonde, imposing woman, somewhat overweight, with a wide mouth and bright eyes. The mouth was hard to read; it was somewhere between friendly and intimidating. Not a woman to cross. She was wearing a tight green T-shirt and light purple slacks. Her feet—well her feet didn't look right at all. They were in black shoes, but turned sideways, almost backwards in fact. And she was hovering a few inches above the floor. Our gravity didn't seem to have any effect on Momo.

"Greetings," she said in that rich, low voice of hers. "Joe Cube,

Jena Bonk, Spazz Crotty. I'm Momo from the fourth dimension."

Jena gave a little shriek of fear and surprise.

"What?" said Spazz, looking at Jena. "She's not with you?"

"Oh yeah, Momo's a friend of ours," I said, trying to wallpaper over things. "Let's go, Momo. If you want to talk, we can do it in the car."

"So you're off for some card sharping," said Momo. "Most excellent. I relish your low cunning, Joe Cube." She must have picked up on my noticing her feet, for now she smoothly turned them around and settled to the floor.

"Cool moonwalk," drawled Spazz, observing the move. "This woman is—who? One of your relatives, Joe?"

"She's an alien," said Jena, who'd backed off all the way to the other side of the room. "She did something to Joe last night while I was asleep."

"Gnarly!" said Spazz happily. "Joe's girlfriend from the psycho ward. This is turning into an interesting day after all. What was that about a dimension, Momo?"

"I'm a four-dimensional woman," said Momo quietly. "Like a god compared to you, Spazz. Not Joe's girlfriend. Not a psycho. Perhaps Joe was right in saying that I should augment you. It might be well to have more than one agent in your world."

"Not me," said Jena, her eyes defensively slitted. "Don't augment me."

"Don't augment either of them," I said. "One of us is enough." I didn't want to see Spazz horning in on my new-found power.

Spazz cocked his head oddly, obviously trying to execute a difficult mental reset. It did my heart good to see his confusion.

"Fourth dimension like time?" said Spazz finally.

"Not time," said Momo firmly. "Yes, one can model time as a higher dimension. But I'm from a fourth dimension of space. Time is a different type of dimension entirely. I'm as subject to time as you are."

"If your fourth dimension isn't time, then what is it?" asked Spazz.

"We call our world's cardinal directions up, down, East, West, South, North, Ana and Kata," said Momo. "But just as do you, we have a somewhat different set of names for the directions relative to our own bodies. In daily life, we speak of up, down, right, left, back, front, vinn and vout."

"Flatland," said Spazz suddenly. "What you're saying reminds me of that book about a world that has polygons living in a plane. The hero's called A Square."

"Exactly," said Momo enthusiastically. "I know this book well. It's one of Spaceland's finest works. I'm like the sphere who intersects A Square's plane, Spazz. What you see before you is but one of my three-dimensional cross sections." Momo gestured at her ample body.

"Why aren't you all crooked and bulgy?" I interrupted. "Why do you look different from last night?"

"Last night I didn't take the trouble to come in at a right angle," said Momo. "I wasn't quite perpendicular to your space. Nor was I standing so still as I am now. Think once again of the prime analogy. Four is to three as three is to two. If a cube cuts a plane at a right angle, it forms a square cross section. But if the cube is tilted, the creatures in the plane see something else. A rectangle, a trapezoid—"

"Or a triangle or a hexagon," put in Spazz. He'd regained his composure. But he still thought we were kidding him. "Great rap, Momo. Where did you really meet her, Joe?"

Momo stepped towards Spazz, no longer holding herself rigid. A great bulge moved down her arm, and when it reached her hand, the hand disappeared like a melting ball of wax. She was lifting it vout of our space.

As I watched Momo in action, I paid attention to the ways in which my new subtle vision affected my view of her. My third eye projected Momo's unimaginable four-dimensional shape into a very odd three-dimensional form. I could see a whole solid, just like when I looked at Jena—but I didn't see innards. Momo was, rather, like the tangled roots of a stump, with her arms and legs and torso seeming to grow through each other. Very gnarly, very hard to describe.

Momo must have noticed me staring at her, and she answered my unspoken question, even as she continued bearing down on Spazz. "There's more of me up above your space, Joe, covered with skin just like the cross section in your space. That's what your subtle vision is showing you. You can see inside Jena and Spazz because your extra eyes up above space peek over the three-dimensional shells of their skins. They are quite open to the fourth dimension, on both their vouter and vinner sides. Unlike you, in your newly augmented form." As usual, Momo's explanation didn't make much sense to me.

Right about then Spazz made a muffled noise and began trying to spit something out. With my subtle vision I could see one of Momo's fingers inside his mouth, a pink fingertip resting on his tongue like a stone sausage.

"Oh my god," said Spazz after Momo removed her finger. "The attack of the hyperdimensional dental hygienist." The guy never let up on maintaining his cool. You had to hand it to him. "Suppose I believe you're from the fourth dimension," said Spazz to Momo. "So then what? Are you here to conquer the planet? Eat our brains? Rape us? Or is this just a sightseeing trip?"

"She wants me to teach about her world," I said. "She calls it the All. I'm supposed to organize a start-up to develop a new kind of technology." The idea was starting to appeal to me. With the proper use of sound business principles, there was no reason I couldn't start my own dot-com! That was a hell of a lot cooler than cheating at blackjack. "Maybe you could be, like, my assistant," I told Spazz.

Spazz guffawed in just the same way that Jena had when I'd mentioned my plans before, the guffaw shading into a long series of wheezy chuckles.

"Shut up," I said. "I could do it. Momo augmented me last night. Vinn and vout. I have subtle vision. I can see the pipe and the bud in your pants pocket, for instance. I could fire you for that. The Kencom campus is a zero-tolerance drug-free zone, in case you'd forgotten. It's in the contract you signed."

"Um—" Once again Spazz was at a loss for words. I was loving it. He gathered his wits and changed the subject. "So, Momo, can we see the rest of your cross sections? Can you move completely through our space like the sphere does for A Square in *Flatland*?"

"Indeed," said Momo. And then she did it.

She quickly shrank out of sight—and then she came back, slowly showing us one cross section at a time.

What did it look like?

The first thing we saw was a little ball of light purple, hovering in the air at waist level. The silky fabric of Momo's pants. Her belly. The ball expanded and a cap of light green appeared on top like a polar ice cap. Her shirt. Quickly the pants lengthened and the shirt grew, gently swelled by Momo's breasts. This was all in miniature to start with; the initial cross section of Momo was no more than three feet tall, hanging there a foot or two above the floor. Her arms sprouted from the arms of the shirt and a little head-ball appeared, hovering above the body, not yet connected. No eyes or mouth on the head, just a ball of skin. A neck grew in to fill the gap between body and head. A mouth bloomed in the bottom part of the head, and then a pair of eyes appeared. It was a child-sized Momo, with a face that was finer and more delicate than before. The tip of Momo, as it were. As yet, she had no hands or feet.

"Unbelievable," murmured Spazz, nervously touching the stud in his ear.

I was kind of tuning in and out of my subtle vision while this was happening. When I looked at Momo with my third eye, the successive cross sections were overlaid on top of each other, nested together like Russian dolls.

Momo's cross section continued to grow in stature, with the curves of her figure growing more pronounced. Finally her hands and feet appeared. As she continued moving through our space, the shadings of her skin kept subtly changing through different tints of pink. She was wearing lavender pants and a green blouse all the way vinn and vout. Before long she'd reached her greatest size, which was even a bit larger than what she'd shown us before. The maximum Momo was a heavy-featured blonde just a bit under six feet. A statuesque woman. Momo moved on with her passage, shrinking and growing less rounded, and then her arms and legs were gone as well. Her face blanked over with skin, and then her head separated off, shrank and disappeared. Her arms drew back into her shirt, and the striped ball of her shirt and pants dwindled to the size of a bowling ball, an egg, a grape—and stopped at that size.

"Unbe-freaking-lievable," said Spazz.

"She's an angel?" said Jena.

The grape gave a sudden sharp jiggle, as if something had poked it. It warped, twisted, and split in two. And now, more hurriedly than before, Momo came back through our space. This time she showed us a different sequence of cross sections. It was a disturbing sight.

It started with two irregular leather shapes hanging in the air, folding and flexing. The combined feet of all the cross sections we'd just seen. The foot-things were bowed down in the center, just far enough to touch the floor. Like casters. The feet drifted upwards and morphed into lavender balls: pieces of Momo's legs. The balls rose and merged to become a version of Momo's butt, big and bouncy, but sculptured in warped planes and twisting curves. Some familiar looking globs appeared beside it: fingertips. The fingers merged and became pieces of hands; a cap of green grew down over the purple butt and it became belly and breasts. The hands turned into sections of arm that drifted in towards the pale green blouse. In an abrupt transition, all this collapsed into the glob of Momo's neck, which quickly grew out to a head-ball that was, to start with, just blank skin. The skin's color flowed and morphed through shades of pink and tan, the colors drifting across it like clouds across the Earth. And now the head split and grew a mouth, crooked and uncommonly wide.

"Are you three beginning to understand my power?" said the great mouth. Teeth glittered inside it—far too many teeth. "Do you accept that Joe Cube must build a company to develop the technology of the fourth dimension?"

The head wagged to one side and warped down to a fraction of its size, becoming a tan cone with a mouth around its rim: a version of the trumpet shape I'd seen last night. A wart on the side of the trumpet bulged out, forming a lumpy projection with an eye in it. And then the lump with the eye crawled over to the other side of the cone. A second eye-lump appeared, then a big beak of a Picasso nose, and the mouth shrank down to a little triangle-shaped corner. A cloud of bright lines began swarming around the nightmarish head. Momo's hair: brown and blonde. The hair thickened up and covered everything, then shrank to—nothing.

Looking at Spazz and Jena, I could clearly sense how they felt. They were scared to death. As was I. And then Momo was back again, only her head this time, lumpy and crooked and cubist.

"What steps will you take to commence the Great Work, Joe?" asked Momo.

"I don't see why we shouldn't still go to Tahoe," said Jena in a small voice. She was way on the other side of the room, squeezed into the corner and biting her nails. "Listen, Momo, if you want Joe to start a company, he's going to need seed money. Even before the first round of funding. We're not just talking research and development, we're talking focus groups, marketing studies, prototypes, and a business model." The touchstone words put Jena on familiar ground. She ran with it.

"We'll start out with a proof of concept," continued Jena, her cheeks growing pink again. "Then do some surveys to figure out the best way to productize. And meanwhile we're getting a buzz going. If we do this right, the venture capitalists will call us instead of us calling them. Maybe a stunt of some kind to whet the public's interest. Free media exposure. How about a contest to raise the profile? We'll have Web of course, Web from the start, but if we wanna hook the front porch folks, we'll need to get direct mail and telemarketing campaigns in place, all ready to go as soon as we can pull the trigger. You're talking about a serious budget, Momo. Millions. I could work it up."

"The prophets and holy men we used in the past had no business models," said Momo thoughtfully.

"Joe, a prophet?" said Jena, laughing again.

"Can I get some respect?" I said. "You're right, Momo, business is the way to go. And we're the ones to do it for you. And as for funding, if you don't make a scene in the casino, Jena and I can win mucho dinero in Tahoe. Nothing like what we'll need, but at least enough to start. Once we've got some seed money, we'll think of a way to make it grow. Blackjack's just for openers."

"You only have six hundred dollars in your wallet," said Momo. "That's a rather small stake for gambling."

"It's enough. If I keep winning it'll build."

"I'll obtain some additional cash," said Momo. "A proper amount to start with. I see some nearby. Wait." She disappeared.

"It's gotta be Vegas," said Spazz.

"What the hell are you talking about?" I said. I was still mad at Spazz for laughing at me.

"Vegas is where the high-roller games are. You win more than a hundred grand at Tahoe or Reno, they'll throw you out and maybe stomp your butt in the parking lot. If we're talking about winning a million off quality people, it's gotta be Vegas." Spazz gave a brisk cough for emphasis.

"What's this 'we,' Spazz?" I said coldly.

"Didn't you say you needed an assistant, man? Hell with that, I'll be your Chief Technology Officer. Or how about your—*apostle*. I heard that stuff about prophets. Momo's tried this before, right?"

"I don't know if it was Momo herself. It might have been one of her ancestors. She said her trick for giving me my third eye was a family secret." I lowered my voice and took Jena aside, hoping Momo wasn't watching us from somewhere vout there.

"You're smart to build up the budget estimate," I murmured to Jena. "If Momo's machine works, great—and if it doesn't, we've still helped ourselves to a big chunk of the cash flow. We work this thing, and we get rich either way. You think I should really cut Spazz in?" Jena nodded enthusiastically. I was going to have to keep an eye on those two.

"Where did Momo go just now?" asked Jena loudly. "Where would she get money?"

Right about then the stacks of bills started dropping out of the air. Seventeen thousand bucks in all. Momo swelled up into the room and stood there smiling at us.

"I obtained these from the building across the street," she said. Meaning Wells Fargo. "They were inside the great metal safe."

"Oh my god," said Jena. "Did anyone see you?"

"By no means. The building was empty and the vault was locked. I went over it and reached vinn to pull the money out. Nothing more than my fingertips was visible. These flat pieces of paper are very important to you, are they not?" She fixed me with her all-seeing eye. "I can read your lips, Joe Cube. I know of your ignoble wish to amass great wealth." I started to mumble an apology, but Momo held out a calming hand. "I recognize your qualities, both good and bad. I accept you as you are. But let there be no thought of shirking the Great Work."

"And the Great Work would be something relating to the fourth dimension?" said Spazz. "Are you talking about an educational product? Not much money in that."

"I don't bring the fourth dimension as a theory," said Momo. "I bring it as a *fact*. No one who beholds me can doubt."

"The point of all this being what?" asked Spazz.

"That's right," put in Jena. "We need a clear mission statement for the business plan."

"It is well that you have so practical a turn of mind," said Momo. "My mission is that you make use of some very remarkable technology."

"To do what?" pressed Spazz.

"The situation is this," said Momo. "My family can produce a certain class of simple devices that we'd like to see you Spacelanders make use of. Rest assured that the technology is quite out of your normal ken. I'd rather not say more until I've decided upon the best application."

"We'll definitely need a sharper message," said Jena. "Before we go out and pitch."

"I'll tell you soon," said Momo. "I'm researching a variety of things."

"About Vegas," I put in. "Why should I bother going off to cheat at blackjack, when you can fetch us as much money as we want? Did you think of looking in the safe-deposit boxes?"

"I will countenance no shirking," said Momo.

"I'm not shirking," I whined. "It just seems inefficient to gamble when you can steal." That didn't sound good, so I amended it. "Not that I'm for stealing."

"It'll be fun at the casino," said Jena. "Like a team-building exercise."

"Vegas kicks butt," added Spazz.

"It will be interesting to observe how you three comport yourselves," said Momo. "And it's not certain that I can keep visiting you. The Empress's troops—well, never mind about that for now. It is well that you learn how to provide for yourself without me. Give a man a fish, and you feed him once. Teach him to fish, and you feed him for a lifetime." She grew larger again, a body flowing out of her head like hot wax. "Shall I transport you to Las Vegas?"

We three looked uneasily at each other.

"I think we'd rather take an airplane," I said.

"Let's do it," said Spazz. "We'll drive up to the airport and get the next flight. We're not gonna need reservations. Nobody's gonna be booked on any flights today."

"Should we bring Tulip, too?" I suggested. I liked Tulip a lot better than I liked Spazz. I kept thinking about how she'd felt when we'd danced together. Her spicy smell, her heavy gold earrings, her oily, kissable skin.

"Can't," said Spazz. "She's gone to spend a couple of days with her sister in Fremont. Took off this morning. We had a little falling-out over breakfast, sad to say."

"What happened?" asked Jena.

"I told her I'm head over heels in love with you, Jena," said Spazz in his softest, hoarsest voice. I could hardly believe my ears. And then Spazz was letting loose one of his grating laughs, right in my face. "Just joshin', dude."

The three of us got in my Explorer and swung by our house to get some stuff for the trip. While we were at it, we switched cars; we drove to the airport in Jena's shiny new frost green VW Beetle. Jena said it would be easier to park, and she was right. We got a great compact-sized space right by the elevator to the gates.

Las Vegas

Jena had brought her deck of cards along, so we played practice hands on the whole flight down, with Jena dealing and Spazz acting like another player. While we were playing, Spazz wrote a little Java simulation on his laptop to figure out precisely how much my subtle vision was going to improve my odds. The tattooed snake on his right forearm writhed as his fingers typed. A few hundred thousand hands scrolled by in cyberspace, Spazz quietly clearing his throat as he watched.

"In standard play, you win against the dealer forty-six percent of the time," rasped Spazz. "With subtle vision, you never have to bust, and your win rate goes up to almost sixty percent." Three-fifths of the hands, just as I'd thought.

"That's puny," said Jena.

"Well, Joe *could* look way down in the deck and save his big bets for the hands he's sure to win. Do you want to try that, Joe?"

I doubted it. I'm a businessman, not an engineer. "Sixty percent is fine," I said dismissively. "It'll pile up."

"Unless a run of bad luck cleans you out early," said Spazz, touching his ear stud.

"Are you sure you'll win, Joe?" asked Jena.

"Trust me," I said. "The main thing is that we're very cool in the casino. I'm scared of those casino guys. Don't you two be hanging on me."

"You need us!" said Jena. "We're your good luck!" She and Spazz leaned their heads together and laughed. They were getting along really well. This seemed like it could turn out to be fun—Jena knew how to handle a wolf like Spazz.

The conversation turned to where we should stay. Spazz and me had been in Vegas for COMDEX in November; we'd been booked into the three-thousand-room Vegas Hilton right next to the convention center. I suggested we just go there.

"Too plastic," said Jena. "Anyway, this is on our own tab. I know this great funky place called the Hog Heaven. They call it the Hog for short. It's an old casino on the Strip with the world's largest motel right behind it."

"When were you in Vegas, Jena?" asked Spazz.

"I was here in '95," she said. "I was doing research for a project on Indian Gaming." I happened to know that she'd done that trip with Buck Sawyer; it had come a week or two after Jena and I had first met, back when we were working together at a CompUSA in Denver. "I'm half Yavapai, you know," Jena told Spazz.

"Bitchin'," he said. "I like Native American stuff. A woman at Acoma sold me a little round pot with a hole in it, and with a tiny figure of someone crawling out of the hole. But she didn't explain it to me. Did you ever hear any legends about anything like that growing up, Jena?"

"Jena grew up Norwegian," I said. "She doesn't know much about being Native American."

"Shut up, Joe, you sound like my stepfather," said Jena. "And, yes, Spazz, I know exactly what you're talking about. A lot of the

Pueblo tribes believe people came from under the ground. They think the Earth's hollow."

"Seeing in the fourth dimension is kind of like seeing inside of things," I said, tapping the plane window. I didn't like the way I kept losing control of the conversation. "When I look down, I can see under the Earth," I continued. "News flash, guys, it's not hollow." But now Jena was watching Spazz draw a picture of the pot he claimed he'd bought.

It was early evening by the time we got onto the Strip. I rented a Lincoln Navigator SUV, just to compare it with my Explorer. The Navigator was another Ford Motors product, but higher end. It turned out to be a hell of a nice vehicle, if a bit mushy on the turns.

Jena directed me to the Hog Heaven, up at the north end of the Strip. Once we were inside, it took about fifteen seconds to pay a clerk for a couple of rooms next to each other. Outside the casino's back door was a maze of asphalt lanes, all lined with pre-fab beige rooms, stacked two high all along the endlessly branching avenues and side alleys of the Hog Heaven motel complex. There might have been a thousand rooms. The clerk gave us detailed instructions on how to drive to our assigned cubicles, but even so it took a couple of tries. Every row of rooms looked alike. Once we'd parked the Navigator and used our bathrooms, we took off on foot for Nero's Empire.

What a place. Nero's was like a city inside, complete with malls and restaurants, even bigger than Caesar's. It was designed kind of like a fish trap. Once you'd walked in twenty feet past the entrance, you couldn't see how to find your way back out. The slots were whooping and blinking and there were lights on the ceiling to steer you to the gaming tables. I stopped and watched one of the slots for a minute; I could see its insides. If I'd had more of a mechanical bent of mind, maybe I could have figured out how to tell when it was about to pay off. But blackjack was the sure thing. According to Jena, the casino didn't have to tell the IRS about winnings at the gaming tables. Jena said no matter how many chips you won, the casino would redeem them for cash and send you on your way.

I stepped up to the cashier's cage and bought seventeen of Nero's one-thousand-dollar chips with the cash that Momo had given us. They were impressive-looking things, shiny and gold, unlike the lowlier denominations, which were plain colors.

At Jena's advice, I took a seat at a shoe-dealt blackjack table with a minimum bet of a hundred dollars. At the shoe-dealt tables you didn't touch your cards at all, so there was less chance of my doing something wrong.

With the exception of the dealer's hole card, all cards were dealt face up from the fat wooden shoe, which held something like ten decks. The dealer was a sharp-faced, heavily made-up woman with a stiff red wig and a starched white shirt. In her forties. One of those hard-bitten Wild West types; Mom had had co-workers like her back in Matthewsboro. With my subtle vision, I noticed a tear gas aerosol in little holster inside her blouse.

"Howdy do!" she said, eyeing my stack of thousand-dollar chips. "Bettin' the farm." She gave me an encouraging smile. "I admire that."

"Today's gonna be my lucky day," I said.

"Don't forget to take care of the dealer when you win."

On my first hand, the dealer had an eight showing. Using my subtle vision, I could see that her turned-down hole card was a ten. To beat her, I had to get a total between nineteen and twenty-one. I got a six and a jack, both dealt face up from the shoe—no hole card for the players. Sixteen points. The face cards count ten in blackjack, and an ace can count either one or eleven, whatever the player likes. The best hand is a face card and an ace: blackjack.

The dealer looked at me. Did I want another card? With my subtle vision I could see the seven of clubs face down on the top of the shoe's fat deck. If I stood pat, my sixteen would lose to the dealer's eighteen. If I drew, I'd have twenty-three: too high, busted. Lose-lose. I drew a card; I figured it might look suspicious if I never ever busted.

"Joe!" said Jena sharply. She was watching over my shoulder. "You're not supposed to go over twenty-one! Maybe your sixteen would have won!" Had she already forgotten everything we'd discussed on the plane? Like about being cool in the casino? All I had was an edge, with no certainty of winning any given hand.

"Easy, Jena," said Spazz, who was watching over my other shoulder and making a little throat-clearing noise at each card I got.

The dealer glanced over at us, then finished giving the other players their extra cards. The woman next to me stood pat with nineteen. She'd bet two hundred dollars.

The dealer flipped over her hole card, showing her eighteen. If you're not used to casino blackjack, you might think the dealer would want to draw another card to try and beat the player's nineteen, but the rules are that the dealer has to act mechanically. Fairer all around, with less chance for collusion or rancor or massive dealer error. With one exception, the dealer always draws to a total of sixteen or less, and stands pat with a total of seventeen or more. The one exception to the rule comes if a dealer's seventeen includes an ace counted as eleven; in this case the dealer must take a hit as well, changing the ace to a one if necessary.

But right now the dealer had eighteen, so there was no question of taking a hit. The woman with nineteen points won two hundred dollars—blackjack pays the same as your bet—and I lost my first thousand.

As the dealer took my chip. I stared at the shoe of cards, trying to see ahead to the next hand. If I was going to win the next one, then why not bet five thousand? But just now, counting that far into the deck took more concentration than I had. The situation was too stressful. And having Jena hover over me and be doubtful wasn't helping things a bit. To make looking ahead even less practical, players kept coming and going, affecting which card I would get. Keep it simple, stupid. I bet another thousand.

This time the dealer had a three in the hole and a seven showing. I wasn't going to be able to predict what she'd end up with, because she'd be drawing after all the players got done, so this time I'd just draw as many cards as I could without going over twenty-one. I got a ten and a seven for starters. When I got my chance to ask for a hit, I saw that the facedown card on the top of the deck was a queen, which would have busted me. So I stood pat. When all the players had taken their cards, the dealer flipped over her hole card and drew a ten. She had twenty to my seventeen. Another thousand gone.

"You're not doing this right, Joe!" said Jena.

I really didn't like it when Jena doubted me. I lost my temper. "Shut up, you bitch," I hissed. "Leave me the hell alone."

"Hey, let's chill," said Spazz. "Joe knows the rules, Jena. Don't stress him out. And watch your mouth, Joe. That's your wife you're talking to. The woman you love."

"Go away," I repeated. "Both of you. You're bad luck."

Jena glared at me, hooked her arm into Spazz's, and stamped off.

I started winning then. As soon as I was up two thousand dollars, a cocktail waitress appeared, wanting to give me a drink. I asked for ginger ale. When she got back I was four thousand up.

"Here's your drink, honey," said the waitress.

I took a sip. It had rum in it—a lot.

"I wanted plain ginger ale," I said, setting the drink back down onto her tray.

"Oh, I'm sorry," she said, giving me a lingering pat on the back. Maybe feeling me down for a weapon or a computer.

I had a streak of good hands and then I was twenty thousand ahead. A skinny talkative guy with nicotine breath and a New York Jets T-shirt sat down on my left. "I been watching you," he said. "I'm gonna do just like you do." He had a pile of thousand chips as big as mine. Even though he kept losing, it didn't seem to bother him. And he was talking to me all the time. His name was Gus. A low-class loudmouth.

The waitress came back with a new drink for me. This time it was ginger ale and vodka. I complained again.

"What is wrong with me tonight?" she said, laughing and leaning way down so I could see her breasts. "Can't you just be a good boy and drink this one up? I'm gonna get in trouble if I keep taking drinks back."

"No," I said.

"Dude's a lightweight," said skinny Gus. I almost went for the challenge, but then I remembered something Jena had told me on the plane. The further I got ahead, the more the casino would mess with me. Gus was a hired shill whose sole purpose was to screw up my concentration.

"I don't drink like a fish," I told Gus, tossing a thousand-dollar tip to the dealer. "But I play like a whale." Clever line, Joe. I was feeling pretty cool. I wished Jena was there to hear me. I shouldn't have been so harsh with her.

Just to teach the shill a lesson, I put down twenty thousand for my next bet. If I lost, I'd still have the seventeen I started with. Sixteen, minus the tip. The dealer gave me a look, and the pit boss walked over. A handsome, muscular guy with a good tan. The kind of casino heavy I was scared of. His name tag said Sante Machado.

"Pardon me, Mr. Cube," he said. "We're gonna have to close

down this table. Come on over here; we've got a fresh table and dealer all set for you."

I tried to think if I'd told anyone my name. I'd had to show ID and give my name at the Hog Heaven, but I hadn't mentioned it to anyone at Nero's, had I? Oh yeah, come to think of it, Gus the shill had gotten a business card out of me. He'd mentioned COMDEX and out of reflex I'd given him a Kencom card. I guess he'd passed it up the chain. Gus stayed right on me as we switched to the new table.

The new dealer was a black guy with a shaved head. "Let's keep it going now," he said to me encouragingly. "Don't let up, Joe. Break the bank." The dealer always acted like your friend. I set down my twenty-thousand dollar bet again.

The dealer drew a nine face up and a jack for his hidden hole card. Nineteen. I got a five and a three. Tuning out Gus's manic chatter, I focused my subtle vision on the cards in the shoe. A king was next. "Hit me." Eighteen. Not enough to beat nineteen. The obvious strategy was to stand pat, but my subtle vision showed me that the card face-down on the top of the deck was a two. "Hit me," I said again. Twenty. Home free.

"The guy's got brass balls!" shouted Gus, slapping me on the back. Gus busted his hand, the dealer flipped his hole card to show his nineteen and now I was forty thousand dollars ahead.

"You're lucky!" said Sante the pit boss, looking me over once again.

"Clean living," I said, my heart pounding in my chest.

The waitress was at my elbow again with a rum and ginger ale. "Could you just get me a large coffee?" I asked her. "And a hamburger?" I gave her a hundred dollar bill for encouragement. She patted the inside of my leg. Frisking me some more, no doubt. This was all so unreal.

By the time I'd finished my burger I was up a hundred thousand dollars. Time for a break. I gave the dealer a chip and put the rest of the chips in a little cloth sack he gave me. I walked around in the dizzying noise, peering through things to look for Jena.

I found her and Spazz in a bar off the main room, deep in conversation. Their hearts going pitter-pat.

"Hi guys," I said. "It's the Vegas whale."

"How much have you won?" asked Jena, not smiling at me. She'd had a few drinks by now. She looked unhappy.

"A hundred large," I said.

This didn't seem to impress her as much as I'd thought it would. Again I lost my temper, again in front of Spazz.

"Are you still mad at me, Jena? Coming here was your idea in the first place, so for Christ's sake you ought to be happy."

"You called me a bitch and said I was bad luck," said Jena, staring down at her margarita. She began chewing on her thumbnail. "Fine. I'm staying away from you. I don't want to be hurt again. I'm sick of being your keeper and your scapegoat."

"I'm sorry I snapped at you, Jena. I was uptight. Maybe we should call it a night."

Spazz interrupted with a loud cough. "I thought you said you were going to win a million," he insisted. "Jena needs that much for the PR campaign."

"The what?" I was losing track of why we were doing this. Gambling wasn't fun, it was just some kind of weird and stressful work. And meanwhile this freak was doing his best to get it on with my wife.

"Let me talk to him alone," said Jena, still not looking up, still nibbling her nails.

"I'll be back," said Spazz in the *Terminator* voice, and headed for the bathroom.

"Show me the chips," said Jena with a flicker of interest.

I set my little Nero's carrying sack on the bar next to Jena's drink and she peered into it. "Not nearly enough for a house," said Jena after a minute. "With a million, we'd have enough for a decent house and a little left over for the PR campaign. I think you *should* win a million tonight. We can keep most of it."

"Careful," I said. "Momo's probably watching us. This might be some kind of test."

"Who cares?" said Jena. "It's our money. We're the ones who live here. You and me, Joe, chained together."

"Not chained, Jen," I snapped. "If you're sick of me, you're free to leave. And vice versa." Why was I talking like this? I rubbed my face and took a deep breath. "This is all messed up, Jena. I hate it here. Let's go home."

She looked up for the first time. She touched my cheek with her hand, her clear hazel eyes searching my face. Like she was saying good-bye. "Win the million, Joe. We've come this far. No matter what happens, a million's a good thing to have. Do you promise to split it with me? Fifty-fifty?"

"All right," I said, hoping to see her smile. Why was this turning into such a bummer? Here came Spazz walking back across the room, fingering his nose ring. "Don't get too tight with him," I cautioned Jena.

"I like Spazz. He makes me feel young again. Can I come watch you play?"

"Well—better not. I think maybe you really are bad luck. If I'm gonna do this, I have to focus. Will you wait here?"

A long pause. "I guess so," said Jena finally. "If you don't see me later on, that means I got tired and went back to the room. Give me the key just in case."

Back to work. By midnight I had two hundred thousand dollars; I'd switched over to ten-thousand-dollar chips. They changed the dealer and table two more times on me, but pretty soon I had eight hundred thousand. There was a big crowd of people standing behind me watching me play. I was still drinking coffee. Gus had gone to take a leak, and for the moment it was just the dealer and me—which was great, as now I could look ahead into the deck and really see what was coming so I could tune the sizes of my bets accordingly. I was wired like you wouldn't believe.

Here came my chance to reach a million. I bet two hundred thousand dollars. The dealer had a ten in the hole and a ten showing. I started out with an ace and a five, which was sixteen, counting the ace as eleven. I drew a four, and that made twenty, which still wasn't enough to beat the dealer—they didn't pay you for a tie. But my subtle vision had already told me I could do better. "Hit me." A king, which still gave me twenty, now counting my ace as one. A step back? Not really, for now I had the chance to take one last hit and get that second ace waiting down there. *Twenty-one.* I had my million.

"That's gotta be your last hand, sir," said Sante the pit boss, tapping me on the shoulder none too lightly. His eyebrows were angled in this weird, stagy way. He looked like a weary, pissed-off Dean Martin. "Nero's can't handle no more losses tonight."

I took my chips to the cashier and got paid in honest-to-God cash. A hundred packs of a hundred hundred-dollar bills each. Whoops, not quite a hundred packs. Seventy-two packs.

"Where's the rest of my money?" I demanded.

"Federal withholding, Mr. Cube," said the cashier. "Twenty-eight percent. We've filled out the form for you. Just sign here."

They already had my social security number written onto the form. I guess they'd been busy checking me out.

"My wife told me there's no tax on blackjack!" I protested.

"There is if you win more than five thousand dollars, Mr. Cube," said the cashier in a bored tone. "You could look it up. Section 3402 of the tax code. Paragraph Q."

To finish the transaction off, they sold me a shiny metal Halliburton Zero attaché case for nine hundred dollars.

I was a big winner. But meanwhile my wife was nowhere in sight. While I'd been playing, she'd swung by my table once or twice to peek at me, each time looking more desperate. But I'd kept shooing her away. Who needed that noise? Being in a fight with her was ruining the joy of my big score! And now she was gone.

I got a cab back down the Strip to the Hog; I didn't want to be walking around this time of night with a million bucks in an attaché case, minus taxes. But a million just the same! I was riding high. When I got out behind the Hog, I realized I didn't know our room number. I could have looked for a desk clerk, but I felt like I remembered well enough where the room was.

I walked around in the maze of the motel streets for half an hour, getting thoroughly disoriented. Finally I thought of using my subtle vision to peek into the rooms and look for Jena. A lot of people were still awake, doing all sorts of sleazy Vegas-type stuff. Sex, booze, drugs, you name it. One memorable thing I saw was a male stripper wearing nothing but a starched little bib-and-tucker thing and a red silk bow tie. He was closeted with a bachelorette party of three lumpy women from Wyoming. His dancing was over, but he was still at work, earning the little stack of twenty-dollar bills sitting on the TV.

Jena was nowhere to be seen in any of the rooms near where I thought we'd stayed. And then I realized I'd been looking in the wrong alley. I went down to the next one, still no Jena, and then finally, with my regular vision, I spotted my Lincoln Navigator parked by our rooms. I used my subtle vision to peek inside.

Jena was awake. She and Spazz had opened the door between our rooms, and Jena was in Spazz's bed, naked, her eyes squeezed into lustful slits, her arms wrapped tight around him.

Of course.

I stood there on the asphalt watching for two or three minutes, struck dumb, filled with sick fascination. With my subtle vision, I was right in the room with them. It was hot. I'd never seen Jena so excited before in my life. I was, like, hypnotized. But when they paused to switch positions, I pulled my attention away.

Much more than being a turn-on, this was like getting punched in the stomach. I felt cringing and hollow, sadder than sad. Jena and Spazz—it knocked the wind out of my sails. I felt like lying down on the sidewalk and crying. Oh Jena. And now the anger came up too. I wanted to kill Spazz.

What to do? Pound on the door and confront them? Shouting, violence, the cops? That's what my low-rent relatives back in Matthewsboro would have done. But I was educated, civilized. Should I slink away and come back when they were done? Pretend that nothing had happened? It sickened me to imagine lying down next to Jena right after Spazz.

Someone tapped me on the shoulder. A mugger! I whirled, clutching the case of money to my chest. Nobody there—or—wait, yes—it was Momo's hand.

One of her womanlike cross sections swelled up and stood on the pavement beside me. "I see that you're upset about your wife, Joe Cube."

"You got me into this," I said. "Tell me what to do."

"Would you like to get away from here?"

"Yes." That was the best answer for now. Leave.

"I'll take you back to your house."

Momo stepped towards me and gave me a hug. God knows I needed a hug about then. It felt good. Her flesh flowed all the way around me and I felt pressure in every part of my body: in my stomach, in my chest, all down my arms and legs. There was that weird rotating sensation again, and everything got bright. We were outside of Spaceland, just like we'd been when Momo carried me through the wall of my house, floating in the funny higher space that Momo lived in. The All.

The fourth dimension still didn't make much sense to me, but, thanks to having been augmented, I could see in it better than before. There was four-dimensional pink stuff squeezed around most of my body: Momo's flesh. I was kind of sticking out of her like a baby bird in a nest. By leaning out and looking down, I could see that Momo was perched on her shiny little flying saucer. I turned my head and looked up above us.

We were in some kind of immense cave with, I guessed, four-dimensional walls. The walls had a way of morphing their shapes as my head moved. The cave was lit up like the inside of a fluorescent light tube. Evidently there was some kind of air, as I could still breathe. But my main interest was our own world, spread out next to me. My regular eyes could only see cross sections of things—slices taken parallel to the ground, more or less like floor plans. But my third eye could see everything, just like I'd seen into all of our townhouse back home.

"Behold your Spaceland," said Momo.

Right beside us was the Hog Heaven parking lot with the asphalt and my Lincoln Navigator. I wasn't looking at a *view* of the lot, I was looking at the actual lot itself. And it wasn't like an aerial view, either. Relative to the people in Spaceland, I wasn't *above* the lot, I was *vout* from it. Off in the universe next door, you might say. Our motel rooms were open to my view, with, ugh, Spazz and Jena still going at it. I wished I was dead.

I looked past those two at the Texas Texas casino next door; I could scan through every room of it. The gaming tables, the restaurant, the strip show, the offices, a woman smoking a cigarette and counting money in a back room, two cooks in the kitchen joking around, one of them putting his fingers up by his head and imitating a bull. Focusing in on the cooks did me good; it took my mind off Jena. But now the casino was moving past us. Momo was heading for Los Perros.

The Strip went flying past, but not like we were over it, more like we were next to it. It was a little like being in a theater with a big screen showing a drive through Las Vegas. Several times it looked like we were going to ram a car, and I'd wince, but then we'd breeze right past it, me and Momo on her little chrome saucer.

We roared through downtown Vegas with all its lights, and then we were blasting past the desert. When we hit the Sierras, Momo didn't rise up over them. We flew right through them. But not really *through* them of course, as we were a few yards removed from our regular world.

Like I said, there was four-dimensional light all around, and it even lit up the insides of the mountains. I'd always enjoyed hiking in the Rockies as a boy, and it was pretty amazing to see what mountains looked like inside. They're more interesting than you might expect, with lots of big, muscular bends and folds, not to mention the occasional tubes of quartz, the fanned-out mineral growths and now and then a ragged, secret cavern. Not that I could concentrate very well. Every beat of my heart was saying, "Jena." To cover the pain I did my best to look around and notice things.

We raced across the Central Valley, Momo's little flying saucer buzzing steadily beneath us. The surfaces of things were lit by the moon, and their insides were lit by the higher light of the All. The beauty of it was soothing to me. We passed barns, farmhouses, rivers, freeways, and 7-Elevens. And then we were following Route 101 into the south side of San Jose, with a fair amount of traffic even at this ungodly hour—what was it now, three AM on Sunday morning? Pitiful early risers out to beat the morning rush, and there was a rush, even on Sundays.

I could see each and every passenger in each and every car, and

each person in every bed in every house of the suburban develop-
ments rushing by. All the little lives, as pointless as my own.

Finally, we were closing in on the friendly interior of my home,
lit up by the heartbreaking kitchen light that Jena had left on.
Momo plowed on in there and then shoved me over into regular
space. I was home. Me and a metal case with a million dollars in
it. I would have given every bit of that money to roll the clock back
a few hours. I'd been a fool to yell at Jena. I started crying.

"You are weary," said Momo, a crooked cross section of her head
peering into my living-dining room.

"Just go away. Don't ask me for anything more."

Momo left and I got in the shower and stayed there till the crying
stopped. And then I put the case with the million next to the bed
and lay down. I was feeling calmer. I'd say it was all my fault. That
I'd driven Jena away. Tomorrow I could fix things. I'd get her back.
And then I'd get even with Spazz. I fell asleep.

A Dream Of Flatland

In the night I had a memorable dream. I was flying beside a huge vertical plane with something like a painting on it. The flat round image showed a full-size cross section of planet—glowing red in the center, and with mountains and shallow seas on its rind. I flew towards the disk's top border, driven by an urgent feeling that there was something I had to do.

I stopped just short of the plane, which was more like a soap film than a canvas. Looking over at the rim of the disk, I saw movements. It wasn't a painting, it was a world of life. A Flatland. It had the East/West and up/down directions, but it was missing what we'd call North/South.

The top rim of the disk was a strip of land with two-dimensional buildings piled on it, making up a town I somehow thought of as my hometown of Matthewsboro, Colorado. It was like a cross section of Matthewsboro, a jumble of stuff set upon the line of a flat planet's gently curved rim. The town wasn't flat like an aerial view, it was flat like a vertical slice of a city. A cartoon skyline, with the insides of the buildings open to my view. It had dirt below, sky above, a row of buildings with little pieces of street between them—and flat people everywhere.

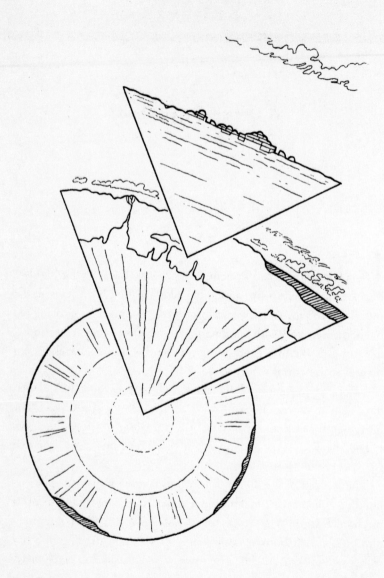

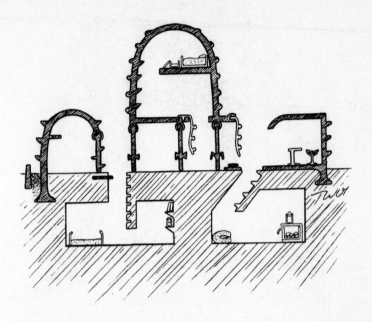

The people of Flat Matthewsboro were nearly as tall as me. Each had two arms, two legs, and a head; they were like silhouettes, like animated Egyptian hieroglyphs. Their heads had an eye on either side and the slit of a mouth on top. The eyes were flat gleaming triangles, and the fronts of their eyes bulged. Their flat skins wrapped around their edges like rinds on slices of salami. Their clothes were stringy wrappers outside their skins, like threads of icing on the rims of gingerbread men and women.

Though these Flatlanders were as tall as me, they were no thicker than their film of space. Seeing a flat man on his own in an underground room, I flew down next to him. I said a few words to him, but he didn't seem to hear me. Would it hurt his space if I reached into it? I thought of an ocean's surface or a soap film. Maybe the surface would give way and stay tight around my fingers. I went ahead and stuck my two hands into the room with him. Just as I'd hoped, the space harmlessly gave way.

The flat man saw the cross sections of my fingers in his room; he darted around in terror. I cornered him against the eastern wall. From my viewpoint in the third dimension, I could see his insides: his muscles, his bones, his brain and his desperately pounding heart. Curious to get a really good look at how he was made, I grabbed hold of his skin on either side and lifted him up.

What a disaster. He fell apart like a hot slice of pizza with too many toppings. As his skin came up out of his plane, his innards spilled out and scattered. Some pieces drifted off into space, some fell back into the plane. I tried to put the man back together, but it was hopeless. There was nothing more to do for him. Sadly I stirred his remains with my hands, trying to get a feel for this flat world's matter. It was like the objects in this world were scraps of cellophane embedded in a soap film. They had a weak kind of solidity to them, but mostly they depended on the upper and lower sides of their space to keep them together. The flat man had been like a mosaic held together by the pressure of his space.

A Flatland woman appeared outside the room's door, which was hinged on the ceiling like a pet door. The door was like a line instead of a rectangle—a fat line that bulged out to a ball at the top end, the ball held by a socket on the ceiling. The vibrations of the woman's knocking and of her voice traveled up my arms and into my ears. "Hey Custer, it's me, Mindy!" she cheerfully called.

The door swung open and her greetings changed to screams. I pulled my guilty hands up out of the room, but not before she glimpsed their pink cross sections. She ran up the carved-out stairs and onto the main street of Flat Matthewsboro, shrieking out the news.

I offered dead Custer a silent apology, and moved along next to the main street of Flat Matthewsboro myself, heading the opposite way from Mindy. Flat Matthewsboro's street ran East/West, punctuated by the town's buildings. It was more like a series of courtyards than a street. The buildings had staircase outlines, big on the bottom and small on top, with basements and sub-basements as well. I could see inside everything.

The citizens of Matthewsboro moved along the streets by walking upon their weirdly jointed legs and occasionally leaping into the air. They were nimble as fleas. The gravity of their world was so weak that they usually chose to clamber over a building rather than finding their way through its passages. And when two of them encountered each other going opposite ways, one would somersault over the other. It seemed customary for the westbound one to hop over the eastbound one.

The building's doors were sturdy affairs, with leaf springs to hold them closed. It occurred to me that if anyone ever left a one-room building's eastern and western doors open at the same time, the building could collapse. To make this less likely, the buildings with more than one door had more than one room as well, so that there were a series of doors. There even seemed to be some kind of signaling system to prevent the all-doors-open-at-once disaster, a system of strings rigged up along the ceilings between the pairs of doors.

The buildings had markings in the form of colored dashes and dots along their outer walls. Thanks to the magic of dreams, I could read the signs. I saw a hot dog stand that I remembered from my boyhood: Cowboy Zeke's Dawg 'N Suds. I watched a man eating a Wrangler Dog; he chewed it up and swallowed the pieces down into the sack of his stomach, washing down the food with a two-dimensional bottle of root beer. The woman behind the T-shaped counter had popped off the two-dimensional bottle-cap for him; the cap was a neat little thing shaped like a staple.

In my dream I knew that the flat man was my Dad. This hadn't mattered at first, but now it did matter. Dad reached up high to wipe off the mouth on the top of his head, then leaned on the counter of the hot dog stand, pointing his mouth towards the shapely young counter woman, bulging out his eyes so that he could look at her. They got into a lively conversation. I reached out and gently touched the surface of the flat world so that the sounds of their voices could travel up my arm and into my inner ear. The Flatlanders sounded country, just like the folks back in the real Matthewsboro.

The woman's name was Dawna. Dad wanted Dawna to come for a walk and let him "pitch some woo." Dad often talked that way, using that forties kind of big-band slang. Some women liked it. Dawna sealed up the hot dog stand and they set off, scrambling over building after building until they'd found their way into the woods to the east of Matthewsboro.

The woods were like the cross section of a broccoli plant: green and filled with nooks and crannies. Beyond the woods lay the shallow bowl of a lake—a water-filled dent in the planet's surface. People were swimming in the lake, diving to pass under each other when necessary. There was steady foot traffic back and forth over the woods between Matthewsboro and the lake, but the daytrippers stuck to the outmost edges of the vegetation rather than pushing down into its depths. Dad and Dawna were as private as a pair of aphids in a tea rose.

I watched them bend their heads to rub their mouths together, and then they peeled off their clothes, the thin strings they wrapped around themselves to hide their skin. How small their clothes were compared to their bodies.

Dad's penis stiffened between his legs. He and Dawna folded and bent their double-jointed legs so they could have sex. Dawna helped Dad insert tab A into slot B. It looked so strange from the third dimension.

A teenage girl was passing westward over the outer edges of the woods, on her way home from swimming in the lake. She looked familiar, but for the moment I couldn't place her. She wore her

hair glued into two ponytails below her eyes, one ponytail on either side of her head. She had a little pet with her, a small darting animal like a dog. The pet unexpectedly burrowed down into a narrow inlet of the woods, and the girl followed after it. Perhaps the dog was drawn by Dad and Dawna's rustlings. The ponytailed girl saw the two lovers, but they didn't see her. Very agitated, the girl grabbed her dog and took off towards Matthewsboro.

A bit later, Dad dropped Dawna off at the hot dog stand and ambled home, pausing on the way to vomit the digested remnants of his meal into a special public trough at the side of a building. In this flat world, people didn't have full digestive tracts. Dad bumped into a friend at the trough. I touched my finger to their plane in the shadow of the trough so I could pick up their sound vibrations.

"Howdy, big gaaah," said Dad's friend, another cowboy-type character. He, too, was squeezing out the waste from his belly. "Nothin' like emptyin' yore gut before dinner, hey Ed?"

"Urp, yep," said Dad. "After some lovin' it's pretty good too, Jed."

"You devil," cackled Jed. "I noticed you slippin' outta town with that little Dawna from Zeke's. I guess you been too busy plowin' to hyar the big news."

"What all's that?"

"Some kind o' weird cult killin'. Custer. He was butchered like a flat pig. His waaf Mindy found him, she said they was things like hands rootin' around in his bloody guts. Spirit hands without no body."

"Mercy me," said Dad. And then, without missing a beat, he began wondering aloud how this might affect Mindy's sexual availability. "Widders gets lonely pretty fast, I hear." Same old Dad.

I followed Dad to his humble home—which turned out to be a Flatland version of the house I'd grown up in. What a pang it gave me to see it, flat and open as the back of a dollhouse. Inside were

Mom and my sister Sue, a loudmouth with a lot of attitude. Seeing Sue and her ponytails, I suddenly realized that she was the girl who'd seen Dad and Dawna. And, yes, her flat dog was with her, fuzzed with orange and white hair just like my boyhood dog Arf. Mom looked angry; her motions were jerky and angular. Sue had already spilled the beans.

I had a sinister feeling of things coming together. My dream was turning into the day when my mother had stabbed my father in his stomach. The worst day of my life. Maybe this time I could do something to keep it from happening. I touched a finger to the corner of the room beneath the couch and listened to them.

As soon as he came in, Dad started telling Mom about Custer's killing. "Seems Mindy found Custer all hacked up, with his innards all over the room!" he exclaimed. "People are gittin' nastier all the time. Mindy's about off her nut; she's sayin' she seen hands crawlin' around inside the remains. Hands without nothin' attached to 'em, all wobbly and changin' their shapes like clouds."

Mom wasn't going to be distracted. "I suppose you'll be slippin' around to comfort Mindy next," she snapped. "Too bad them crawlin' hands didn't git her too." Mom knew her husband. "You and your tramps," she yelled. "Your sluts! I know what you got up to this afternoon with Dawna!"

"Why do you have to run around with other women all the time, Dad?" said Sue in a shaky voice. "It's ruining my life. People tease me about you at school."

"Some day you'll know the score," answered Dad in his slow, Western drawl. "A fella's got his needs." The maddening thing about my father had been that he never seemed to feel guilty. He was like Arf: one whiff of an available female and he was gone, not a thought in his head but burying his bone.

"Oh, let him be, Sue," said Mom, suddenly turning listless. "It don't matter none." She'd often gotten like that towards the end of

the marriage—too sad and crushed to make a fuss. Deflated. But I
knew how much rage was inside her. I knew she was about to snap.

I had to do something to stop the disaster. I stuck my hand
further into the film of Mom and Dad's living room. As before, the
space gave like the surface of a pond, easily letting me poke through.
I moved my hand and waggled my fingers, moving them around in
the air above their floor.

Seeing the little pink circles where my fingers crossed their space,
the three flat people jerked in surprise. Inside their bodies, their
two-dimensional Valentine hearts pulsed faster. Mom screamed,
"It's them hands!" She darted into the kitchen next door, dragging
Sue by the hand. She hooked the flap of the kitchen door behind
her; the barking dog was with her too.

I backed Dad against the other wall, herding him with my fingers. Once or twice I bumped him. He was lighter than the thinnest scrap of paper; my slightest touch sent him flying. When he stopped trying to escape, I lowered my head sideways down into the space and talked to him.

"Don't be afraid, Dad. I'm Joe. Your son."

"Git!" said Dad. "Don't touch me!"

"I'm from Spaceland," I said. "The land of three dimensions."

"What's that crap supposed to be?"

"Spaceland has up, down, East and West like your Flatland," I said. "But we have North and South, too."

"That don't mean a thing. North. Where's it at?"

"It's the other direction of your body. Not up or down, not left or right—it's what you might call back and front."

"Back and front ain't words neither. You gonna tear me apart like you did Custer?"

"That was an accident," I said. "I only want you to understand me. I'm your Spaceland son. Maybe if you understand me, then I can understand the fourth dimension."

"You not my son," said Dad, squeezing shut his eyes. "I'm not seein' you a'tall."

"I'm real," I insisted, with a catch in my voice. "Look at me."

I was weightless; I could fly in any direction I liked. I floated through the house's living room front-on, making a cross section that was first the oval of my stomach, then a two-dimensional outline of my arms, legs and head, then the rounds of my butt, and then nothing. Dad didn't say anything.

I turned and drifted through Dad's space again, this time feet first, like Momo had done. The plane intersected my legs in a pair of circles. The circles grew and joined to make a cross section of my waist, accompanied by the cross sections of my arms. The arm circles merged with my body circle, and shrank down to my neck.

And then I showed Dad some outlines of my head. Still no reaction.

I turned my head at an angle, holding it so that both my eye and my mouth were in Dad's space again. The cross section I made was an irregular blob.

"You a freak," said Dad. "A space monster. You kilt Custer."

"Maybe so," I said. "But Mom's about to knife you."

"Say what?"

"I remember, Dad," I told him. "I've been through all this before. Here, let me help you. I'll augment you."

In my dream I knew I had to make my father wet and then shock him. It seemed I was holding something like a cattle prod, and now, to wet him down, I found myself peeing onto him. My urine spurted into Dad's space from the third dimension, dousing him all over. I touched the electrode of the prod to the center of his brain and—lo and behold—a stalk grew up with a bright black eye at its tip. I ran the prod around the edges of his body and his skin writhed and then spread across his exposed surfaces, a higher skin closing off his exposure to the third dimension.

And then I pulled myself out of their space and watched, with a listening finger resting behind the couch. After a minute, Mom reappeared from the kitchen. Sue and the dog had escaped out the back door.

"Are you all right, Ed?" said Mom uneasily. "Where'd them devil hands go? Did someone put a hex on you and Mindy?"

"I—I can see over your skin," said Dad, staring down at her with his third eye. He could indeed see over her skin and into her guts.

"I can see inside you, Mary. I see your blood and your crap. You as dirty inside as me."

"Oh, I hate you so much!" cried Mom. "You make my life filthy!" She ran into the kitchen and grabbed a long sharp triangle. The carving knife. She stabbed at Dad, but Dad instinctively humped up the middle of his body, making a little arch that the knife could stick through without actually touching him.

From Mom's point of view it was as if Dad's middle had disappeared. She screamed and ran out of the room. Dad's stomach sank back into his flat space.

"You still hangin' around, Space Joe?" he asked. "How in tarnation did I disappear my stomach like that?"

"You lifted it towards the front side of your body," I said. "Into the third dimension. Would you like to see what it's like up here?"

"Okey-doke," said Dad. "And when we done, you set me down somewhere's far away."

After the way I'd torn Custer's skin right off his body, I was a little nervous about lifting up my flat Dad. But he'd been augmented now; his front and back were covered with skin. I took a delicate hold of his leg and jiggled it. It lifted up fine—though his sock and his shoe stayed behind.

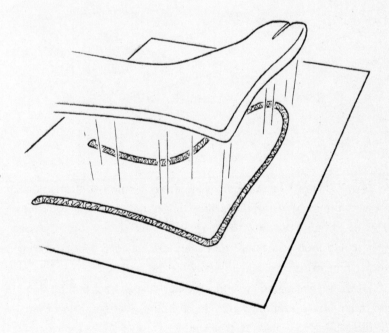

I pulled harder, and then Dad was up above his flat world. He had trouble seeing much of it with his regular eye. The problem was that his flat eyes only saw things that lay in the plane of his body.

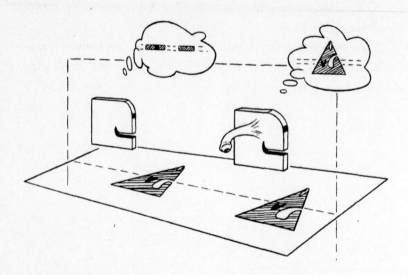

In my dream I knew he was able to get a true two-dimensional view of things by using the stalk of his extra eye. But it took him a while to figure out how to interpret this vision. For him it was as if he could look at a thing from every side at once. I began trying to get him to see my face, to really see me at last.

Down in Flat Matthewsboro, the flat people were boiling down the main street, climbing over the buildings like an army of ants, heading for Dad's place. A lynch mob.

I thought I was safe from them, but the three-dimensional space around me started collapsing, squeezing in from either side, crushing me and Dad down into the world of two dimensions, down into that dull, level wilderness.

I came down in our flat house's backyard. I'd been smashed

flatter than road kill. My arms and legs could still move, but only left/right and up/down. I was a Flatlander, with my vision reduced to a single bright line.

I heard the flat locals coming closer, yelling for my blood. I took off over the neighbor's house, and over the house after that, on and on, with the yelling coming closer. I was doomed.

6

A Narrow Escape

I **woke** to the beeping of my cell phone. For a second I lay there, gathering my wits. The long, complicated dream dropped right out of my head.

I could tell from the sound of the traffic on 85 that I'd overslept. Nine-thirty on a Sunday morning. I could see the traffic with my subtle vision. The bed felt cool and empty and quiet. No Jena. I didn't want this day to begin.

It was her on the phone. "Joe! I've been worried sick. I thought something had happened to you. How could you leave without telling me?"

"I saw you together with Spazz, Jena. Don't you understand I can look through walls?"

It took her a second to formulate her comeback. "You were *spying* on me? Like a pervert?"

"Don't try to turn this around, Jena. I saw what you were doing, and I left. It's over." I was just saying this for effect. I pretty much expected she'd contradict me. But she didn't.

"It's been over for a while now, Joe," she said softly. "I didn't want to admit it to myself. But I can't live with you. You're too cold. Too selfish."

"Go to hell." I cut the connection and started getting dressed. Khakis, a clean blue shirt and a beige V-neck sweater. My hands were shaking. It was hard to button my shirt. A minute later the phone warbled again.

"What?" I answered.

"I think you should move out," said Jena. "I don't want to live with you for one more minute. I'd like you to vacate by the time I come back this afternoon."

"Why should I be the one to move out? Why not you?"

"I don't want to get cheated out of my share of the house." I heard Spazz coughing in the background. And then the sound of his voice. He was advising her. "Vacate, Joe," repeated Jena.

"Fine," I said coldly. "I'll rent someplace better. Or maybe I'll buy. I've got a million dollars, you know. Seven hundred and eighty thousand, actually. You were wrong about them not collecting taxes."

"Half of it's mine," said Jena.

This time I didn't curse. I turned off the phone and put it in my pocket. I opened my metal attaché case and looked at my million dollars again. It made me feel better to see it. The money meant I was still someone. Not a loser. The shaking ebbed away and I began to feel cold and strong. If the bitch wanted me to vacate, I was gone. I went outside, taking the attaché case with me.

It was a sunny day, reasonably warm for the start of January. I drove down to the corner shopping center. On the way there, I tried to take my mind off Jena by getting into the subtle vision thing. You always have a kind of image of what's around you. By glancing this way and that, you keep this full three-dimensional map of the world reasonably well updated inside your head. But with my third eye looking vinn at Spaceland from its stalk, I didn't have to be glancing. I had the whole image, right there, all the time, and my mind's eye could pick out whatever viewpoint I needed. I could see what was behind things and inside things and underneath things. I didn't even need to look at the road while I was driving. I could point my face in pretty much any direction I liked. My third eye could always see where everything was.

It should have felt nice to be seeing all around me all at once. But thanks to Jena, I felt unhappy and numb.

At the shopping center I got a pack of cigarettes at the drugstore. It was time to start smoking again. Jena hated for me to smoke. Too bad. And then I filled up the back of my Explorer with empty boxes. I could pack and be out by noon. Not being home when Jena got back was starting to feel like a really good idea. Vacate. That was so Jena to fixate on a word like that.

On the way back home, smoking a cigarette, I drove slow so I could soak up what all the people were doing in their houses. It was comforting to see them. They were eating breakfast, showering, watching TV, yelling at their kids, like that. And then I noticed a couple doing it. What was the big deal about sex anyway? It was always the same. Why cheat on your partner? I'd always dreaded ending up like Mom, all stiff and bitter and crazy. If Jena was going to do me this way, maybe it was really better to get free. But I couldn't visualize my life without her.

My dream came back to me then. My flat Dad had bucked up into the third dimension to escape the knife. I wondered if there was any way I could lift my own augmented body into the fourth dimension. I felt around inside myself, but couldn't seem to find a way to do it.

But all this time, more than anything else, I was thinking about Jena and Spazz. Jena—well, maybe I could forgive her. I'd been treating her poorly, and perhaps this was what I had coming to me. She'd been drunk. It didn't have to count.

But as for Spazz—I wanted to kill him, pure and simple. I even got to the point of wondering if I should go buy a gun. That would be something. Walk right up to the smug son of a bitch and pump a clip into him. Shoot him in the heart and stomach so I could watch his face. And, yeah, use my subtle vision to look into his body and see his punctured heart pumping his blood into his abdominal cavity and see his stomach acid digesting the adjacent organs. Thinking this way made me start shaking again. I did my best to push the hate thoughts back. If I killed Spazz I'd go to jail instead of ending up rich. If I was rich I could get a better woman than Jena. A woman who wasn't moody and didn't get drunk all the time. I looked over at my attaché case. I needed to stay focused.

Back at the house, I switched on my phone and saw on its screen that I'd gotten three messages from Jena's phone. I deleted them without listening. I needed to vacate. I remembered then that Ken Wong had scheduled a series of special Y2K meetings with staff members today. Sunday morning meetings to iron out any problems before the real work started on Monday. My meeting was in an hour. I wasn't going to make it.

I phoned Kencom and got hold of Ming Wong, the secretary. I told her I was taking a sick day. Ming was Ken Wong's cousin. Ken was a product of Cupertino High School and Stanford, a Silicon Valley smoothie, but Ming was a recent immigrant from Taiwan, and she didn't speak very good English. She was strict and bossy anyway.

"You know where is Spazz?" Ming demanded. "He missing meeting with Ken right now. Bad start for Western New Year. Has Spazz make report to you?"

"Spazz is in Las Vegas," I said. "And Ming, I may not make it in tomorrow either."

"This very bad."

"I've got gastroenteritis. There's diarrhea all over my sheets. Have a nice day." I'd learned long ago that the more disgusting your sick-day excuses were, the less likely it was that anyone would call you on them.

When I turned around to start packing, Momo was there, big and pink and womanly, wearing a gold dress cut open in back. She was sitting on her little metal dish, the saucer thing she used to travel long distances. "Are you and Jena going to start on the business plan today?" asked Momo. Seeing Momo made me mad. She was the cause of all my troubles.

"Plan for what?" I snarled. "For Jena doing it with Spazz?"

"I see you're upset with your wife," said Momo, settling down on my floor as if for a long chat. "I've been reading up on Spaceland business styles, you know. Jena's suggestions about the marketing campaign were very apropos."

"Forget Jena!" I snapped. "It's all over between her and me."

"I think you two could still work together," said Momo. "I'd rather not have to bring more and more people in on our secret, you know." She took on a coaxing tone. "Surely your subtle vision has increased your empathy. How can you refuse forgiveness to someone whose very innards lie open to your view?"

"We have a phrase that might apply here," I said. "It's called hating someone's guts." But did I really hate Jena? Hard to say. At this point I really didn't know anymore. "Leave it alone," I said. "Right now I have to find a new place to live. And, Momo? Before you come nagging me, why don't you figure out exactly what the hell kind of product we're supposed to be developing."

"But this is precisely what I've come to discuss!" exclaimed Momo. "Calm yourself and hear my plan, Joe Cube. Our product will be the key hardware for a third generation cellular phone system. 3G broadband wireless, as your fellows say. We'll send wide-band, packet-switched, hundred-gigahertz radio signals through the fourth dimension. There's an unlimited band of unused frequencies out here, and our air doesn't scatter your signals. They'll travel parallel to normal space, but exactly one millimeter above it. Our core business will be providing little antenna crystals that project vinn from your space. Vinn to the fourth dimension. Little loop antennas in hyperspace. For signals in the ten- to hundred-gigahertz range, an antenna can be a mere centimeter long. We'll kink the antenna wires with two right angles so they run your signals along your vinn/vout axis. The sending antenna shunts the signal vinn to our All where there's no smog, no buildings, no mountains, no other signals, no interference. The signal flies along parallel to your space. And then the receiving antenna shunts it back vout to your world."

"My God!" I knew a killer pitch when I heard one. "You're talking the talk, Momo!"

"My family and I formed the notion of the hyperspace antennas before I came here, but we weren't quite sure yet of the application. While you were asleep, I read the contents of your local bookstore, with particular attention to the business and technology magazines. And then I had my idea. I feel this proposal is very much of your time."

"It's dynamite, Momo." I was pacing around the room, my heart pounding with excitement, all thoughts of Jena temporarily on hold. I had the better part of a million dollars and a great piece of technology. My big break at last! And then a brainstorm hit me. The perfect name.

"The Hyperphone!" I exclaimed. "You like?"

"I'll trust your sense of business on such details, Joe," said Momo in a neutral tone. "That's why I picked you to be our Spaceland representative."

"The Hyperphone," I repeated, still hoping to get my nugget of praise. Actually, come to think of it, maybe I'd heard that word used before? I pressed on. "We'll sell—who knows—maybe a million of them!"

"Most excellent," said Momo, brightening. "A very wide distribution was my intent. Though perhaps a mere fifty thousand antennas would be enough, were people to use them sufficiently."

"Enough for what?" It occurred to me that I hadn't given much thought to Momo's motives for helping me. "Why are you really doing this, Momo?"

"Therein lies a complex and tangled tale," said Momo. "I'll recount it to you at a more propitious time. But we have many tasks before us, so rather than discoursing any further, I'll set off for Klupdom."

"Why?"

"To initiate the fabrication of your—Hyperphone antennas. My husband Voule is quite an accomplished craftsman. I'll return anon. Meanwhile you might ponder the best fashion in which to organize your new business. And you'd better think of a different name. I believe that when I read your bookstore, I noticed that Hyperphone is already trademarked."

"Um—how about Metaphone?" I said after a minute.

"That's taken too," said Momo immediately.

"Christ."

"Name it after me," she suggested.

"How do you mean?"

"The Mophone. Nobody's registered that one yet."

"Not bad," I said, turning the word over in my mind. I was used to this kind of spitballing from endless hours of meetings. I was good at it. "Mophone has mobile phone in it straight up. Kind of retro, which fits in with the idea that we'll make life simpler. There's a black thing going on too. Mo' phone. That works." I tried the word a few more times. "Mophone. Mophone. Mophone. I'm hearing a touch of mofo in there? Kind of a rough word. But that's not a bad thing. Makes us edgy. I can see the ad. Black dude, initially menacing, but then he takes off his shades and he's smiling at you. He's your friend and he's talking to you. He likes you, even though you're a rich white geek. 'Static? Bad signals? Dropping your calls? Get a Mophone, mofo!' " I thought a bit more. "I guess the only things I worry about are the gayness and the drugs."

"Your reasoning is obscure," said Momo.

"Morphine. Homo phone. Morphodite."

"Might such connotations hurt your sales?"

"Oh, probably not. Morphine, well, who cares. And gay is hip. Let's go with it. Mophone. I love it!"

"I really must be on my way," said Momo. "What will be your next step towards our Great Work?"

"I'll look for a place to rent," I said. "And then I'll see about incorporating Mophone."

"It is well," said Momo. "And Joe—remain vigilant. I've seen some signs that—well, never mind. Just remember that you're augmented. That should get you through the day." She was gone before I could ask questions.

The phone chirped. Jena.

"What now?" I asked. "I'm busy vacating." Despite Momo's unsettling warning, I was feeling pretty chipper. Unlimited phone spectrum! The Mophone!

"Joe, it's about Nero's Empire. You were so huffy that I didn't get a chance to tell you before. One of their guys was at our room first thing this morning. He woke me up. Very buff, very tan, very crooner. He said he has to talk to you."

This sounded like the pit boss from last night. Sante. "You told on me?"

"No! I was surprised you weren't there. I told him I didn't know what was happening."

"What did he say then?"

"He said he'd find you." Her voice had an anxious edge. "He said he knows where you live. And then he left, and I called you, and you hung up, and Spazz and I had breakfast, and now we're on the way to the airport."

"Was it Spazz who put them on me?" I demanded. "Did Spazz tell?"

"Nobody told Nero's Empire anything, Joe. Let's try and stay centered. You're blowing everything all out of proportion. It's probably something innocent. I only called to give you a heads-up. Maybe they want to take your picture. Like to advertise about their big winners. Or maybe they want to comp you for your next trip."

"Thank God I'm clearing out. They might already be on their way. I'll hurry. And—Jena?"

"What."

"Be careful."

"You be careful too, Joe. I'll call you again when I get up to Los Perros."

"Okay," I said. "I'm gonna be all over the place today. Momo's got an idea that's completely off the hook."

There was a pause. "We can still work together, Joe. Even if we're split up." Hearing Jena on the phone, I could visualize her so well. She'd be staring down at her fingernails, nibbling at them a little. Her nose would be sharp and her cheeks would be pale. Her eyes slitted. Nervously pursing her lips. Checking her face in the sun-visor mirror. She was so touchingly unsure of herself.

"We'll see," I said softly.

"Don't forget that half the money's mine."

I'd been thinking about this one. Like it or not, I'd told Jena last night that I would split the winnings with her.

"I remember what I said, Jena. But first we'll see what happens with the Nero's Empire guy. And as for the rest of it—who knows. Nothing's final yet."

"Great." She made a kissing noise and hung up. I felt better now.

I got into a packing frenzy, and in a little less than an hour I was done. Everything I owned fit into a suitcase and seven cardboard boxes, except for the computer and the stereo which were loose on the car floor. I had my desk and my desk chair too. There would have been fewer boxes, but I had some books and papers I'd never unpacked from the last move. I didn't let myself think too much about why I was packing. I just did it.

Right as I was stepping out the door for the last time, my phone rang one more time. I was pretty eager to be on my way before the gangsters showed up, but I answered just in case it was Jena with more news. But it was someone different.

"Hello, this is Tulip Patel. I'm calling for Joe Cube?" Her voice was warm and vibrant.

"Um—hi, Tulip. It's me. How did you get my number?"

"Spazz left your card here." She stopped, seemingly not sure how to continue.

"And you're looking for him?" I coaxed.

"Yeah," said Tulip. "How was the big trip to Vegas?"

"Jena and Spazz aren't back yet," I said. I heard a car in the street, and quickly checked it out with my subtle vision. Just a neighbor's BMW. Those were nice cars. Jena kind of wanted one. Maybe I should get her one for—but wait, Jena and I were supposedly through. I kept forgetting, and in the shock of the brutal memory, I blurted out the truth. "They spent the night together. It was really painful."

"*Damn* it," said Tulip. "I knew this would happen. Well, that's all I needed to know, Joe."

"What are you going to do?"

"I'm moving out on him," said Tulip. "He's done this kind of thing before. God's gift to women."

An obvious thought formed in my reptilian male brain. "I'm moving out, too," I said. "So maybe I'll see you around."

"Maybe." She didn't sound too interested.

"I won a million bucks at blackjack last night," I bragged.

"That's nice," said Tulip. "But you lost your wife."

That popped my bubble pretty fast. "I'm feeling kind of suicidal," I said. A useful line, partly true. "It would help to talk with a woman."

"I don't know you, Joe."

"Can I call? Maybe we could get together."

"I'll think about it," said Tulip, and gave me her number. Good good. Jena wasn't the only fish in the sea.

In my car, I peeked in my attaché case at my tax-bitten million dollars one more time, making sure I really did honest-to-God have it, and then drove back to the shopping center, smoking two cigarettes on the way.

So I'd gotten out of my house before the Nero's guys showed up. No way they'd find me now. What was with that, anyway? If Jena or Spazz hadn't squealed, Nero's had nothing to go on. I'd had a lucky night, that's all. That's what gambling was all about. Were they sore losers all of a sudden? I bought a paper and sat down in the local Starbucks to study the classifieds.

Real estate was insanely tight in the Valley these days. Los Perros listed a total of ten houses for rent, half of them to hell and gone in the mountains. I decided to go for the most expensive one actually here in town, a two-bedroom house right on Los Perros Boulevard. It rented for more than our monthly mortgage payment. Big deal. I had seven hundred and eighty thousand dollars in the Halliburton case sitting on the table in front of me.

I made a call and got a Kay Harmid at Welsh & Tayke Realty.

Even though it was Sunday, they were open. Yes, the house was available for immediate occupancy. It had just gone on the market today, I was lucky, I was Kay's first caller on this. She'd be able to show it to me this morning if I liked. But I needed to understand that I'd have to come up with three months rent to move in: first, last, and deposit.

"No problem," I said, even though she was talking about a serious amount of dough—almost enough to buy a car. But, hey, I was a player.

"Bring a contract," I told the Realtor. "If I like what I see, we can sign off right away. I'm starting a new company and I need a temporary base of operations."

"I have some prime office space I could show you as well," said Kay Harmid.

"I'll be working out of my home until we finish our next round of funding," I said. "That won't be a problem, will it?"

"Not at all. The house is on a corner lot. You and your partners can come and go as you please. I'll meet you at the property in fifteen minutes."

The house was a small, frail, one-story wood structure on a corner next to a traffic light, with the Route 17 entrance ramp a hundred feet away. A fifty-year-old summer cottage, planted in such a crappy location that nobody had ever bothered to scrape it off the lot and build something new. The house was painted a brave light yellow, with green and brown accents on its spidery Victorian trim. The paint was totally coated with grime from the traffic. Kay Harmid was waiting in the house's large parking area, sitting in a white diesel Mercedes with tinted glass, talking on her cell phone. There was a tiny one-car garage by the driveway, its door overgrown with glossy Algerian ivy. I pulled in beside Kay Harmid and she got out, a stocky woman with a large, double-jointed black leather purse. She had shiny skin, short hair, and an expensive suit cut from folk-art fabric. Little pictures of burros and farmers. Her smile was cursory. Real estate was a seller's market these days. Take it or leave it.

I'd thought the traffic was loud at our house, but this was a different story. Just now a truck was idling at the light, and the noise was pretty much all I could think about. It was too loud for talking. And this was only Sunday! The Realtor and I stepped inside the house, me toting my cash-filled attaché case.

"It's kind of busy here," I said.

Kay closed the door and the sound level dropped down. "Not to worry," she said, handing me a business card. "There's double-paned glass and a brand-new heating-cooling system. I love these hardwood floors."

The house did indeed have hardwood floors, reasonably clean and shiny. All the walls and ceilings were painted white—not fresh painted, mind you, but not too scuffed either. It took about a minute to peek into the four tiny rooms: the front living room, the kitchen, and two bedrooms. Ancient fixtures in the kitchen. Back in Matthewsboro I could have flat-out *bought* this house with what these Californians wanted for a few months rent. Jena wasn't going to be at all impressed. In fact she'd probably make fun of me.

But to hell with Jena. I needed a place to stay. With the right furniture, I could make the front room look like a real office. And it would be easy for investors to meet me here. Take the Los Perros exit off Route 17, and your first right turn is my driveway. I walked around the place again. One of the bedrooms in back wasn't all that bad; it looked out onto a row of messy eucalyptus trees that pretty much hid the sight of Route 17. The long, curved leaves were green in the sun and the sky beyond them was blue. I used my third eye to form a full image of the house, and then let my viewpoint fly all around inside it. It felt like home.

The only thing was, I couldn't shake the feeling that I was going to be moving in here with Jena. In recent years it had always been the two of us looking for housing together. What the hell was I doing renting a house without asking Jena? But that was over now.

I hardened my heart and told Kay, "Let's do it."

"You're going to love it here, Mr. Cube," she said. "Now if you want to give me your social security number, I can run a credit check while you look over the paperwork."

Kay phoned my number in to Welsh & Tayke. While we waited for the call-back, I filled out a rental application form and read through the fine print rental contract. Reading it calmed me down. I'm a businessman; I like contracts. As Kay looked over my form, her phone rang. She listened for a minute, then hung up and gave me a thoughtful look.

"You're co-owner of a townhouse at 1234 Silva View Crescent?" she said.

"That's correct. My wife and I bought it together. We're splitting up." It hurt to be saying it out loud. I half expected Kay Harmid to contradict me, to try and talk me out of it, to recommend a marriage counselor.

"I'm sorry to hear that," was all she said. She glanced down at my form. "Will your wife be taking over the mortgage payments?"

I hardened my heart again. "That's correct. And we'll be putting the house on the market." I'd just decided that. Might as well get my equity back. Let Jena really see how it was, being on her own.

Kay brightened at this bit of news. "Well that should work out, then. I hope you'll consider using me as your agent. I've sold a lot of properties in the Silva View neighborhood. I think you'll be pleasantly surprised at how much your home there has appreciated in just these past few months. Now, regarding the move-in payment. I think I mentioned the amount on the phone?" She jotted it down on a piece of paper for me, as if not wanting to say the absurd figure out loud. "If you want to drop a certified check by the office, one of us can give you the keys."

"How about cash?" I said.

Not even a ghost of surprise on her face. Things were crazy in the Valley these days. "No problemo," said Kay Harmid pleasantly.

"Just a minute," I said, and took my case out to my car. I didn't want her to see how much I had in there.

The traffic noise was overwhelming. A bit like the ocean, or like a high wind through the trees, but without that wholesome natural quality. Jena would have talked me out of this, made a scene if necessary. But I was alone now, free to do everything as stupidly as I pleased.

The case shifted in my hand a little as I got into the car. And I almost thought I heard the sound of the money rustling. I set the case down on my lap, opened it—and screamed.

There was a giant red spider in there—a tarantula? I threw my hands up in the air, trying to squirm away. But the spider didn't come for me. Actually it wasn't a spider. It was a red hand. Long, skinny red fingers with pointed black nails. Talons. Like a devil's hand. There were still a few bills in there with it. The hand gathered up the bills and made a crooked, twitching motion, shoving the bills vinnward into the fourth dimension. And then the hand paused, gave me the finger, and disappeared.

I sat there, my heart going a mile a minute, the empty metal attaché case in my lap. Finally I closed it up and went back in the house.

"On second thought, I think I'll bring the money by your office," I told the Realtor.

She looked me over again. "How soon?" she said finally. "We've had two other calls on this property already. It wouldn't be fair to the owner to—"

I glanced at my watch. It was eleven. "I'll be there by one," I said.

"We can hold it for that long," said Kay. "But let us know if you'll be late. If I'm not in, the girl at the desk will take care of you." She shook my hand. "It's been nice working with you, Mr. Cube. And don't forget to call me when you're ready to put your Silva View Crescent house on the market."

The Realtor drove off, leaving me standing there next to my car. What now? I needed to talk to Momo. The sun was going behind some clouds. I put on my leather jacket and walked around behind the house to its weedy backyard. There were some back steps and a little porch—a bare platform of warped gray boards.

"Hey Momo!" I called, sitting down on the edge of the porch. "Come talk to me. One of your friends just stole my money!"

No answer. I guessed she was still off fetching those antenna crystals she'd been talking about. Well, hopefully she'd be back soon. She could always get me more money. I opened the attaché case again, checking that it was really and truly empty, then lit a cigarette and sat there thinking. That red hand hadn't looked like Momo's hand one bit. Presumably the thief was some other kind of being from the four-dimensional All.

I had a vague memory of Momo mentioning a race called the Dronners. Momo was from the Kluppers; they lived up above our Spaceland—"up" in Momo's sense of the word. She'd said something about the Dronners being another folk who lived down below. Like Heaven and Hell, with Earth in between. If that red devil hand had been a Dronner's, I wasn't looking forward to seeing any more of those guys.

For the moment I was all alone in the yard. I hate being alone. I focused in on my subtle vision, checking out my surroundings. Next door was a complex of doctor's offices; not regulation MD doctors, but rather counselors, chiropractors, massage therapists, holistic healers and wellness consultants. And back behind the lot were the eucalyptuses and the bank down to Route 17. My third eye noticed some homeless people camped in a culvert under the highway. Just kind of sitting there staring at a strip of sky. They didn't care about the traffic. If all else failed I could join them.

I turned my attention to the house, checking it out again. For some reason my third eye seemed to be getting misty, but with a little effort I could still focus it. There wasn't any basement to the house, and the attic crawlspace didn't have anything in it but wires and insulation. The tiny, sealed garage was dusty and empty. And the house, well, it wasn't that bad. I kept on sitting there, not knowing what else to do.

Traffic wasn't all that loud just now. It seemed to come and go. I could do worse than live here. Just then my shaky subtle vision noticed a Lincoln Towncar turn off from the 17 exit and roll into the lot in front of the house. There were two guys inside it, one of them very fit and tan, with a Latin-lover look to him. The pit boss from Nero's. He was holding a cell phone like he was taking instructions from somebody as he drove. The other guy was pale and thin with a gimmie cap pulled down low over his eyes. Gus the shill. They were both wearing shades and, thanks to my third eye, I could peek under their coats to see that they were carrying guns in shoulder holsters. Gus had something like a knife strapped to his leg as well. Oh no. They jumped out of their car, one of them heading around either side of the house. It was like they knew I was back there.

I headed for the eucalyptuses, but Gus caught up with me before I got there. He was fast.

"Joe Cube," he shouted. He'd pulled out his gun. "Don't make me hurt you, bro."

I stopped and turned to face them. Gus's gun had a silencer, like in the movies. Sante was standing a little behind him.

"Hey, Joe," said the pit boss smoothly. "Sorry to bust in on you like this."

"Sante," I said, trying to smile. "You guys scared me. What's the problem?"

"Health problem," said Sante. "You feelin' okay? Can buy a lot of good care with a million bucks. Don't stand over there by the trees like that. You look scared. Whatsamatter? There don't have to be no problem. Come on and let's go in your house."

"It's not my house," I said. "Nobody lives there. I was just looking at it."

"Nice and private here," said Sante, looking around the yard. "This is a real good part of town. I grew up in downtown San Jose. My Mom's still livin' there. But enough with the light chit-chat. Let's sit on the back steps. Where you was sittin' before."

"How do you know where I was sitting?"

"Little bird phoned me," said Sante. "Little pigeon. You don't got such good friends, Joe. Fella told us you cheated at the big game last night. Nero's don't like that. Good thing you got the case with you."

"Go on," said Gus, gesturing with his gun. "Go on over there and sit down." He took the case out of my hand as I passed him.

The three of us sat down on the edge of the porch. It pretty much had to be Spazz who'd phoned them. But why? He already had my wife. And I'd said I'd give her half the money. Why was Spazz doing this to me?

"It's empty," I said, just as Gus flicked open the case. Gus cursed and threw the empty case halfway across the yard.

Sante did that thing with his eyebrows. Looking all mature and long-suffering. A this-hurts-me-more-than-it-hurts-you kind of face. Jerk. "Help us out, Joe," he said. "You cheat at Nero's, you pay Nero's back."

"I didn't cheat," I protested. "I don't know who you've been talking to. It's a lie. I got lucky is all. How would I cheat? We played with your cards. I didn't even freaking *touch* the cards. You can't just go threatening everybody who wins at your casino." I was hitting my stride now. "You can't do this, Sante. I'll tell the cops."

"You ain't goin' to no cops, Joe," said Sante. "We know where you got your seed money."

"What are you talking about?" I said, trying to keep my voice level.

"The seventeen thousand dollars you used to buy your chips," said Sante. "You stole them from the vault at a Wells Fargo in the north part of San Jose. We checked the numbers on your bills and matched them to a report come out on the police wire. Nero's is connected, Joe. We got friends all over the place. We ain't passed the word on you yet, though. None of us needs to snitch to no cops. You give us back our million and we keep your seventeen. It's like a gentleman's agreement."

"Gee," I said, a little recklessly. "Will you comp me next time I come to Nero's?"

Gus grabbed me hard by the arm. "You think we're playin' with you, Joe? You ever step in a casino again, you're a dead man. Where's the million at?"

"It's—it's not here. Maybe I can get it for you."

"Maybe?" said Sante, grabbing my other arm. "You're disrespecting us, bub." He pushed me down onto my back. "Show him the pick, Gus."

Gus pulled up his pant leg and pulled out the knife—or no, it was an ice pick. The dull gray of its steel was shiny silver where the tip had been ground to the sharpest of points. Gus pulled my shirt tail out of my pants and ripped my shirt open, popping the buttons and uncovering my bare belly. I tried to roll away, but Sante had me pinned tight. And now Gus sat down on my legs.

"Don't," I said. My voice wasn't as loud as I wanted it to be.

"Don't," I shouted, finding my volume, and then I broke into a shriek. "Help! Someone help me!"

"That's loud traffic, huh?" said Sante pulling a rolled-up pair of cotton sweat socks out of his coat pocket. He forced them into my mouth, wedging my jaws so far open that the hinge made a pop. "We're gonna give you a taste of what your Mom did to your Dad. What a piece of work she musta been, what a psycho. Yeah, Nero's knows all about you, Joe. We done our research. Boss was laughin' about this. Gut-stab this Cube guy, he was sayin'. That'll get his attention. Boss is like a psychologist, he likes to tailor our approach, know what I mean?"

I tried to scream, to beg, to make promises, but nothing was coming out past the socks. I threw myself against Sante and Gus, struggling like never before.

"Take it easy there, Joe," said Sante, enjoying this. "Don't have a coronary. It ain't really nothin', gettin' stabbed with an ice pick. We know a nice spot so you won't even need a doctor. But next time we use the knife. Do him, Gus."

"Right here?" said Gus, patting a spot on the left side of my pale, trembling stomach. Sante nodded, his eyebrows slanting down to the sides. I tried again to squirm away, but they had me completely immobilized.

Gus poised the ice pick like he was about to throw a dart, and then whipped it down towards me. With all my will, I drew my stomach away from the point.

I heard the ice pick thud into the wood of the porch. The musical sound of it quivering. Suddenly I remembered my dream of last night. It was like the dream had gotten me ready for this, had prepared me so I'd know what to do.

"What the—?" said Sante. "He broke in two?"

"Jesus, Sante," said Gus. "We've killed him."

I lay still, watching things with my feebly functioning third eye. A foot-wide strip of my body had disappeared; it had bowed vout into the fourth dimension. My legs had slid up the steps a little to take up the slack. I'd done just like Dad had done in Flatland. The spots where my body bent away into higher space were sealed over with tough pink hide—the hyperskin I'd gotten when Momo cattle-prodded me. There was a big pink oval at my waist and another at the bottom of my chest. With nothing in between.

I let my head loll to the side like I was dead. I was having a bad enough day that acting dead felt natural. Sante and Gus stood over me, not sure what to do next. And then Momo appeared in the yard, looking for all the world like an overgrown yuppie homeowner on the warpath.

"Foul villains!" she exclaimed, striding towards us. "You'll pay for this crime!"

"Waste her," said Sante. Gus already had his pistol out; he leveled it at Momo's head and fired off a shot. With the silencer, the gunshot was nothing but a hissing pop. Like an air gun. The bullet struck Momo right in the forehead. A little dimple formed where the bullet hit; the bullet popped out and fell to the ground; the dimple smoothed over. She kept on coming. Sante got out his gun and shot Momo too, this time in the chest. The bullet had no more effect than a finger poking a loaf of dough.

Sante and Gus took to their heels. With my spotty subtle vision, I watched their Towncar go fishtailing out of the driveway and onto Route 17. My stomach slid back into visibility. I got to my feet.

7

Klupdom

Well done, Joe," said Momo, walking over to me. "Practice the motion again, before you forget the trick of it."

I looked down at the ice pick, still stuck in the wood of the porch, and tried to reproduce my feelings of terror. But for the moment, my bare stomach stayed stubbornly in place, butt-white in the pale winter sunlight.

"Come come," said Momo taking the ice pick in her hand and waving it at me. "You can do it."

Seeing the ice pick move towards me was enough. It was like that first instant when your skis unfreeze and you start sliding down a run. It takes only the slightest twitch to get started. With a steady, even motion, my midsection rose vout into the fourth dimension.

"Now your arm," said Momo.

It was easier this time. The trick was to take a part of my body and to want it to be somewhere else. My arm disappeared from view, starting at the hand and working its way up. Oddly enough, the sleeves of my shirt and coat stayed behind. I looked like an amputee, but I could feel my hand off in hyperspace somewhere, and I could dimly see it with my failing subtle vision.

"Your head," said Momo.

That went too. And now, like a magnetic sticker peeling off the side of a refrigerator, the rest of my body joined me. And all of my clothes stayed behind. Khaki pants, underwear, Banana Republic shirt, Patagonia jacket, socks, shoes—everything stayed on that back porch. Even my Swatch. I'd slipped vout of everything I owned and landed naked in another world.

It was nice being vout beyond our world. It was just warm enough to be comfortable. The four-dimensional All was filled with four-dimensional air, and I was augmented enough to breathe it. The air was bright, though nowhere did I see a higher Sun. As I'd noticed before, our Spaceland seemed to be floating inside an enormous four-dimensional cavern, fully blocking off half of the view.

I turned to look at Momo. Though my subtle vision was ever weaker, my third eye showed Momo as a solid three-dimensional form resembling a translucent mass of coral. Her eyes were down inside the flesh like raisins in a muffin, but now, as she turned towards me, the eyes migrated out to the closest part of her. Her arms and legs stuck out of her middle like the branches of a mutant forked radish. She was sitting on that comical little chrome saucer of hers.

She reached out toward me with one of her flowing pink arms. To my regular vision the arm seemed to break up into pieces as it moved; to my third eye it looked like a long water balloon being filled at one end and emptied at the other. Momo's hand was holding out something like a small, mildly glowing dinner roll, pale blue in color. It was a roll in my own three-dimensional space, that is, but just a few inches vout from there it was a bagel. My third eye combined the two versions, showing the object as a bagel nested inside a translucent roll, with both shapes clearly visible.

"You must be famished," said Momo. "All you've been getting is three-dimensional food. Your third eye and higher musculature need four-dimensional nourishment. Eat this. We call it grolly. A great delicacy with tremendous strengthening powers. It's a sort of fruit that grows only in the Cave Between Worlds, that is, upon these walls around us. Grolly is the foundation of my family's fortune." She gestured towards the distant sides of the cavern, which indeed had some pastel patterns that could have been growths of plants.

I took the grolly and bit into it. It was satisfying like nothing I'd ever tasted before. It was like having a whole long meal all at once. All of my augmented body's parts were enjoying it. This food of the All was a bit like a higher form of bread, but firmer, springier, and with a taste that combined the moist succulence of fresh sliced peaches with the melting sweetness of fine chocolate. I ate my way through the middle of it, gnawing it in two. I wished Jena was there to try some too. The pieces drifted away, but I caught hold of one and ate some more, making new grolly fragments that all escaped from me. I was clumsy at holding onto things in the fourth dimension. My hands seemed as awkward as cardboard pincers. Momo snagged the loose pieces and ate them herself.

As I was wolfing down the grolly, my subtle vision grew strong and clear. I'd been weak with hunger, that's all. I looked around for more food. Off in the distance were the walls of the cave, spotted with those pastel patches, the colors a shimmer of pale blues, purples, and yellows. The patches looked a lot farther than I wanted to go into the fourth dimension. It seemed wise to get back to Earth soon. Jena and Spazz would be in town. I still needed to figure out where I stood with Jena. And as for Spazz—more than ever I felt like killing the guy. The business with the gangsters had gotten me into a really disturbed state of mind.

"What happened to my money?" I asked Momo, remembering my emptied-out attaché case. "Was that a Dronner who took it?"

"It was Wackle," said Momo. "An hydra-headed enemy indeed."

She paused, and again I studied her form, thinking about the difference between subtle and regular vision.

With my regular eyes I saw three dimensional cross sections of four-dimensional things. Well, strictly speaking, I saw two-dimensional patterns on my retina which my brain, through lifelong habit, knew how to interpret as three-dimensional things. By twitching my higher muscles in a certain way, I could turn my head a bit in the vinn and vout directions, and by wobbling vinn and vout I could see complete sequences of cross sections. If I looked at one edge of Momo, I saw a little ball, and as I moved my head, the ball changed into her full womanly form.

My subtle vision was a different story. I was still getting used to my third eye, perched on that stalk from the center of my brain. It was a little disgusting to even think that I had such a thing; it made me feel like a crab or a lobster. But the third eye's subtle vision gave me a much better view of the fourth dimension than any series of three-dimensional slices. If an ordinary eye's images are like photographs, my third eye's images were like stacks of film frames, with one frame for each layer of four-dimensional space. To my third eye, the world resembled an art-glass paperweight filled with colorful blobs.

I saw Momo as a solid mass with subtle shadings all through her. That was one of the odd things in my third-eye images up here. Shadows went right into the middles of things. The third dimension was no barrier at all. Momo's eyes were buried inside her flesh like dots of blue inside pink glass. But the things that looked as if they were inside Momo weren't really inside her. They were vinn or vout, that's all. Not that I understood all this right away.

Momo was talking to me about Wackle, gesturing with a hand that bloomed out of her insides. It was like seeing a sandy spot in a tide pool open up into a sea anemone.

"Wackle is most troublesome," she was saying. "Not only did

Wackle take your money, it was Wackle who telephoned those ruf-
fians. I plan to kill Wackle—at least as much of him as I can. You'll
be of use in this matter."

"What? No way!" Did she really expect me to get in the middle
of a four-dimensional feud? I ran my hands over my face. I needed
to be patching things up with my wife, not starting in on some
weird new battle.

"Let's go back," I said, turning towards Spaceland. It was no
more than a few feet away. Rotated out into the fourth dimension
as I was, my regular eyes saw Spaceland very poorly. My regular
eyes could only see ghostly slices of that back porch I'd been sitting
on. But my third eye could see the porch and house and yard as
clearly as before—a familiar three-dimensional shape that looked as
desirable as a dock would look to a drowning man. My watch and
my clothes were lying there. I reached out towards them, not sure
how to move myself through empty hyperspace.

"Not yet, Joe," said Momo. "As long as you're up here in the
All, let me show you my home. Don't worry about your things—
here, I'll put them into your car." She reached down and grabbed
my stuff, getting a tight grip on my watch so its innards wouldn't
fall out, and then she used her saucer to dart us over to my locked
car, easily setting my watch and clothes onto the seat. "We'll be on
our way, then," said Momo. "To Grollyton in the mighty land of
Klupdom. We'll fetch your cell-phone antenna crystals while we're
there. I'm sure Voule has a batch by now."

"You still didn't bring them?"

"It takes some time," said Momo. "It's delicate work. I came
back down to check on you because I had a feeling that Wackle
would start making trouble as soon as I was well out of the way.
Oh, before we go, let's bring something for you to give the Empress.
Pick something from your car."

"Um—what does the Empress like?"

"You decide." One of the things I'd put into the car was an old mouse from my computer. For Christmas, Jena had given me a new improved cordless mouse with optical tracking and a mouse wheel, and I didn't know what to do with the old one. It still worked, so I hadn't thrown it away. But I didn't have any use for it anymore. I reached vinn towards my car and snagged that. My gift for the Empress.

"How do I carry it?" I asked Momo. "I'm naked. I don't have any pockets."

"You can have this," she said, and gave me a four-dimensional sack with a four-dimensional cord that I tied around my waist. The sack was of a soft cloth like dark blue velvet. The mouse fit easily inside. The sack's mouth was a sphere that the cord was somehow able to pull closed.

Momo reached out and took hold of me, then tucked me under her arm like a painter carrying a canvas. "Klupdom ho!" she cried, and sent her little saucer darting upwards towards the great spotted walls of the cavern. Though I had no way to judge distances here, it seemed as if they might be several miles away.

In fact the cliffs were farther than that, and it took some time to approach them, even though the saucer seemed to move incredibly fast. It had a nice high windshield that automatically curved further around us as we accelerated. Finally the cliffs were close enough that I could make out some details. The gray stone of the rocks was mottled with the patches of pale glowing light that Momo said were colonies of grolly. Many of the grolly patches had been partly cleared away, leaving a beige stubble. In the midst of some of the half-cleared patches I could see Kluppers at work. Each group of workers was accompanied by a large, trucklike saucer that they were loading up.

"Your people harvest the grolly?" I asked Momo.

"Indeed," she said. "Grolly is more than a victual; it's an elixir. As it happens, my family owns the rights to harvest from all the grolly fields in these parts. We manage our plants with great care. You'll notice some guards about; they watch for Kluppers who might think to come down here and poach from what is my family's. Our guards watch for Dronners as well. There's no grolly left in Dronia. The fecund and profligate Dronners have eaten their plants into extinction. They're like a race of locusts. It's a common thing for them to sneak up through Spaceland and steal from us. We can't see through Spaceland, you know. The Dronners use it to hide from us." Momo's tone was stern and unforgiving. She reminded me of someone, but for the moment I couldn't place the memory.

"I'm surprised there aren't a lot of Klupper tourists around," I said. "Don't you guys like to come down here just to look at Spaceland?"

"The Empress and her High Council discourage travel to the Cave Between Worlds," said Momo. "Her Highness fears that some casual visitor might harm Spaceland. She lends great credence to an ancient legend that links Klupdom's well-being to the health of Spaceland. As above, so below, eh? She cares not that the cover of Spaceland makes it so easy for the Dronners to get within striking range of my family's grolly."

Momo was a fanatic on the subject of Dronners and grolly. Instead of answering I kept looking around. I needed all three eyes to make out what I was seeing.

To my regular eyes, the walls looked like rock, except that, as we moved, the rocks were morphing into different shapes. A minute ago, for instance, the closest outcrop had looked like a range of mountains, but as Momo's saucer moved us onward along some direction that was a combination of up and vout, the mountains smoothed over into rolling, lavalike mounds, and as we traveled further, the valleys between the hills deepened into ragged canyons.

It wasn't like these landscapes were next to each other—no, they were all in the same direction. It just depended on where in hyperspace I looked at them from. It reminded me of a computer-animated ad I'd seen for an SUV. In the ad, the hills around a guy in a car got big and turned into snow-capped mountains. The fourth dimension was like an animator's morph knob.

My third eye was able to see all three versions at once, the mountains, the hills, and the canyons. My third eye saw them as inside each other; the mountains inside the hills inside the canyons. I think the order had to do with how far away they were.

A shape flew past. It was a muscular, gray-suited Klupper on a ridiculous little flying disk like Momo's. He was carrying a tube that looked like a weapon: a science-fiction bazooka with wires and radiator fins. I wasn't into science fiction, but for some reason Jena got a kick out of *Star Trek*, so we'd seen every one of the however many *Star Trek* movies made. She'd like imprinted on the show when she was growing up in Arizona.

What with being four-dimensional, the hyperbazooka looked pretty funky. I assumed the gray-clad Klupper was one of the family business's guards that Momo had been talking about. He called some kind of question to Momo and she answered. The Kluppers' native speech sounded a little like Chinese and a little like a tape played backwards—tuneful swoops of sound with unexpected long pauses.

After some more conversation, the guard saluted Momo and continued on his way. I was a little disappointed that he hadn't come closer to marvel at flat Joe Cube from the land of three dimensions. Well, maybe he hadn't noticed me. Momo had me squashed as tightly to her body as a sticker on a banana. Looking out into the distance I noticed more Kluppers in the air between Spaceland and the cliffs.

"Do they all work for your family?" I asked Momo.

"Perhaps half of them do," she said. "The others are minions of the Empress, stationed here to watch over your precious Spaceland. You can distinguish the soldiers by their crimson uniforms and gold-colored saucers. Although it's our taxes who support them, the Empress's troops don't even help us chase the Dronners. And woe betide any of our guards who happens to shoot in the direction of Spaceland—not that our power-beams affect your flat matter. The Dronners know of the Empress's injunction, and they take advantage. They're devilishly cunning."

Suddenly I remembered who Momo sounded like: a rich kid I'd known in business school. He was in line to inherit the ownership of a big logging company, and he had had that same sense of divine entitlement. Any threat to his inherited wealth was an attack on the natural order of things, to be exterminated by any means necessary. He used to talk about having the Earth First tree-sitters shot for trespassing. On top of that, he was after Jena all the time, and she was slightly interested in him. I was liking Momo less all the time.

We continued flying upwards and the walls of the cave drew closer. They were larger and more imposing than I'd imagined, far bigger than the Rockies. I felt like an ant. Draped all down one of the nearest cliffs was a tangle of glowing cream and lavender fingers, gently waving in the air. There was a nice smell coming off them. As they moved, their shapes altered in a lovely way. Viewed with my regular eyes, their long, tubular stalks would bulge up at the tip to form a ball that opened up a hole inside it. Then they'd sway back, the hole would close, and the big ball would melt back into the stalks. That morphing thing again, which meant I was seeing different slices in the fourth dimension.

"Grolly?" I asked Momo, half worried I'd set off another of her rants.

"That's right," she said expansively. "It's all my family's property. Go ahead and take some." She swung in close to the grolly thickets, but not close enough to touch. Maybe twenty feet off.

"Closer, Momo," I urged.

"No," said Momo, enjoying herself. "Time for your flying lesson. I warrant that you can do it. There's legends of our ancestors teaching Spacelanders to fly. Flap your whole body in hyperspace. You're flatter than one of your stingrays. It should work quite nicely. Lift your stomach vout like you did before, and then push it rapidly vinn. Employ your arms and legs, as well. In the manner of swimming."

"This is for your entertainment, or what?"

"Perhaps. And think, Joe, should we be separated at some time, you'll be glad for this skill if you want to make your own way back to Spaceland."

"Why not just give me a flying saucer like yours?"

"They're too valuable."

It took me a while to get the knack of the proper bucking motion. As far as the fourth dimension went, I was a thin hypersheet of skin and muscle. It made me an efficient flapper. My third eye bobbed around like mad, making me so seasick that I stopped paying attention to what I saw with it. In my regular vision, pieces of my body kept drifting in and out of view.

I soon got hold of a grolly plant and pulled off the fruit at its tip. Depending what angle I looked at it from, it was like a dumpling or a doughnut. To my third eye, it was a dumpling inside a doughnut. Or the other way around. I nibbled at it, enjoying it just as much as my first sample. One other thing worth mentioning is that the grolly seemed—how to say this—more *aware* than plants usually are. The stalks of the plants were reacting to my motions, leaning towards me as if to offer me their fruits. It was like they were dancing with me.

At this point I noticed a couple of grolly guards floating on saucers nearby, both armed like the one I'd seen before. They didn't look any too happy about my eating the grolly. But for now they were just watching.

I glanced back down towards Spaceland, that giant glass paperweight with busy little Los Perros inside it. I revolved it in my mind's eye, looking at it this way and that. I wondered if Jena was back yet, and if she was looking for me.

"Would I really be able to flap all the way home on my own?" I asked Momo.

"I would deem so," said Momo. "You have a highly advantageous ratio of surface area to mass." She guided her saucer to a lush clump of grolly plants some thirty yards away from me and began picking some of the fruits for herself, stashing most of them in the folds of her dress, but eating a few as well. The grolly stalks around her began swaying and dancing with excitement.

Finally one of the grolly guards flew over. His skin was of a purplish tinge. He spoke sharply to Momo—on a second hearing, the Klupper speech sounded less like backwards Chinese and more like birds and car engines. Momo answered him, gesturing towards me as she talked. The guard said something else, and finally Momo dug down into her gold dress and handed him a shiny sphere that might have been a coin. "Come on now, Joe," called Momo. "This fellow's new, he doesn't quite believe that I'm one of his employers. Fly after me and my saucer. It'll be good practice for you." The guard glared at me and made a get-going gesture with his gun. Maybe he thought I was some kind of Dronner.

I flapped after Momo, gasping with the effort. She idled along, tauntingly just out of reach, leading me up and vout to where the mountains and hills broke into canyons. We flew into one of great ravines, and just when it looked like we'd hit a dead end, Momo veered vinnward. I curved my body and sailed after her, cutting the air like a knife. The wall ahead of us opened into a huge vertical tunnel that seemed to go up forever. All at once I was too scared and tired to go on. I wanted to be home talking things over with Jena. I hung there in the overwhelming vastness, feeling like a dust speck in a mineshaft. Far beneath me I could still glimpse Spaceland, ringed all around by the rocks of the canyon that led to the shaft.

I was in fact sinking downwards towards Spaceland. Though I'd felt weightless before, up here there was a faint gravitational pull back towards the center of the Cave Between Worlds. Momo was far above me, high into the great bright tunnel. It seemed the air up there was glowing like the air in the rest of the Cave. The walls around me were jagged rocks with a few grolly seedlings, everything shifting and morphing as I moved. What was I doing here? I continued to drift down.

"You're lagging, Joe," said Momo, swooping back down to join me. "Are you weary?"

"I want to go home now."

"Pish," said Momo, gathering me into her arms. "Tush. Piffle. You still haven't seen the town where I live. It's called Grollyton— the gathering and distribution of grolly is our region's most important business."

"How much further is it?"

"Eight hundred miles."

"What!"

"Look out!" Momo darted to one side, and three Kluppers on an oversized boatlike saucer came sailing down the shaft, barely missing us. They veered vout and disappeared around the lip of the canyon we'd come in through. "They're here to ferry up the grolly harvest," said Momo. "This tunnel is the principal path from our part of Klupdom to the Cave Between Worlds. My great-great-great-grandmother Helga discovered it. At top speed, it's a half hour's flight to the top, and perhaps twenty minutes to fly back down. A bit of a labyrinth, but easy enough for those who know the way."

"I don't want to go!"

"You must experience the glory of Klupdom, Joe," said Momo. "Once you familiarize yourself with my land, you may come to love it more than your Spaceland. To my family's way of thinking, Spaceland is, after all, just a troublesome curtain which hides the machinations of the filthy Dronners."

It disturbed me that Momo had this odd resentment towards my universe, but before I could come up with an answer, we'd taken off upwards, as if on some nightmare elevator. The saucer's windshield curved far around us, but even so, the air beat against me, threatening to tear me loose. I pressed my body against Momo. The walls flew by, a steady blur. I could feel myself getting heavier as we rose. As we moved, my third eye saw a textured mass of solids and gaps in which everything was streaming outwards from the center. We swerved left, right, vinn and vout with sickening lurches. Soon I could see a ball of light up above, and then we shot out of the tunnel's spherical mouth.

There was a cluster of buildings near the tunnel's mouth: Momo's family grollyworks and two barracks, one for the gray-suited grolly guards and one for the Empress's crimson-uniformed troops. Some of the grolly guards were unloading one of the barge-like saucers of freshly harvested grolly sent up from down below. Others were setting neat packages of grolly into a smaller saucer with a cover on it. A delivery van.

Momo didn't stop to talk with any of the guards and soldiers, and they freely let her go. I don't think they noticed me at all. Their buildings looked like great sturdy boxes that flexed and warped as we flew past—it would take me some time to get the knack of understanding four-dimensional perspective. Just a bit further on, we touched down in a field.

It was a pleasant, grassy landscape, with rolling meadows and a river. A flock of small animals was hopping around where we landed, things with transparent wings on bodies like balls of rubber bands that shimmered with every color of the rainbow. They were busy pecking at the ground, digging into it with conical beaks. As we approached, they squawked and flapped away. In the middle distance were the towers of a town. Grollyton. Jena would have liked seeing this.

Momo set me on the ground and I immediately fell over onto my vinn side, feeling the rocks and grass against my higher skin, the ground pressing against all of my muscles and organs. A nasty sensation. Momo was laughing at me. After a minute's struggle, I managed to right myself. I bent one leg vinn and one leg vout, giving me some stability. To my regular eyes it looked as if my legs disappeared in the middle of my thigh, but my third eye could make out the way I had them splayed apart. In this world I was like a cardboard cut-out of a man, and it was hard not to fall over.

I walked around a bit, getting the feel of things. As well as being able to step to my left, right, front, and back, here in Klupdom I could take sidesteps in the vinn or vout directions. My regular eyes saw an Earthlike landscape, but it was just one of an endless number of landscapes parallel to each other in the fourth dimension. For instance I'd see a tree in one of the landscapes, but it wouldn't be there anymore when I walked a few yards to my vinn.

My third eye was able to combine all the images into one; it was a little like looking at a series of translucent landscapes overlaid on top of each other. In this view I could clearly see a dirt road that led towards us from the town, a path that my regular eyes saw only in bits and pieces.

Some Kluppers were coming along the path towards us. In the
lead was a coffee-colored man with smooth, powerful motions. His
shape was much fuller than Momo's. He was followed by a tense,
smaller man talking urgently to a calm, plump woman, and behind
them was a bent older woman with white hair. Not that they were
really men and women. Their arms and legs seemed to move right
through their bodies as they walked. They wore richly colored
clothes. Prancing along behind them was something like a dog. I
felt very naked.

Momo called a cheerful greeting in her native language as the
dark man strode up to us. He returned the greeting and gave Momo
a loving embrace. He walked around me, looking me over. "Behold
the Spacelander," he said in English after a minute, talking the same
old-fashioned way as Momo. "Welcome to Klupdom, Joe Cube. I
am Voule."

"Hello, Voule," I said and held out my hand. His grip was strong.
He gave a big coarse laugh, whirled me around, and slung me high
up into the air. I was completely disoriented by the spinning, but
when I felt myself falling back down, I was able to start flapping
hard enough to keep from smashing into the ground. I landed near
the plump young woman.

"Don't be so mean, Father," she called to Voule in English.
"You'll frighten him." She reached out and ran her hand across my
higher skin. I felt it as a tickling in my lungs. "I'm Kalla," she told
me, enunciating very clearly. "Momo and Voule's daughter. Voule
didn't hurt you, did he?" Her dog sniffed at my leg and then gave
me a lick that I felt all the way down to the deepest part of my calf
muscle. Kalla pushed the dog away and scolded him. "Leave the
Spacelander alone, Gogo. You'll frighten him."

"I'm okay," I said, though in fact I was starting to feel desperate.
The mouth of the tunnel was only a few hundred yards away.
Maybe I should jump in there and hope for the best? I looked at

Kalla with my third eye. The tense man was muttering something
to her. For a moment, Kalla looked almost like a person, but then
she moved her head in some way that made it turn inside out. Her
eyes, mouth and nose sank into her skin, tunneled through her head
and emerged on its opposite side. Four-dimensionally speaking,
she'd rotated her head to look at her mother Momo.

"That's right, Kalla," Momo was saying. "This isn't easy for the
Spacelander." She turned her attention to me. "So now Joe, you've
been presented to Voule, and this fellow next to Kalla is her husband Deet, and this fine lady is my mother Eleia." Spindly Deet
saluted, and the gray-haired woman curved herself in a solemn bow
that brought her head down into her chest. I passed up on shaking
their hands, in case they too wanted to throw me like a Frisbee.

The five of them talked in their native language for a few
minutes. Though four-dimensional sounds weren't quite as odd as
four-dimensional sights, they were pretty strange. The noises had a
way of seeming to tune in and out like a weak signal on a radio,
but when they were tuned in they shook every bit of my body. Like
loud, deep organ notes. Old Eleia took a shot at talking English to
me.

"Momo informs me that a Dronner's been meddling," she said
to me.

"It was Wackle," put in Momo. "A cunning antagonist indeed.
Wackle stole all the Spaceland money that we'd gotten, and then
proceeded to instruct some other Spacelanders to attack our Joe
Cube."

"That's right," I said. "And I was thinking. Maybe this is all a
big mistake. I'd be happy to forget the whole freaking thing."

"You're only fortunate the Dronners are such skulkers and cow-
ards," said Voule. "Otherwise Wackle might act more directly." He
chuckled and gave me a poke in the stomach. "I can't get over how

flat you are. How can you Spacelanders stand it? It's hardly like living at all."

"Spaceland is God's mistake," added Deet. Kalla and he made a striking pair; like the dot and comma of a semicolon, with Deet constantly whispering to Kalla. He had a fixed, twisted smile. "Were there no Spaceland, the Dronners wouldn't find it so easy to sneak up and steal our grolly," he said. "Isn't that right, Grandmother Eleia?" I had the feeling Deet was a recent addition to Momo's family. A gung ho yes-man. I acted a little that way myself when I was around Jena's mother. She owned a ranch, and I'd grown up in a rented crackerbox.

Thinking of the house I'd grown up in reminded me again of that dream I'd had about Flatland last night. At some level the dream had helped keep me from getting stabbed. I tried to remember what else had been in it. Maybe there was something I could use now.

"Don't let's try and tell him the whole story at once," Eleia was saying. "Remember, his poor brain is but three-dimensional. Come with us now, Joe Cube, we'll repair to Momo and Voule's dwelling. Your special antenna crystals are ready. The sooner you disseminate them, the sooner we can put an end to the Dronners once and for all."

"Cannons open fire!" cried Deet. "Deet at your service!" He did a little war dance. Gogo the dog pranced around him, joyfully barking.

"Yes, yes, we have a golden opportunity," said Momo cheerfully. "How do you like Klupdom, Joe?"

"The real question is how do *you* like Spaceland," I said. "You guys keep talking about my universe like it was a scab or something."

"Ah, but wait till you see the antennas I made," said Voule. "They'll make your fortune."

"You aren't out to hurt Spaceland are you?" I asked.

"Of course not," said Momo—too quickly? "The Empress would execute anyone who dared to harm Spaceland."

"What was that about the antennas helping you to eliminate the Dronners?"

"Well, if you must know, I'll tell you," said Momo, and then paused for a moment. To make up a lie? Voule said something to her in their native language and she resumed talking. "The antennas will project towards the Dronners' half of the All—to your vinnward side, the side that lies hidden beneath Spaceland. Our notion is that the presence of your telephone signals darting about next to Spaceland will frighten away the timid Dronners. And, yes, they're sensitive enough to notice the electromagnetic radiation. It's just as one might repel marauding crows from a cherry tree by tying bright pie plates to the branches. That's the whole of our plan. And your role? That was my brainstorm of this morning. Although it would be easy enough for us to implant the antenna crystals in your film of space, we need for Spacelanders like yourself and your future customers to pump energy through them. You'll get rich by selling the new broadband 3G cell-phone technology! We'll do something for you and you'll do something for us. It's what you'd term a 'win-win,' Joe."

The others listened intently to this explanation, and then burst into speech in their own tongue. I had no idea what they were saying. At least they weren't outright laughing. As they were talking, some of the birds came back. With everything morphing and appearing and disappearing and turning inside out I felt like throwing up.

"Come this way," said Eleia regally, and started off towards the city of Grollyton, followed by Momo and Voule, Kalla and me, Deet and Gogo the dog. Momo's little saucer tagged along on its own. As we walked through the fields, Momo handed out her fresh grolly to her family members; they all ate it eagerly. Even though they controlled the grolly import business, the stuff was still a treat to them. I got a piece too; Deet and Voule guffawed at the messy way I ate it. I did my best this time not to lose any of the pieces.

Our path dipped down near the river; it was like many rivers at once. The sight of the four-dimensional water made me uneasy. I had the feeling that if I fell in there I might have trouble finding my way back to the surface. And then of course a gust of wind knocked me over onto my vinn side again and my grolly went all over the place. I screamed for help, afraid I was going to slide into the river. Old Eleia suggested that I ride in Momo's saucer if I was going to make such a fuss every second.

Kalla lifted me up into the shiny, hovering vehicle and handed me a piece of the grolly I'd dropped. For the rest of the way to the city, I drifted along behind Momo and the others, still nibbling on my grolly. I felt as helpless as a little boy in a stroller with his lollipop. Come to think of it, the saucer resembled a coin-operated ride like a kid might sit on outside a supermarket, a tiny round thing with a double seat. But the seat was four-dimensional, and in the absence of Momo, I had more space than I could possibly use. My four-dimensional cloth sack rested on the seat next to me.

I thought of Jena again. If I'd had her there to talk to, I wouldn't have felt so lost and bewildered. And she would have noticed a lot of stuff that I didn't see. We could walk down a block together, and at the corner Jena would be able to tell me some little story about everyone we'd passed, while I—I wouldn't have even noticed any of them unless they happened to be beautiful women, and even then all I'd really have seen would be whether they'd noticed me back. Jena was always telling me I had a problem with seeing anything that wasn't about Joe Cube.

I sighed and turned my attention to the saucer's controls. It was a simple ball on a stick, like a gearshift knob. Apparently you pushed

it left/right, up/down, forward/backward and vinn/vout to move. I
could have tried pushing on it—perhaps to fly back down the tunnel to Spaceland on my own. But it seemed overwhelmingly likely
that I'd smash into a wall. Better just to see what happened next.
Momo would take me back soon. The more grolly I ate the better
I felt. Even if I didn't have Jena, it was pretty amazing to be vout
here in the All of hyperspace.

I relaxed into my seat and gazed comfortably at the green fields
of Klupdom. They were dotted with unearthly flowers. One flower
had overlapping crystals for its petals, another was knots of worms,
another was a nested series of spiral cones like calla lilies, another
had a single blossom that was a big angular doily with small doilies
at each of the big doily's corners—and a lot more corners involved
than you might expect. And then I saw some hyperspace roses. The
blossoms were like every stage of a rose at once: the tight bud, the
perfect bloom, the seed pod surrounded by blowsy, dropping petals.
It was wonderful. Of course the thought of roses sent me back to
Jena again. Would I ever get over her? Could I get her back? Let it
go, Joe, I told myself. Live in the moment.

That lasted for about a minute and then I started worrying again.
Assuming time was the same here as in our own world, I figured it
to be almost two o'clock. There was something I'd said I'd do by
one o'clock—oh yeah, give that deposit to Kay Harmid. Not that
I had the money yet. It suddenly occurred to me that—once I got
back—I could peel myself vout into the fourth dimension and take
money out of bank vaults as easily as Momo had. Just for a loan
till the Mophone started making money, you understand. But there
was still the problem of Wackle. Would he rob me again? Maybe
this time Momo could stop him.

The buildings of Grollyton were up ahead. We were just close
enough now for me to make out some details. It looked to be a
tidy, walled town of stone houses and spires, with the grassy fields

running right up to the town wall. The wall was set with towers, spaced to the vinn and vout as well as to the left and right. A few hundred of them in all, ornate spiky stone things like you'd see in Europe, but with brilliant, complex crystals at their tops.

Jena and I had gone to Austria one summer; it had been awesome, every single little thing different from what you were used to. Actually Jena had liked it more than me, but seeing her wake up happy and excited every day had made it worth it. I'd been hoping to do some more traveling with her after Kencom went IPO, maybe something easy like England this time. But who knew if we'd ever even go out for coffee together again.

Enough about Jena, dammit! Like I said, Grollyton looked kind of medieval. I could make out a big dark spot in the wall, probably the town gate. It was still a ways off. We paused and Momo dug around in the saucer to produce a rope.

"I must bind you now," she told me. "Please stick out your hands."

"What?"

"It will be easier if I tell the guards that you're my captive. Otherwise they might ask too many questions."

"You're not going to hurt me, are you?"

"Of course not, Joe. If I wanted to hurt you, I could have done so a thousand times already. I'll release you as soon as we get to our family's house. The binding is just for show."

So I stuck out my hands and Momo tied them—or started to until I cried out in fear. The pressure of the rope crumpled my wrists in some four-dimensional way. It didn't hurt exactly, but it looked disgusting. Momo undid the rope, wrapped a bit of cloth around my wrists and tied me again, not pulling the rope as tight as before. And then our little procession went onward.

We were starting to pass other Kluppers and they exclaimed and waved when they saw me, their flopping four-dimensional mouths

forming every kind of what's-that and gee-whiz and haw-haw expression you could think of. The way things warped with every
motion was still making me feel sick.

The gate was higher than I'd imagined; I leaned back to stare up
at it. There was a stone sculpture of a grolly plant over the highest
point of the arch; the stone captured the four-dimensional variations
of the plant, with its fruit that was both a ball and a doughnut. A
group of the Empress's crimson-uniformed soldiers surrounded us,
and Momo started talking. The soldiers treated Momo and especially Eleia with great respect, but even so, the discussion took quite
some time. They were curious about me, and came over several
times to touch me. I got the feeling it wasn't quite kosher for me
to be up here at all. Deet said something to the soldiers that made
Momo snap at him, so then he went back to muttering with Kalla.
Finally Voule handed over some coins and chunks of grolly to a
soldier who must have been the captain, and we were through. But
when I glanced back, the soldiers were still gesturing in my direction.

We proceeded down a street paved with cobblestones, ran into
what at first looked like a dead end, but then shifted to the vinn
and continued on our way. Momo and her family were walking a
lot faster than they'd been going before. It was like they were in a
rush now, as if something was going to happen soon. Meanwhile I
looked around, taking in the sight of a four-dimensional city.

Even though the town hadn't looked all that big from the outside, it felt huge on the inside. Streets kept branching off every
which way. The houses had this weird way of seeming to turn inside
out as I rode past them. Not that I could see inside the rooms; the
inside-out thing had more to do with how I was reading the fourth
dimension. Each of the houses was a whole lot of houses at once,
and all their layered-together walls added up to huge solid blocks
that had a sickening way of rotating through each other.

Finally we came to a big stone mansion with carved decorations on it; the carvings were like three-dimensional image loops of Kluppers waving pieces of grolly. Letting my third eye's viewpoint browse through one of the carvings was like watching a movie.

"This is our family home," Momo told me.

There was this incredible fountain in front of it, the ultimate transdimensional cosmic ideal of a fountain—layer after layer of water dripping and squirting and splashing and running down in sheets, totally hypnotic. And then, just to bug me, Deet splashed some water on my face and I started choking. Old Eleia made a sharp comment to him. Deet got a hangdog look, and even went so far as to wipe me off. Of course if he hadn't splashed me, I might never have stopped staring at that fountain. I turned my attention to the house.

It was three stories high, three rooms wide, three rooms deep, and three rooms across in the vinn/vout direction. Though I couldn't see through the walls, I could gauge the size of the house by counting its windows. Three by three by three made eighty-one rooms in all—I multiplied it out in my head. Three to the freakin' fourth power. This was a lot of rooms for not all that big a family—a house beyond a dot-commer's most bloated dreams. What with that fourth-power thing going on, hyperspace had more room in it than regular space.

On our way through the town, we'd picked up a little procession of followers, mostly kids. They kept darting up to touch me, running their hands over my vinner and vouter sides. Several of them made it a point to touch my penis, laughing like maniacs to see it flap. I covered my privates with the velvety cloth of the carry-all at my waist, but still the gawkers kept touching my body. Their hands felt like big worms crawling around inside my guts and my flesh.

"Stop it!" I hollered at one particularly intrusive curiosity-seeker, a stumpy little Klupper boy with a shock of red hair. The sound of me trying to boss him made everyone laugh. The kid seemed to be a favorite of Momo's family, and no matter how much I yelled at him, he wouldn't stop touching me. So, what the hell, I started screaming as if I were being killed. Throwing a tantrum in my stroller. Momo and Eleia opened their house's front door, and Kalla pushed me and the saucer in after them. We were in an entrance hall. Deet stayed outside to deal with the crowd, but Voule and that red-haired kid had come inside too. They took off towards the back of the house. Kalla untied my hands. I hopped out of the saucer and left it in the hall. The three women of the family ushered me into a sitting room. I sat down on a couch next to Kalla.

There were over a hundred pieces of furniture in the room, but nothing was crowded. In your normal ostentatious-type mansion room, you might have twenty-five pieces of furniture, loosely arranged in a five by five grid. Chairs, couches, tables, china closets, like that. But here the floor had room for five by five by five pieces of furniture. Left/right, front/back, vinn/vout. Nice comfortable-looking furniture, too. Jena would have loved seeing this stuff. She was always dreaming of ways to get inside rich people's houses. We'd toured all the palaces in Vienna.

There was a huge rug covering the floor, a beautiful oriental-style carpet with patterns that morphed off into endless variations along the vinn and vout axis. Like in a carpet store where they have a giant stack of rugs in the middle of the floor and you can flip through them. But in here, all those rugs were on the floor at once. The grolly business made a nice profit, all right.

A butler in a complicated black and white outfit came angling across the room and handed me a glass of something bubbly. Though I felt queasier than ever, I tried some, hoping it would settle my stomach. But then when I took a drink, the glass slipped out of my hyperthin hands and fell on the rug. At least it didn't break. The butler was staring so hard at me that Momo had to remind him to clean up my mess.

A little Klupper came trotting in—that red-haired kid again. His four-dimensional nose looked like a pig snout. It turned out he was Momo's son, Kalla's little brother Torsten. I think he was sorry about having upset me; he had a toy he wanted to show me. Torsten didn't speak English; he just held out the toy.

I took the toy in both hands and examined it. It seemed incredibly complicated. Looked at from one angle, it resembled a cube with each face a different color. But when I rotated it, sloping terraces bulged out of a few faces. As I turned the toy further, the terraces grew, kind of sucking the rest of the cube along with them, and then it smoothed out and I was holding a new cube with a different set of colors on its faces. The faces swung around as smoothly as if they were on hinges. But yet the thing felt rock solid. I studied the clever gimcrack for a minute.

"Isn't that cute," said Kalla. "Torsten gave Joe one of his blocks."

"That's all it is?" I said, amazed that this bizarre object was something so simple. "A block?"

"It's a hypercube," said Momo. "Like our house."

"Oh, of course," I said, just to cover my butt. But then all of a sudden I finally got it. The block stopped looking like it was made of hinges. It was a hypersolid, that was all. I walked across the room, still holding the block, and looked out the window.

Up until now, everything had been seeming to warp and turn as I passed by. It's like when you're walking down a street—if you kind of zone out, you see the patterns around you as flat shapes that are deforming as you move. Normally your brain does some kind of reconstruction thing with your two-dimensional input images and you get the idea of three-dimensional objects. But every now and then the filter stops working.

I remembered it happening to me on a poorly planned ski-trip with some party-hearty college buddies. I'd been up studying for three days but my friends were tripping on E, and they talked me into being the driver. I never take psychedelics; I guess I'm afraid of losing control and ending up like my mother. So I was the natural choice for designated driver. Anyway, there I was driving a van of spaced-out buddies, with a couple of quarts of coffee in me, and I started seeing the road as a two-dimensional videogame. The effect was especially strong inside tunnels. I drove us all the way to Aspen like that, finding my way like an ant walking on a photograph.

And now, here in Grollyton, maybe thanks to all that grolly I'd been eating, the opposite thing was starting to happen, a higher-order brain-filter was kicking in and I was really starting to see the fourth dimension. With my third eye, I could see the buildings outside as four-dimensional boxes instead of as flopping shapes. The warping was just changes of perspective. For the first time since I'd gotten to Klupdom, my stomach calmed down.

Voule appeared, carrying a hypercubical box filled with hyperthin sheets of plastic. The sheets were dotted with little squares of a hyperdimensional substance that glittered like silicon. Like tiny glass cookies sitting on trays.

"These are your Mophone antenna crystals," said Voule. "They're hyperprisms."

"Cool," I said, not that I had a clear idea of what he was talking about.

Voule took out a sheet and peeled off one of the square things. To my normal eyes it looked like a thin rectangle of silicon, perhaps half an inch long on either side and a couple of millimeters thick. It had a pair of sturdy copper wires protruding from its edge. The pair of wires ran into the center of the crystal and seemed to disappear there.

My third eye could see that the crystal extended a slight amount into the fourth dimension. It was actually a continuous trail of crystals. A hyperprism, a four-dimensional box.

"Look what the wires do," said Voule, handing me a four-dimensional magnifying glass that resembled, loosely speaking, a ball on a stick, not that I bothered to waste much time trying to think about it.

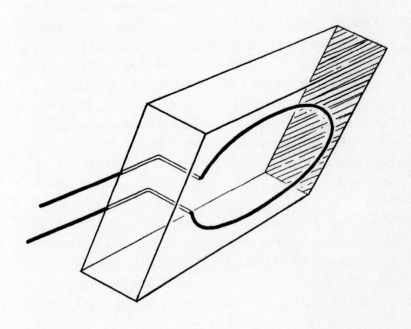

Peering through the hyperlens with my third eye, I could see how the copper wires entered the crystal and disappeared near its center—like I'd noticed before. But now my third eye could see that the wires had a right-angle vinnward bend in them at the center. Remember that this four-dimensional crystal was a vinn/vout stack of crystal cross sections. The wires left the center of the "top," or voutmost, crystal to run a short distance vinn to a "bottom," or vinnmost crystal, there to bend back into a normal space direction. In the bottom crystal, the two wires branched apart, circled around and hooked up with each other, making a flat loop that was parallel to the space of the top crystal where the wires originally fed in.

"A loop antenna," said Voule. "But with the loop in a vinner space that's offset precisely one millimeter from the space of the vouter crystal." He chuckled and rubbed his hands, which was a bizarre thing to see in and of itself. Like two dark-skinned snakes eating each other. "I've machined these all to have the exact same hyperthickness," continued Voule. "There's ten thousand of them on these sheets. Momo will set them down into Spaceland with you when she takes you back."

Just then Deet opened the front door and shouted something to us. A warning? Looking out the window, I saw a whole company of the crimson-suited soldiers by the fountain, with an incredibly ornate flying saucer floating in their midst. It looked like this monstrous bronze cradle Jena and I saw in the Hapsburg Treasure Chamber in Vienna.

"Oh my goodness, the Empress is already here," said Momo. "Quick, Voule, secrete Joe's crystals in my saucer. Come, Joe, I'll bind your hands again." I let her do it.

Voule ran into the entrance hall and stashed the sheets. And a moment later, Deet opened the door, grinning and bowing. A tall, greenish-skinned woman came striding in.

Momo and her family all bowed deeply, and then the Empress

started asking questions. She had a deep, furry voice. Her jewelry was just unreal, with these incredible gems made up of vinn/vout trails of geometric solids. I would have liked to have gotten one for Jena.

Of course the Empress wanted to get a good look at me, and Kalla urged me forward. The Empress ran her gnarled old hand across my vinner and vouter sides, then said something to Kalla.

"She wants you to pirouette," said Kalla. "She wants to see just how thin you are."

So I did a pirouette to my vinn, and of course I had to trip over my feet and fall down onto the floor, unable to break my fall thanks to my tied hands. The Empress exclaimed in wonder and pity. At her urging, Momo helped me back up and untied my hands. The Empress quizzed Momo for a while. Momo answered in her sweetest tones, with many gestures in my direction. Finally the Empress turned her attention back to me. She asked me a question in her native language, and Kalla translated.

"She wants to know what you think of Klupdom," said Kalla. "Say something nice. And offer her your gift."

"Klupdom is wonderful," I told the Empress. "It's very big. You have a lot of room." Kalla relayed my answer and the Empress let out a peal of laughter.

Meanwhile I got the mouth of my hypersack open and took out the old mouse. The ball from inside it had fallen out. I bowed and handed the empty mouse to the Empress.

The Empress held it up by its wire, looking at it from every side, perhaps marveling at our flat Spaceland workmanship. But then she got a stern look on her face and told me something else.

"She wants you to promise not to come up here again," Kalla told me. "Momo told her you'd escaped from Spaceland on your own. She thinks you're a sorcerer. Momo said you came up here to steal our grolly."

"Oh thanks a lot," I said. "Tell the Empress I'm just a poor slob who wants to go home."

Kalla said who knows what, and the Empress nodded. She made a commanding gesture, and then Momo tucked me under her arm and hopped into her saucer, making a show of putting the rope back around my hands. The Empress made a parting speech that nobody bothered to translate for me. Eleia ran into a back room and came out with one of those hyperbazookas for Momo. The Empress shook a warning finger at me, and then Momo and I were on our way, with two military saucers flying in formation with us.

We swept over Grollyton and the river and the field and then we were roaring back down the tunnel to the Cave Between Worlds, the military saucers trailing us on either side.

"What was that last thing the Empress said?" I asked Momo as the long miles of the tunnel swept past.

"She said that I'm to watch over you," said Momo happily. "She also said you'd do well to forget the black arts you employed to escape your proper space."

"So you blamed it all on me, huh?" I said. "I notice you didn't show her the antenna crystals."

"I don't think the Empress would understand if my family told her of our plan," said Momo. "The Empress is not very technically inclined. But she thinks you're good luck. Like a mascot. She authorized me to ensure that the Dronners don't get you."

"Lucky me," I said. The fact that I was finally heading home made me giddy with relief. Compared to all this, my problems with Jena seemed very small potatoes. Surely we could patch things up. "The Empress didn't scold you for bringing me to Grollyton?" I asked Momo.

"No indeed," said Momo. "She praised me for catching you. As I said, she's deputized me to care for you. And, Joe, I'm allowed to shoot towards Spaceland if needs be. This is working out even better than I'd hoped. I can come and go in your vicinity as I please, with the full approval of the Empress's troops. And the next time Wackle interferes—I'll blast him!"

"You're sure it won't hurt our world if you shoot into it?" I asked, eyeing her massive, complicated weapon.

"Of course not," said Momo. "It'll be like light through a windowpane."

And then we were flying into the Cave Between Worlds, us and the two saucers with the Empress's soldiers.

"Where should I set you down?" asked Momo. "In the new house you found?"

"Well, no, I haven't rented it yet," I said. "I guess in my car is best. Where you put my clothes. But first can we swing by my real house? I want to see if Jena's home."

Jena was home all right. And, God help me, she was in bed with Spazz again. In the middle of the day. And this time she wasn't even drunk. They were in our bed, cuddling and kissing. The air went out of me like from a slashed tire. It was truly over. I was crushed, yes, but at some other level I felt—I don't know, maybe I felt like I was getting out of jail.

"I'm sorry, Joe," said Momo as we flew away from there. "Should we try and get the money for your rent again?"

"I'll borrow it or something," I said quietly. "Just put me in my car." And that's what Momo did, with the two crimson-clad soldiers watching. One of the soldiers said something to me right before Momo untied me and put me back into space, and Momo translated it for me.

"If you come vout into our space again, he'll kill you." The soldier hadn't sounded angry or anything. Just stating a fact. And then I was down in our flat little world again, naked and with that hyperdimensional cloth carry-all still tied to my waist, various jiggling cross sections of the hypersack visible as it jounced up and down along the vinn/vout axis. The sky had clouded over and the wind was picking up. Nearly dusk already. I picked up my watch and looked at it. Ten minutes to four in the afternoon. And Jena was in bed with Spazz. I felt lost and alone.

Momo wasn't quite done yet. She carefully set the antenna crystals down inside my car with me. What I saw was a tidy array of little chips appearing over my seat, and then there was a ripping sound, as Momo pulled the backing sheet loose from them, and the chips dropped to the seat cushion. I sighed, unable to get excited about this. Momo did it a few more times, and then I had like ten thousand little squares of crystal in the bucket seat next to me. The same seat where Jena always used to sit.

A Date With Tulip

Something big had changed inside me when I saw Jena in our bed with Spazz. It was like there'd been a rope or a vine or a leash from Jena to me—and now it was gone. Suddenly I was done with wanting Jena's approval. For the last however many years, I'd been getting my personal validation from her. I'd been counting on Jena for my self-esteem. And now I realized that if I was ever going to feel good about myself, it was solely up to me.

I was naked except for the sack at my waist, sitting in my SUV on the clothes that Momo had mounded onto my front seat right before our trip, the SUV sitting in the driveway of the whipped old rental house. There weren't any pedestrians to notice me, so I didn't bother to dress just yet. I lit up a cigarette and sat there thinking.

Obviously I didn't make Jena happy, or she wouldn't be getting it on with another guy. In my old mode, I would have begun cursing myself for not trying harder; I would have scolded myself for being a self-centered, number-skulled, numb-nuts businessman. But, hey, I was who I was. Why be down on myself?

It was probably a childhood thing. When I was growing up, Dad was mentally a million miles away, scheming about his girlfriends

and his business deals. And Mom wasn't emotionally available either. She was consumed by her neuroses, practically nuts. Between
the two of them I grew up feeling invisible. But Jena—the first time
I met Jena, she laughed at everything I said and she looked at me
like I was her hero. It was just what I needed.

Jena wanted admiration back from me, plus financial security,
plus something else I could never quite put my finger on. Something
she needed to feel happy. Over the years I'd come to devote more
and more of my energy to her, always trying to make Jena happy
and, when it didn't work, trying harder to try. I wasn't doing it out
of any basic goodness or generosity of spirit—in fact, I'd come to
resent Jena's demands, to despise how quick she was to throw out
everything and lapse into depression. But pleasing Jena had become
the only game in town. My only path to love and approval. And
the more I needed her, the less she needed to give.

But now we'd reached the end of the road. The leash was broken.
My new deal was this: It was up to me, and me alone, to tell myself
I was okay. I said it out loud.

"You're okay, Joe. You're good. God loves you." God? Why not.
Saying the big word seemed to help. Not that I'd turned religious
all of a sudden. Mom's half-hearted attempt to raise Sis and me in
the Catholic church had barely left a trace. But after the trip to
Klupdom—well, it was pretty clear that the world was a hell of a
lot bigger than I'd ever thought it was.

And me too, I was bigger than I used to be. I was augmented. I
was the only one on Earth who'd been to the fourth dimension.
Until now, I'd never felt like I was big enough to help myself. But
now I was ready. Next topic.

I looked out the windshield at the grimy yellow clapboards of
the future headquarters of Mophone, Inc. The green and brown
trim was kind of pretty. I was already feeling proud of the dump.
Be it e'er so humble, there's no place like home. What I needed to

do now was to make my way over to the local Wells Fargo and—
make a withdrawal. I hadn't told Momo, but I was planning to hit
the vault.

I was on the point of starting my car, but then I realized I could
just as well flap over to the bank once I was in hyperspace. Much
smarter not to be seen at the scene of the crime. I'd gotten pretty
nimble with my higher muscles up in Klupdom, and the grolly had
me feeling strong. It would be easy to peel vout into the fourth
dimension.

No wait, better peel *vinn*. The Empress's soldiers had instructions
to shoot me if I came back vout. So I'd go vinn to the Dronian
half of the All. The other side of Spaceland from the Kluppers. No
soldiers or grolly guards there to hassle me. Though there was of
course the little matter of Wackle and the Dronners. Oh well, what
the hell. I'd started getting the feeling that some of the things Momo
said weren't true. Maybe the Dronners wouldn't bother me at all.

I switched to my third eye so I could see all around me and
check if anyone was watching me in my car. Not hardly. There was
a steady stream of traffic stopping and starting at the light, but each
and every single Silicon Valley ant was intent on his or her mission.
Work, work, work, buy, buy, buy. If anyone noticed me and my
SUV at all, they probably thought I was a Realtor. And nobody
paid attention to Realtors.

My third eye still stuck vout of Spaceland into the Klupper side
of the Cave Between Worlds, and it took only a slight twitch of
my eyestalk to be able to look and see what Momo and the Empress's soldiers were up to. They were hovering not too far off,
apparently in a discussion. It definitely wouldn't be good to go vout
there right now.

I felt down into my augmented body and made sure I remembered how to twitch myself to the vinn. It was important to get
this right the first time. Once I had the motion all set in my mind,

I did it. And then, whoa, I was out of Spaceland again, floating in the Dronner side of the Cave Between Worlds. It felt different right away; the air on this side was cool and thick, almost like water. Even so, I could breathe it.

I flapped a bit, rolling over so that my third eye pointed vinnward towards Dronia. Just as on the Kluppers' side, there were some things like cliffs a few miles away from Spaceland. But while the Kluppers' cliffs were gray with a few pastel patches of grolly, the rocks of Dronia were like a tropical reef, covered over and over with bright growths that, given their distance from me, must have been enormous. I noticed some things like lacy, city-sized coral fans, and next to them was a cluster of mountainous—anemones? Immense bunches of waving tentacles. I planned to stay away from those guys for sure. The whole vicinity of the cliffs seemed to shimmer; each nook and cranny was filled with the darting flashes of small moving things. And the air was a clear, sparkling jelly. It was like being deep undersea: fascinating, but scary.

Though I'd been doing my best not to think about Jena, she came back to me now on a wave of memories about the time last year we'd flown down to Cabo and taken SCUBA diving lessons together. On the third lesson we'd gone down to ninety feet and I'd freaked out. Everything had turned heavy and slow and sinister, with the bubbles like devils' laughter in my ears. The surface had looked way too far away, a wrinkled mirror high above me as a cloud. I'd swum straight up to the top, barely remembering to breathe out on the way. The guy waiting in the boat had hauled me in, and down below Jena and the guide had finished the dive.

By the time Jena surfaced, I'd calmed down. Jena had been in a really up mood. That night we'd had a candlelit dinner on the hotel patio, our skin tight from sunburn. And Jena had told me how much she loved me. Reached out and touched my cheek. I could still feel her fingers. If only—

I stopped right there. It was up to me to validate myself. And even though Jena was gone, there were plenty of other women out there, and I'd find one before long.

If the Dronners didn't kill me, that was. One of the big anemone things was stretching out its tentacles to alarming lengths. I hung there in the thick Dronian air for a while, staring vinn towards the living walls, waiting to see if anything was going to come for me.

But for now nothing did. Maybe the Dronners weren't as interested in me as Momo claimed. So now I rolled myself back voutward, turning my third eye's attention to Spaceland. There was Los Perros, with everything open to the fourth dimension, everything at my mercy. I flexed my augmented body and flapped like a bat. Count Joe Dracula.

In a minute or two I was next to the Wells Fargo on Santa Ynez Avenue in downtown Los Perros. I scooted in close to Spaceland, right beside the Wells Fargo vault, not the main vault, mind you, but the vault where the safe-deposit boxes were. Most likely, the serial numbers of the bills in the safe-deposit boxes wouldn't be in the bank's records.

I used my third eye to scan back and forth across the boxes till I found a big one that was loaded with hundred-dollar bills wrapped into ten-thousand-dollar packets with yellow paper bands. Dozens of packets. Good deal. I'd had a feeling I'd find a box like this. Hidden money from somebody's shady deals. Not that I was in a position to call other people shady. I made a mental note of the box number, promising myself that once I got good and rich, I'd put the money back. And then I reached vout and grabbed three packets and stuffed them into the four-dimensional sack that I still had tied to the cord around my waist.

When I reached vout for more, my hand banged against the metal side of the safe deposit box, and it made a big noise down in Spaceland. You would have thought the bank would be empty on a Sunday afternoon, but there were a bunch of tellers and managers there, I guess to check things over for Y2K bugs. One of the tellers on the other side of the vault wall cocked her head, stopped what she was doing, and walked into the vault, looking around to see what had made the noise. Damn. I held still, watching the teller, a good-looking Latina woman. I looked at her skin inside her clothes, and at the calm inner workings of her body. I could see inside the other bank employees as well, and for a minute I had this odd sensation that they were all parts of a single organism that just happened to cross Spaceland in different places. The Mystical Body of Christ, as they called the Church in parochial school. I'd always wondered how a bunch of different people were supposed to be part of one body, but now, looking down at my fellow Californians in the bank, I could get a feeling for it.

The teller took out her compact, fixed her lipstick, and then started on her eye makeup. This was going to take a while. Longer than I wanted to be floating here with my naked butt an easy target for the Dronners. Maybe I could have sneaked more money out of the boxes with the teller still there—after all, my hand would only be appearing on the insides of the boxes—but I decided not to take the chance of making another noise. It would be easy enough to come back later on.

I flapped a little distance vinn from Spaceland, and then I rolled myself over and stared again at the overgrown Dronian cliffs. The more I looked at them, the creepier they were. The colors of the cliffs were shivering and rippling like the grain in a field of wheat. And some of those anemone tentacles really did seem to be reaching out in my direction. Time to quit while I was ahead.

Hurriedly, I flapped my way back to the car. First I pulled the money out of my four-dimensional bag and set it down into my front seat. The packets of bills snapped themselves back into ordinary reality as soon as I held them vout at the correct angle to

Spaceland. And then I had an awkward minute trying to get my own bod back into the car; the first time I tried, I banged myself against the roof and got bounced back into hyperspace.

Another try and I was in the front seat of my SUV. Winter's early dusk was setting in; the wind was blowing the trees around. There was a chill in the air. I got my clothes on and counted the money. Thirty thousand bucks. I filled my wallet to the point where I had to rock over at an angle to sit on it, and I stuffed the rest of the bills into the front pockets of my leather jacket. It looked like I had breasts. But I didn't want to park any money in the haunted attaché case. I wondered if Momo was watching over me, and if she'd be able to stop Wackle from robbing me again. The sooner I could spend my money, the better.

I hustled over to Welsh & Tayke Realty on Santa Ynez Avenue, practically across the street from the Wells Fargo I'd just robbed. Kay Harmid was just stepping out the door, locking the place up.

"I got my deposit!" I cried.

She gave me and my car a thoughtful look. "I was just about to show the property again," she told me. "A third client. I showed it to someone else earlier this afternoon. I noticed that you'd left your car in the driveway?"

"I have friends near there," I said vaguely.

"Well, nobody else has signed on yet, so it's still yours to rent. Come on in and we'll settle up."

So that took care of about ten thousand bucks. And then I went down the street to a new bank I'd noticed that was open on Sundays, a place called the eBank. They got around the state laws about banking hours by having you interact with a terminal. But there were people there to help you. Like in a video arcade. They called themselves bankpersons. I opened a business checking account in the name of Mophone, with me on the signature list. It seemed like a good idea to get the money onto a bank's books before Wackle could make off with it. I fed fourteen thousand into a machine and kept sixty of the hundreds in my wallet.

I asked a bankperson about finding a lawyer to draw up some quick incorporation papers for me, and she told me about a local guy who worked late on Sundays in the Latham Building at the corner of Main Street and Santa Ynez Avenue. Business was so important in the Valley that things never fully closed down.

The Latham Building was an old two-story granite building, kind of Wild-West-looking. The lawyer was on the second floor over a home decorating shop called Yupnip. Yupnip was filled with over-priced furniture and clever, highly expensive gewgaws made of things like rocks and wire and sticks. Hundreds of bucks for some-thing you could find lying on the ground. Like a dot-com company, in a way. Jena liked Yupnip; in fact we'd gotten a lamp there. It was basically a two-gallon tin can with seashells epoxied onto it.

Upstairs from Yupnip I met with a tall, soft, curly-haired lawyer called Stu Koblenz, and we had the incorporation papers drawn up in less than an hour.

"What's Mophone's core business gonna be?" Stu asked me when we were done.

"We're still in non-disclosure," I said.

"I hear a lot of that," he said. "Give me a call when you're ready to talk patents or IPO. I can do it all."

And then I hit Kinko's copy shop and made some Mophone business cards with the address of my new house and my cell phone number. I listed myself as Chief Executive Officer. It felt good to be the boss.

I drove to my new house and hauled the boxes in from my car. The traffic was noisier than ever. People coming home from their Sunday outings. I took out my business card and looked at it again. It gave me the confidence to phone Tulip.

"Hare Krishna," answered Tulip.

"Um, hello," I said. "This is Joe Cube."

Tulip burst into embarrassed, reckless laughter. "I thought you were my sister calling," she explained. "We always say Hare Krishna for a joke. Actually I'm Catholic."

"Me too," I said. "Hail Mary."

"Oh, I don't joke about the real Church," said Tulip. "I take it quite seriously."

"I'm calling to ask you to have dinner with me," I said. "I'd like to make you an offer."

"Offer to do what?" said Tulip. "This morning you told me you were suicidal. Are you looking for an executionress? A hangwoman?" Reckless laughter again. "I have just the right outfit. It's this black sari my great-aunt gave me when I graduated from high school. Nothing shows but my nose."

"Oh, I'm feeling much better now," I told Tulip. "In fact I've incorporated a new company. Mophone. We could use an engineer like you."

"A business date," said Tulip. "Very Silicon Valley. We'll synergize, prioritize, and productize. Can I pick the restaurant?"

"You got it," I said.

"Let's try Ririche in San Jose," she said. "I've been meaning to go there. Eight o'clock?"

"Sure."

"Hang on," said Tulip. "I'll multitask." A rapid series of beeps and hisses came over my cell phone and then I heard Tulip's voice again. "Done," she said. "I just used the Web to get us a reservation."

"You've got the Web on your phone?" I asked.

"Doesn't everyone?" Tulip laughed again. "I'm glad you called, Joe. My sister thinks I'm depressed about Spazz. I've been watching horror movie videos all day. Never a good sign." A pause. "Any more news of our exes?"

"I saw them together at my old house this afternoon," I said, sparing her the details. "And then I rented a new house of my own."

"Fast work," said Tulip. I sensed a hint of pain in her bright, joking tone. "Me, I'm stuck in Fremont. They have the biggest Indian language movie theater in the Bay Area. The Naz. But that's about it. And I like Hollywood movies. The pure product."

"Maybe I could sublet you a room here."

"Oho. The alliance of the rejects. We'd better continue this discussion face to face, Joe."

"Eight at Ririche," I said. "I'm looking forward to it."

I killed the next couple of hours getting my place set up. I put my desk and computer in the front room—this would be the office. And I stacked my boxes in one of the bedrooms, leaving the second bedroom vacant just in case. And then I made a quick trip into Los Perros to buy a futon to sleep on. The easiest thing I could think of was going to Yupnip. Hey, I had seventeen thousand dollars in the bank, and I knew where to get more. I got a futon with a holder made of bolts and weathered gray lumber, a folding butterfly armchair with a seat made of an old canvas tent, a couple of UFO-style lamps, a fancy rug with this bitchin' design of hundreds of little pastel TV sets printed on it, and a couple of plastic tractor-seat stools for the kitchen. It felt festive to be shopping after dark. Like buying Christmas presents.

And then I got ready for my date. Showering was a little tricky as I didn't have any soap or towels. I was a couple of minutes late getting to Ririche. Tulip was already there, sitting at the bar drinking an orange juice, her gold earrings glinting in the dim light. She looked prettier than I remembered. Her lips made me think of chocolate ice cream. In this light, I couldn't see the blemishes in her skin. She was wearing a gray power suit and a pale orange silk blouse. I'd gone for slacks, sport coat, and tie—a special lavender paisley tie from Macy's.

Ririche was exquisite, all white table cloths and heavy silver, chic waitpersons and posh customers. With my subtle vision seeing everything, I could barely keep track of which customer was me. At the same time I was politely making an effort not to look under Tulip's clothes. Actually sitting down with her got me so flustered that I missed whatever it was she was saying to me. I thought I heard the word "elephant."

"I've always liked them," I said. "We didn't have a zoo anywhere near Matthewsboro, but I saw them in the circus. That's where I grew up, a small town in Colorado."

"What are you talking about, Joe?"

"Elephants?"

"Do you expect every Indian to discuss elephants?" said Tulip, frowning a little. A loose hank of hair escaped her barrette and fell across her cheek. "I was talking about testing out new *elements*. For doping the chips at our fab. I was trying to tell you about my job."

"Reset," I said. "You don't like elephants?"

"Not really. My mother had statues and paintings of Ganesh all over the house. He's a god who looks like an elephant. He's also the god of rats. Very fleshy, he's kind of disgusting." A sour twitch at the corner of her mouth.

"You said you're Catholic?"

"I went to Holy Names Academy in San Jose. You're new to the area, you probably don't know about it. It's a very good Catholic preparatory school. Yes, I've come to prefer monotheism. It's more rational. I was president of the Cardinal Newman club at Stanford."

"Stanford? I'm impressed." I glanced down at my menu. All the entrées were thirty bucks. "This is on Mophone, Incorporated, Tulip. Order whatever you want."

"Even caviar?" she said, a little teasingly.

"Whatever it takes to float your boat. We're in heavy recruiting mode at Mophone."

The waitress showed up and we ordered stuff, starting with caviar. Tulip gave me an amused look.

"When you say *we*, Joe—who else is at Mophone besides you?"

I offered my impression of a cocky Tom Cruise smile. It was a look I'd practiced in the mirror back in college. "Just me," I said. "But I've got a new technology you're not going to believe." I handed her a business card.

I saw a flash of pity in Tulip's eyes as she glanced at the card and put it away. "Maybe we should just call this a date, Joe," she said. "Not everything has to be a big business deal. What were Spazz and Jena doing when you saw them this afternoon?"

"They were lying down naked and kissing each other," I said. "In what used to be my bedroom."

"Oh," said Tulip, staring down at her glass. The skin below her eyes looked almost black. "What does he see in her, I wonder?"

"She's sexy," I said. "And she's new. I think that's the main thing for Spazz, isn't it? Another conquest. He's so into himself I don't think he looks any deeper than that. Jena's hot, and she wants him, and that's enough."

"And Jena?" said Tulip in a brittle tone. She wasn't liking this. "Why does she want Spazz? I'd peg Jena for picking someone—" She paused to choose the right word. "Someone more conventional."

"Yeah," I said. "Someone like me. A weak, conventional person that she can dominate. But—you know what, Tulip? I'm changing. I've been through some heavy stuff recently."

"I still don't get why Jena wants Spazz," repeated Tulip, seemingly unwilling to talk about me. "She's a goody-goody little junior exec."

"That's how she likes to present herself these days," I said. "But she's more chaotic than you realize. Spazz validates her chaos." Usually I didn't think this much about relationships. Maybe my subtle vision had opened my mind to more than just the fourth dimension. "Jena going to Spazz is like a flip-flop," I said. "I guess I can tell you that Jena had some major problems with her stepfather growing up. Sex became this power thing for her, always about master and slave. I—I let her be the master, and I think now she's ready to be Spazz's slave." Was this me talking? "I don't really blame her," I concluded. "I wish her well."

"I'd like to wring her scrawny neck," said Tulip in a matter-of-fact tone. And then she raised her voice to imitate Jena. "Oooh Spazz, you're so smart. Oooh Spazz, I like your big bad motorcycle."

"Spazz is the one I want to kill," I said. "But maybe we should be talking about us. Truth be told, Tulip, you're much sexier than Jena."

"Thanks," said Tulip, accepting the compliment but not passing one back. She didn't seem too interested in me. The waitress brought the caviar and we had some fun with that. It was in a bowl on a plate of ice with little dishes of minced onion and hard-boiled egg. I'd ordered champagne to go with it.

"What was all that about offering me a job?" said Tulip after we toasted each other. "Were you serious? What is Mophone, anyway?"

"I've gotten hold of about ten thousand special cell-phone antenna crystals," I said. For the moment I wasn't going to try explaining where they came from. "They're very small, and they pipe the signals out into—oh, call it a superchannel. There's no other signals in the superchannel, and no interference. You can use whatever frequencies you like."

"I've never heard of any superchannel," said Tulip. "And where would you be getting cell phone hardware anyway? I hope you're not buying chips on eBay. Some of the scuzzier fabs are dumping their defectives there. They're not good for much besides really lightweight apps. Things like musical greeting cards."

"These aren't chips," I said. "They're antennas. They stick out into the superchannel. Here, look." I handed Tulip an antenna crystal that I'd brought along. Her face looked happy and confident as she took it. Hardware was her thing. She gave the crystal a once-over and then pulled a magnifying glass out of her purse.

"I always carry this in case I find a beetle," said Tulip, gesturing with the lens and not really looking at my crystal yet. Once again I noticed the dark acne scars on her cheeks. "You never know when one will turn up. Have you ever heard the story about what the biologist John Burdon Sanderson Haldane said to the clergyman?"

"Can't say as I have," I said, putting on a bit of a cowboy accent.

"The clergyman goes, 'Professor Haldane, as a naturalist, you have an exceptional familiarity with the Creation. Might you draw any conclusions about the Maker?' " Tulip paused, raised her finger, and delivered Haldane's answer in a drawling, upper-crust tone. " 'He has an inordinate fondness for beetles.' "

"Shucks howdy," I said, slapping my thigh to get a smile out of her. I was really enjoying Tulip.

Now she turned her attention to the antenna crystal. "No number on it," she said. "Was this highjacked from some fab by a Vietnamese gang?"

"Stop worrying about where I got it," I said. "Can you see what it does?"

"I don't think it does much," said Tulip after a bit. "There's nothing to it. These two wires just go in and disappear in the middle. The chip looks like plain silicon. It's a square of glass with two wires in it."

"Ah, but the wires don't really disappear," I said. "They make a right-angle bend out into the superchannel. There's a connecting loop that you can't see."

"You're not technical at all, are you?" said Tulip, handing the antenna crystal back to me. "I hope you didn't pay much for these."

"Just trust me on this," I told Tulip. She seemed so competent and practical that I was hesitant to tell her my crazy story about the fourth dimension. She'd think I was nuts. It would be better to tell her after she'd seen the crystals in action. "This *is* an antenna," I said, tapping the crystal. "And it uses a non-standard transmission channel. I'm ready to pay whatever it takes for you to spend a day or two making a pair of prototype Mophones for me. Once you see that I'm right—well, we can take it from there."

"I could do it," said Tulip, twisting the stray rope of hair that hung across her cheek. "It would be easy. Would you pay me—oh, four thousand dollars a day? Even if your antennas don't work?"

"Done," I said, happy to play the big shot. We were finishing off our main courses now. "I can pay you cash in advance for your first day, if you like."

Tulip looked up from her plate. "Pay me right now?"

"Sure," I said. I used my third eye to look around to see if anyone was watching us, but everyone was into their own personal dinner dramas. I counted forty hundreds out of my wallet and forked them over. Tulip tucked them into her purse. Finally she looked impressed.

"Can you do it tomorrow?" I asked her.

"The first Monday of the new Millennium?" said Tulip. "Oh, I guess I could. It's just going to be stupid Y2K meetings. Nothing will get done. I'll call in sick." The corners of her mouth looked determined.

Over dessert I asked her again if she wanted to sublet a room.

"We can talk about it tomorrow," said Tulip, glancing at her watch. She tossed her head, making her earrings jangle. "I've got to get back to my sister's. She and her husband want to go to a midnight concert by Turbans Over Memphis and I promised to babysit. The Turbans are playing at the Naz, that Indian movie theater I told you about, with a Satyajit Ray film in the background. Very retro. All the cool Indian engineers will be there."

I paid the check and we went outside. "It was nice to have dinner with you," I told Tulip.

"You bet it was nice," said Tulip with a big smile, her cheeks shining. "You really cheered me up. I'll come by around ten tomorrow morning? To the address on your card?"

"Beautiful," I said. As she walked off, I peeked into her fine body. Was her heart beating just a little bit fast?

The wind was blowing harder than ever, like it was trying to rain. When I got back to my house I was too excited to go to bed. For some reason it struck me that this might be a good time to get some more money from Wells Fargo. Go ahead and get enough cash to pay Tulip for her second day. Wackle hadn't showed up again; maybe Momo was keeping him away.

The blue velvetlike sack was floating next to my new butterfly chair, slowly changing its shape as it drifted vinn and vout. I'd tied its shiny gold-colored rope to the chair's leg to keep it from floating off into the All. I untethered the sack and peeled myself vinnwards. Once again all my clothes stayed behind. Going into the fourth dimension was like jumping right out of my socks. I wrapped the sack's cord around my waist and started to flap.

Even though it was nighttime in Spaceland, the higher light of the All filled Dronia and bounced off the objects of our hyperflat world. I could see fine. I wondered if Momo was still over on the Klupper side, trying to watch over me. I'd forgotten to check on her before taking off into Dronia. And now that I was over here, Spaceland blocked the view of the Kluppers' half of the Cave Between Worlds.

Flying alongside the village to Wells Fargo seemed like more work than it had before, and by the time I got there I was too tired to think very hard. I just went to the same stuffed safe-deposit box and cleaned it the hell out, not bothering to count how many bundles I took. Maybe half a million bucks, all stuffed into the hyper-sack tied to my waist.

I backed off from Spaceland. And then something thumped me in the middle of my spine, pressing from my vinner side. I shrieked at the top of my lungs, twisting and flapping as hard as I could. I swung around towards Dronia to see what had touched me and—oh God, it was a red devil-shaped monster. I knew at once that it was Wackle.

He was red and rubbery and constantly changing his shape. He had quite a few arms, or legs, and he had a tail that led vinn and vinn—a miles-long tail vanishing off towards the writhing anemones on the reefy Dronian cliffs. The horns on his head were soft and flexible, like snail horns. Eyestalks. He didn't have any regular eyes in his face, but he had a mouth and a nose.

"The pig fat Kluppers are anti than you know," said Wackle. He didn't talk at all like Momo. While Momo sounded Victorian, Wackle came across like an overexcited nut. "Momo's freeze-minded, Joe Cube, anti life and anti free. Listen to my tentacle of me. I'm red as your heart, true blue. Stop helping the Kluppers—or else what? A Wackle cackle!" And then he did cackle, long and loud, trying to scare me. His mouth resembled a giant clam shell, with rows of teeth inside.

"Get away!" I yelled. "Don't steal my money again!"

"I make cosmic cause against Joe's filthy paws," said Wackle, coming towards me, his mouth opening right up around his head, and a new face coming out of his throat. "No no dough dough Joe Joe," he said, catching hold of my bag of bills. A third face came out the mouth of his second face. His head was continually turning inside out.

"Help!" I hollered and pulled back on the bag. I needed Momo. But she couldn't help me here in Dronia. I had to get back into

Spaceland where she could see me. Even though I was pointed away from Spaceland, I knew it was right behind me. I twitched like a crawfish backing under a rock and then, bingo, I felt myself locking back into Spaceland. I was standing naked on the lit-up sidewalk outside Wells Fargo. It must have been a little past midnight; nobody much was around, other than a few smokers in front of the Black Knight bar down the street.

Things looked somehow weird, but before I could figure out why, two of Wackle's hands were there in Spaceland with me, still grappling at my bag of bills. I yanked the bag, Wackle tugged back, I pulled some more, and now the bag opened and all the money fell out, the packets coming undone, and the bills swirling off down the street in the cold, damp gusts of wind. Damn!

More of Wackle appeared in front of me, standing there like an over-the-top Halloween monster. He came for me, still talking in that jabbery way he had, and I screamed again, and then, all of a sudden, there was a big flash of light, like the biggest camera flashbulb you ever saw. Yet there was no sound of an explosion. Just this immense H-bomb of a flash, brighter than white, more like pale purple. It blinded me for a second, and while I was blind, something smacked into me and slid down my leg.

When my vision slowly faded back in, I saw I'd been struck by a bloody chunk of Wackle. The jiggling glob drifted off through the pavement and disappeared. Wackle was gone. But my troubles weren't over.

There were sirens in the distance and shouts from down the street. The people outside the Black Knight—three men and two women—were running towards me, running towards the naked guy next to where the big flash had happened. And more people were coming out of the bar.

Meanwhile hundreds of thousands of dollars were blowing down the sidewalk like fallen leaves. Of course when the barflies noticed this, they forgot about me and started gathering up the bills as fast as they could, shouting with excitement.

"There's money all over the place! Hundred dollar bills!"

"Grab some, dude! Before the cops get here!"

"Yeeee-haw!"

Flashing police lights were coming up the street. I needed to get away. But this was no time to go back into hyperspace. I thought I knew a good combination of back streets and pedestrian walkways to get me home. I ran down into an alley beside the bank—and instantly got lost. Instead of being on my left, the parking lot I was expecting was on my right.

"This isn't real money," came a shout from Santa Ynez Avenue. "It's all backwards!"

"Where'd the naked guy go?" shouted someone else. It seemed like they hadn't noticed me going into the alley.

I crouched down and ran through the parking lot, keeping myself behind the cars. I knew there was a bike path back here—but it, too, was in the wrong position, off on my right when it should have been on my left. I took it anyway, running with all my might. So far so good. Nobody was on my tail.

A minute later I was on a pedestrian bridge over Route 17. I glanced down at the traffic—what the hell? The cars were all driving on the wrong side of the road. And the sign over the freeway that said Los Perros Next Exit was on my left instead of on my right. And—the writing on the sign was backwards. Somehow the world had turned into its mirror-image.

My new house was close enough to the pedestrian bridge that I was able to find it. I just went from landmark to landmark, still wondering why left and right had changed places.

All the doors to my house were locked, of course. A little hop into the fourth dimension would have gotten me in easily enough, but I still wasn't ready to try that again. But then I remembered

I'd left my bedroom window open. I scampered onto the back porch, with the window on the wrong side now, and climbed in.

I'd sort of hoped my room wouldn't be backwards, but it was. Everything the opposite of how I remembered it. The business books by my bed were in mirror-writing. I unfastened the tattered blue velvet hypersack from my waist, and, as I did, a few stray bills fell out of it. Unlike all the other writing around me, the bills looked normal. They weren't reversed.

That last shout I'd heard came back to me. "This isn't real money. It's backwards." But the money was the only thing that *wasn't* backwards. It didn't make any sense.

I crawled into my bed and pulled up the covers, trying to imagine I was safe. But of course I wasn't. Every nook and cranny of Space-land was completely open—to the Kluppers on the vout side and to the Dronners on the vinn side. They could come for me anytime. A creepy feeling. I focused in on my third eye to see what I could see out in the All. But where I expected to see Momo and the soldiers, my third eye was instead aimed towards the cliffs of Dronia. I could almost grasp what had happened, but not quite. Hell with it. I was too tired to think about dimensions.

Lord, it had been a long day. I'd moved, traveled to Grollyton, robbed a bank, started a company, hired Tulip, been attacked by a monster from the fourth dimension, and seen the world turn into its mirror-image. I wondered what Jena was up to. Cautiously I tested my feelings. My new resolve was still holding up. I was okay without Jena. I was really going to be okay.

I fell asleep smiling.

9

Mophone, Inc.

The next morning I got out of the wrong side of bed—or started to, but then I slammed my elbow into the wall. Damn. The world was still backwards. I used my third eye to peer out at the highway and, yes, all gazillion Monday-morning cars were driving on the wrong side. As long as I was using my third eye, I glanced into the All, hoping to catch sight of Momo. I'd forgotten that my third eye was sticking vinn towards Dronia, with its distant, writhing anemones. I definitely didn't want to go there again.

I walked to the 7-Eleven, only two blocks from my new digs. I could have walked five blocks to the Los Perros Coffee Roasting, but I personally didn't care all that much about what kind of coffee I had in the morning. That was more Jena's thing.

I had to be careful to walk in what seemed like the wrong direction, and I almost got run over when I crossed the street. I picked up some coffee, a muffin and a mirror-reversed newspaper that was too much trouble to look at just now. I wasn't sure whether I should pay with one of my new regular-looking hundreds or with some of the older mirror-reversed money in my wallet. So I hung back and watched another customer. Mirror-money was the way to go. I was glad I could still speak and listen.

Outside I took a bite of my muffin, and found myself reflexively spitting it onto the sidewalk. It tasted like soap, or worse, like the smell of Pine-Sol floor cleaner in an airport men's room. I tried to wash away the janitorial taste with a sip of coffee, but the coffee was nasty too, a brew of nose drops and coconut sunblock, even worse than 7-Eleven coffee usually is. Something told me there was no use going back into the store to complain.

When I got home, I drank a couple of glasses of water, but even that didn't taste quite right. The water had a faint hint of gasoline in it. I tried nibbling at some mints I had; they tasted like hot chili peppers. At this rate I would starve to death. Where the hell was Momo when I needed her? Again I peered out into Dronia, again I was scared to try going there.

I sat down in at my desk to study the paper, the ꙄＷꓱИ ＹꓤUꓛꓤꓱＭ ꓱꙄOႱ ИAꙄ. Right on the front page was a picture of the Los Perros Wells Fargo with an inset image showing some fanned-out hundred dollar bills. The bills in the picture didn't look reversed to me, but by now I was realizing that I was the only guy who was out of step. If something looked right to me, it looked backwards to everyone else. I took the paper into the bathroom and held it up in front of the mirror so I could read it.

"Mirror Million Blows in Wind," is what it said. "Bankers Check Coffers."

Just then there was a knock on the front door. I lowered the paper and examined my face in the mirror. I looked kind of crooked, but not all that different. I went to the door.

"Hi Joe," said Tulip, not really looking at me. She had her six gold earrings on, but she wasn't wearing any makeup at all this morning. The old acne scars on her cheeks stood out very clearly. I finally grasped that this woman was a science geek. An engineer.

"I brought some things," she said, setting down two boxes of tools. She trotted back to her car for more stuff. A brown Nissan wagon. I noticed there was a statue of the Virgin Mary on her dashboard.

Tulip returned with two new cell phones, still in their boxes. "I'll put a couple of your antenna crystals into these, and we'll see what's what." She glanced at my face and did a double-take. "Is something wrong, Joe? Didn't you sleep? Are you worried about Jena?"

"I just feel weird today," I said. I longed to confide in her, but it didn't seem safe. "Is the kitchen counter all right for you to work on? You can sit on this new stool."

"Okay," said Tulip. The bags under her eyes were darker than ever. "I didn't sleep so well myself. I even tried to phone Spazz, but he wasn't home. It sucks to be rejected." That long black lock of hair was hanging down across one of her cheeks.

I brought Tulip some of my antenna crystals and she settled in with the cell phones and her tools. She had special thick glasses she put on for the close-up work. Her mouth was calm and serious. How wonderfully competent she seemed.

I dialed up my email on my desk computer, just to seem busy, but it was too hard to read the backwards writing. So then I hand wrote some notes towards a business plan for Mophone, Inc. Time passed. Tulip was quietly tinkering in the kitchen. I went in and looked at her, enjoying the curve of her back and the shine of her cheeks. She gave me a blank, preoccupied glance. I took a glass of gasoline-flavored water and went back to my desk. I was getting really hungry. Much as I hate thinking about science, it was time to figure out what had happened to me.

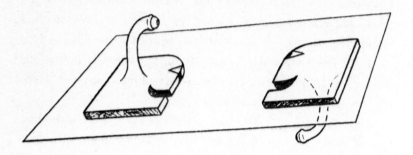

Momo had said it helped to think in terms of Flatland. I found some scissors in my desk and I cut out a little paper profile of a man, a man with feet and a body and a mouth and nose, with the feet and mouth and nose all pointing to the right. I set the flat man down on my desk and looked at him for a minute. I drew a dot in the middle of his head to stand for his third eye. And then I flipped him over so his third eye was pointing down into the desk. His feet and mouth and nose were all pointing to the left. Flipping the flat man over in the third dimension made him into his mirror image. That's what had happened to me. I'd started out with my third eye pointing towards Klupdom, but then I'd turned it towards Dronia. And thanks to Wackle, I'd come back into Spaceland without re-orienting myself.

"Playing with paper dolls, Joe?" asked Tulip. "You'll make a perfect CEO."

"I'm doing some out-of-the-box thinking," I said, sliding the cutout man into my desk drawer. "Previsualizing our users. Are you making any progress?"

"Well, your antenna crystals do have some functionality," said Tulip. "If I pass current in through one wire it comes out through the other. Even though the wires don't seem to touch each other. It's like there's an invisible loop. So maybe they really are antennas. Before I can test them, I'll need to dash out to Fry's. I need a couple of wiggywaggy-frammistat-bilgebulge-777-converters." That's not the exact phrase she used, but I'm no techie.

"Fine," I said. "Get yourself a snack while you're at it. I don't have any food here."

"Do you want to come along for the ride?" said Tulip. This was the closest thing to a friendly overture she'd made. But I needed some time alone just now.

"I'm kind of busy," I said.

"With your paper dolls," said Tulip, laughing and shaking her earrings. "Rrright! Okay, Joe, see you later."

As soon as she was gone, I went back into my bedroom, closed the door and the shades, and peeled myself into Dronia. No sign of Wackle. With a quick flip of my augmented body, I turned myself over so that my third eye was pointing back towards Spaceland. And then I touched down.

Nothing was backwards anymore. My bed was on the proper side of the room, I could read the titles of my business books, and my face looked normal again in the mirror. Time to eat! I jumped in my car and jammed down to our local fast-food strip to stuff my gut. The food tasted great but when I got home I still felt a little wobbly. Grolly—I needed grolly for my augmented bod. I peered up into Klupdom. No sign of Momo anywhere nearby, but I did see a saucer with one of the Empress's crimson-dressed soldiers. There was no hope of me trying to go vout there and forage for grolly just now. I'd have to wait for Momo and beg her. Where was she, anyway?

Around then Tulip came back. "Feeling better, Joe? You look more like your old self."

"Yeah, I'm good now. I got some lunch. How was Fry's?"

"It's the key sight to see in Silicon Valley," said Tulip. "Even though it's rather ordinary. I always take my visitors there. You'll find almost anyone in Fry's. Last month I saw Clement Treed buying four PowerBooks. The maximum dot-commer. He's tall and thin. He looks like a Muppet. A big mouth on a little head. He's not that old of a guy either."

"The *MeYou* Clement Treed? The richest guy in Silicon Valley? Did you talk to him?"

"I went, 'Hi,' and Treed went, 'I'm sorry, but I'm busy right now.' I was with my cousin Amita who's just come over from India to take Computer Science classes at San Jose State. So then I put on my Indian accent and I said very loudly to Amita, 'This is the *pandit* who defiles our *Mahatma*. He compares himself to Gandhi for material gain. For shame, Mr. Treed, for shame!' "

Tulip was referring to an ongoing MeYou ad campaign that had shown a picture of Gandhi and Clement Treed with the MeYou logo and web address. The ad was one of a series. They'd used Gandhi, Picasso, John Lennon, and Einstein, all blue-chip personalities like that, each of them Photoshopped in with Clement Treed. It was kind of gross, but the numbers showed the campaign was helping. As if MeYou needed to get any bigger. I'd read about the campaign in the business magazines. Instead of laughing along with Tulip, I drifted off for a second there, scheming about the Mophone. Maybe we could get some venture capital from Clement Treed. Even if Tulip had insulted him, he'd remember her. And that was half the battle.

"Are you even listening to me?" snapped Tulip. Her eyes were big and shiny, the pupils dark brown in the white orbs. "You keep it up, and I'll charge you double tomorrow."

"You're not going to finish today?"

"Money, that always gets their attention," said Tulip. "The pointy-headed bosses of the world. Come talk to me while I work, Joe, I'm getting bored." Another overture. Not riding to Fry's with her had been a good move. It had made me more of a challenge. Women like a challenge.

So now I sat on the other stool in the kitchen, chatting with Tulip. She'd pried the two cell phone cases open, and she was replacing the old antenna assemblies with my antenna crystals and those whizzbang-whatever chips from Fry's. She had her thick glasses on and she was using a soldering iron.

"I'm going to start out with a peer-to-peer architecture," said Tulip. "Like walkie-talkies."

"Are walkie-talkies different from cell phones?"

"Cell phones use the client/server architecture. If you call me on a normal cell phone, your phone sends a signal to a telephone company's antenna, the telco does some digital munging on the signal, and then a telco antenna broadcasts the signal back out for me to pick up. We're clients and the telco is the server. Walkie-talkies send signals directly to each other without any third party. Peer-to-peer instead of client/server. Peer-to-peer is only practical for short distances. But if this so-called 'superchannel' of yours works as well as you say it will—maybe we can stretch it out. In terms of hardware it also happens to be easier to implement. And since I don't think it's going to work anyway—"

"You're saying the Mophone could work without a phone company to back it up?" I said, getting excited. "The users wouldn't have to pay a monthly service charge?"

"Would be nice, huh?" Tulip crimped in the corners of her mouth and gave me a serious look. "What's the story with the superchannel, Joe? And where did you get the crystals?"

"I guess I can tell you now," I said. "A creature from the fourth dimension gave them to me. Her name is Momo. The wires in the middle don't actually disappear; they stick into the fourth dimension. They make a loop on the vinn side of our space."

"So you're going to be like that, huh?" said Tulip, leaning over the phones. She totally thought I was kidding. A little blue plume of smoke spiraled up from her soldering gun. "Never mind. Did you hear anything from Jena today?"

"No. I guess she went in to work."

"I don't think so," said Tulip, brushing aside a hanging twist of hair. "I cruised by 1234 Silva View Crescent on my way back from Fry's." She rolled her big eyes my way, regarding me over the lenses of her glasses. "Jena's Beetle and Spazz's motorcycle were both there. I guess they're having a honeymoon."

"They missed work?" I exclaimed. "I wonder if something's wrong with them."

"Why do you say that?" asked Tulip. "You didn't sneak over there and kill them, did you, Joe? The house looked awfully quiet." There was a slight smile on her full, chocolate lips, but she wasn't completely joking. She was a little afraid. She wasn't quite sure what I was like. She had this skittish, almost paranoid side to her.

"I'm not a violent guy, Tulip."

"Last night you said you wanted to kill Spazz."

"And you said you wanted to wring Jena's neck. We were venting. Commiserating. Look, I am so over Jena, you wouldn't believe it. I've wasted too many years looking to her for my self-esteem. I'm okay. I know that now. I'm okay just as I am. Do you have good self-esteem, Tulip?"

"Of course," said Tulip. "But that's not the right way to think. I'm more concerned about my relationship to God."

This was kind of jarring. I hadn't heard a single person talk seriously about religion in the whole time I'd been in California. Not like back in Matthewsboro—I remember one time there I'd picked up a hitchhiker from the local Bible school, and as soon as he'd gotten in my car, he'd said, "Have you heard about Jesus?" Just to be a wise guy, I gave Tulip the same mock-innocent answer I'd given the hitchhiker.

"Who?"

"I told you I'm religious, Joe. It's the center of my life. God is the living core of everything around us. We're the clients and God's the Server. He has an inordinate fondness for people as well as beetles." She laughed easily. "Yes, I'm different from most people. I care about God and about my fellow humans. I hope you don't have a problem with that, Mr. Self-Esteem."

"I totally respect your opinions," I told Tulip. "But I do have a little trouble seeing how you fit in with Spazz."

Tulip was quiet for a minute, thinking. "Spazz's attraction for me? You know how we met? We were both buying earrings at an Indian store. Spazz makes me laugh. And—well, I've always been a very good girl, you know. Spazz represents, oh, chaos, disorder, creativity, bohemianism. He excites me. I guess I had some hope of reforming him a little bit. But it didn't work."

"Spazz—he's not religious at all," I said. "He's a stoner."

"Well, Spazz claims getting high is a way to see God," said Tulip. "But enlightenment isn't about getting high. It's about compassion." She'd been working all this time. Now she set down her tools, took off her glasses, and got up from her stool. She gave me a full, frank look. Her dark mouth was level and serious. There were shiny high-lights from the window on her large, thoughtful eyes. I'd stopped noticing the scars on her cheeks. I wished I were more bohemian. "Here," said Tulip, handing me one of the cell phones. It looked the same as ever, but she'd put the antenna crystal inside it. "Take this outside and try to call me."

"You're done?"

"For now. The way it works is that when you press the Send button on either of these phones it makes the other one ring."

I went out into the backyard and pressed the Send button on the Mophone. I heard a ringing from inside the house, and then, over the phone, a click and silence. Tulip had answered my call.

"Mr. Watson, come here," I said. "I want you."

"Mr. Bell," came back Tulip's voice, crystal clear. "I heard every word you said—distinctly!" We'd both seen that old movie about the invention of the telephone.

"Terrific!" I cried. "I wonder what kind of distance we can get? Should be pretty much unlimited. There's nothing to get in the way in hyperspace. No buildings, no curvature of the Earth."

"Hyperspace," said Tulip's voice in the Mophone. She was ready to take me seriously. "You really say a creature from hyperspace gave the antenna crystals to you?"

"Momo," I said.

"Did she ask you to worship her?" Tulip stepped out onto the porch to look at me. The bags under her eyes were dark and tired. "Did she ask for your soul?" I remembered Tulip's mentioning that she watched a lot of supernatural horror movies. She seemed like one of those people for whom a fear of the devil was the downside of their love for God. My mother had been like that; in fact she'd thought about the devil a whole lot more than she'd thought about God. I'd never seen the point. Believe in a loving God, fine, but why scare yourself with stories about Satan? It's not like you need

Satan to account for evil. Ordinary people pump out plenty of it on their own.

"It wasn't like that at all," I told Tulip, turning off the Mophone and looking at her. "There's nothing supernatural here. This is science and business. Momo's basically a plantation owner from the fourth dimension. Like a saucer alien or something. Her family grows this stuff called grolly."

Tulip shook her head. The idea of Momo seemed to upset her. "I think I've done enough for one day," she said. "Four thousand dollars worth. I'm going home."

"Will you come back tomorrow?"

"Maybe." She fingered one of the dark bumps on her cheek. "Will you cut me in for stock?"

"Sure I will! You can really take another day off from work?"

"Yeah," said Tulip. We walked back into the house and sat on the stools in the kitchen. "I phoned ExaChip while I was at Fry's," she explained. "They're not doing jack this week. I told my boss I'm going skiing, and he said it was fine." She hefted her Mophone. Her mood was brightening again. "I'm starting to believe in the antenna crystals. The fourth dimension. I guess anything's possible. The Mophone could be a killer product. How much stock would you offer me?"

"You can be the Chief Technology Officer," I said. "I'll give you, I don't know, a tenth of our founder's stock? But then I'd only want to pay you like five hundred dollars a day."

"I'm getting two hundred thousand a year at ExaChip," said Tulip. "So you'd have to go at least a thousand a day."

"I could do that," I said, maybe too quickly. I really wanted Tulip in on this. She was smart, I was attracted to her, and—if I could win her over, it would be a way to get back at Spazz. Show him I was as much of a man as he was. "I could give you my extra room, too. If you need a place to live."

"Let's take a look at it."

We walked through the tiny hall to the unused bedroom. Tulip gave the room the once over and peered out the windows. She turned her big eyes on me and brushed back her loose-hanging hair. "It would be handy, for a while. But I wouldn't want you to have any unrealistic notions."

"I don't, Tulip," I lied. "Not at all. Strictly business. Though if you change your mind—"

"It's no good to rush into a new relationship just to get back at someone," said Tulip, as if she were reading my mind. She fingered the three hoops in her right ear, thinking. My subtle vision had gone fuzzy, but I managed to glance inside Tulip's body: she was still and calm. "This would be a lot nicer than my sister's," said Tulip presently. "I have to sleep on the couch there. And Sis always expects me to baby-sit. Did I mention that Fremont bites? I have to drive on the Nimitz to commute from there." The Nimitz was the worst freeway in the whole Bay Area. At just about any time of day, it could take you an hour to go five miles on the Nimitz. Hooray for the Nimitz! Thanks to the Nimitz, Tulip was going to move in with me! "I'll do it," she said. "And no Satanism."

"Don't worry!" I said. "It'll be great. We'll get rich together."

"I'll tell you what," said Tulip. "I'll drive up to Fremont right now and get my stuff. And I'll take the Mophone with me and we can check if it keeps working when I'm far away."

So that's what we did. Tulip launched her Nissan into the traffic, and for the next hour and a half she called me every five or ten minutes. The connection held up fine. No fading, no tearing, no cut-outs, no drift. We had a peer-to-peer phone that scaled over intercity distances! Every time we talked, Tulip got more excited. She asked me again about how the chips worked, and I told her a little more about Momo and the fourth dimension. She was believing it, but she still didn't like the idea of Momo. And then she was at her sister's house and she hung up for a while.

I got to work on my computer, making up a business plan. If we were going public with Mophone, we couldn't fund it with stolen money. Sooner or later some auditors would be looking at our books. We were going to need some honestly scammed venture capital. I felt a little dizzy at the thought of this. The uneasy, wobbly feeling I'd had after lunch came back to me. I went and lay down on my bed.

The phone started ringing—not the Mophone, my regular cell phone. It was Tulip.

"I'm just starting back, Joe," she said. "But—something funny happened. The Mophone disappeared."

"How do you mean?"

"It was in my purse in the car, and when I went back out it was gone."

"Maybe your nieces and nephews took it?"

"No, the car was locked and I have the only key. I don't see what could have happened to it. Could this have something to do with that—that supernatural creature you were talking about? Do you think she might be from the Evil One?"

"Relax," I said. "Those nuns made you too superstitious. If Momo took your Mophone she'll give it back. She might just be checking out your engineering. Maybe even improving it." I sounded more confident than I felt. If it was a Dronner like Wackle who'd taken it, I was screwed. Doubly screwed if Tulip ever got a glimpse of a hypercreature who looked like Beelzebub himself. I might need to go looking for the missing Mophone. "If I'm not here when you get back, you can let yourself in with the key under the doormat," I told Tulip.

"Okay." Now that she'd dropped her bomb, she sounded calm.

"I'll take my time. The traffic's gridlocked. I'm going to stop off at the Great Mall and pick up a bed and stuff. See you later."

I found my hypersack and tied it to my belt in case I was going to have to go out into the All to find Tulip's Mophone. And right then my Mophone rang. It was Jena. I wasn't really surprised. Jena and phones went together.

"How did you get it?" I asked as soon as she'd said hello.

"Momo's here. She gave us a bunch of antenna crystals this morning. Spazz has been trying to wire them up all day, but it's not happening for him. Momo brought us one of your Mophones so Spazz can see how you did it."

"Goddamn it!" I yelled. "Let me talk to Momo!"

"I think we better talk in person, Joe," said Jena. "Come on over. And bring my half million."

"It's gone," I snapped. "Didn't Momo tell you?"

"You've got more," said Jena. "I saw the paper."

"Shut up!"

"Come on over. Don't take too long, or I might make some more calls." Jena hung up.

It took me a minute to get my head back together. What was all that crap I'd been telling myself about being okay? I wasn't okay at all. Jena was pushing me around as much as ever. I drove over to my old house, cursing and fuming.

Spazz met me at the door. He wasn't wearing his nose-ring anymore; maybe Jena had already talked him out of it. But he still had the big silver stud in the top of his ear. I felt like ripping it out.

"Dude," said Spazz, but nothing else for the moment.

Jena was sitting on the couch biting her nails, and next to her was Momo, looking like a fat, naked Picasso woman. Momo nodded in my direction, and one of her eyes crawled across her face and winked at me. Meanwhile Spazz sat down at my old kitchen table. He had some tools there, though not nearly so clean a kit as Tulip's.

Tulip's pried-open Mophone was lying next to two more cell phones
that Spazz had been tinkering with. Spazz was avidly studying the
details of what Tulip had done.

"Hi, Joe," said Jena to break the ice. "I hope you're not mad at
me. I appreciate your having moved out without a fuss." I felt a
flush of pleasure at her kind words. Her face across the room looked
as crisp and clear as ever. Her pink cheeks, her bowed lips, her far-
seeing eyes. I felt the same old need to make Jena happy, to win
her approval. I was very far indeed from being okay.

Not trusting what I might say to Jena, I turned to Momo. "Why
are you helping them?" I asked her. "I thought you were on my
side. That's my Mophone you gave Spazz. Tulip invented it for
me." Across the room, Spazz gave a sharp cough, but he didn't look
up from his circuitry.

"Calm yourself, Joe Cube," said Momo. Her voice took on a
cozy, soothing tone. "You'll be the better for some grolly." A shiny,
lavender bagel appeared at the tip of her outstretched hand. I walked
over and took it. I needed grolly like a man in a desert needs water.
I gnawed at the chunk, trying to keep too much of it from sliding
off into the fourth dimension. Though I'd kind of meant to save
some for later, I kept right on chewing the grolly until I'd eaten
every bit of it. It didn't take me long.

I wasn't wobbly anymore, and my subtle vision was sharp. I could
see the rest of Momo vout there in hyperspace, Momo and her
saucer. I used my third eye to take a quick look at Spazz and Jena.
I could still see inside them, which meant that Momo hadn't augmented them.

"Why are you helping Spazz and Jena?" I asked Momo again.

"I wanted to ensure the timely creation of a Mophone," she said.
"It seemed wise to have two separate teams working on it. After the
fiasco last night, I wasn't feeling so confident in you, Joe Cube. You
should understand that what happened to you served you right.

You've no business going down into Dronia alone. They're evil, evil beasts. It's dangerous—and inappropriate—for you to converse with Wackle."

"No worry of that happening again," I said. "You killed him."

"That was just one instance of him," said Momo. "There's no end to Wackle. He's like the fingers on a hand, or like the tentacles of an anemone. But let's not trouble ourselves with Wackle just now. I'll deal with him should he approach us. Let's make plans for Mophone, Inc. You four must work together."

"Did you bring my money?" interrupted Jena.

"It's gone, dammit," I told her. "Wackle took it yesterday morning right after I vacated for you. And yes, I took a little extra from the bank, but that's all mine. I tried to go back for even more, but then Wackle came for me and Momo splattered him. Steal your own money if you want some, Jena. Get Momo to augment you."

"I'll not augment anyone else," said Momo. "The Empress's soldiers are watching my activities too closely for that."

"Good," said Jena, then turned back to me. "I saw the mirror money in the paper, Joe. Weird. How many good bills did you actually get?"

"None of your business," I said.

"Seventeen thousand dollars," said Momo. "And he's right, Jena. That's his money now. If you want money you're going to have to earn it."

"What about the mirror money?" asked Jena.

"I think I'll take it from the police station, turn it right way round, and put it back where it came from," said Momo. "What was the box number, Joe?"

I told her.

"Good," said Momo. "And once you get some funding, I'll put the rest of the money back as well."

"You think we'll get funding?" said Jena.

"Of course," said Momo.

"Aha!" exclaimed Spazz, still bent over the cell phones. "Now I get it. I'm gonna make a run to Fry's."

"No man steps in Fry's but once," said Jena cheerfully. It was one of her sayings. She'd noticed that whenever I got some hardware at Fry's I always had to go back and exchange something the next day. She gave me her prettiest smile. "We three will make a good team, Joe. I'll be the Director of Corporate Communications. You know darn well that I'm the only one who can pitch to the venture capitalists. It's me who's the cheerleader type. You can be the CEO, and Spazz can be the Chief Technology Officer. We don't really need that other girl, do we? What's her name again? Rose? Violet? Daisy? Alfalfa?"

"Tulip's the CTO," I said. "Spazz is the one we don't need."

"Hell you don't," said Spazz, finally listening to us. "This little kludge of Tulip's is fine if all you've got in your network is two phones. But once we scale, we're going to need packet-switched CDMA. Code Division Multiple Access, dude. Each and every spoken syllable has the target phone's number on it, that's the way CDMA works. No way Tulip can write the program for that. It'll run as a distributed parallel computation on all the Mophones. Like the Internet, but with no servers, just a zillion peer-to-peer clients. It's an idea that Tulip and I have been talking about, actually. Tasty. You know I'm the one to hack it. It'll be fun. And as for titles, hey, you can call Tulip the Chief Technical Officer if that's what it takes to make her mother happy." He paused to cough, and then continued. "I don't give a squat what you call me. High Llama, Beauty School Dropout, Just In Time Compiler, Alligator Wrassler, whatever. Just so I get the same money as everyone else." He gave me one of his cocky, sarcastic smiles.

"A bastard is what I'd call you," I said, the anger welling up in me. "A jerk. You stole my wife. You son of a bitch." I took a step towards him.

"Time warp," said Spazz, getting to his feet. "Neanderthal zone." He circled around to the other side of the kitchen table. He was holding one of his screwdrivers. He was tall, but I outweighed him.

"Don't, Joe," said Jena, her voice breaking. "It's not Spazz's fault. It's my fault." I had this funny moment of subtle vision just then. Instead of seeing Jena as some calculating evil tormentor, I saw her for what she really was, a wistful, not-particularly-bright person who didn't know what the hell she was doing. A person like me. I was nuts to get so uptight about this. Couples split up all the time. I was acting mentally ill. I flopped down on the other end of the couch from Jena, with Momo sitting between us. Spazz regarded me for a minute.

"Hunky-dory?" he said, setting down his screwdriver.

"We'll see," I said. Deep down I still had some mentally ill thoughts about what I might do to Spazz. But not here and now. I could at least pretend to be okay. Momo was right. If we were going to make a go of Mophone, we four would have to work together.

"Hark!" said Momo, who'd just been peeking vinn at the Dronner side of Spaceland. "A Wackle approaches!" She stuck one of her arms vout into Klupdom and got the hyperbazooka from her saucer. Jena and Spazz exclaimed when she pulled the weapon down into the room with us. It was awesome, a three-foot hypercylinder covered with a filigree of tubes and wires. Since it was four-dimensional, it looked particularly bizarre, getting thicker and thinner and with bits and pieces of it appearing and disappearing as Momo moved it around. "I'll pot him from here," said Momo, and now most of her disappeared on the vinner side of Spaceland with the hyperbazooka. Her butt and legs were still on the couch, but rounded off at the waist.

"It's like she's ice-fishing," said Spazz. "With a rocket launcher. Who's this Wackle you keep talking about?"

"I saw him last night," I said. "When I was trying to rob the bank. He looks like a devil and he talks funny. He scared me so much that I came down mirror reversed. And then Momo shot him. He was like the tip of a tendril from an undersea anemone thing on the cliffs of Dronia. I guess there's a new tendril coming for us right now."

"Yikes," said Jena. "We're not safe anywhere, are we?"

"Momo and the Empress's troops are watching over us," I said.

"So creepy," said Jena.

"Can you see what Momo's doing down there?" Spazz asked.

"No," I said. Because my third eye was sticking vout into the Klupper half of the All again, I couldn't see into Dronia.

Momo's legs tensed and braced themselves, then jerked as if in recoil. A bloody scrap of Wackle tissue came streaking across the living room and disappeared through the bedroom wall.

"This is so *X-Files*," said Spazz. "I love it."

"One less Wackle," said Momo, reappearing on the couch with her weapon cradled in her arms. "If it weren't for Spaceland we could be shooting Dronners all day long."

"Spaceland is our world, right?" said Jena.

"It divides the All in half," said Momo. "Klupdom above and Dronia below. The problem is, we can't see through Spaceland."

"But you can come down and stick your head through it," said Spazz.

"Indeed," said Momo. "But normally it's forbidden by the Empress. She doesn't like for us to interfere with Spaceland. It's only safe for me to be talking to you now because I bribed the soldiers to leave me alone. They're very poorly paid, you know."

"Does your Empress know what you did to Joe?" asked Spazz. "Giving him that third eye he used for the blackjack game?"

"The Empress views Joe as a powerful sorcerer," said Momo. "She thinks he became augmented all on his own. She views him as—

how to say this—a sacred monster. I've been authorized to do what's necessary to contain—and protect—Joe Cube."

"The Empress doesn't know about the Mophones," I put in. "Momo says their radiation will help keep the Dronners away. They'll stop sneaking up through Spaceland to raid Momo's family's grolly fields."

"Speaking of my family, it's time for me to go spend some time with them," said Momo. "I'll rejoin you in a few days. But no need for worry. I think I've taught the Wackles a bit of a lesson. And here's a little more grolly to tide you over. Good luck with your new business, you three." Momo handed me another shiny lavender doughnut of grolly, a rather small one this time. Her body began melting away into hyperspace.

"Just a minute," I said, feeling uneasy. "How long are you going to be gone?"

"The sooner you set up some meetings with investors, the sooner you'll see me again," said Momo. "That's the next time you're likely to need me. I can't be meddling every minute."

"What about bringing me more grolly before that?" I said. I hated to think I'd be running out of the stuff so soon again.

"Find your investors, then you'll get your grolly," said Momo. "May your craving serve as an extra impetus towards rapid initiatives." What was left of her was drifting down towards the floor like a leaking helium balloon. At the last minute she paused and pointed a little mouth-trumpet up at me. "Remember, Joe, whatever you do, stay out of Dronia." And then she was gone. I took a little nibble of my grolly.

"What is that stuff?" asked Spazz. "Can I try some?"

"It's food for my higher body," I said. "I don't have nearly enough of it. I can't spare any at all."

"Now I'm really curious," said Spazz. "You sound like a coker talking about his stash. Let me taste just a crumb."

I pincered off a literal crumb and handed it to him. He bit into it and winced.

"Ow!" he exclaimed. "It's hard. Like a piece of sand. Or a rock." He spit the purple speck out into the palm of his hand.

"Not for me," I said proudly. "I'm different." I crunched down one last bite, enjoying the sweet, rich, fruity taste, and then I forced myself to put the rest of the grolly into the hypersack at my belt. I was feeling really good. That last taste of grolly had put a spinning flywheel of energy into my head. Working with Spazz and Jena had begun to seem like the perfect idea. I discussed business plans with them. They were all smiles. After a bit, I decided to call Tulip on her cell phone and let her in on the plans. Turned out she was back at my new house, busy putting her bed into the extra room.

"Guess where I found your Mophone?" I said to Tulip. "It's with Spazz."

"What? That rat! He was following me? He stole it from my purse?"

"No, no—Momo took it. Just like I thought. She reached in from the fourth dimension."

There was a silence. "Have you actually seen Spazz?" said Tulip finally.

"I'm with him and Jena right now. I think the four of us should talk things over."

"Really?" There was an upward surge in Tulip's voice. A hopeful lilt. Maybe she thought Spazz wanted her back again.

"Just to talk about business," I said flatly. "About the Mophone. You head the tech, Spazz writes the software, Jena does the VC pitch and the marketing."

"I don't know if I'd be comfortable with that," said Tulip, her voice chilling over.

"Why don't we four sit down and talk about it. We'll be right over."

"No," said Tulip quickly. "I'm about to go out for supper."

"Stay there. We'll come over. I'll bring beer and pizza."

"Oh, all right. Bring juice and ice cream, too."

So we held our first team meeting at Mophone world headquarters.

To start with, we got ourselves psyched up to the point of faxing in resignation letters to our real jobs.

Next, Spazz drafted us a patent application for me to take to Stu Koblenz. He said it didn't matter if the patent didn't actually explain how we made the antenna crystals.

And then we sent out some emails to try and set up meetings with possible business angels—including Clement Treed. We told everyone we had an "operational and patented technology for broadband comm with low power and no EM spectrum conflicts." In the current Silicon-Valley-speak, a venture capitalist was a buttoned-down manager who invested other people's money for them. They were, of necessity, somewhat cautious. We were looking for rich guys ready to plunge in with their own cash. They were the business angels.

Over the course of our evening, Tulip went out of her way to pay a lot of attention to Spazz. Smiling at what he said, sitting next to him, telling him things. So it was pretty awkward when, around ten o'clock, Spazz and Jena left together, leaving Tulip and me alone. Tulip looked at me, burst into tears and disappeared into her room as fast as she could.

The next day, Tuesday, January 3, 2000, I ran around like a chicken with its head cut off.

At nine A.M. I went to Kencom. Before Ming would give me my termination papers, I had to undergo an exit meeting with Ken Wong. This was a minefield to be carefully crossed. Though Ken came across as polite and preppy, he was a tiger when it came to business. But I knew how to say the right things. I taped the conversation to make sure that the other three would follow exactly the same line in their own exit meetings, which were scheduled a little later in the day. Inside his desk, Ken had a tape recorder going too; I could see it with my third eye.

I was frank with Ken about the reasons Spazz and I were leaving. I told him that we were founding a start-up named Mophone to productize a new idea we had. Ken feigned anger and brought out the intellectual property rights waiver I'd signed when joining Kencom. I stated that our new technology had nothing at all to do with Kencom research and that it was something which Spazz, Tulip, Jena and I had developed completely on our own time.

Ken threatened to sue me, and I said Mophone would vigorously defend itself and that he would lose. And then, as I'd hoped, he changed his tack. He wondered if I might be interested in making my new company a subdivision of Kencom. I said that we wanted to be fully autonomous—but that we would certainly be open to letting Ken and his backers be on the list to see the pitch for our upcoming round of seed funding. I pointed out that this would also be a good way for Ken to reassure himself that we were not using any Kencom technology. Ming Wong phoned Jena and signed up Ken for a slot.

Back at the Mophone headquarters, I played my meeting tape for the others, and then they went off for their own exit meetings: Spazz to Kencom, Tulip to ExaChip, and Jena to MetaTool.

That afternoon, we four met up again. Apparently Ken Wong had pressed Spazz really hard to stay on, but Spazz claimed he hadn't wavered. Stu Koblenz came over and we four worked out our deals with each other, as well as setting an antenna crystal patent application in motion. And meanwhile Jena was on her laptop and cell phone, playing the investor nibbles that were coming in. We lined up seven meetings for Wednesday, starting with Ken Wong at eleven and ending with—yes!—Clement Treed at five o'clock.

After Stu left, Jena and I set up a computer spreadsheet to plan our marketing and distribution, while Spazz and Tulip started hand-drawing some Unified Modeling Language diagrams for the classes and interaction sequences needed for the embedded Mophone firmware.

Even though we were working together, Jena was kind of holding me at arm's length. She was plenty talkative about all the business things, but if I asked any kind of personal question, she'd brush it off with a short, neutral answer. And I couldn't get her to smile. I couldn't help noticing that Spazz and Tulip in the kitchen were having more fun than we were; their voices were going up and down, exclaiming, interrupting, laughing. What it came down to was that both the women liked Spazz and neither of them liked me.

I felt in my pocket for my grolly, but I'd eaten it all.

"I've had it," I told Jena. "I'm ready to knock off. Should we get something to eat?"

"Oh, I think I'll go home," said Jena blandly. "Tomorrow's going to be a big day." We peered into the kitchen, where Spazz and Tulip were bent cheek-to-cheek over a sheet of paper with lines and boxes on it. Spazz was drawing an arrow, and Tulip playfully yanked the pencil out of his hand to add a label to the arrow. Spazz chuckled.

Jena didn't like it any more than I did. "Come on, Spazz," she said. "Let's go home."

Tulip snapped her head around and glared at Jena. "Just a minute," she said.

"Yeah," said Spazz, glancing our way but not really seeing us. "We've almost worked out the class inheritance tree."

"You want to walk to 7-Eleven with me to get some cigarettes?" I asked Jena.

"Oh, all right," she said. "Get ready to leave in ten minutes, Spazz."

"Okay," he mumbled, leaning over the diagram.

So then Jena and I were outside together in the early January night. It was dry, with a damp breeze. Out of reflex, I tried to take her hand, but she shoved hers into her pocket.

"Don't, Joe," she said. "Just really let it be over."

"I know you're right," I said. "We've been making each other miserable. But, still. When I see you . . ."

She stopped and looked at me. Her pink cheeks, the bow of her lips, her narrow eyes seeing into me as clearly as if she had subtle vision. She was motionless as a picture, waiting for my next move. I had a sudden odd image of her as a video game I'd lost my last quarter in. Yes, yes, it really was time to let go.

"We'll be friends," I said. "That's all."

"Good," said Jena. "I'd like that. I need friends."

I got my cigarettes and we started back.

"I do have to ask what you see in Spazz," I said. "He's like the opposite of me."

"Duh?" said Jena, and finally laughed. "I don't see Spazz and me lasting very long," she added. "He's like—like when someone gives a prisoner a cake with a hacksaw blade inside it? Spazz was my hacksaw blade. As long as we're being nosy, what's the story with you renting a room to Tulip? You're after her, aren't you? That zitty geek."

"She's nice," I said. "But I don't think she's over Spazz."

"I don't like her," said Jena. "The way she glares at me with those big cow-eyes. And her skin! Do you think she ever takes a bath?"

"Lighten up, Jena. You're the one who has Spazz, not Tulip." I lit my third cigarette in a row as we walked up to the new house. I'd expected Jena to say something about my smoking, but she didn't. She went inside while I finished my smoke.

"I can't find them!" cried Jena, suddenly reappearing. Her forehead was an asterisk of wrinkles and she was biting her thumbnail.

I quickly used my subtle vision to go over the rooms of my house. They wouldn't actually be in Tulip's bedroom, would they? No, at least not that. They'd left entirely. Spazz's motorcycle was missing from where he'd parked it beside the house.

"Maybe they went to get more food," I said, trying to stay calm.

"Oh, just get me out of here," said Jena. "Give me a lift home."

We didn't talk much on the ride to 1234 Silva View Crescent. I dropped Jena, drove back to the house on Los Perros Boulevard and then I was home alone. Have I mentioned that I don't like being alone? I tidied up for a minute, checked my email, spell-checked the business plan and printed a dozen fresh copies for the presentations tomorrow. Still no Spazz or Tulip. And, to make things worse, they'd taken along our prototype Mophones. I didn't want to think about what that might mean. It had to be they'd just gone off for sex. I could have phoned Tulip of course, but I didn't feel like it. I didn't want to be a hungry little dog trotting after her for scraps.

I started up PowerPoint and converted our business plan into a series of slides. I even used my scanner to make slides out of the UML diagrams that Spazz and Tulip had left lying around the kitchen. And for a good measure, I lay one of the antenna crystals on the scanner and made a slide out of it too. It was nearly midnight and Tulip still hadn't come home.

By now it was pretty clear what had happened. Spazz had taken her back to his place. I went to bed. The exhilaration of the grolly was gone and I felt depressed. Nobody loved me. If Spazz was Jena's hacksaw blade, I was her jailer. That was my thanks for all those years of trying to make Jena happy. And Tulip—last night she'd broken down in tears at the thought of spending the night under the same roof as me! And now she'd gone back to that sleazy jerk Spazz. Why was I letting Spazz in on the Mophone anyway? It was Tulip who'd gotten the antenna crystals to work. Et cetera, et cetera.

When I woke in the morning the house was still empty. I went over the PowerPoint slides, tweaking them and adding annotations. Jena phoned around nine A.M.

"Well?" she said.

"They're not here yet," I said. "And they have the Mophones."

"Oh God," wailed Jena. "Our first meeting is at eleven. Ken Wong."

"Come over and help me get ready," I said.

"I'm not coming if the others aren't there," said Jena. "This is totally going down the tubes. Why did I let you talk me into re-signing from MetaTool?"

"Phone Spazz," I told Jena.

"I don't want to phone him," she said, her voice rising. "Why don't you phone that nasty Tulip?"

"I don't want to phone either," I said. "It would feel lame. But, you know, I think I'd feel okay with going over there in person."

"To Spazz's house? You know where it is?"

"Not exactly. Do you?"

"Yeah, Sunday afternoon he got me to drive my car there to get some of his things."

"Will you drive there with me right now?" I asked.

"No way, Joe. But I can give you directions. It's not far." She went on to tell me how to find Spazz.

"Promise you'll be here at eleven no matter what," I said when she was done.

"I'm not promising *anything*," said Jena, her voice going shrill. "Call me back after you see Spazz."

I jumped in my car and headed down Route 17 and up Black Road into the mountains. In twenty minutes I was parked outside a mossy shack under some huge redwoods. Spazz's red motorcycle was chained up in front. Rather than rushing right in, I used my third eye to peer through the walls of the house. There was the kitchen, with pot plants growing on the counter by the rear window. Spazz and Tulip were drinking coffee, Spazz in long underwear and a sweatshirt, Tulip looking comfortable in a robe. Spazz was on his cell phone. I wondered who he was talking to. It occurred to me that if I went out into hyperspace I could stick my ear into the corner of his room and hear what was going on.

One of the Empress's soldiers was vout there on the Klupper side of the All, so it wouldn't do to go into hyperspace on that side. I decided to chance another trip through Dronia. I peeled myself vinnward, briefly rolled over to make sure none of those anemone things were reaching out from the cliffs, and then turned back the right way, with my third eye staring down at Spaceland. I flapped over to Spazz's cabin. I leaned voutward to press my ear into Spaceland, under the kitchen table where nobody would notice it.

"... weird ego trip," Spazz was saying. "No, I don't think so either, Ken. Joe Cube isn't anyone's idea of a CEO. Like you said yesterday." He gave a coughing laugh as Ken added something. "Yeah, or maybe a McDonald's franchise. He eats there all the time. No no, Joe's not the man to put together the kind of massive score we're looking at." He paused, listening. "That's what I said, Ken. Unlimited spectrum, with no FCC licenses needed. Low power and an unbelievable signal-to-noise ratio. That's right. Tulip and I just finished prototyping it yesterday." Another pause. "Well, sure, you might as well show up for today's meeting anyway. It's at eleven o'clock? Joe and his wife will have some dippy little slides. Tomorrow morning, you and Tulip and me can get together and have the real meeting." Another pause. "Oh, that's not a problem. I'll just file a competing patent application. Joe's isn't fully executed yet. Anyhow, it's Tulip and I who have the working prototypes. Joe's not going to be able to do jack about it. It's not like the dude's gonna build the thing himself. Yeah. Totally. It's kind of sad. But, hey, I've got a good feeling about Kencom. Thanks. Later."

He hung up, coughed, laughed, walked over and kissed Tulip on her big, soft, chocolate mouth. I decided to kill him.

I drew back a foot from Spaceland and wriggled along until I was right even with Spazz. I peered into his body. There was his heart.

I shot my hand forward and grabbed his aorta, squeezing it shut. Spazz grunted and clutched his chest. Tulip dragged a chair over and helped Spazz to sit down. They didn't know it was me, because the only part of me inside Spaceland was my hand, and that was hidden inside Spazz's chest. The aorta was tough and slippery and twitchy. I kept up the pressure. Spazz's heart was flopping around, bumping at me. His eyes rolled up and closed. He slumped back in his chair. Tulip was screaming, though with my head out in hyperspace I couldn't hear her. She grabbed the phone and dialed 911. I hung onto Spazz's aorta. His face was starting to turn blue.

Something struck me in the middle of the guts and sent me spinning. Spazz's aorta slipped out of my grasp. I was tumbling through hyperspace and now something grabbed me hard and shook me.

Yes, it was Wackle. Another Wackle, that is, another red devil figure at the end of a long, winding tentacle thread that led all the way back to the distant Dronian cliffs.

"Peace and love, bro Joe," said Wackle, his crimson face pushing close to mine. He smelled like the ocean. His mouth was like a clam shell and his eyes were on little stalks. "Killing kills the killer. Be gentle in the lonely night."

Though Wackle was terrifying to look at, his tone was sweet and his words were reasonable. Maybe the Dronners weren't really the bad guys? I paused and caught my breath.

Down in Spaceland, Spazz was back on his feet, coughing. Tulip gave him a glass of water. Spazz picked up the phone, punched in 911, and talked to someone to cancel Tulip's call for help. I could see Tulip arguing about it, but Spazz's gestures clearly indicated that he didn't want cops and medics poking around his house. He was already completely recovered.

I was glad. It was good I hadn't killed Spazz. I would have felt bad about it for the rest of my life. I'd been crazy to go after him like that.

"You were right," I told Wackle.

"What it is," said Wackle. "You're thick as pie, a Klupper-fed guy. The fattened-up Spacelander, yas. For shame to be a shark. There's a reason, there's a rhyme, there's a season, there's a time. What it is Momo do with you?"

"I don't know what Momo's really up to," I told Wackle. "It's complicated. She says her family wants me to make the Mophones so the antenna crystal signals will keep you Dronners from stealing their grolly."

"Bullpoo," said Wackle. "Grolly's junk. What Kluppers got, Dronners don't want. Nohow. Just want they leave us alone. Worrisome they're working you, is what we thinky-thunk." He gave a cackle and formed some stubby arms which pretended to shoot a hyperbazooka. "Blooey! Wackle kerflooey! Scatter my smeel, a favor indeed. Those splatters put new me trees on the grow there and there and there and there and there and there and there and there and there . . ." He pointed twenty arms towards the Dronian cliffs. "Bud me, baby! Simpler than your two go." Down in Spaceland, Tulip and Spazz were embracing.

"I—I guess I'll go back down," I said, when Wackle didn't say more. "And—thanks."

"Ding the dong," said Wackle. "Old trick, new dog. Glad to save your soul, little fatty. I'll keep out an eye, ever so many an eye. You can count on me when the Klupper runneth over."

"All right," I said, and flopped back into my car, making sure not to come down backwards. I sat there and honked the horn.

Spazz peered out, did a double take, gestured that I should come talk. I got out of my car and spoke to him from the yard. I'd decided to play my hand strong.

"How's the heart?" I said straight up. I reached out towards him and made a squeezing gesture with my hand.

Spazz winced and his jaw dropped a little. He put his hand on his chest.

"What it is," I said, half-imagining I could hear a Wackle cackle. "Hurry up, dude, we've got our meeting with Ken at eleven." I started to get back in my car, then paused and glared back at him. "Call Ken and tell him the meeting today is the real thing, okay? And, dude, don't forget to bring the Mophones." I made another violent grab with my hand, and this time I really did hear a Wackle cackle. But it was me making it.

I drove off, giving Jena a cell phone call on my way home. I kept it simple, just told her that Spazz and Tulip would definitely be there.

"I'm at the Los Perros Coffee Roasting," Jena told me. "Tell you what. I'll run over and get a computer projector and a little movie screen at OfficeMax." She was back into the program. She was good at this stuff. "Showing PowerPoint slides on your desktop is bush."

"Good idea," I said. "Mophone will reimburse you."

When I was nearly home, a lump of Momo appeared on the car seat next to me. Back in town.

"You were in Dronia again," she said accusingly. "Where you were expressly forbidden to go."

"Just for a minute," I said defensively. "To eavesdrop on Spazz."

"I witnessed your actions," said Momo. "I saw your hand grasping his heart, and I peeked into Dronia. Do you presume to play the higher being, Joe?"

"I just wanted to scare him," I said. I glanced over at the lump of flesh next to me. It was the size of a small dog, with a mouth,

an ear, and a hank of blonde hair. The mouth looked angry. "Spazz
was trying to ruin the company," I added, "It's me who's working
things out for you, Momo. I'm your man."

"You spoke with a Wackle as well," she said coldly. "That's what
caused you to release your rival's heart. It was a Wackle who
knocked you loose. You and he engaged in a colloquy, his goal
being, I well know, to undermine and subvert."

"Maybe," I said, barely moving my lips. "I don't know. I have
to watch the road. I have to think about the meetings today. I'm
doing them for you."

"You blotch, you stain, you cartoon," said Momo. A tendril of
her flesh reached towards me and seemed to sink through my skin
and into the fibers of my spine. I felt a shiver of pain, like the
lightest of notes struck upon a harp. Another twinge, stronger this
time. And then a true spasm that forced me to pull the car off the
road and bend forward moaning in agony. "Don't presume!" said
the blob on the seat next to me. "Don't pick and choose which of
my orders you should obey."

"I won't, Momo," I whispered. "I won't do it again." I felt a
thousand needles in my back.

"What won't you do?" insisted the blob.

"I won't go into Dronia again."

The pain stopped, and the mouth formed a smile. "Very well
then. Remember this: I'll be close by."

The day's meetings started very badly. Ken Wong and some old
Taiwanese guy showed up before any of us had had a chance to
talk and clear up our unresolved issues. The room was so tense it
felt like the air was tied into knots.

Spazz had made another call to Ken Wong on his way into our
Mophone headquarters, and with all the crossed signals, Ken didn't
know what to believe or who to listen to, which is not a state of
mind conducive to dropping a bundle of cash on anyone. He

stopped Jena halfway through her presentation and remarked that Spazz and I would be welcome to come back to our old jobs if this didn't work out. And then he and his partner were gone.

We had twenty minutes till the next prospective business angel, and now I had a chance to coach Jena about the slides. She'd done Ken's presentation cold. While we were going over the slides, Spazz started heckling me, saying I'd scanned the wrong UML diagrams.

"We don't have time to change them," I snapped. "Maybe if you'd stuck around and helped last night instead of taking off."

"I just can't believe you think you're running this show," said Spazz. "Pinhead. Nazi. Murderer." He broke into a long bout of coughing.

"Don't get so angry, Spazz," said Tulip. "You'll make yourself sick again."

Evidently Spazz hadn't yet told Tulip what had really happened in the cabin. But now he spilled the beans. "It was Joe who made me sick," Spazz told Tulip. "He went up into the fourth dimension, and he reached down inside my chest to squeeze my heart. Or he got Momo to do it for him." His face still looked a little blotchy, and he hadn't shaved. He glared at me. "If you pull that again, Cube, I'll tell the cops."

"There's not a jail that can hold me," I said, feeling cocky. I really had him on the ropes.

"You put a curse on Spazz?" said Tulip, shrinking back a little. "You and your familiar hexed him in the cabin?"

"*What* are you talking about?" asked Jena, looking up from the computer.

"Spazz was all set to double-cross Joe with Ken Wong," Tulip told Jena. "And Joe gave Spazz a heart attack. It was dreadful. I think maybe all of this is black magic."

Jena's eyes got narrow. "We're getting ready to pitch to six prospects in a row. Our big break. So *stop freaking out*. All of you. We can fight later. I'm the one who should be mad anyway. With Spazz running out on me like that." She pouted her lips and trembled her chin a little. "I thought you were tired of Tulip, Spazz."

"I am," said Spazz weakly. "I'm sorry about last night."

Tulip threw down the Mophone she was holding and disappeared into the kitchen. There was a knock on the door.

The business angels were all over the map in appearance, approach, and behavior: a gray-haired fatherly blood-sucker from the chip industry; a shrink-wrap billionaire bent on collapsing the self-confidence of anybody with the ambition of following in his footsteps; a seen-it-all portfolio manager ready to rewrite our business strategy as soon as he met us; a shy, liquid-eyed Colombian who said he was a rancher looking to diversify; and two twenty-year-old day-traders who said they'd spent the morning playing volleyball on the beach. I talked a little volleyball with the day-traders—volleyball was one of my things, too, though I didn't get in as many games as I would have liked.

Jena's presentation got better and better—it was like a dance, like the miniature theatrical performances that airline stewardesses do to accompany the safety messages, like cheerleading. Spazz was mesmerized, but none of the investors were buying it. The chip guy didn't like our staffing, the shrink-wrap guy thought our Mophones were fakes, the portfolio guy didn't like our numbers for scaling to the mass market, the rancher—if that's what he really was— couldn't understand the point of our product, the day-traders thought our timeline to a hundred percent profit was way too long.

And then Clement Treed showed up. There were footsteps on the porch, the door swung open, and it was him, tall and lanky, his froggy mouth bent in the shape of a smile, his eyes alert behind his glasses. He had a surprisingly small head, made smaller by his monkish haircut. He was wearing preppy J. Crew clothes so new they looked like they were right out of the UPS box. Compared to

Clement, I was almost grungy. He gave a high sign to his limo driver and came on in. He spotted Tulip right away.

"We paid to use Gandhi's image, you know," he told her in a quiet tone, as if continuing a conversation from two or three minutes ago. "A charity in Calcutta. His family picked it."

"Oh, I'm sorry I ever brought that up," said Tulip, twisting a long strand of her hair. "I was just having a little fun at your expense to impress my cousin."

"Fun at my expense," echoed Treed, snagging my desk chair and lightly sitting down. He was a thin man with a slight paunch, in his late thirties. "That's something the government likes too. You'd think the public would be more appreciative of what MeYou has done for everyone. And I'm not done yet. I'm out to diversify. Who's the CEO?"

"Me," I said, stepping forward. "Joe Cube."

Treed shook my hand, his grip firmer than I'd expected. "You've got ten minutes," he said. "Amaze me."

Jena did her cheer routine. Treed interrupted only once, to volunteer a detailed correction to one of the UML diagrams. When Jena was done, he sat staring at the last slide, the one with the picture of the antenna crystal. And then he started polishing his glasses.

"Can somebody tell me more about this so-called superchannel?" he said, still looking down at his glasses. "How does it work?"

"That's our core trade secret," I said.

"I signed your non-disclosure form," said Treed in a mild but impatient voice. "And now I need to know if you have something or not."

"Tell him, Joe," said Spazz.

"It's—it's the fourth dimension," I said. "The antenna crystal has a wire that sticks into hyperspace."

"Cute," said Treed, his long mouth spreading in a rueful smile.

"Science fiction." He put on his glasses and got to his feet. "I have to ask—that thing in the paper yesterday, the mirror-money hoax. Was that a set-up for this?" It was like Clement Treed's tiny head held an all-seeing web-crawler that ran a thousand times as fast as my brain. "Which of you four is the one who convinced the others?" he demanded.

"Me again," I said, attempting a debonair smile. "You have to listen, Clement. The money really did flip over. I was trying to take it from a bank. Of course I'll pay it back once we're funded." I walked over to where the image of the antenna crystal floated on our screen. "The fourth dimension is real," I said, pointing at it. I tried to remember how Momo had explained things to me. "Think of a Flatlander trying to imagine a third dimension," I added, waving my hands. The shadows of my arms on the screen looked lumpy and odd. "It's a different direction completely."

Treed turned away from me. "Good luck," he told Tulip. "I really do admire Gandhi, you know."

I used my third eye to peer up into the All. Momo was right there watching us. "Come help us!" I cried, beckoning wildly. "Show him, Momo!"

There was a wavering on the screen. The image of the chip seemed to swell and fatten, as if the screen had developed a big bulge in it. The bulge was a sphere of Momo's skin, a round ball appearing in front of the screen with the projector shining the image of the chip onto it. And now the Momo sphere floated across the room to bounce upon the floor at Clement Treed's big feet, bouncing up and down like a basketball, a basketball with an eye in it, a big blue Momo eye. The eye winked.

"Oh my yes," said Treed, settling back into my chair and actually smacking his lips. "I'm in for this one. Consider yourselves funded. Better than that. If you can bring this thing to market, MeYou will take care of daily operations."

10

Bad News

After New Year's Day came and went without a peep, the Y2K-bug consultants had started predicting a worldwide software seize-up for Leap Year Day. As chance would have it, they were right to worry about that particular day, not that the problem was going to have anything to do with the computers. No, it was thanks to the Mophones that humanity would face the end of the world on Tuesday, February 29, 2000. But I'm getting ahead of myself.

Before he'd sign over the bucks, Treed got Momo to agree on an exclusive contract to supply her antenna crystals only to us. He also wanted to know what was in the deal for Momo, and she told him about the supposed Dronner-repelling qualities of hyperspatial radio waves. This was a time where it was good to be working with a single rich business angel instead of a due-diligence, managerial-type venture capitalist.

Wednesday, January 5 was the day Clement Treed funded Mophone, Inc., and Monday, February 28 was the day we started shipping product. It was a wild eight weeks, a business major's wet dream. The richest guy in Silicon Valley was funding me to set up production, distribution and marketing for a water-walking product with an off-the-hook buzz. There weren't enough hours in the day.

I told people I was loving every minute of it, but that wasn't true. The "loving every minute" line was the kind of rah-rah, can-do bull that a guy like me feeds his boss. Not that I had a boss anymore—I was the CEO. I was doing the cheerleader thing out of reflex. Treed didn't care if I loved Mophone or not.

My business plan projected Treed's take at ten million bucks. The way our deal worked was that Clement had forty percent of the founder's stock, while Jena, Tulip, Spazz and me each had fifteen. These weren't options, mind you, these were fully-paid shares. They weren't worth anything at all yet, but after the IPO, according to my spreadsheets, Clement's cut would be good for that ten million. And we others would get three point seven five mill each.

Yes, things were looking good. The Mophone advance orders were pouring in as fast our three-tier website could pass them from the web page to the server to the database and back. A San Francisco service provider called monkeybrains.net was hosting our site and handling the billing for us.

The Mophone cases were being injection-molded by a plastics factory in Taiwan, using a slippery, metallic-looking red alkyd resin that Clement Treed had picked up at a fire sale price from a refinery in Indonesia. The redness of the Mophones was a branding thing, part of the campaign worked out by the advertising agency Jena had hired.

I'd found a maquiladora in Juarez to assemble our Mophones; they were using the same production line someone had used for knockoffs of Motorola StarTacs. The big difference was that each Mophone included a four-dimensional antenna crystal and a call-routing "Motalk" chip. Tulip had used a firmware compiler to instantiate Spazz's Java design for the Motalk chips, and ExaChip was fabbing them for us.

At first we'd thought it would be more dramatic for Mophones not to have the old-style antennas, but it made production easier to leave them in. Another win in taking this route was that we were able to put a dual functionality into the Mophone. If you subscribed to a regular cell-phone service, a Mophone could use its old-style antenna to access that, too. Clement got us a deal with PacBell to resell their standard cell-phone services for those who wanted them as a Mophone add-on. At least for now, it was worth having standard cell so you could call people who didn't have Mophones.

Everything depended on everything else; it was like a dance floor that was rising into the sky lifted by a dozen giant balloons spaced around its edges, and I was the guy racing around the parquet adjusting the balloons to keep the platform level. Like I said, it was a business major's wet dream.

Why wasn't I loving every minute? I had three issues.

My first issue was that I didn't have a woman to love me. Jena had successfully retaken Spazz from Tulip; every night the two of them were going back to my old house together. Though Tulip was still renting a room from me, nothing romantic was happening between us. Tulip was depressed about Jena and Spazz; I could hear her crying almost every night. I wanted to comfort her and cheer her up, but she'd been even more distant since my number with Spazz's aorta. She still hadn't let go of her idea that Momo was an evil spirit who'd bewitched me. In fact, I think she felt a little guilty about helping with the Mophone at all. In other words, there was no hope with Tulip or with Jena. And I didn't have time to look further afield until we got the Mophone shipped.

My second issue was the sinking feeling that maybe Momo really *was* an evil spirit—even though she did come from the Aladdin's lamp of modern science and not from the cesspool of old-time superstition and magic. On the plus side, Momo had used some of Clement Treed's cash to square things with the banks, but I kept having the feeling she was leading me down the garden path to a pit of poison punji sticks. New versions of Wackle kept showing up in my bedroom to give me heavy, incomprehensible warnings,

but Momo would always hyperbazooka the Wackles before they
could finish. She killed with an ugly glee, and I hadn't forgotten
the cruelty with which she'd sent pain into my spine. I would have
liked to have heard what the Wackles had to tell me, but with
Momo around I didn't dare go vinnward to Dronia to talk to them
alone.

My third issue was the realization that I'd become clinically ad-
dicted to grolly. Whenever I wanted more grolly, all I had to do
was step into my bedroom, pull the blinds and close the door. I'd
hold out my hand with my thumb and index finger making a circle,
a sign for Momo, who was usually watching these days. She'd appear
with a little pastel bagel for me, telling me to work harder. She was
a killer, a tyrant, a pusher. The upside of my addiction was that I
could work unbelievable hours, but I was using three or four bagels
of grolly a day, and I felt like crap whenever it started wearing off.
An odd side effect was that I'd completely stopped dreaming. I'd
lie down to sleep and I'd stop moving, but all night my mind would
be going over business plans. I wished I'd never met Momo; I
wished she were dead.

My life was a loveless desert of work and grolly and I had the
sick feeling there was big trouble ahead. After a while, the only
thing keeping me going was Clement Treed's plan to have MeYou
take over our operations once we made it past product launch.

The Mophones went on sale the morning of February 28, and
by that evening, we'd moved twenty thousand units. It was all over
the news. People were using Mophones in every corner of the country, and some ultrasurfers had already found a way to use Spazz's
open Motalk architecture to hook a Mophone to a computer and
send real-time, uncompressed, full-screen video. No more lurching,
muddy, low-bandwidth, postage-stamp video. With Mophone, your
computer screen was a window looking at a scene a thousand miles
away. We were the only broadband communication channel that

mattered anymore. Our competitors didn't have a chance.

We watched the news together at the office: Jena, Tulip, Spazz, Clement Treed and me. Channel 4 had filmed an interview with us that afternoon. While we watched ourselves, Clement Treed busted out a magnum of Cristal champagne and five crystal glasses. We toasted, the news ended, I muted the TV, and then what?

You'd think we'd be all chattering and cheerful, but we were burnt out from the big push, and more than a little sick of each other. Jena and Spazz in particular hadn't been talking to each other all day.

Clement drank half a glass of champagne, flopped down on our soft, low couch, took out his Mophone, and began calling up associates all over the world, using his Palm Pilot to time and chart the connection latency speeds. His knobby knees stuck up nearly as high as his shoulders.

Spazz had his Mophone hooked to his laptop and its digital camera. He sat at the kitchen counter alternating between videophone conversations with excited programmers and cruising the Web looking at airplanes. The first thing he wanted to buy himself was a private jet.

Tulip watched over Spazz's shoulder for a minute, then got on her own Mophone and drifted into her room, talking with her brother-in-law in Fremont about going out tomorrow to get a good deal on a new Mercedes. We didn't quite have our money yet, but Lord did we have good credit.

I sat in my chair with my feet on my desk, my computer turned off for the first time in two months, enjoying doing nothing. The business was in MeYou's hands now. I'd crossed the desert and made it to the oasis. All I had to do now was wait for the IPO. The price of our stock would shoot up and up, and when I couldn't stand it anymore, I'd sell off my founder's shares. Jena sidled up to me and refilled my champagne glass.

"Are you happy, Joe?" she asked.

"I should be," I said, and left it at that.

"I should be happy too," said Jena, sitting down on the edge of my desk. Her face looked a little out of focus, a little lost. "I'm footloose and fancy free. Spazz is leaving me."

"How do you mean?"

"He's not going to be staying at our old house anymore. All he wants to do is get his new plane and fly around the world. Alone. Find a girl in every port or something." She drained her glass and poured herself another. "But don't worry about me. You guys are really going to give me my shares, right, Clement?"

Treed looked up from fiddling with his Mophone and Palm Pilot, his eyes lively in his little head. "Not to worry, Jena," he said. "I never stiff a start-up collaborator. You're in high clover." He smiled down at his little screen, now and then poking a virtual button. "If we IPO every bit as expeditiously as the SEC allows, my current trends equate your worth to the total real-estate value of, hmmm, Rwanda. Belgrade could be next."

"I should be happy," said Jena again, and rubbed her face. "Would one of you guys please take me home?"

Treed regarded her alertly, as if studying a visual illusion or a chess puzzle. "If this is a not-driving issue, I'd be glad to drop you off. I'm leaving in a few minutes." He turned his attention back to his Mophone, placing a test call to a friend called Kelvin in Switzerland.

Meanwhile Jena pursed her lips at me in her best come-hither way. "Maybe it's time for us to make up and be friends," she said to me very softly. "I mean *not* friends. Be like we used to be. I've been missing you, Joe. I'm lonely."

"I'm lonely too," I said, almost melting. But not quite. I remembered too well how it was to live with my sense of well-being perpetually linked to Jena's whims. I wasn't all that happy these days, but at least I wasn't being jerked around. I hardened my heart. "Go on home," I told Jena. "Let Clement drop you off. It's time for bed."

"Thanks for nothing," said Jena, hopping off my desk. She flounced into the kitchen and knocked Spazz's laptop off the counter so hard that its case smashed open on the floor.

"Oops," she said.

"You bitch," yelled Spazz. "I just finished getting the video configured! I'll kill you!"

"That's an actionable threat," said Jena. "Did the rest of you hear him? He's a violent, abusive man, and if he ever talks to me again, I'm going to sue this company." She put on her coat, jingled her car keys, and went outside.

I was out the door after her. "Don't drive, Jena," I said. "You've had too many drinks for that."

"Come home with me, Joe."

Before I had to answer this one, Tulip was out there too.

"Do you think he's your dog, Jena?" said Tulip. "You think you can kick him out and whistle him back? Joe's too good for that."

"Thanks," I told Tulip.

"Limo Service," said Clement Treed, out on the porch too. "Come on, Jena."

"Everyone hates me," said Jena, not very emotional at all. It was like she'd been messing with our heads just for the hell of it. Or to be the center of attention. "Let's go, Clement," she continued. "We have to stop by the supermarket, okay? What do rich people eat at home?"

"I recommend port and preserved kumquats," Treed told her as he folded himself into the back of his limo. "With brandy-soaked plum pudding. But I'm not coming into your house."

"Oh, Clement, you think I'm too rich for you?" Jena closed the door after her and they motored off, leaving Tulip and me on the porch. I could have used my third eye to peer after them, but I didn't want to.

The door to the house flew open once more. Spazz shouldered his way past us, too angry about his laptop to speak. He jumped on his motorcycle and roared off towards Santa Cruz.

I looked at Tulip and Tulip looked at me. "I meant that," she said. "You are good. All this time I've had too low an opinion of you."

"Are you finally ready to kiss me?"

"Sure."

It was just as I'd hoped. Tulip's lips were soft, her smell intimate and spicy, her skin warm and smooth, her voice a friendly music in my ears. She called me her dear sweet Joe. She spent the night with me in my room.

I woke early, and wondered at having a woman in bed with me again, enjoying the bone-deep comfort of having a fellow human to cozy up to, a pleasure even deeper than sex. It's a mammal thing; we're meant to sleep with partners. Tulip shifted against me, with her dark hair fanned across her pillow. She was still asleep, dreaming, her eyes moving beneath her eyelids. She was naked except for a chain around her neck with a little gold cross. Delicious.

I'd slept with Tulip, the Mophone was a success, and I didn't have much work to do today. Just a little hand-off meeting with some guys from MeYou; they were coming over this afternoon. It was rainy and windy outside, the kind of weather they called a "storm" in California. In any other state they would have called it a gusty spring rain. The raindrops pattered against my bedroom window. It was cozy in here. Everything was perfect. Well, not quite. Physically I didn't feel too good.

The problem was that I'd neglected to eat any grolly the night before, and now I was jonesin' for it. I had a trembly, leafy feeling, kind of like I used to get when I'd exercise a lot in the morning without eating breakfast or lunch. I hadn't had time to exercise yet this whole new year, by the way.

I watched Tulip for a minute. Her eyes had stopped moving beneath her lids. She was quite deeply asleep. I tried to stop myself, but before long, I made a circle with my thumb and forefinger and stuck my hand up in the air. Sure enough Momo was nearby. A glob of her appeared over me, a crooked head with a hand sticking out of its temple, the hand holding a little doughnut of grolly. It dropped gently onto the blanket over my stomach. I picked it up and nibbled. Ah. As always, I promised myself I'd kick the stuff tomorrow. Momo smiled knowingly at me. She knew better than to make noise and wake up Tulip. Now everything really was perfect.

And that's when things went crazy.

A big red devil shape appeared next to my futon, a Wackle. Momo shifted her shape, bringing a section of her hyperbazooka into visibility. All this still in silence, like a dream.

But now it got loud, way loud. Three more Wackles appeared on the other side of Momo and let out a battle cry. An ambush! The Wackles sprang at Momo like tigers; they clawed at her; they pried the hyperbazooka from her hands; their voices were a stuttering roar. The weapon went tumbling across my room, and still another bellowing Wackle arrived to catch it. The first four Wackles had tight hold of Momo, they were dragging more and more of her into the room with us. The fifth Wackle raised the hyperbazooka and aimed. Their yells kept starting and stopping as their writhing mouths moved in and out of our space. It was like listening to a fight over a cell phone with a gappy signal.

"Joe!" screamed Tulip. She was bolt upright, squeezed back into the corner where my futon met the wall, the sheet pulled across her breasts. "Make it stop, Joe!"

"Look out," I yelled. "Gonna flash." I lunged at her and got my hand over her eyes.

And right then the fifth Wackle fired the hyperbazooka. I closed my eyes just in time to block out the insane, bright-beyond-ultraviolet blast. It was brilliant orange through my eyelids. Out in hyperspace the pulse dazzled my third eye. I heard the wet sound of Momo coming apart, the hoots of triumph from the Wackles.

"Help me God!" screamed Tulip and twisted away. "Help me! He's possessed!" When I reached towards her, she actually held up her little cross.

I tried to calm her, but she was off the futon and backing away. Bloody pieces of Momo were bouncing around the room, flexing and changing their shapes with the four-dimensional tumbles. The five Wackles had joined hands and were dancing around in a circle, first one way, and then the other, their heads turning inside out. I was kind of relieved to have bossy, menacing Momo out of the picture, but to Tulip none of this looked good.

"Devils dancing widdershins!" she shrieked. "Save me, sweet Mary, dear Mother of God!" She was out of the room in another second. There was a brief clatter next door, and then she was pounding down the front steps naked, carrying her purse, a dress, and a pair of shoes. I watched her with my third eye. Her car peeled out and drove away. So much for my new thing with Tulip.

I should have been bummed out, but with the grolly in me nothing much mattered. I sat there eating the rest of it, enjoying its resilient texture and its peachy chocolate taste, watching the Wackles. It was awesome, seeing five of them together. They fit together like the points of a snowflake, though, yeah, I know snowflakes have six sides. But five made better sense for the Wackles. The old devil and pentagram thing. Maybe people had been seeing Wackles throughout history. From what I knew of them so far, they didn't deserve their bad rap.

"Good luck dead Klupper," said one of the Wackles, flinging the hyperbazooka and some pieces of Momo vinn towards Dronia. Another Wackle was sticking his head high vout into the Klupper half of the All. "No grolly guards near," he reported, lowering his mouth back into my room. "Dance with us, Joe. The Wackle war whoop!"

Two of them reached out for me, and now we were a circle of six, prancing around my room. Insanity. My Mophone rang. The Wackles stopped and stared at it. I answered. It was Jena.

"Hi Joe," she said. "Sorry I got so emotional last night."

"Nothing new," I said. "Things are kind of weird here right now, Jena. Can I call you back?"

"How's *Tulip?*"

"She left. She thinks I'm evil. Bye."

"Wait, wait. The reason I called you is that gangster's back in town. Sante? He just called me. He saw about us on TV last night. He says he got fired because of you and your million dollars. He says you owe him a favor."

"Ask Clement Treed," I said, irrationally angry at Jena for the bad news. "You got Treed to go to bed with you, right? Tell *him* to pay Sante."

"Don't be like that," wailed Jena. "Clement never came in at all last night. I was being a jerk, okay? But listen. Sante said if you won't talk to him, he's gonna talk to *me*."

"Christ," I said, the rage draining out of me. Poor Jena. "Hold on."

I looked over at the Wackles. "That million you took from me last month," I said. "Can I have it back?"

"Where's my sneeze?" said one of them, and the others laughed.

"Yesterday's gone," added another.

"Why did you steal it?" I asked despairingly.

"To kill your phone in its cradle," said another. "Too late now. Ringing in what change is the today question."

The first Wackle was moving his head in and out of our space as he watched my Mophone. "Little piece of light so what?" he mused. "Peeping chicken."

A big curved piece of metal came drifting through the room. One of the Wackles grabbed hold of it, steadying it. The cross-section grew round and full, as big as my futon. It was Momo's flying saucer. Jena's voice was quacking from the Mophone. I put it back to my ear.

"I really have to go," I told Jena. "But don't let Sante get you. Get out of the house right away."

"Should I come over?" Her voice was small. "Who's there with you?"

"Wackles from the fourth dimension. Don't come just yet, it's already too nuts. Maybe in an hour. But get out of the house right now. Hurry. Get some breakfast and then, yeah, come here. It'll be safe. If Sante comes here, I'll do him like I did Spazz. Except this time I won't stop."

"*Oooooooooooooooooooooooooooooooo,*" went the Wackles. Their preaching of nonviolence seemed kind of hypocritical after what I'd just seen them do to Momo.

"You care about me, Joe?" said Jena.

"Yeah," I said grudgingly. I knew this would lead to something else.

"Can you come get me?" asked Jena then. "You made me leave my car last night."

"Jena, no. Ride your bike. Or walk." They didn't have taxis in Los Perros.

"Thanks a lot. It's raining, creep."

I sighed and hung up. Talking to Jena always brought me down. She knew so well how to push my buttons. A ruthless exercise of her wiles. Was the Sante thing even for real? Hell with it. Enough about Jena for now. What was more interesting was that I had five hyperdimensional aliens and a flying saucer in my bedroom. I had a sudden brilliant thought.

"Let me keep the flying saucer," I proposed. What a thing to have!

"Pluperfect proof of Momo's massacree," said one of the Wackles. "A tasty cowflop for the horsefly Kluppers. Buzz they'll come and sting. Hide it fast, Joe."

"Park it in Dronia," said another Wackle. "Beneath notice."

"Joe's garage!" said a third. "Tether it with smeel of me!" He tugged at his body, pulling out a long strand of pinky-red flesh like bubblegum. He snapped the strand free with a hollered "Ouch," then looped one end of it through a hole in the rim of the saucer.

"Vinnwards!" yelled the Wackles, and disappeared, dragging the saucer after them—or trying to. The strand of Wackle flesh simply stretched and stretched, and the saucer moved nowhere. The Wackles reappeared, and this time took hold of the saucer. I peeled myself vinn and followed along.

It had been weeks since I'd been out in the All; it was as amazing as ever. The air of Dronia was thick and sparkly clear. I rolled over to look vout towards Spaceland. The little bit of perspective my eyestalk gave me from inside Spaceland was nothing compared to how things looked from out here. Everything visible from every side at once, not under me, not beside me—but voutwards. It was beautiful to know how well our world fit together.

"Flubba geep," said one of the Wackles. I had the feeling they sometimes made noises just for the fun of it, not meaning anything in particular. "Foo da boo for you." He'd found a proper, non-stretchy, four-dimensional rope coiled up inside Momo's saucer, and now we used that to tie the craft to a rafter in my sealed-up garage. The saucer hung there in hyperspace, twenty feet away from Spaceland.

"Thanks, boys," I said. "I'm going to enjoy having this thing.

Maybe I can use it to get grolly. Is there grolly on your cliffs?" I glanced over at the great, teeming wall of Dronia, that endless reef. From certain angles I could see threadlike lines leading out to my new friends.

"Klupper slave food," said one of them, sternly. "Absolutely not. Grolly versus Wackle. Plantimal war. We want grolly space, grolly want Wackle space. You should kick it."

The thought of truly giving up grolly made me uneasy. "I need it for my augmented body," I protested.

"No," said the biggest Wackle. "Any hyperfood will do. I say! Eat smeel! Eat me! Goo for you!" He pulled a piece of his flesh loose, formed it into a little hypersphere, and handed it to me.

"Smeel?" I said. "That's what you call your flesh?" I sniffed it. It smelled like musky tofu. I took a little bite; it was slippery in my mouth, tasting of salt and fungus. I spit it out, though some of it had already coated my tongue. The little ball of wackle flesh twitched out of my grasp, hopped onto my left shoulder, grew a mouth, and bit me, drawing blood. I caught hold of it and threw it as hard as I could at the big cackling Wackle; it merged right back into him.

"You eat me and I eat you," said the Wackle. "Very fine."

"I'd rather eat plants," I said, trying to stay calm, dabbing at the little cut on my shoulder, telling myself it was really nothing much, just a weird Wackle joke. "Grolly's a plant."

"*I'm* a plant," said the Wackle. "Look far to see my giant beanstalk."

"Not plant," put in another Wackle. "Animal."

"Plantimal," said the first, and they left it at that.

I moved my third eye vinn and vout. Yes, as I'd noticed before, there were long smeel strands leading from the Wackles to giant anemones on the cliffs of Dronia. So far as I knew, an anemone was an animal that stayed in one place like a plant. There were some other things by the Dronners' cliffs that most definitely weren't plants. Shimmering things that darted about like fish.

I wondered what it was like in Dronia. With Momo gone, I was free to go there if I wanted. It was hard to believe the Wackles had really killed her. What were the other Kluppers going to do when they found out? The soldiers probably wouldn't care, but Momo's family—that would be another story. If they came looking for her and saw I was missing from Spaceland they'd suspect me.

It was time to go home and lie low. Eat something, talk to Jena, see about Sante, talk to the people from MeYou, like that. Lie low— what a laugh. As if there were any way of hiding when four-dimensional eyes could watch my every move. The trick was to play dumb and act normal. Keep on just as before. Hopefully we wouldn't run out of antenna crystals before the IPO. As far as I knew we still had about twenty thousand of them that Momo had brought last week. Which reminded me of the big question that had been nagging me for weeks—what was the real reason for the Mophones?

"Do the Mophones bother you or not?" I asked the Wackles.

"Do radio bother you either too?" said Wackle. "No they don't. So for why the Kluppers make Mophones? Deep dish question."

"Momo said the phone signals would keep you from coming through Spaceland to steal her grolly," I said. "But the Mophones don't bother you and—and you don't even like grolly. You're not interested in Klupdom. Momo was lying about everything. So why *did* she give us the Mophones?"

"To end in tears you bet," said a Wackle. "To plow us under. Get rid of them now, Joe. This we ask."

"Not yet," I said quickly. "Nothing bad is happening. The Mophones are a great invention. And we still have to do our IPO." I glanced down at Spaceland just in time to see Jena walking onto my porch wearing a yellow Patagonia slicker. It was raining harder than before. She looked anxious and bedraggled. "I'm going back now," I told the Wackles.

"Our smeel is one," said the biggest Wackle, miming a bite in the air and patting the spot on his body where he'd pulled loose the ball of flesh. Whatever *that* meant.

I turned myself the right way round, and settled back into my room, standing there naked. Immediately Jena was walking in my door, water dripping off her slicker, her woman's eyes seeing everything. Her hair was straggly and she'd left home in such a hurry that she hadn't put her lipstick on.

"Tulip slept with you?" she demanded. "What's that cut on your shoulder? Did she bite you? Hussy. What if she has AIDS?"

"Hi, Jena." I still had my calm center from being in the All. "I have to shower and get dressed. Don't forget the MeYou folks are coming by for the hand-off at three o'clock." I got past her and into the bathroom before she could continue. First thing, I put rubbing alcohol, antibiotic cream and a band-aid on the spot where the Wackle ball had bitten me. It was a little half-moon nick in the skin, out on the very end of my left shoulder. If I turned my head I could see it. Nothing much, but it was kind of disturbing. I brushed my teeth twice to get the taste of the Wackle flesh out of my mouth. *Our smeel is one.*

By the time I was dressed, Jena had settled in, eating leftovers from my refrigerator. She'd brushed her hair and fixed her makeup. She was wearing a bright yellow blouse and some electric blue slacks. She looked good.

We made some plans for how to deal with Sante, and then we did a little work in the office, tying up loose ends. It was still raining. There weren't any calls from Sante and, equally nice, Spazz didn't come in. Jena kept trying to get an argument going, but I didn't rise to the bait. It was like I was finally getting over her.

Sleeping with Tulip had helped a lot. It made me realize that there really were other women in the world for me.

Around two o'clock I started needing some more grolly. I was weak and achy all over. I drank a couple of Cokes, but it didn't help. Finally I told Jena I was taking a nap, and I went into my room, locking the door behind me to keep her out.

I'd kind of hoped I might find some scraps of grolly on my floor, but there weren't any at all. I was feeling worse all the time. Feverish, sick to my stomach. I used my third eye to peek into the Klupper side of the All, not quite daring to think about what I was about to do. There weren't any of the Empress's soldiers or any grolly guards around. The soldiers hadn't been watching Momo at all; she'd long since paid them off not to observe how flagrantly she was meddling with our world. And it seemed she'd been telling the grolly guards to leave her alone as well. Nobody had seen her get shot, nobody knew I had her saucer, and the space between me and the Klupper cliffs was flat-out empty. I decided to go for it.

I peeled vinn to Dronner space, losing my clothes as usual, and flapped over to the garage. There was my saucer. Some Wackles were watching nearby, more of them than before, but they didn't say anything to me. The way their shapes kept changing, I couldn't be quite sure they were the same guys I'd talked to before. I steered clear of them. Just untied the saucer and got into it. The Wackles still didn't say anything. I got the feeling they were curious to see what I was about to stir up.

I took a deep breath and took hold of the stick that controlled the saucer. It was pretty much like an old-time floor-mounted gearshift. I pushed the knob a bit and—*ZOOOM*—I flashed through Spaceland and into the Klupper half of the All. Wow. I pushed the stick a little further, and felt myself rocketing towards the cliffs of Klupdom. I jiggled the knob this way and that, getting a feel for the controls. They were incredibly responsive; I veered left, right, up, down, vinn and vout, always keeping my course aimed roughly towards the cliffs.

As I got closer, I homed in on a particularly bright patch of chartreuse and lavender. A fresh, unharvested grolly field. I managed to stop the saucer without slamming into the cliffs, and then I undulated over to the field. As usual, the grolly plants—or animals?—were happy to greet a harvester. The fronds stretched towards me, lining up like the stalks of wheat in a crop circle. I could see how they might be distant relatives of the Wackles. Plantimals. But the grolly didn't talk crazy, and it tasted good.

I starting picking grolly buds, snapping the lovely little ball/bagels off the friendly fronds. I'd brought my hypersack with me, and I used it to ferry load after load of grolly to the saucer, my full mouth munching all the while. Before long I had like ten pounds of the stuff, easily a month's supply. I would have gotten more, but now another silver saucer came flying towards me—one of the Momo family grolly guards, a bulging fellow in gray.

Quick as a knife, I turned myself to stare straight at him, which aligned me so that—to his eye—I was only the thinnest of lines. I was like an angelfish that hides from a shark by pointing towards him. The purplish-skinned guard pulled up next to Momo's saucer, looking it over. Clearly he recognized his mistress's vehicle, for now he started calling her name. Moving with incredible grace and cunning—at least to me it felt that way, high on grolly as I was—I kept adjusting myself to be edge-on towards the guard. He bellowed Momo's name a few more times and then, to my horror, he took out a rope and prepared to tie her saucer to his own, as if to tow it away.

Before I'd really thought through the consequences, I gave a great flap of my body, sending myself into the seat of Momo's saucer. I leaned on the control, yawing the machine around and roaring it back towards Spaceland. It took the guard a second to get the picture, and then he came after me in hot pursuit. He didn't catch me, though. I had a good head start and, unlike the guard, I had no qualms at all about flying through Spaceland into Dronia. By aiming carefully, I crossed Spaceland through the empty space inside my garage. So the neighbors wouldn't see.

The Wackles cheered to see me reappear. There kept being more of them, as if they were massing here for something. Like in *The Birds*. I slowed, looped around, tethered my saucer to the garage beam again, and flapped back to my room, bringing along as much grolly as I could stuff into my hypersack. The rest could wait in the saucer till later. Still the Wackles just watched.

Back in my room, I put on my khakis and paused, fingering the bandaged Wackle-bite on my shoulder. It felt itchy and sore. I was about to take off the band-aid and have another look at it, but now Jena started knocking on my door.

"Joe! Are you finally awake? I heard something. What did you lock yourself in for? Lucky for you the MeYou people are running late. Clement called half an hour ago. But listen, Joe, I heard something in the garage."

I used my third eye to peer vout over the door at Jena. She looked energetic and nosy. "Open up," she repeated. "There was this big whoosh and thump. What if it's Sante?"

I undid the lock and pulled on my shirt, a burgundy linen number. I could check my cut later.

"Since when do you get undressed for a nap?" Jena wanted to know. "Are you trying to seduce me?" She gave me a pert, inviting smile. Should I respond? No. I put on my socks and shoes.

"Don't worry about the garage," I said. "That was me out there." I hefted my hypersack. "I was vout in Klupdom replenishing my stash. I've got my game face on now, Jena. I'm ready to rock and roll."

"That grolly stuff's not good for you, Joe," said Jena. "You're not the same anymore. You've gotten so—cold. Cold and heartless."

"Maybe I'm just that way around you," I said. "Protecting myself. You wiped your butt with my heart, I seem to recall."

"What if we go to a marriage counselor?" said Jena, nibbling on one of her fingernails. "Give ourselves a fresh start. We'll both be rich after the IPO. Maybe we could be happy again. You'd have to quit grolly, though."

"As if your drinking wasn't an even bigger problem." In my normal state of mind, I might have welcomed Jena's offer. But right now it was the grolly in me doing the talking. Cold and heartless. "Forget it. The point is, Jena, I really don't want to get back together with you. All we do is make each other miserable. It's hopeless. Now lay off me, okay? We'll do this last meeting and it'll be adios. Stu Koblenz can help us get the divorce."

"Go to hell!" shouted Jena, and stormed out of my bedroom, slamming the door behind her.

I looked around the room for a good place to hide my grolly. I had this uneasy feeling that Jena might find it and throw it away. Finally I wrapped it in some dirty laundry and slid it under the far corner of my futon.

As I was bent over doing that, somebody kicked me really hard in the butt. At first I thought it was Jena, even though I hadn't heard her come back in. But no, it was a wiry little figure from hyperspace. A Klupper. Momo's son-in-law Deet. His cross section looked jagged and mean. He hit me in the side of the head before I could get up. The blow knocked me all the way across the room.

"Jena!" I shouted. But the only answer I heard from Jena was the slamming of the front door. Deet grabbed me by the shoulders, shaking me so hard that I was bouncing in and out of space. I heard Jena's Beetle start up and putt away.

"You killed Momo, you flat piece of dirt," hissed Deet.

"It was the Wackles," I cried. "They ambushed her. It wasn't my fault!"

"You helped them," said Deet, jabbing a finger into my body and sending a preliminary tingle of pain up my spine. "One of our guards saw you in Momo's saucer. Degenerate fool. Do you think you can trifle with the Kluppers?"

"I found the saucer floating around," I protested. "I thought Momo didn't need it anymore."

"Give it to me," said Deet.

"Huh?"

He adjusted his head so that I saw something like a human face. A thin face with a small, twisted smile. "I have no saucer of my own. I borrowed Voule's to fly here when we got the word. I deserve to inherit my mother-in-law's saucer. Give it to me and I'll tow it home."

"I—I don't know where it is," I said.

A huge jolt of pain raced down my spine and out into every nerve of my body.

"It's in Dronia," I shrieked. "Right vinn from my garage. Go and get it."

Deet stopped, thinking. "Another ambush," he said finally. "Your Wackle friends lurk vinn there, do they not?"

Moving quickly, he fattened up one of his arms and drew a hyperbazooka down into the space of my room. Like Momo had done before, Deet shoved his head and shoulders vinn to Dronia, clutching the weapon and blasting away. A red piece of Wackle-smeel bounced off my bed and disappeared vout into Klupdom.

Deet kept up his shooting until, apparently, the hyperbazooka had used up its charge. He drew a partial cross section of his head back in the room with me, leaving some of his head still on the vinnward side of the All, to watch for Wackles. "They're obscenely numerous," he remarked. "Ever more of them approach." He looked crooked and anxious.

"I can fetch the saucer for you," I offered. If I could peel vinn to Dronia, I'd be safe from Deet.

"Scum," he said slapping me again. "Trifler. I'll claim the saucer in a few hours time. The Empress will see fit to properly clean out the Dronners once your Spaceland is no more." He looked at me, gauging the effect of his words.

"No more?" I croaked. Somehow, deep down, I'd known this was coming.

"Indeed," sneered Deet, pulling himself back from Dronia. "Your filthy membrane of a world will be gone before you sleep again. Even as we speak, your chattering fellow apes destroy the integrity of your cosmos. It's safe to tell you now, I deem. The Mophone antennas send out more energy than they receive. Your Conservation Law is broken, your film of space wears thin. It is as my family planned. Spaceland will burst, and we'll rain destruction upon the Dronners. Their kingdom shall be ours. The cliffs of Dronia can become one vast grolly farm."

The red snout of a Wackle came pushing into my room; at the first sight of it, Deet was gone.

Pop!

Using my third eye, I could see Deet vout on the Klupper side of Spaceland, frantically trying to recharge his hyperbazooka with a cord from his borrowed saucer. In the distance, a couple of grolly-guard saucers were approaching.

The Wackle snout in my room grew to a full devil-sized body. He'd heard what Deet said about destroying Spaceland. "Kill the Mophones fast," he told me. "We'll cover you. Our smeel is one." The last phrase sent a tingle through the bandaged spot on my shoulder.

The Wackle dwindled, heading voutward after Deet. But he wasn't going alone. A cascade of red flesh went pouring through the space of my room like a midair cattle stampede. Wackle after Wackle appeared, swelled up, and then shrank down to the size of a persistent golf ball. My room was abuzz with the red balls of smeel, a hundred of them or more, each ball the cross section of a long tail connecting a Wackle to his home cliff. With my third eye I could see the horde of Wackles vout on the Klupper side of Spaceland; they were tearing the hapless Deet into little pieces. The grolly guards were just starting to arrive—too late to save Deet, but not too late to fight the Wackles.

I snatched up my Mophone—surely one more call wouldn't matter at this point—and called Spazz. He answered on the second ring.

"Yo?" It was hard to hear him; there was a whistling roar in the background. Was space already coming apart?

"Spazz, we have to turn off the Mophones!" I shouted. "It's an emergency! I know you made a script for pumping out Motalk upgrades to the users. How can I use it?"

Spazz answered something, but with the background noise, the only word I could make out was "uptight." I fumbled at my Mophone, turning up its volume.

"Talk louder!" I screamed. "We have to shut off the Mophones immediately!"

Spazz's voice floated free of the drone, finally audible. "Why?" he asked in a lazy drawl. "Some kind of snag in the MeYou meeting? You need to put a scare into Clement Treed?"

"No, no, we've got a disaster, Spazz! One of the Kluppers just told me the Mophones are a trick. The antenna crystals are draining our energy away! Space is gonna pop."

"Pop?" I thought I heard Spazz chuckle.

"Like a bubble film that gets too thin," I said. "Like a mildewed sail in a gust of wind. Spaceland's gonna tear open and disappear. Nothing'll be left. We gotta turn off those Mophones!"

"What you smokin', dog?" said Spazz, still not taking me seriously. "Or is it the grolly?" The cross sections of the Wackle strands were flailing all over the room, bashing holes in my floor, ceiling and walls. One of them shattered the glass of my window and swooped outside. Several others followed. A floorboard at my feet splintered.

"Please please please help me, Spazz. Can you come to the office right now?"

"I'm a mile high, dude. Taking a test ride in a jet I might buy. Look up, you can probably see me. I'm the Gulfstream IV-SP over Los Perros. Heading southwest. I'll be over the beach in thirty seconds."

"Make them turn down the engine, Spazz! I can barely hear you! I'm going to sit down at my computer now. Tell me what to do."

"Hold on." I could hear the faint sound of Spazz talking to the pilot. Instead of damping down, the background roar grew shriller and louder.

I walked out of my bedroom and into the office area. The Wackle balls followed me, some going through my open door, but most of them crashing through the wall. Plaster dust went flying. Another platoon of Wackles came tumbling through the room on their way vout to fight the Kluppers, their shapes shifting like flames. The strands of their tails made more balls in the room. A few of them had even made holes in the roof, and rain was starting to drip in. My house wasn't going to last much longer.

I sat down at my computer and for a horrible second, I couldn't remember the first thing about how to use it. "Spazz!" I yelled into the buzzing Mophone. "Help me! Are you there?"

The background roar slid down the scale and finally I could hear Spazz properly. "We're at ten thousand feet now," he said. "Coasting. The ocean looks great. I was just thinking about what you said. That the vacuum's gonna decay? Dude, I saw a physics article about that once. Written up as a hypothetical scenario. That maybe our vacuum is only metastable, and maybe somewhere it'll tunnel down to the true zero, and once that happens the decayed state will fill a sphere that expands forever. Supposedly the hole would grow slowly at first, but then it would speed up. Destroying everything in its path."

"Pop," I said. "Space is gonna pop. We're pumping energy out the antennas, more than they're taking in. You know that law in physics? The Conservation of Energy? The Mophones are breaking the Law."

"Funny Tulip didn't think of that," said Spazz. "Her kind of thing. Why didn't you ask Tulip to help you, instead of asking me? She knows how to access the user Mophones as well as I do."

"Tulip thinks I'm possessed. She saw some creatures from the fourth dimension. She left. You got no idea what's been going on today, Spazz. The Wackles killed Momo. Jena was here after that, but now she's gone too. We had another fight. And—oh no, I forgot—that gangster Sante's back in town. I have to see about Jena."

"Poor Joe," said Spazz, breaking into his wheezing laugh. "Such the loser. Married to Jena. Phew. Look, can't we stall on crashing the phones? I want to buy this jet. Let's wait a week till we scam our money from the IPO. You and me are talking on Mophones right now and I don't see any like ball of Nothingness eating up the fabric of reality."

A Wackle glob thumped me in the back, rolling my chair away from my desk. There were more of them darting around outside the window and in my front yard. Cars on the street were slowing to look at my house, at the weird red balls and the fleeting devil figures.

"Things are coming apart fast," I said. A hole in the ceiling had dripped a puddle of water onto my desk. "Please please tell me what to do. For the love of God, help me, Spazz."

"Oh, all right," said Spazz. "Begging is good, Joe. I like it. You should always talk to me that way. And, what the hey, if this is bogus, I can always turn the Mophones back on. I wonder if—"

"Come on, Spazz! Please! Let's shut 'em down!"

"Okay, okay, all you have to do is go to this web address I'm gonna tell you, enter my name and a password, and then type something into a form you'll find there. I've got a script on the server that sends what you type to all the Mophones."

"Tell me."

Spazz walked me through the steps. His secret controller web page had a graphic of the vintage soft-porn queen Bettie Page holding a whip; the tip of the whip led to a field where I could type in Spazz's real name, which I'd never actually heard before, and then this weird, hard-to-hack password pΛh#re@ky?DEF6. A little Motalk upgrade window appeared.

"Type helo mophone:* and press ENTER," said Spazz. "One l in helo."

I did it. Meanwhile sirens were coming towards my house, a fire engine and a rescue vehicle. The rain picked up as the fire engine pulled up and the firemen jumped off. Suddenly a big metal disk materialized in my front yard, rolling around on its edge like a twenty-foot hubcap, gouging a muddy trench in the ground and changing its shape as it rolled. That would be Deet's borrowed saucer. It dinged the truck, smashed my garage and disappeared into Dronia. Another wobbly wave of Wackles flickered through my front yard, on their way to Klupdom. The firemen stood there in shock, with no clue what to do next, the rain streaming off their helmets and their yellow slickers.

"Type halt-a," said Spazz.

I did it. The window at the tip of Bettie's whip printed an echo line:

done

"It says done," I told Spazz.

"Gnar gnar," said Spazz, meaning something like "Good."

A question occurred to me. "If the Mophones are off, why can I still hear you?"

"We're like superusers," said Spazz. "You and me and Jena. Our three Mophones don't accept downloads. They were the first three we built, before Tulip put the download feature in."

"Well turn off your Mophone and don't use it again! I'll tell Jena and we'll be done. Oh, thank God, Spazz, thank God. We're safe."

Just then something cataclysmic must have happened up in Klup-dom, for a dozen dead Wackles flew across my office and crashed through the house's front wall like it was tissue paper. I yelped with surprise.

"You're really losing it, Joe," said Spazz on the Mophone. "I better be the one to call Jena."

"Don't!" I shrieked. But he'd already hung up.

There was a heavy creaking from overhead, as of thick, rusty nails being slowly pulled from old beams. I pocketed my Mophone and ran out into the front yard just before the ceiling of my office collapsed.

There was a sharp twinge in my shoulder. From the corner of my eye I could see my burgundy linen shirt bulging upwards. Something was growing out of the spot where the Wackle had bit me! I didn't like to think what it might be. But right now I had the fire chief to deal with, a handsome guy with a dark mustache.

"What's going on?" he asked. "Is this a toxic spill?"

"It's—it's computer graphics," I told him, wiping the rain out of my eyes. "A three-dimensional projection unit gone out of control. There's nothing we can do to stop it. Just keep people back from the house." A Wackle ball thudded into me, very nearly making me lose my balance.

"Is there anyone else in the house?" asked the chief.

"No," I said. The Wackle strands were smashing it to bits. Pieces of wood and plaster were flying; the walls were wobbling.

"Where's your utility boxes?" asked the chief. "We need to cut your power and gas."

"In back," I told him, and he splashed off.

I pulled out my Mophone and dialed Jena's number, leaning over the Mophone so the rain wouldn't get on it. Busy. Talking to Spazz. When Jena got going, she could talk for half an hour. And Spazz would let her—just to drive me nuts. He didn't really buy into how serious this was.

I'd have to find Jena in person before it was too late. Maybe she'd gone back to our old house? Not likely, given how worried she was about Sante. Where else did Jena like to go? The Los Perros Coffee Roasting. She loved to sit there drinking nonfat decaf lattes and talking on her cell phone.

I decided to drive there. Even though I could walk to the Roasting in five or ten minutes, I didn't want to do it in this rain. My shirt was already soaked. The scene here had gotten so chaotic that none of the firemen moved to stop me from getting into my car.

But before I could pull out of the driveway, a limo blocked me in. Clement Treed and the MeYou transition team. Oh, Christ. I honked, but the driver didn't move. I jumped out and ran back. Clement got out of the rear and unkinked his lanky body, looking around.

"Bad news?" he said, ducking his head against the rain.

"I turned off the Mophones," I told him. "They were a trick. The Kluppers gave them to us so we'd pop space. They want to get rid of us so it'll be easy for them to shoot the Dronners. I have to go find Jena. I couldn't turn off her Mophone."

Clement scowled down at me. "Turned the Mophones off? The day after product launch? That's a showstopper, Joe. Hurry up and turn them back on."

"Didn't you hear me, Clement? We're talking about the destruction of the cosmos! The Mophones violate the Law of Conservation of Energy. They'll make a hole in space. The decay of the vacuum."

"What's your source on this?" he said sharply.

"Them," I said, pointing to the swarm of red balls. "The Wackles."

"I was wondering about those things," said Clement. "Bad business. They're wrecking our office. You won't restore Mophone service?"

"Maybe—maybe we do a bait-and-switch," I said frantically. "We slam our users over to PacBell."

"There's no *we* anymore," said Clement grimly. "You've lost it, Joe. I'm taking control. And you're fired."

There was a blinding flash of light: a hyperbazooka beam passing through our space. Some of the red balls disappeared, and a few more dead Wackles went flying by, rapidly phasing through a series of nightmarish shapes you weren't really sure you could see. Losing my job didn't seem too important just now.

"Gotta go," I shouted. I jumped into my Explorer, put it into four-wheel drive, and circled through the yard to get to the road. I headed for the coffee shop as fast as I could go, using redial on my Mophone to call Jena over and over. Busy, busy, busy. I should have killed Spazz when I had the chance.

The lump on my shoulder gave a sharp twitch. What the hell? I reached under my linen shirt and peeled off the band-aid. I felt a round bump with two sharp, wiggly little projections on it. It moved when I touched it, and, oh gross, was it making a sound?

But now there was a siren behind me, a cop car with its flasher on. Either I was speeding or Clement had sicced him on me. Whatever. I wasn't stopping. Looking in the mirror at the cop, I realized that a bunch of the red Wackle balls were following me, swarming all around the outside of my Explorer. Protecting me from the Kluppers. I felt a deep wave of affection for the Wackles. Truly our smeel was one. I'd worry about my shoulder later.

I got a parking space right in front of the Coffee Roasting. I peered in past the rain, looking over the customers, my mind running at unbelievable speed.

In the window were a couple in identical blue and yellow biking jerseys, blue and yellow shoes, black spandex shorts, like they were on a team. Behind them was a blonde woman handing an accordion file organizer filled with separate small folders to a nerd who held his lips pooched out in moronic concentration. Beside them was a man with a long straight nose, fine teeth, curly hair, and a strong chin, holding forth to a trio of older CEO-type guys, his girlfriend silently gazing at him like a flower enjoying the sun. Just now he'd said something to make the older guys laugh, and the girlfriend had ducked her head and was looking openmouthed over at them, milking the moment. The CEOs were dignified silver-haired guys in turtlenecks and jeans. I noticed all of this in the split second I was scanning the room for Jena. I was amped like you wouldn't believe.

And then I saw her, sitting at a table in a corner near the rear. She was just setting down her phone; thank God she was off the line. We were almost home free!

The cop had double parked next to me. He was a fit, craggy guy my age. Intense-looking, short dark hair, mustache, acne-scarred skin. The kind of guy I might have played beach volleyball with on a different kind of day. "Sir," he called, peering past the Wackle globs between us. "Sir!" In California, whenever someone called you "Sir" it meant they were going to hassle you. Back in Matthewsboro it had been a term of respect.

Though the window I saw Jena picking up her Mophone again, pushing the buttons to make another call. Wanting to say one more thing to Spazz.

"Don't!" I shouted, jumping out of my car. "Don't use the Mophone!"

"Sir!"

The flock of Wackle balls smashed the Coffee Roasting's plate glass window, sending the customers scattering. In the aftermath of the tinkling glass came a moment of silence, broken only by the quiet pooting of jazz from the coffee shop's sound system. And then I heard a tiny little voice from my shoulder: a high voice, a Wackle voice.

"It's gonna pop, Joe!" it cried.

I believed what it said. I flung myself into the shop, ran to the corner of the room, and dove across Jena's table, knocking her Mophone from her hands. Jena gave an angry exclamation, jumped to her feet and stepped back. She thought I'd gone nuts.

Pop!

It was a small sound, clear and distinct. The Mophone had been replaced by a sinister black sphere. The sphere was matte black, so utterly nonreflecting that it looked like a flat disk, or even like a flaw on my cornea. It was a hole in space, slowly and implacably increasing its size. Soundlessly the sphere dug through the tabletop and ate away the side of Jena's coffee mug. At the ball's touch, matter disappeared like a burst bubble's rainbows, objects evaporated like the pictures in a burning reel of film.

The ball gave off a vibe of pure Nothingness, a vibe that I recognized as Death. I knew Death a bit from seeing my mother's brother Vick die of a stroke at Thanksgiving dinner one year. This was after my parents had divorced, when drunk Uncle Vick had taken to spending the holidays with us. One minute old Vick had been bragging and bullying, inflating himself with our attention; the next minute he'd been dead on the floor with his tongue sticking out and his little eyes gone milky blank. I'd seen Death convert Vick into Nothing. And now Death was here again.

The ball's rate of expansion was picking up. The whole table was gone and the ball was nearly as tall as me. It was starting to dig into the floor. Jena was hemmed into the corner of the room. There was an instant when she still could have darted out, but she'd hesitated and missed it. There wasn't any possible way for her to get out past the ball now. She could smell the Death in it, too.

"Help me, Joe!" she cried.

There was no question in my mind that I had to save my Jena. Nobody else was going to do it. The mustached cop who'd been so interested in me was standing outside on the sidewalk, busy calling for backup on his cell phone. It was all up to me. But I found it hard to step forward and reach for the ball of Nothing. Logically, I knew I was augmented, hyperthick, and probably impervious to the dissolution of Spaceland—but the deathly sphere terrified me.

Jena screamed again. I stopped thinking and leapt into the ball. My outstretched arms went in first, and then my head. It was fine for my body, but as I left the fabric of Spaceland, my watch and my clothes disappeared.

Yes, despite my fears, it was fine for me inside the ball, just plain old hyperspace. I could see Klupdom and Dronia to either side. I was breathing the air of the All.

"Grab the edges," piped the voice from my shoulder.

Right. I groped around at the edge of the ball, turning my hands vinn and vout. There was a kind of hyperthickness I could catch hold of. It felt like slippery latex. The stuff of Spaceland. I clamped onto either side of the ball, turning my hands around and around, knotting them into the fabric of space. The ball tried to grow further; I was barely able to hold it back. Without releasing the grip of my hands, I kicked out and found the ball's edges with my feet. I jiggled my feet in a four-dimensional way and got swatches of our space wrapped around them. And that was enough.

I was holding the ball in four different spots. My arms were stretched out to the left and right, and my legs were doing the splits from front to back. The ball of Nothing had stopped growing. Joe Superhero.

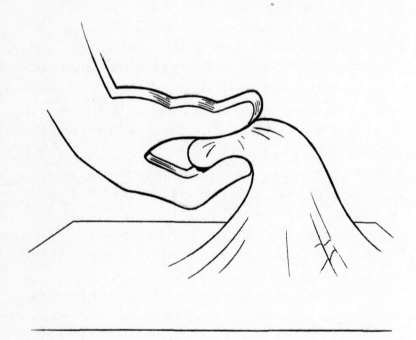

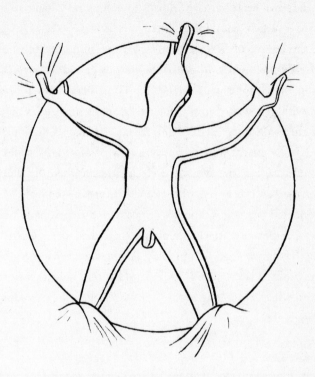

"A pyramid of forces," said the voice on my shoulder. "Perfect, Joe."

I glanced over and finally allowed myself to see the little Wackle head growing out of my flesh. The head was the size of a thumb, four-dimensional, with its shape changing as it moved. It had soft little devil horns. At its neck, its crimson hide blended into my pale skin. Gnarly gnarly gnarly. I looked away from it.

I used my third eye to see into Spaceland. There was pandemonium in the Coffee Roasting. Jena was sobbing and shouting my name. She couldn't see me here inside the ball; she thought I'd sacrificed myself for her. Good! Like being at my own funeral. But—not so good—she was still trapped in the corner by the curve of the ball.

I turned my head back and forth, looking vinn towards Dronia and vout towards Klupdom. There was a lot to see. Hundreds, maybe thousands, of Wackle strands were reaching out towards me from the Dronian cliffs. Many of the strands passed through Spaceland into the Klupper part of the All. Vout there I saw four silver saucers with gray-suited grolly guards. Momo's husband Voule was among them: dark, powerful, loud. At his commands, the purplish-skinned grolly guards were attempting to wipe out the Wackles with hyperbazookas, but the Wackles were frustrating them by the sheer force of their numbers. For the moment it was a stand-off.

I wondered why the Empress's crimson-clad troops hadn't come. It must be that the attack upon Spaceland had been carried out without her knowledge. If our only enemies were Momo's family and the grolly guards, the Wackles could surely hold them off un-til—until what? How long was I supposed to float here holding my world together?

"Yoo-hoo," said the Wackle head on my shoulder, trying to get me to talk to it.

I still didn't want to; I didn't want the head to be real. Mean-while the steady straining of the Nothing-ball was starting to wear on me. I noticed that if I flexed my knees and elbows, I could make the ball a little smaller. But my muscles could only hold so long, and each time I'd let up, my limbs would snap back to their max-imum extension, with the sphere of Nothing patiently pulling at my joints. At some point I was going to come apart.

"Help," I said softly.

"Me?" said the Wackle head on my shoulder.

"I guess so," I sighed, finally acknowledging it. "Can you call the others?"

The little head let out a piercing whistle, and one of the Wackle strands drifted into the ball. It flowed and thickened until a fat, devilish Wackle section was squeezed in there with me, the rest of him sticking vinn and vout on either side.

We were mashed together like lovers in a sleeping bag. "Our smeel is one, Joe," said the Wackle, his face pressed against mine.

"Are you the one who bit me?" I asked. The Wackle shrugged, as if to indicate this was a pointless question. I was beginning to understand that individuality meant nothing for the Wackles. They were all part of one great SuperWackle, including the extra head on my shoulder, and speaking of the head, how in hell was I going to get rid of it?

"A handy head for wander wonder," said the Wackle, as if he were reading my mind. And perhaps he was. Certainly I was understanding the Wackles a lot better than I'd been able to a few hours ago.

The Wackle petted my extra head with a tendril from the tip of a folded-up arm. "Atop High Dronia you soonest fetch a patch," he said. His motions were jiggling the ball of Nothing, pulling that much harder on my joints. I couldn't stand it much longer.

"Stop jouncing," I snapped. Now that we were practically brothers, there was no need to stand on ceremony. "Fat slob. Why don't *you* hold the ball for a while? Or can we sew it up?"

"Fetch a peachy patch, flatty," said the Wackle. "Drabk the Sharak of Okbra can do. If. You bark to doggy Drabk beyond beyond the Dronia." He made a vinnward gesture and the ball jounced again. Hard.

"Grab the ball and let me out of here, idiot."

"Negatory," said the Wackle. "Boneless stretch taffy pull me whoops it would."

"Then do this," I hissed. "Bring the rope we used to tie up Momo's saucer. And be careful when you slide out. Do it smooth, pig."

The big Wackle eased himself out of the hole and swooped off through the clear air of Dronia. Thanks to my garage having been crushed, my saucer had drifted quite some distance off, but it didn't take the Wackle long to return with the rope. He grew half a dozen arms and nimbly pulled out a series of mounds from the edges of the Nothing-ball, knotting the rope around each one of them. Soon the pressure was off my arms and legs and I could let go; I eased myself into the space of Dronia.

The Wackle tied off a few more spots on the ball—by now he'd made at least twenty links. The sections of rope stretched back and forth between the knots, making a kind of three-dimensional star, five or six feet across. Around the ball was Spaceland, that is, the Los Perros Coffee Roasting with its broken front window and its customers on the sidewalk. The rough-skinned cop was in the shop, uncertainly looking at the tip of his nightstick where the ball of Nothing had melted it away. He wasn't going to do much till reinforcements arrived. Jena had stopped crying for me and was trying to figure out how to get out without touching the ball.

Here in Dronner space, there were Wackles on every side. Thanks to the parasitic head on my shoulder, I could easily tune in on their conversations. They were talking about the Kluppers, the hole, and about me. About how I had to fly my saucer up to High Dronia to fetch a patch from Drabk—whoever or whatever he was. The main image of Drabk I could pick up from the Wackles was of some object like a thick, dark worm—a caterpillar?

The tied-up ball of Nothing was an open window to Klupper space. Looking through it, I saw other Wackles still fighting with Voule and the grolly guards. The group of Kluppers were down to only one hyperbazooka now. It seemed as if two more Wackles were arriving to take the place of each one the hyperbazooka blew away. Voule and the guards were getting back into their saucers; they were about to retreat.

As the enemy saucers got underway, big, coffee-colored Voule noticed the web of ropes we'd woven into the hole in space. He made a commanding gesture, and one of the guards flew his saucer straight at our little cobweb. I made a pushing gesture towards it with my mind—a bit like the way a football fan might wish a rival team's touchdown pass to tumble from the air. My wish had legs. The Wackle head on my shoulder sent it out, and instantly a score of Wackles converged on a spot between the hole and the saucer. The saucer slammed into them, and was trapped by the sticky smeel of their flesh. In moments, the guard had been shredded and his saucer had been tossed over to the Dronian side of the All.

"Full speed," hollered Voule, and the three silver saucers sped away.

"They'll be back," warned the head on my shoulder. It didn't speak as oddly as the other Wackles. Maybe it knew English better from being part of me. "Rush to Drabk the Sharak of Okbra and beg him for a patch."

Suddenly I found it unbearable to have this thing growing on me and talking to me. I reached over, grabbed the head and pulled at it. Its neck stretched like gum, and when I let go, it snapped back to where it had been before. I stretched it again, determined this time to bite the little neck in two, but now a big Wackle intervened, slapping my hands away.

"Two heads are better," cried the Wackle. "Your pirate parrot!" He started dragging me towards Momo's captured saucer. "Hurry scurry, Cap'n Joe!"

"Hold on," I said. "You can bring the damn saucer over here for me if you're in such a rush. I have to do something first." I turned back toward Spaceland. I didn't want to leave Jena trapped in the corner and thinking I was dead. She might do something rash. I caught hold of the tight-stretched ropes inside the ball of Nothing and flapped my body as hard as I could. Yes, I could move it relative to Spaceland. Like scrolling a view. The ball shifted towards the center of the Coffee Roasting room, swallowing up a strip of floor, a chair and half a table.

While I was moving the ball, I noticed a couple of shiny little crystals floating in its center. Antenna crystals! One from Jena's Mophone and one from mine, which had been in my pants pocket. Everything but the four-dimensional crystals had been melted away by the disappearance of three-dimensional space. That meant there was only one working Mophone still in existence. Spazz's. If only he didn't decide to turn his on again. Another hole like this, and we'd be toast. I definitely had to talk to Jena.

"Hunker down and keep quiet," I warned my extra head.

And then I lowered myself into the Coffee Roasting. The customers were outside, milling around with more cops and some newly arrived firemen. They were disturbed about the latest motion of the ball. For her part, Jena was eyeing the new space I'd made between the ball and the wall, wondering if it was safe to make a run. She hadn't noticed me yet.

"Jena!" I called, stepping around from behind the big black ball. "You can get out now. Hurry!"

"Sir!" a policewoman shouted at me. She had short curly blonde hair and a middle-American face, plain as a piecrust. She was holding a gun. I was naked, and my left shoulder was crowned by the bump of a little red devil head.

"Joe!" exclaimed Jena. She darted past the ball and threw herself into my arms. "You saved me! I thought you were dead!"

"Sir!" shouted the mustached cop.

"I have to take off again," I told Jena. "I'm supposed to find a patch to cover that ball of Nothing. Whatever happens, don't let Spazz use his Mophone. It's the only one that still works. Call him right now on his regular cell phone and tell him what happened. He'll listen to you. He thinks I've gone nuts. And tell him not to even think about turning the other Mophones back on."

"Get away from him, ma'am," ordered a heavyset policeman with extra braid on his shoulders. The head cop. He had a shaved head and a fat wattle at the back of his neck. "He's dangerous."

"What's that thing on your shoulder?" asked Jena.

"It's—it's like my parrot," I said. "I'll get rid of it when I can."

"I kind of like it," said Jena. "It's bitchin'. I always wanted you to get a tattoo."

That was nice of her to say. I was glad I'd saved Jena. But I wasn't sure what came next. On the one hand, I still had the feeling that I didn't want to go back to her. On the other hand, Jena was like the Wackle head grown onto my shoulder. Part of my flesh. Did I really truly want to split up?

On a sudden impulse, I kissed Jena good-bye right before peeling myself vinn towards Dronia. It was the first time we'd kissed in two months. Despite all my reservations about Jena, my lips were the very last thing to leave Spaceland. Out there I paused, looking down at her standing there holding her hand to her mouth, remembering the kiss. Why couldn't I ever straighten out my feelings about this woman?

A Wackle pressed up to me, Momo's saucer in tow.

"Drabk now you," he urged.

"Exactly where is he?" I asked.

"Atop Dronia and beyond. Seek and ye find."

I looked over at the great shimmering reef of the Dronian wall, with the thousand red Wackle strands tapering back to it. The wall's details changed with each motion of my head.

"Is there a tunnel to the top?"

"None of us Wackles has ever been there," said the little head on my shoulder. "You'll have to find your own way. I'll watch." It was a complete parasite, in other words. At least it spoke something like standard English.

I got into the saucer and felt around in the cockpit for the extra grolly I'd left there. I needed something to calm my nerves. Naturally the grolly was gone.

"We threw it back through Spaceland," the growth on my shoulder told me. "We didn't want its spores to get loose and start growing on our land. Grolly's bad for you, Joe Cube. It's a Klupper slave drug. You need your true self to meet Drabk the Sharak of Okbra. Truer than true."

"Great," I said angrily. "This is just great." I slammed the saucer control forward and we blasted towards the huge, four-dimensional cliffs.

Drabk

I drew closer to the cliffs, at first following along beside the hundreds of red Wackle strands that stretched from there to Los Perros. I could see more clearly than ever that the individual Wackles were tentacles from a group of giant anemones, each of the creatures the size of a village. Off to the side of the red anemones I noticed some big, darting shiny shapes, pointed at either end. I thought of them as hyperfish. They seemed agitated by the approach of my saucer. But I kept on coming. There was, after all, something of a rush. Before long the Kluppers would manage to cut the ropes tying off the hole, and Spaceland would be gone.

I was only a mile or two from the cliffs now. They looked solid up ahead, with no sign of a tunnel. I pushed my saucer's control stick vinnward, hoping to find a passage. My four-dimensional side-step sent the red Wackle anemones morphing down to nothing. And before long a promising rocky canyon appeared, opening up in the wall like a smile. Schools of hyperfish were hovering down in there, shining with every color of the rainbow. The smaller ones were like streamlined tunas, but the large ones had frilly, undulating fins around the circumference of their bodies and bunches of tentacles at their mouths. They were like the cuttlefish I'd seen at the Monterey Bay Aquarium—except for being four-dimensional and really, really big. I veered towards one of the hypercuttlefish, and the canyon walls morphed with my motions. Suddenly an orange anemone popped into view upon an outcrop nearby. It was even bigger than the Wackle clumps had been.

As soon as the orange anemone sensed my presence, its thick tentacles came writhing out towards me. I fumbled at my control stick, but I was too slow. The anemone caught hold of my saucer, the same way that the Wackles had grabbed Voule's craft before.

My saucer wrenched and pitched. I went flying out of my seat and tumbled through the thick, watery, Dronian air. A pair of orange anemone tentacles swooped in and took hold of me on either side.

They weren't exactly Wackles, but like the Wackles, they had mouths set into their ends.

"Flat Klupper pig," said one of them in a woman's voice. To talk with me, she'd formed a section of her tip into a doughy humanoid shape with a face like a jack-o'-lantern's. Her triangular eyes glowed greenish white. My other orange captor was nothing but a tapering cylinder with a little round toothy hole in her swollen tip—no sign of face at all. She had four hands, all of them clamped to my bod.

"Die now," said the second tentacle's round mouth, the words a faint, high-pitched hiss.

"I'm a Spacelander," I cried. "Not a Klupper! I'm trying to save you!"

"It's true," piped the red Wackle head on my shoulder. "This is Joe Cube. He travels to High Dronia to petition Drabk the Sharak of Okbra!"

"Parasite filth die," whistled the round-mouthed second tentacle and, faster than it takes to tell it, she bit down and yanked the red Wackle right out of my flesh. It was like having a bad tooth pulled.

A twinge of pain followed by great relief. Oddly enough there was no blood.

"Wackles try spawn everywhere," said the first tentacle, the pumpkin-faced one. She watched with approval as her sister-tentacle chewed the shrieking little red devil-head into bits. And now that second tentacle began nuzzling at my shoulder with her toothy hole, rasping away the last traces of the parasitic Wackle from my shoulder.

The Halloween face of the first tentacle watched me, her white eyes bouncing around inside the volume of her head.

"Tell your sister thanks, but that's enough," I told her, putting a protective hand over my shoulder. "Everything else is me. I'm Joe Cube. Nice to meet you two."

"Jacqui I am, and Loplop my sister," said the first tentacle. She turned her head inside out and let her eyes slide around on its surface. "True Spacelander you?"

"Truly," I said. "The Kluppers made a hole in Spaceland, and I have to find Drabk to get a patch. Otherwise—no more Spaceland. The Kluppers will bomb you day and night. Their grolly plantimals want to grow all over your cliffs. Can I have my saucer back now?"

"No," said Jacqui, echoed by a breathy, whistling, "No," from Loplop. And even as they answered, I saw my saucer flying back towards Spaceland, flung at some incredible speed by a whipping motion of the orange anemone's vast tentacles.

"What am I gonna do now?" I cried.

"Come to Mother," said Jacqui. "Merge."

I didn't like the sound of this at all. The thing they called Mother was a stadium-sized mound of slimy orange flesh. I tried to twist away, but Jacqui and Loplop were holding me tight, their hands clenched into puckers. The two tentacles began shortening themselves, pulling me down to the writhing orange mass.

Mother was waiting for me. In her center, amid all the tentacles, was a gaping four-dimensional hole, an intricate structure of chambers and passageways, flexing and folding as we drew closer. Mother's mouth. Somehow I could pick up a faint sense of what she was thinking. The Spacelander was too tasty a morsel to be eaten by a mere tentacle-tip mouth. Mother's tummy, that was the place for the Spacelander.

"Help, help!" I screamed, like some hyperactive cartoon character hanging from a thread above a lion's open mouth. "Someone please help me! I have to find Drabk!"

Ask and ye shall receive. A hypercuttlefish the size of a zeppelin came flying towards us, fixing me with its large, intelligent eyes. The creature's tan flesh was filled with glowing stripes and dots. The undulating four-dimensional fin around its body was like a dancer's spangled skirt, with the powerful beating of the fin bunching the body's spots into impossibly beautiful curves and surfaces. In the midst of the light show was the hypercuttlefish's enormous mouth, wreathed by its creamy tentacles and rimmed by a sharp-edged black beak.

The zeppelin was too fast for the giant anemone. The great jaws severed the tentacles of Jacqui and Loplop, and the three of us were carried off inside the hypercuttlefish's mouth, a space the size of a large, high-ceilinged room.

"Damn!" said Jacqui, her bitten-off end quickly sealing over. She and Loplop were still holding onto me.

"Let go," I said.

"Yes," whistled Loplop. "Crawl now, Jacqui. We land new place and grow." The two of them took off like a pair of big worms, humping their way across the damp floor of the hypercuttlefish's mouth. They made it out just before the beak fully closed. And now I was alone. It smelled like baked potatoes in there, not at all what I'd expect. There was something else mixed into the steamy potato smell, a whiff of perfume. Lavender?

The darkness was lit by the glowing spots inside the hypercuttlefish's flesh. I walked and flapped my way over to the polka-dotted wall of the mouth, pressing my flat vinner side against it so that I'd be hard to swallow. It was nice and smooth, and the overall touch of it sent a tingle through every part of my body. The hypercuttlefish flesh reacted to my presence; the lights inside it drew closer to me. But for the moment nothing else happened. I could feel a vibration in the hypercuttlefish; it was flying somewhere fast.

I lay still, catching my breath. I'd been going full out for the last couple of hours. I had a vague feeling I should be making plans, but things were too out of hand to know where to begin. I leaned against the cheek of the hypercuttlefish, too tired to move. The vibrations of its flesh were like music; I found my mind drifting back to New Year's Eve at the Black Watch, with golden oldies blasting on the speakers and colored little Christmas lights tacked to the black plywood walls. Jena and Spazz and Tulip there, the four of us dancing. Dear Jena. I seemed to see Jena right in front of me, decked out in a shining little red dress, her lipstick bright, her hair full of glitter.

Jena leaned forward to talk to me, but her voice came out like noises. "Wuh guh rabba. Yama yava flan." She looked very receptive, very friendly. I nestled against the hypercuttlefish's cheek, wanting to sink further into my nap. Maybe I could dream about Jena making love to me.

"Is this better?" said Jena, reaching out to tap me on the shoulder. "Can you understand me now?" She was glowing all over like a lightstick.

I let out a grunt of surprise. I wasn't asleep at all. There was a real Jena shape, right here with me. Had the hypercuttlefish put her there?

"You can talk to me," said the Jena. The lights in the cheek-wall were twinkling in Christmas colors and, by God yes, the vibrations of the cheek were making a damn good imitation of Nirvana playing "In Bloom." Too weird.

I craned towards the Jena, still not saying anything. I was worried that she might be planning to eat me. As soon as I had that thought, the Jena smiled at me and I could see her perfect, luminous teeth. She wiggled the tip of her tongue, dark pink against the glowing pale pink of her face.

Using my third eye, I figured out that the Jena was connected on her vinnward side to the cheek of the hypercuttlefish. As far as my regular eyes could tell, she was a free-standing three-dimensional figure, but my third eye could see that in hyperspace the Jena was the vouter end of a hyperbump. Like one of those wart-on-a-tendril lures that anglerfish dangle near their mouths. She was part of the cuttlefish.

"Don't hurt me," I said, cringing away from the Jena thing. "I'm trying to save your world from the Kluppers."

"I know," said the Jena. "I read your whole mind through your hyperskin while you were lying on my cheek."

I jerked myself away from the cheek, but the Jena gave me a gentle shove, pushing me back against the soft, fleshy wall.

"Relax," said the Jena. "I'm not out to hurt you. I've already swallowed you, right? What more could happen? My name's Kangy by the way." The more she talked, the clearer her voice became.

"You sound so normal," I said finally. "Kangy. Not like the Wackles or those orange tentacle things."

"I'm a lot smarter than them," said Kangy/Jena. "They're almost plants." She came over and leaned up against me. She felt good, though her luminous skin was slicker than Jena's. She didn't smell like Jena, but she didn't smell bad. Like hot tea with lemon. The smell went well with the lavender and roast potatoes scent of the hypercuttlefish's mouth.

"Why don't you love your wife?" asked Kangy in a gentle tone.

"She's always running games on me," I said. "I do things for her and then she sulks. Nothing's ever enough. I'm tired of trying to please her. And the real dealbreaker is that she went off and slept with another guy."

"Deal?" said Kangy. "The deal is you give her money and she grows you a baby? That's not a deal you can make. Paper is two-dimensional, Joe, life is infinite-dimensional. Love comes first." She cocked her head and smiled impishly. "I'd be interested to see exactly how you Spacelanders *do it*. Seems like you'd keep falling out." She slipped off the red dress—or rather the dress merged into her skin. Kangy had gotten Jena's proportions one hundred percent right. That showed what a clear mental image of Jena I must be carrying around in my head, loyal husband that I'd once been. Could I start loving instead of dealing? This Jena looked good enough to—

But of course she wasn't Jena. She was Kangy. I pushed her away from me. I thought of hidden beaks.

"Maybe that's from your fear of your mother," said Kangy, responding to my last thought as if I'd spoken it out loud. "Never mind. Let's talk about your plans before we get there."

"Get where?"

"I'm flying us to the top of Dronia. To find Drabk. Like you asked." Her bright skin had covered itself with another of Jena's outfits, the yellow blouse and the electric blue slacks she'd been wearing this afternoon.

"You heard me shouting Drabk's name?" I asked.

"Drabk lives in all who hear. He answers when he's needed."

"Jacqui and Loplop didn't seem to care about Drabk."

"Plantimals," said Kangy with a touch of contempt. "All they know is eating and spawning. That's *dealing* for you, Joe. The Wackles want to grow on the Klupper cliffs, and the Kluppers' grolly wants to grow down here. If we didn't have Spaceland to split the Cave Between Worlds, there'd be a terrible war. But you know what? The Dronners would win. We're smarter and tougher. Compare me to those two-legged Kluppers. Compare a Wackle to a grolly plant. We'd kick their cheesy butts. Spaceland's for *their* protection, not ours. I bet the Klupper Empress knows that. That's probably why she doesn't want those greedy morons in Momo's family to try and get rid of Spaceland." She was sounding more like Jena all the time.

"How do you know so much?" I asked Kangy.

"Like I told you, I touched every part of your brain through your hyperskin. The skin's not that thick. Momo should have done a better job augmenting you. Anyway, I made a mental copy of your flat brain and I watched it think, so that's how I know everything you know. I ran my copy of your brain in high speed, forwards and backwards like a—videotape." She handled the last word like someone picking up dog doo with a shovel. "It's ridiculous how dependent you Spacelanders are on your dippy little machines."

"Don't you Dronners have machines? The Kluppers do."

"Machines suck," said Kangy. "We haven't used them for ten thousand years. Whoops, hang on, Joe, I see some food up ahead."

"What about finding Drabk?"

Kangy made a Jena-type gesture, holding her Jena-hands up at chest level and flapping them up and down in my direction. It meant "calm down." The Jena stepped over and pressed against me, as if to make sure I didn't come unglued from the inside of Kangy's huge cheek.

The great hypercuttlefish's jaws opened up and I could see outside past the fringe of her tentacles. We were in a long cave, flying along at a tremendous speed, presumably on our way to the surface of Dronia. The space was illuminated by the glowing air of the All. Rather than being solid, the walls were an intricate filigree of mineral formations, just like in the famous Indian Caverns three miles west of Matthewsboro. My hometown's big tourist attraction, which drew hundreds of visitors each summer.

I recognized the upward-growing stalagmites, the downward-growing stalactites, the helictites that grew in any direction at all, and the sagging sheets of drapery we used to call cave bacon. The walls were covered with formations like soda straws, popcorn nuggets, and coral. The floor was rippled with slumping sheets of flowstone and dripstone.

And of course it was all four-dimensional. The stone columns, antlers, cascades and nubs were continually changing their shapes and sizes as we moved vinn and vout among them. I was glad to be flying inside of Kangy; I would have crashed the saucer in here for sure. It was beautiful. Kangy was nice. As I thought this, the Jena kissed me on the cheek.

Far ahead were some pinky-gray shapes moving among the mazes of rock. They had long feelers and stalk-eyes, any number of little flipper-legs, and curved bodies with fanned-out tails. They were moving along backwards, powering themselves by repeated snaps of their tails, their frightened beady eyes watching Kangy's approach. Hyperprawns!

Just as it seemed we'd cornered one, it disappeared through what looked like a solid wall. Kangy veered vinnward and the wall opened up into a space like a cathedral, with the hyperprawn streaking across it. Kangy gave a huge flap of her fin, and a moment later we'd caught up with the prey. Kangy's tentacles seized it, her beak bit it in half, and then the two twitching pieces of the hyperprawn went skipping across her mouth and down her gullet. The Jena held me tight lest I be pulled along.

"Yum yum," said Kangy, opening her jaws again so I could still see the view. "We're almost there." The nave of the stone cathedral narrowed down to another tunnel, which arced upwards to form a vertical shaft. I saw a bright ball up above, and then we powered out of the tunnel's spherical mouth and into a hilly landscape of heavenly beauty.

The sky was the perfect bright blue of autumn, the hills the fine, crisp green of early spring. Thanks to some oddity of the fourth dimension, many of the hills seemed to float up in the sky. Conversely, there were holes in the ground holding patches of blue. In this part of Dronia, earth and sky were mixed together.

Weaving from hill to floating hill were the thick, brownish-purple stalks of enormous vines. Everything in Dronia seemed almost weightless. I guess it was the thickness of the air.

The vines had great heart-shaped leaves and pale white flowers. Gently drifting among them were legions of hypercuttlefish, feeding upon the fruits of the vines. These were the Lords and Ladies of Dronia, or so it seemed.

"There's my husband," Kangy told me through the Jena. "His name is Stool."

"That's nice," I said in a strained voice. Something about my relief at having made it up here made me want to burst out laughing, and Stool's absurd name almost set me off. I was trying not even to *think* of laughing. For I knew that Kangy could read my mind.

Stool came sailing over to greet Kangy, propelled by his frilly body-fin. He approached in silence, with his tentacles tidily bunched to a point over his mouth. A riot of colors was playing across his body, and even from inside Kangy's mouth, I could see that she was flashing with patterns as well. This was how they talked. Stool docked against Kangy as quietly as an airship, twining his mouth-tentacles with hers. One of his thinner tentacles reached into Kangy's beak and felt me. A sudden bright blue eye opened up on its tip to examine me. He didn't smell quite as pleasant as Kangy. There was the same baked potato smell, but it was mixed with ammonia instead of with lavender.

"Stool says 'Howdy pardner,'" said Kangy's Jena, laying her hand upon the tentacle. "He wants to know if you'd like to ride on his back. He'll be better than me at taking you the rest of the way to Drabk."

"All right," I said. The idea of getting out of Kangy's mouth sounded pretty good. "But can Stool talk to me like you do?"

"He'll be able to if you let him touch you for a minute. He can model your brain even faster than me. Stool's smart."

So I held still while Stool broadened his tentacle tip into a flat paddle that he laid along the vouter side of my body, right against my brain. I felt a creepy tingling all over the inside of my skull, and then the tentacle drew back and formed itself into a shape like a Western saddle.

"You can get on him now," said Kangy's Jena. "Good luck!"

"Thank you," I said, seating myself on Stool's tentacle. He'd even grown little stirrups for my feet. "Will one of you take me back to Spaceland after I meet Drabk?"

"Drabk can put you there himself," said Kangy. "Distances are nothing for him. God speed your journey, Joe Cube. And remember. Love, don't deal."

The two hypercuttlefish released each other, and Stool swept me up to a spot on his head between the two bulging mounds of his eyes. It was like an elephant lifting up his rider. I felt pretty grand up on top of Stool. His endlessly changeable flesh shaped out a seat for me there, with a hole for my legs, a back for me to lean against, and handgrips on either side. And right there in his skin near my knees was the vertical slit of a mouth.

"We're gonna hightail it to that there Sharak of Okbra," said the mouth in a cowboy accent. "Hang on tight, you hear me, pardner?" Stool sounded like my Dad, or like Dad would have sounded if he'd been a slit in the back of a four-dimensional cuttlefish named Stool.

That last thought finished me off. "I'm r-ready, S-stool," I said, the giggles growing into guffaws. Nothing seemed to matter anymore. This was so far beyond anything that made sense.

"What's so all-fired funny?" said Stool in mock anger. He was beating his big fin, flying up into the sky. Since the back of the chair was touching the vinner side of my brain, he could feel everything I was thinking. "My name means 'turd' to you, eh? I been called worse'n that, boy."

"I'm sorry," I said, tears of laughter running from my eyes.

"Don't make no never-mind," said Stool equably. "You here to do a good deed. Savin' your world, and protectin' the Kluppers from gettin' their asses handed to 'em. I'm right proud to help you."

We rose higher and higher. The floating hills were like islands, each of them seemingly rounded off and grassy on every side. Only by moving my third eye could I see the Doctor-Seuss-style natural bridges connecting them to the ground.

Some other Dronners were flying along with us, their hyperskins flowing with the colors of their speech. The patterns included tilings, paisley swirls, networks of light, photorealistic images—all at once. The patterns were three-dimensional; they were modulated all along the vinn/vout axis of each Dronner's hyperskin.

It occurred to me that Stool was probably showing the others my thoughts. Well, that was fine, for I had nothing but pleasant feelings about this place. It was a paradise—the clear sky, the graceful vines, the floating hills, the hypercuttlefish aglow with 3D colors—it was paradise, and I was happier than I'd ever been.

Still we mounted higher. There was only one more island of green, all by itself a half mile above us. The air was getting thin, and Stool's fin was working harder than before. One by one, his companions turned back, unable to continue the ascent.

With a last push, Stool reached the final floating hill. It was no more than a hundred yards across. There were small white and yellow blossoms in the bright green grass. Stool latched onto the grass with his mouth tentacles. "End o' the road, pardner," he said. "I expect you'll find ole Drabk here."

I scooted down the sloping backs of his tentacles and set foot upon the floating hill. We were maybe two miles above the surface of Dronia. The little ball of a hill slanted down on every side. I felt distinctly uneasy about the possibility of slipping off it. On the crest of the hill, one of those thick vines rose up into the air before swerving into another dimension and out of sight. I decided I'd sit next to it. Something to hang onto.

"Take 'er easy, son," called my father's voice from the slit in Stool's back. "God bless."

"You're leaving me up here?" I said.

By way of an answer, Stool let out a "Yee-haw!" He released his hold on the hill and dropped fin-first towards Dronia. I peered down, watching him enjoy the fall like a sky-boarder, steering himself through spirals and loops.

And now it grew very quiet. I made my way to the vine and sat down at its thick base, waiting to see what would happen next. The stalk was thick, with a barky texture. Almost like a tree. There was a slight whisper of wind in its large, heart-shaped leaves. I wondered how the Wackles were doing in keeping the Kluppers away from that hole in our space. I hoped to God that Jena had managed to convince Spazz not to turn on his Mophone again. Even though the Dronners didn't care all that much about Spaceland, for me Spaceland was everything. My heart lived there. My Jena.

More time passed, and finally I thought to call Drabk's name aloud. Something like a face with a heavy mustache popped out of the trunk of the vine, a little knob of a face with floppy pointed ears and a thick, Middle Eastern kind of mustache. The mustache—

that was the caterpillar thing I'd seen in the Wackles' minds. Drabk's face had bright, bulging eyes with slanting slits for their irises. The overall effect was of something old and wise and sly.

"Drabk?" I repeated.

"You have traveled far," he said in a low, silky tone. His accent matched his mustache. "What is your purpose?"

"I need a space patch," I said. "The Kluppers made a hole in Spaceland and I need a 3D piece of space to cover it up."

"This one wonders where we might find such a patch," said Drabk, cocking his head to one side and blinking.

I had a sudden mental image of the RCA Victor dog, harking for His Master's Voice. But Drabk was supposed to be the Master here. The Sharak.

I figured that when he said "this one," he meant himself. Running a guru routine. I didn't much like gurus. When I was growing up, there'd been one who'd gotten his followers to buy up some ranches near Matthewsboro. We'd see the followers in town sometimes, educated people who talked softly and kept their mouths set in smiles. But they'd turn mean as snakes whenever there was any kind of disagreement, like over sewage or cattle or dogs or property taxes.

"The Wackles and the Dronners said you'd know how to make a patch," I said carefully. "They said you could do anything."

"*You* can do anything," said Drabk, his eyes glinting. "You have the patch already."

"No I don't," I said, feeling impatient. "That's why I came here. They said you could give me a patch and that you could set me down next to the hole in Spaceland. You do know what Spaceland is, don't you?"

"This one knows nothing," said Drabk flatly. "This one doesn't think. Climb past the words and thoughts, Joe Cube. You already have the patch."

"That crummy significant crud doesn't mean jack to me," I snapped, suddenly losing it. "So thanks for nothing."

"You don't have it yet," said Drabk, and twinkled at me while I figured that one out.

And then the bump that was his face began sliding up the vine. He paused just before the bend where the stalk disappeared into another dimension—the fifth? Drabk stared provokingly down at me, his mustache unreadable, his floppy ears hanging over his brilliant eyes. "Follow this one," he said. "Climb the beanstalk." And then he moved out of view.

I sighed and looked longingly down at Dronia. I was feeling weak and shaky. It had been too long since my last piece of grolly. Maybe I should go home.

If I turned my third eye far enough to my vinner side, I could just make out a narrow path of green land leading down and down from my tiny hill, an inches-wide strip that forked and merged with other airy paths like lace. Theoretically I could scoot along it and make my way back down. Or, hell, I could probably just jump off and sky-surf my way down like Stool had. But then what?

I put my hands on the vine to nowhere. I was scared to climb it, but deep down I knew I had to. I took hold of a coiled, dangling tendril overhead. When I pulled on it, the tendril pulled back, helping me. It was like the vine wanted me to climb it. I started on up, from tendril to leaf to tendril.

When I hit the fifth-dimensional bend in the vine, I bent with it. Dronia disappeared. There was nothing left but the taut blue sky and the purplish stalks and green leaves of the vine.

"Drabk!" I shouted. "Wait up! I'm coming."

A bump in the vine bulged out right in front of me, forming that same knowing, mustached face.

"Keep climbing," Drabk told me. His breath smelled like cloves. "Climb without thinking."

"And then you'll get me the patch?" I insisted.

"Not get," said Drabk. "Be. Climb past thought to Okbra."

So climb I did, for who knows how long. Every now and then the vine would veer off in a new direction, and I'd follow along with it. The new directions weren't left, right, forward, back or even vinn or vout. They were new dimensions, each one different from all the ones before. I don't know how I could tell exactly, but I could. For one thing, the sky changed from dark blue, to pale blue, and eventually into white. For another, it got harder and harder to see anything except for my own body, and my body was all in streaks and patches. But I kept on climbing, kept on reaching out into the uncertainty and having the next tendril or leaf slap reliably into my palm.

As I labored on, my mind emptied out. I was but a set of pumping legs and arms, an ever-less-significant twitch in the vastness of the All. I no longer had any expectations about what I was doing this for.

And still the vine led onward, taking me up through a seemingly endless series of higher dimensions, the lurching bends coming ever closer together. At some point, time itself became just another dimension I'd passed. And scale as well. Was I shrinking? Was the vine growing as fast as I climbed? Was I even climbing anymore? Not that I was asking myself these questions. Without really meaning to, I'd fully followed Drabk's advice. I'd climbed beyond words and beyond thought.

Some sort of jump-cut discontinuity must have happened around then, for the next thing I remember is being perched on a silvery little cloud. Me and Drabk sitting there facing each other, the two of us with our legs crossed like cartoon hermits atop the Magic Mountain. Not a thought in my head.

"Joe Cube," said Drabk.

When he said my name I remembered myself. The first thing I thought was that I wanted some grolly.

"Expel your addiction," said Drabk. He had a body now, a spindly little wiseman body with dark-colored arms and legs. He stuck out a knobby finger and tapped me on the forehead.

I coughed and something loosened in my chest. I coughed harder, and the object moved up my throat, scratching all the way. I spit it out into my hand: a prickly round dark purple thing like a burr.

"The grolly roots," said Drabk. "Your patch."

"You—you did it!" I exclaimed.

"You did it," said Drabk.

I paused to look around. The cloud we were sitting on was like very fine fuzz. It was the tip-top, infinite-dimensional ending of the vine we'd climbed. The air around us was a glowing bright white.

"Where are we?" I asked.

"In the Presence," said Drabk. "As always."

I understood something deep then, but what it was is hard to say. The world going on all over the place all the time—it is the Presence. And the Presence cares; the Presence loves me. I was surprised.

"I love you," I told Drabk, not knowing I was going to say this. Drabk smiled and nodded.

We sat there for another timeless interval and then the burr in my hands caught my eye. I had to go patch Spaceland.

"How do I get back?" I asked Drabk.

"Jump into the void," he said. "Infinity is zero in Okbra. From here, you'll pass through Pointland to Lineland to Flatland to Spaceland. Your noble heart will be your guide."

I got to my feet. The cloud of fuzz was soft beneath my naked feet. Walking was hard; my legs felt like they had a thousand knees and ankles. I made it over to the edge of the cloud and poised myself for a jump, keeping the grolly root burr clenched in my hand.

"Good-bye," I told Drabk, glancing back at him still sitting there. He gave a friendly wave and disappeared.

I jumped.

Return To Spaceland

Everything changed the instant I jumped off of Drabk's infinite-dimensional cloud. My world collapsed to a point. It was just as Drabk had told me; the way home led through Pointland.

In my Pointland, everything was in one place. Me and the grolly root were mashed in there together. But even though the parts of my body were all on top of each other, somehow the parts were different. Yes, I was a point, but I was a point with *structure*.

My eyes were folded in there for instance, and I could see. Well, not exactly *see*; it was more like I had a mental image of my world, because the world was right on top of the eye. My image held every bit of me at once: me inside me inside me inside me. It was cosmic.

Speaking of cosmic, for the little time that I was in Pointland, I was possessed by the notion that the Presence was me. Yes, in Pointland I was filled with the belief that Joe Cube was God. I, you, he, she, it—all of space was Joe! I was everywhere, I knew everything, I could do anything. I said it out loud, the thinking the same as the speaking: "Let every part of creation praise omnipresent, omniscient, omnipotent Joe Cube!"

And crap like that.

Pointland was about total self-absorption. I was babbling about how great I was, preaching to the choir, and I *was* the choir. Who knows how long it went on.

The way it ended was that I felt a curious stretching, like I was breaking up into pieces. Disturbing. I'd grown used to having all of me in the same spot. My body changed and I started hearing the sound of other voices. A strange, confused chirping. At first I thought it was my subconscious talking, but then, *whammo*, someone barged into me!

The shock traveled along the length of my body, from my head to my toes. I was a six-foot line segment. I'd graduated from Pointland to Lineland. My height dimension had become real.

I had an eye at my top end and the sole of a foot at the bottom. The grolly root was layered into my midsection. Looking through my eye, I could see—a dot. A bright, inquisitive dot. Another Linelander's eye, staring down at me.

"Velcome, new baby," said a woman's alto voice from behind the eye. "Sorry I vas bumping into you. You bloomed zo very fast. I'm Yekaterina. Vat's your Momma's name?"

"Mary," I said, too surprised to do anything but give a straight answer. My voice vibrated within my body and traveled down the line. "Mary Cube," I added. "I don't imagine you've ever heard of a cube."

"No, I don't know dat name," said the Lineland woman. "How far from here she is, your Momma?"

"Um . . ."

"Oh, zorry, you're not knowing nothing yet, are you, my new baby boy neighbor. I missed hearing de song dat grew you. Maybe I vas asleep. It's zometimes hard to be noticing at my age." She raised her voice, and shouted so loud that my body trembled. "Hey, Yitzhak, looky dis new baby boy right between us. Six feet long he is!"

A deep voice responded from beneath my foot. "Good riddance to you, Yekaterina! Going bananas I vas, staring into your eye. Dis much better is. Nice pink foot of a baby boy." I felt a tickling in the sole of my foot, as of something feeling it. "Zpeak up den, bubbala. Vat's your name?"

"I'm Joe," I said. I tried sliding back and forth a bit. My eye bumped Yekaterina's eye, and my foot bumped Yitzhak.

"Don't trample into me, baby," cried Yitzhak, instantly irritable.

"I'm not a baby," I said. "I'm from another world."

"From heaven to us you are coming," said Yekaterina. "And velcome you are." She nudged me with her eye, then raised her voice to talk through me again. "Don't be a stinker, Yitzhak. De boy needs his exercise to grow. Bounce all you like, baby Joe."

"Big enough already he is," bellowed Yitzhak. And then he lowered his voice to talk to me. "Vat you mean, you're not a baby?"

"I'm from Spaceland," I said. "I won't be here long. Soon I'll be moving on to Flatland. A world with two dimensions."

"Vat you mean?" rumbled Yitzhak once again.

"A world where people can move past each other," I said. "Where people don't have to stay exactly where they're born. If we were in Flatland, I could move to your other side."

"Listen at dis crazy baby," trilled Yekaterina. "A lovely voice you've got, Joe. You vant to meet my daughter?"

"Um . . ."

"Tanya!" sang Yekaterina. "Taaaanya." The three of us fell quiet, listening for an answer. I could make out the voices of dozens, scores, hundreds of Linelanders. As I focused in on the sounds, I was able to form an image of the world, mentally arranging the voices in the order of the singers.

And here came Tanya's answering call. Listening to it, I could tell that Tanya was some four hundred yards beyond Yekaterina.

"She sounds very nice," I told Yekaterina. "You and Yitzhak must be proud of your daughter."

Yekaterina let out a peal of surprised laughter.

"I'm not dat noisy Cossack's husband," boomed Yitzhak. "Ve are having no resonance together vatsoever. She's only my neighbor. My vife, half a mile down from here she is." He raised his voice. "Saaaadie!"

"Here, dear Yitzhak," came a faint soprano answer.

"If you don't live next to your wife, how do you, um . . ."

"Harmony is life," chirped Yekaterina. "The right vibration makes a new baby born. Your voice sounds wery nicely with Tanya's, I am noticing. Who knows? Maybe ve a nice match can make vhen you're a little more grown, baby Joe. Vith practice, your voice may someday beat together vith Tanya's and churn up a new segment."

Once again I felt a shifting within myself. I was spreading out into a second dimension. "I'm on my way out," I told Yekaterina with relief. "Bye bye."

Sproing! I was a full two-dimensional man. It felt so good to have room to stretch out. I could move my flat legs and arms up and down and to the left and right. I did a few jumping jacks, shaking out the kinks. I'd been reconstituted in such a way that I had a flat eye on either side of my head. My retinal images were only patterned lines but, being a Flatlander, I was able to use these images to build up a two-dimensional mental model of my surroundings.

I was on a little patch of grass between two houses, each of them with a tight-shut swinging door. There was a lot of noise coming from the other side of the house on my right, like there was a crowd of people yelling. Somebody climbed over the house's roof and looked at me. A flat man. His head was weird. He had his eyes on its sides, and his mouth was up on the top. Come to think of it, my mouth was on the top of my head too.

"There he is!" shouted the man on the roof. "The killer!"

Suddenly it hit me. I was back in the Flat Matthewsboro I'd dreamed about the night after we went to Vegas. Two months ago. I hadn't thought about that dream very often, but now the details came back. I'd accidentally killed a Flatlander named Custer, and a lynch mob of Flatlanders had come after me. Things were starting up right where my dream had left off.

I bent my legs and leapt upwards like a flea. I landed on the roof of the house on my left and scrambled over it. With my left eye, I could see open space up ahead, with greenery rising upwards. I jumped and kicked, moving as fast as I could. With my right eye, I could see the Flatlanders in hot pursuit.

There were some holes in the ground. I jumped over the first five or ten of them, and then I decided to climb down into one. The green stuff underfoot was a giant plant. I wormed down into the tunnel; the leaf-stuff was smooth and green and succulent. The leaf-crack widened into a round dead end. A bit of water was trapped there. I drank some of it and hunkered down to wait.

There was something clutched in one of my hands, a collapsed-down version of the grolly root that I'd coughed up when I'd been with Drabk. Looking at it, I remembered what I was doing here. I was trying to make my way home to patch a hole in space. Sooner or later, I'd pass on beyond Flatland. I only needed to wait this out. And then I'd be home with Jena again.

I could feel the vibrations of Flatlanders overhead. At first I thought I'd escaped them, that they were passing me by. But then I heard a scraping and slithering. Some of them were coming down into the plant after me. In another few minutes they had me by the arms and legs. One of them was carrying a long stick with spring clamps on it. They clipped my legs to one end and my hands to the other and they carried me downtown like a captured tiger.

My head was sealed up between my two arms and I couldn't see where we were going. Apparently I was breathing through my skin, so I didn't suffocate. We jounced along roughly for a while, climbing up and down over buildings, and finally we stopped. Someone unfastened my lower arm so that I could see. We were in a large courtyard between two tall, stepped buildings. My captors flipped the carrying stick over and laid it on the ground. I could see Flatlanders perched all up and down the terraces of the buildings, shrieking out their hatred. The only one to speak on my behalf was flat Dad.

"My boy didn't mean nothin' by it," he said. "Just got a little rambunctious. And who really gave a hoot about Custer anyhow?"

"Shut your crack, Ed," interrupted flat Mom, who was there too. "This killer's no son of ourn. He's a devil thing! Burn him up before he does magic again!" The crowd hollered their assent.

None other than Custer's widow Mindy had been appointed as my executioner. The Flatlanders attached the back of my carrying stick to a kind of crane, and then they hoisted me a few feet off the ground. Beneath me were lumps of wood and oily scraps of paper. Mindy lit a long match and leaned forward to light the fire. I stared down at it, feeling the heat. The flames had a funny way of rippling across the wood; they'd flare up, run out of air, then drop back down. But each time they rose higher. A flame licked along my left arm, charring it.

"Drabk!" I cried. "Save me now!"

I glimpsed the fuzzy worm of his mustache and then, thank God, my flesh shifted again. I was growing back into the third dimension. The cries of the Flatlanders segued into the faint honking and tweeting of coffee-shop jazz. I'd never heard anything so sweet.

Yes, I was back in the Los Perros Coffee Roasting, with the grolly root clutched in my left hand. Despite all the adventures I'd just been through, not much time seemed to have passed. The cops and firemen were still there, and Jena too. Torrents of rain were coming down outside the broken window. It was late afternoon, still light, almost spring. Jena stood out like a flower in her bright yellow blouse. She was talking on the regular cell phone that she carried as a backup for her Mophone.

"Jena!" I shouted. "I'm back." I was naked.

She gave me an oddly guarded smile and said something into her phone.

"Stop him before he gets away," shouted the boss cop with the stubbly roll of fat at his neck. The mustached, volleyball-player-type cop and the pie-faced blonde lady cop stepped towards me, but not very fast. Everyone was nervous about what I might do next.

Quickly I strode over to the hole in space, which was holding steady at six feet across. There were some red Wackle lumps in the room as well, they were guarding the hole and its invisible ropes from the Kluppers. I tried to use my third eye to peer into hyperspace. But, I now realized, my third eye was gone. I wasn't augmented anymore. I'd grown back into three dimensions, but no further. I couldn't see past the surface of the hole.

Even so, I knew what to do. I fanned out the branches of my grolly root as best I could. The root felt much heavier than it looked. Being four-dimensional, the tendrils twisted and changed shape in an uncanny way. With some effort, I pitched the root towards the center of the black ball of Nothing. It sank in, disappearing from view.

For a moment there were no results. The volleyball cop and the lady cop screwed up their courage and grabbed my arms. Had all my recent efforts been in vain? My frantic trip through Dronia to Okbra to Pointland to Lineland to Flat Matthewsboro back to Spaceland—had it all been for nothing? Sooner or later the ropes tying off the hole would likely give, either on their own or because the Kluppers might return in force to cut them. And then Spaceland would be gone. I noticed an odd change in my feelings towards that last thought. Even if Spaceland did disappear, even if I died— the Presence would persist. At some deep level, everything was all right, no matter what.

I took a slow deep breath. A filigree of purple appeared upon the surface of the menacing black ball, splitting and branching till it covered every last bit. With a sudden lurch, the ball began to shrink. Faster and faster it drew together, collapsing in on itself. And then *pop*, the hole was gone. Space was well again.

The Wackle globs flowed and swirled as the Wackle tendrils drew back from Klupdom into Dronia. The fleeting shapes of a dozen cheering red devils flickered through the air so fast that you couldn't be sure you saw them. The onlookers gasped and then the Wackles, too, were gone. You would have thought everyone would have started cheering. But it was like they were too freaked to realize what I'd just done for them. I'd saved the universe, and did I get any praise? Far from it. Nobody even wanted to look at me. I was a troublemaker getting busted.

"We've got a complaint against you, sir," said the mustached cop at my side. The lady cop was holding my hands behind my back and fastening plastic cuffs onto them.

"Here's a blanket," said the fat-necked boss cop, stepping forward. "Cover him up."

"Let's go out to the car now, sir," said the lady cop as she wrapped the blanket around my shoulders, draping it to cover my nakedness. She turned me around and began frog-marching me towards the coffee-shop door.

"Stop," I cried. "What's the charge? I just saved the universe!"

"You can talk about it when they book you," said the roll-necked cop. "Move along quietly, sir, or the officers will have to use force. And, frankly sir, we'd rather not. It's an ugly thing to beat a naked man."

"Let me talk to my wife!" I protested. "Jena! Tell them it's okay!"

"Clement made a complaint about our office getting trashed," Jena told me. "I think he told them you set off a bomb. He's really mad at you. We're having an emergency meeting at MeYou at seven o'clock. I'll tell him to lighten up." She wasn't looking me in the eye.

"What else?" I demanded.

"We have to go now, sir," said the lady cop, giving me another shove. "You can make a phone call from downtown."

"What else?" I yelled at Jena. Where was her gratitude?

"It's Spazz," whispered Jena before the cops could push her away. "He and Clement think we should turn the Mophones back on. For the IPO."

"No!" I screamed. Sure, at some level everything was fundamentally all right, but there was no reason to let some freaking greedheads throw away our whole universe for an IPO! "You have to stop them, Jena!"

She shrugged and maybe shook her head, and then I was in the back of the cop car, cuffed and naked in a blanket, looking out the window with the raindrops running down it. The mustached cop and the lady cop sat in front. Just to make everything the more desperate and stressful, guess who I saw walking up to Jena as the cop car pulled away? Sante the gangster, wearing an Oakland Raiders jacket, a black pork-pie hat and wraparound shades. With all the cops around, Jena took it casually. Sante said something to her and she pointed me out to him. He did a double take, then started laughing, his teeth white against his tan skin. He wagged his finger at me as we drove away. Then gave me a thumbs up like he was going to help me. Right.

The cops headed towards the freeway; they were taking me to San Jose. Right before the on-ramp, we passed the former Mophone headquarters. The building had completely collapsed to a wet, muddy heap of sheetrock and splintered wood. There were some TV reporters in the yard, filming. A Channel 2 van was just heading past us towards the Los Perros Coffee Roasting. They were too late for the real story. I wondered if it was ever going to be told.

It was rush hour. The freeway was gridlocked and the rain was gusting down. The cops didn't talk to me and I didn't talk to them. We were moving towards San Jose at a crawl, even with the driver blinking his lights and burping his siren. I was kind of happy for the chance to rest. What a mind-boggling trip it had been.

I flashed back to the image of naked Tulip in my bed. In some ways the high point of the day. I wondered if Tulip had gotten over thinking I was a Satanist. I hadn't realized she was quite that superstitious. Well, if she thought the Mophones were the devil's work, maybe she'd fight Clement's plan to turn them on. Or would she? After all, she'd been planning to spend today shopping for a

Mercedes. She'd be home at her sister's by now, a family-sized curry cooking on the stove. Maybe they had the TV going, and Tulip was seeing the collapsed Mophone building on the news right now. She'd be wondering if I was okay, maybe worrying about me. She'd called me her dear sweet Joe. Did I have any chance of a relationship with her? Worth a try.

If nothing else, hooking up with Tulip would be a good way of stopping myself from drifting back to Jena. Tulip could be like a Loplop to gnaw the ingrown feelings for Jena out of my flesh. If that's what I really wanted. I thought of Loplop and pumpkin-faced Jacqui trying to feed me to their anemone Mother. And then Kangy the cuttlefish saving me and growing a fake Jena to talk to me inside her mouth. Man oh man, the stuff I'd seen today!

But I was mad at Jena again. What was that number she'd pulled at the Roasting just now? First of all, no thanks or praise, and then she'd been shaking her head when I asked her to stop Spazz—and then she'd pointed me out to Sante? Bitch. Well, maybe she hadn't been shaking her head. I shouldn't always be so fast to turn against Jena. Maybe it had been more of a worried, who-knows-type shrug. And maybe Jena had been right to make sure Sante saw me being hauled off in cuffs. Give the guy a little comradely sympathy for me. Help him like grasp that Joe Cube wasn't carrying around a million bucks in pocket change for the first bullying cheeseball who asked for it. That smile and thumbs-up Sante had given me, what had that been about? Somehow I had the feeling Sante wasn't really going to try and do anything to Jena. In any case, she'd be smart enough to hang with the cops till he was gone.

I turned my thoughts to higher things. To Drabk, and the way we'd climbed that endlessly dimensional vine to Okbra. To the Presence. I tried to bring back the state of mind I'd been in, that feeling of being One with the essence of the Cosmos. Inching along the freeway in handcuffs, I couldn't quite get it back. For that

matter, I was finding it hard to even imagine hyperspace. I'd had
the fourth dimension in my mind for these last two months, what
with my third eye sticking vout into the All to peer vinn at our
world, and me able to see the insides and outsides of everything all
the time. But now that was gone. I could remember the feelings,
and some isolated images, but I couldn't put them together into a
four-dimensional whole. Vinn and vout—where were they?

Even though there was a Kevlar window between the front and
back seats of the cop car, I could clearly hear the staticky messages
crackling over the cops' radio. There was some kind of accident up
ahead. The driver took this as excuse to turn on his siren and swing
into the breakdown lane. We were still only halfway to San Jose.
At slack time on a good traffic day, you could drive to Jose from
Los Perros in fifteen minutes. But we'd already been on the road
for half an hour. The rain still pouring down. Californians had no
clue about how to drive in rough weather. Even this cop wasn't
doing too good a job; I could feel our car fishtailing. Of course if
I said anything he'd probably Taze me or club me. It occurred to
me that I was sick of Californians. Deep down, I didn't really like
it here. In an odd kind of way, being in Flat Matthewsboro had
made me miss Colorado.

We maneuvered our way around the accident, and then the traffic
lightened up a little. I could see the stubby office buildings of San
Jose with an airplane gliding over them for a landing. Seen from
the side like this, you couldn't see the plane's wings. It looked like
a silver pod, settling down like a saucer. That got me to thinking
about the Kluppers. It was kind of a miracle they hadn't stopped
me from fixing the hole in space. If they'd really come after the
Wackles in force, they could easily have driven them away. It must
have been only Momo's family and their grolly guards behind the
plot to destroy Spaceland.

If Spazz and Treed didn't turn the Mophones back on, everything might be okay. It was hard to believe they were even considering doing something so reckless. Like oil companies who wouldn't admit there was such a thing as global warming. But more so, much more. Surely Jena would be able to tell them how crazy their idea was. The hole of Nothing had almost swallowed her, for God's sake. Had she really shaken her head when I'd asked her to stop them?

Oh well. I slumped back into the seat. If I leaned on my shoulder instead of onto my cuffed hands, it was pretty comfortable. My body felt better than it had in a long time. Not only was I no longer four-dimensional, I wasn't hooked on grolly anymore. I was light instead of heavy. Slack instead of tight. Content instead of needy. The Presence was everywhere.

We splashed through the wet, gritty dusk and pulled up at the central San Jose jail, a six-story concrete building on First Street near Route 880 and the airport. It was ugly here; the planes were screaming past overhead. My mood had darkened again. You save the freakin' universe and they haul you off to jail?

A TV crew had gotten there before us; they shot footage of me being taken out of the car. It was live for the six o'clock news, and my two cops walked extra slow to get some camera time. I could hear the newswoman talking as we approached. She was trim, heavily made-up, Vietnamese. She had the perfect sprightly California accent, with each word chirped and bitten-off just so. It was like you were listening to juicy high-school gossip.

"Coming towards us now is suspected bomber Joe Cube. Apparently distraught over his job termination from the high-tech communications start-up, Mophone Inc., Cube has been accused of blowing up his workplace. The blast leveled the Mophone headquarters in Los Perros, temporarily closing down the Mophone service. A low-speed police chase ended at the Los Perros Coffee Roasting Company less than an hour ago. Reports of damage to the popular coffee shop are still coming in. How does this affect the

wildly popular new Mophone? Mophone founder Clement Treed
promises to restore service in twenty-four hours." She held a mi-
crophone towards me. "Are you guilty, Mr. Cube?"

The cameraman had me in his sights. This was my chance to
warn the public. "Whatever you do, don't turn your Mophones
back on," I said, talking fast before the cops could pull me away.
"They made a hole in space. I fixed it. Arresting me was a big
mistake. I'm a hero. I saved the universe!"

The newswoman's eyes stared past me at the camera. "Suspected
Mophone bomber Joe Cube," she repeated. "Live from the San Jose
Courthouse. More on this breaking story on the ten o'clock news.
This is Thu Nguyen. Back to you, Jim."

Up on the fourth story of the jail, they booked me on the bomb-
ing charges. A lady detective read me my rights and asked me to
make a statement. I declined. While I'd been talking to the TV
camera, I'd been able to step outside of myself a little bit and hear
how I sounded, all naked and wrapped in a blanket. I sounded like
I was nuts. Anything I put in a statement would just make things
worse. My best bet was to wait for Clement to drop the charges.
Or for the facts to sort themselves out. And to try, if I could, to
get out on bail. The detective said a magistrate would set the
amount when he came in after his supper. She had one of her
assistants dig up some homeless-shelter-type free clothes for me,
mustard-colored polyester bell-bottoms and a Judas Priest heavy
metal sweatshirt, both of them too small. And some running shoes
that were too big.

Before they locked me up, I got a chance to make my phone
call. It was a pay phone on the wall, with a bored guard standing
a few feet away watching me. No need to call Jena, she knew where
I was. And calling the Mophone lawyer Stu Koblenz seemed like a
waste of time. Clement Treed was paying Stu's bills; he wasn't going
to help me unless Clement told him too. The detective said I'd get

a second call to find a bail bondsman after the magistrate came in. So, what the hell, I called Tulip. Maybe she was the one to talk sense to Spazz.

"Joe!?" she exclaimed. "I just saw you on TV! Are you out of jail so fast?"

"I'm still in here, Tulip. You're my one call. I had to talk to you."

"To me?" Her voice cracked. "About what?"

"You left in such a hurry this morning," I said. "Holding up your cross at me. Get real, Tulip. Those things you saw weren't devils, they were Wackles. Hyperdimensional aliens who happen to be red. They're no more Satanic than house plants."

"I've been wondering all day," said Tulip. "Maybe I did jump to some conclusions. Like I've told you, I've seen a lot of supernatural horror movies. You're not really evil at all, are you, Joe?"

"Science and business, Tulip," I said. "That's all it ever was. Until today anyway. Today—I guess you could say I saw God. There's no Devil out there at all, Tulip. Just the Presence. Infinite Love."

"I'd like to think that too, Joe. But when I woke up this morning there was blood in your room, and shooting and yelling. I don't want to see that kind of thing ever again. It was like my worst dream. How could you make that happen right after—right after—"

"I didn't make it happen," I began. But then I thought back. It was my need for grolly that had brought Momo into the room in the first place.

"Let's go, homie," said the guard next to me. "We're on a schedule here. Gotta take your picture, process you in. We don't got all night."

I ignored him and pressed the phone tighter against my ear. "It won't happen again," I told Tulip. "I'm done with all that. I'd like to see you when I get out."

"When's that going to be?" asked Tulip. "They said you blew up the house."

"The Wackles knocked it down," I said. "You saw how hyper they were. They were fighting with these other four-dimensional aliens. Momo and her family. Kluppers."

The guard tapped me on the shoulder.

"I'm not done," I cried. "Please!"

The guard chuckled and shook his head. "You doin' phone sex, or what?" But he stepped back for another minute.

"You're going to the meeting at MeYou, right?" I said to Tulip.

"Yeah," she said. "I have to leave in a few minutes. Ordinarily I'd hate to drive down there, but I've got my new Mercedes. It's green. Why did you turn off the Mophones? Are you trying to ruin our IPO?"

"The antenna crystals, they were a trick. Momo gave them to us so that we'd make a hole in space. The Mophones send out more energy than they take in. I told Spazz, but I don't think he believes me. And Clement doesn't even want to think about anything that'll hurt the IPO."

Tulip was quiet for a few seconds, putting the pieces together. "Conservation of energy," she said. "I should have thought of that. How soon would the Mophones make the vacuum decay?"

"It already happened," I said. "This afternoon at the Coffee Roasting. There was a hole in space. I got there just in time. I went into hyperspace and tied it closed and then I found a patch. Jena saw it happen, but I don't know if she really gets it."

"She never does," said Tulip contemptuously.

"She's smarter than me," I said protectively. "Anyway, can you make sure that Clement and Spazz don't turn the Mophones on again?"

"I'll think about it," said Tulip. "You realize that if Mophone stays dark, we don't get the IPO. Maybe the hole in space at the

Roasting was a fluke. I bet Jena talks on her phone more than anyone else alive. I'll go to the meeting and we'll do some calculations and—"

The guard reached over my shoulder and pushed down the cradle of the phone. I wanted to yell at him, but I didn't. I'm dumb, but I'm not that dumb.

14

The Empress

So they processed me in and I was alone in my cell. There weren't any windows, just flickering fluorescent lighting from some fixtures in the hall. The cell had a cot and a sink-toilet. Lots of initials and curses and gang signs were scratched into the shiny beige paint. I'd glimpsed a few of the other inmates on my way down the cellblock hall. An anxious gang kid, a sullen drunk, and two maniacal tweakers. Inside my cell, I couldn't see them anymore; there were concrete walls in between us. The cells were kind of like stable stalls.

I lay back on the cot, resting. There was a line of pain on my forearm. When I rolled back my shirt to look, I saw a singed dark line. A welt from the fire in Flatland? Too weird. I rolled my sleeve back down and thought about dimensions.

I was fantasizing how easy it would be to get out of here if I were still augmented. Even though I couldn't visualize hyperspace anymore, I remembered all the things it had let me do. If I were augmented, I could go vinn to Dronia, flap through hyperspace to the sidewalk outside the jail, and pop back into Spaceland. The cops had taken my wallet when they processed me into the jail so, if I were augmented, before leaving the jail area, I'd first flap over next to the valuables locker and reach in, just like when I'd robbed the bank. And then I'd be out on First Street with my wallet. There was a light-rail line that went by here and up North First Street to where a bunch of high-techs like MeYou had their offices in tilt-ups, which were one-story buildings made by hauling in prefabricated concrete walls, laying them flat, and then using cranes to tilt the walls up to the vertical. I'd been to MeYou a couple of times. It was right next to one of the light-rail stops, at Component Drive, if you can believe anyone would ever give a street such a dumbass name. Easy name to remember though. Like a sore place on your gum that your tongue keeps wanting to touch. Yeah, if I were augmented, I'd get my wallet, flap out of here and catch the light-rail to Component Drive. But I wasn't augmented.

Even though I'd lost my watch to the bubble of Nothing, I'd noticed the time when they were booking me. It was a little after seven by now. Jena, Tulip, Spazz, and Clement Treed were at MeYou, deciding what to do. It was crazy for me to be locked up! I went to the barred door of my cell and shook it.

"I've gotta get out!" I hollered. "I've got a meeting to go to!"

"Meeting," echoed one of the tweakers, his voice a fueled whoop. "I've got a meeeeting!"

"Yuppie meeting!" screeched the second tweaker. "Intel down two, Apple down three, Cisco down four, crank up five, Scotty up forty-nine!" The last two meant speed and PCP, which were the big tweaker favorites. Cheap, dirty drugs.

"Forty-niner!" echoed the first tweaker. "I got a meeeeting."

"Shaddup!" hollered the drunk. "Shaddup or I'll kill you bastards. Shaddup shaddup shaddup."

The guards didn't respond to any of this. They had cameras on the ceiling to watch us with. There was no reason for them to come in here. Me yelling was no different than a dog barking in the pound.

I sat down on my cot, staring intently into the empty center of my cell, hoping to see something, ignoring the way my polyester pants cut into my waist.

"Can you hear me, Drabk?" I whispered. "Wackles? Can you hear me? We have to stop them from turning on the Mophones!"

And now, yes, there was a flicker in the air. But it wasn't Drabk and it wasn't a Wackle. It was something green and leathery and wrinkled—a hand, two hands, a face—it was the Empress of Klupdom. She gazed at me and spread her knobby old hands as if in friendship. Her neck was wrapped in a muff that was pinned with a large and intricate gem. Crimson sleeves led part-way from her hands to her invisible body.

"Greetings, Joe Cube," she said in her deep, furry voice. "You did well to patch the hole in Spaceland. Momo's family has been punished."

"It was the crystals Momo gave us," I said quietly. "They weaken the fabric of our space."

"I understand," said the Empress. "Before his end, Voule confessed that he and Momo supplied you with tens of thousands of them."

"That's right," I said. "We packaged them into Mophones. They're turned off now, but they may yet be turned back on."

"I know this," said the Empress. "Even now my troops are watching the meeting of your wife, your lover, your rival, and your master. My marshal relays the news to me as we speak. If I say the word, he will pluck the hearts from all four. Does this sit well with you?"

"No!" I yelped. "There has to be another way."

"You are ingenious, Joe Cube, you are blessed with a Spacelander's low cunning. So I have come to ask you this: What is the other way?"

I was temporarily too panicked to think. "We won't turn the Mophones on again," I babbled. "We'll recall them. Don't hurt Jena. We'll get all the Mophones back."

"From what my marshal is overhearing at the meeting, this is not your partners' intent," said the Empress. "It's hard work to unsow seeds cast to the wind."

"Can't you fix things from vout there? Reach down and take all the Mophones away?"

"Perhaps we could, in time. But if your partners act so unwisely, then of time there is none. It does seem best the four should die. Only then may we have the leisure to hunt down each and every crystal."

"Don't kill Jena!" I cried, so loud that the other inmates could hear me.

"Kill Jena!" cackled one of the tweakers. "Dude! Kill Jena good!"

"Beam me up, Scotty," shrieked the other tweaker. "Beam me and Jena up!"

"Shaddup shaddup shaddup," went the drunk.

There was madness all around me, but once again I felt the Presence. All grew still and calm. I had plenty of time. I thought of Dronia and of her cliffs. I thought of tens of thousands of tentacles, each of them splitting at the tip. "The Wackles," I said to the Empress in a low tone. "They can do it! There's so many of them!" And here came the best part of my thought. "The antenna crystals stick vinn to the Wackle's side of Spaceland, Empress. It'll be easy for the Wackles to find the crystals. They can feel them like stubble. Like rough spots. They look like little squares sticking out of Spaceland. Call the Wackles, Empress, bring one of them here to talk with us."

"I am to bawl an invitation into Dronia?" said the Empress, her hands curling in a gesture of disdain. "I shall entreat vermin?"

"I'd gladly do it," I said. "But I'm not augmented anymore."

"And a good thing too," said the Empress, making no move to call anyone. "You became a menace."

"Call the Wackles, Empress, and all our problems will be solved."

She paused, as if listening to an invisible voice. "My marshal tells me that your wife, lover, rival and boss are now very nearly agreed upon reactivating the Mophones. What folly. Yes yes, quite soon they must die."

"Call the Wackles!"

"You are most importunate, you flat man."

"Please. You owe me this much. After the way Momo used me."

"Oh, very well."

The Empress's shape shifted as she pushed her head and arms further through Spaceland and into Dronia. A lump of her midsection remained in my cell, swathed in crimson hypercloth whose fuzzy nap was thick in some spots and thin in others. Soon she rocked back into the cell—and a Wackle appeared beside her, a full-sized red devil, just like all the times before.

"True Empress of Klupdom?" he said, reaching out to touch the Empress's green hand. "First contact hi."

I glanced up at the camera in the ceiling outside the cell, wondering if the guards would come. Maybe they were napping. I still had the feeling of plenty of time.

"You have to eliminate our antenna crystals," I told the Wackle. "Those things that made the hole before." The Wackle's expression was blank, as in complete incomprehension. "The hole in Spaceland?" I coaxed.

"Memory bank withdraw for who you I do now," said the Wackle. "Replay. Our smeel is one. The hole in space that Drabk fixed. Long long ago this was."

"Two *hours* ago," I hissed. "Listen to me. There's thirty thousand antenna crystals scattered around Spaceland. Each of them projects a millimeter vinn to Dronia. Find them all and pull them out. Hurry! Get all the Wackles on the cliff working together and you can do it in like two or three minutes."

"Why for?"

"So there's no more holes in Spaceland, pinhead! So the grolly doesn't grow all over your cliffs!"

The Empress made a disapproving click. "I can express this more eloquently in our higher tongue." She leaned vinn and made some noises, a series of four-dimensional sounds. Most of her speech went off into Dronia, but some of the sound leaked into Spaceland.

My stomach vibrated so much I almost crapped my pants. One of the tubes in the hall lights went out. The tweakers went ape. The drunk started bellowing.

There were footsteps and the rattling of bolts. The guard was coming. I turned to warn my visitors—but they were gone. And, as it turned out, I never saw them again.

"The yuppie's goin' dark side!" one of the tweakers called to the guard. "The dude is five-oh-one, he's doin' voices like *wuuuuh*."

"No man, he's like *grooooh*, not *wuuuuh*," interrupted the other tweaker.

"You in a condition, homes?" the guard asked me, peering into my cell.

"I'm fine," I said. "Have they set my bail yet?"

"That's it," said the guard, jingling his keys. "You got a bail bondsman came in for you too. Any luck, you're not comin' back to this cell, so don't leave nothin'." He paid no attention to the tweakers or to the darkened light.

Out at the booking desk was the same detective I'd talked to before. She was a round-faced Hispanic woman with deep wrinkles in her forehead and around her mouth. Kind-looking, but serious and worldly-wise. "The bomb squad's report just came in from the house on Los Perros Boulevard," she told me. "No evidence of explosives. Can I see your hands?"

I held out my hands; she turned them over and felt my fingers and my palms. "Soft," she said. I noticed she had a little tape recorder going. "Desk-worker hands. No blisters or calluses. Unlikely that Mr. Cube destroyed the house manually." She glanced up, regarding me with clear, hazel eyes. "Is Clement Treed angry with you?"

"Yes," I said. "We had a disagreement on a strategy decision."

"Dot-commers," said the detective, like she was talking about termites. Guys like me were making people like her pay a lot more in rent. She'd probably been born in San Jose. "I asked the magistrate to set your bail at ten thousand dollars," she said. "That's low. Tell your bondsman to do the paperwork and you can go."

Who was this bondsman they kept talking about? And then he appeared from around a corner of the hallway, carrying a manila folder in his hand. It was Sante Machado, his oily hair shiny in the fluorescent lights. He'd taken his hat and shades off, but he was still wearing his Raiders jacket. His lips parted in a wolfish grin.

"Hey Joe," he said, stepping forward. "I got your bond all set for you." He laid the papers down on a corner of the detective's desk. "Put your John Hancock here and here and here and you're sprung. You need a ride anywhere when we get out?"

"I don't think so," I said. "I'll take the light rail."

The loan fee for the ten thousand dollar bond was eight hundred bucks. Good enough. I was eager for freedom, and I didn't ask Sante any questions in front of the detective. In a couple of minutes we were outside the jail, standing under the overhang with the rain coming down past it. It was dark; the raindrops sparkled in the pink sodium lights of the parking lot.

"C'mon and ride in my car," urged Sante.

"Gimme a break, man." Sante was still taller than me, but I

wasn't scared of him anymore. "You wanted to stick an ice-pick in my guts. I'm not going anywhere with you. And listen up, man, either Mophone's about to go outta business or the world's coming to an end. Either way you don't get your million."

"I got fired from Nero's on accounta you and that million," said Sante, his eyebrows slanting mournfully down. "You owe me. That's why I bailed you out, to remind you to do me a favor."

"Since when are you a bail bondsman? And what exactly do you want?" Eager as I was to get up to MeYou, I needed to finish my business with Sante.

"I grew up here in San Ho," said Sante. "I was a bondsman before I worked in Vegas. When the rubber hits the road, Sante collects the dough."

"Except for my million," I said, unwisely rubbing it in. Sante clenched his teeth and a muscle moved in the side of his jaw. He stared out at the rain for a minute, then glared down at me.

"Don't disrespect me, Joe. I don't wanna do nothin' we'll regret. Let's say the million is water under the dam. Me and Nero's is through. I'm lookin' for a new career, you know what I'm sayin'? This high-tech jazz, I wanna get in on it. Stock options, like that. You gotta find me a job at this new outfit of yours. Mophone. Deal?" He stuck out his hand.

This man I'd been so frightened of—he was asking me for help. He was a son of San Jose, briefly gone wrong in Vegas, now come home to partake in his fair city's boom. My heart opened to him. I shook his hand.

"I'll do my best," I said. "But like I said, there's a good chance Mophone's going out of business. Not to mention the fact that our big money guy fired me and got me arrested. Clement Treed."

"Ah, that's bull," said Sante. "You got an in. You can do it, Joe. Make me head of Security. Or Personnel. I'm good with people." Over on First Street, a train had just gone by. It would be twenty minutes till the next one. "C'mon and let me give you a ride," said Sante, seeing me notice the train. "We're friends now, Joe."

"You got a gun on you?" I asked.

"Always," said Sante. "I'm licensed, bro."

"Let me hold it while we ride," I said. "Just so I'm sure you don't start in on me with the ice-pick."

"My man," said Sante, handing me his pistol butt-first. "We're all learning. Grow or die, hey? C'mon, my car's over here. You're goin' up to MeYou on North First, right? Your little hottie told me. Jena Bonk. Hey Joe, how'd you duck that ice-pick anyway? I never seen anything like it. Was that like some Eastern marital art?"

"Yeah," I said, getting into Sante's black Lincoln. "I learned it from Momo."

"That woman I tried to shoot? Where's she at now?" He wheeled out of the lot and sped north on First Street.

"Rubbed out by a rival gang," I said, trying to sound tough. "The Wackles." The gun felt weird in my lap. I put it in Sante's glove compartment. "From now on we're strictly nonviolent, you dig?"

"That's cool," said Sante. "High-tech, right Joe?"

The reflected traffic lights made long red and green stripes in the rain-wet streets. I imagined hyperspace Wackle tendrils feeling all over our planet like an anemone opening a mussel. Tried to visualize it and make it true. If only it was working. If only Jena was okay. My heart beat faster and faster as we approached MeYou.

I couldn't help but notice that Jena was the one I was worried about the most. Face it, I was stuck on her. Earlier today she'd talked about seeing a marriage counselor. I'd blown her off; I'd been high on grolly and wrapped up in all my resentments. I'd been wrong. I needed to let go a little bit. Learn to stop thinking that every slight change in Jena's happiness was about me. Learn that Jena was a separate person.

"It's up there on the right," I told Sante. There were a few lights in the MeYou tilt-up, and four cars in the lot. Jena's Beetle, the old beater Chevy pickup that Spazz drove in the rain, Clement's limo, and Tulip's new green Mercedes. I strained to see if there were any signs of movement behind the lit windows. "Park in the shadows," I told Sante, thinking ahead to the worst that might happen.

"Okay if I come in too?" said Sante as he stopped the car. "I'll give you backup in case Treed cracks wise. Anyway, if these guys gonna hire me, they may as well see my face."

"Yeah, fine," I said, opening my door. "One thing, though, Sante, there's a chance—" The words caught in my throat. "There's a chance they'll all be dead."

"Them Wackles you talked about? That was a Wackle who phoned me about how you cheated at cards that time, right? Some kind of overexcited nut. I thought you said high-tech wasn't rough. Hell Joe, we're right back in *my* world now." Sante leaned across me and took his gun out of the glove compartment, sliding it inside his jacket. "Anyone's iced in there, we get out fast, right? We don't wanna take no fall. And, Joe—use your handkerchief to open the door. Never leave no prints on a crime scene."

We hustled across the shiny wet parking lot. The MeYou door was unlocked. We went inside. Quiet, quiet, quiet, nothing but computer hums. And then, to my joy, I heard a shout. Spazz yelling, "Goddammit!"

"High five," I said to Sante, and we slapped palms.

A minute later we were down the hall and in a lab room with a conference table, two computers, and four people in the pink of health. Jena, Tulip, Spazz and Clement Treed.

Jena looked over at me, her lips red, her narrow brown eyes bright and excited. I ran across the room and hugged her. "I love you," I told her. "I was worried I'd never see you again. I love you, Jena. And I'm off grolly. Let's try and work things out."

"Um . . . okay," she said, her voice going way high on the second word. And then she giggled. "Why not? I love you, too, Joe. We've been acting so dumb. I've been worried sick. Look at my nails." Indeed, they were chewed right down to the quick. I kissed them.

Tulip looked over at us and mimed a vomiting face, sticking out her long pink tongue and shaking her head so hard that her earrings bounced around. And then she started laughing like she was glad to have me off her case. She was standing next to Spazz, who was, as usual, sitting at a computer. There was that same picture of Bettie Page on the screen that Spazz had guided me to earlier that afternoon.

"Just in time, Joe," said Spazz, his silver nose-ring glinting in the light. "Did you screw up my website or something? Do you remember exactly what you typed in? I keep trying to turn the Mophones on—but they're not working right. And mine's broken too now." He gestured at half a dozen Mophones lying next to the computer. "I can't get anything but standard PacBell service on any of them." He turned and began typing into his dialog box.

"Don't!" I cried, letting go of Jena. "Are you crazy? Didn't Jena tell you about the hole?"

"They didn't think it would happen again," said Jena. "They said they'd have to do more research to see if there's really a problem—but meanwhile it would be okay to run the Mophones. It's good you're finally here, Joe. Sante promised he'd get you out of jail, so I came straight to the meeting. But these greedheads won't listen to me."

I started around the conference table towards Spazz. Clement Treed stepped in my way. "What do you think you're doing here?" he demanded, looking down at me in my too-tight Judas Priest sweatshirt and mustard-colored polyester flares. "Dressed like that? I fired you this afternoon. This is a private company meeting. I'll call Security if you don't leave." His angry big mouth seemed to wrap halfway around his head.

"I'm Security," said Sante, staring Clement right in the eye. "I say Joe stays." Something about the way he said this made Clement back off and sit down.

"You can't fire him anyway, Clement," said Tulip. "You only have forty percent of the stock. Jena, Spazz, Joe, and me, we own the other sixty. And we say Joe stays. Right guys?"

"Of course," said Jena. "I was about to say the same thing. There's no Mophone without Joe."

"Hell yeah," said Spazz. "Now come here and show me how you broke my site, Joe. We gotta get those Mophones happening again or there's not gonna be an IPO. And don't start jabbering about holes in space again, 'cause Tulip and I just ran a simulation in Mathematica and the chances of another breakdown before IPO next week are like—"

"Hold on," I said and picked up one of the Mophones on the table. I pried its case open and looked inside. Yes. The antenna crystal was gone. I checked another and another. "Thank you, Wackles!" I shouted. "Praise the Empress of Klupdom! Hail Drabk the Sharak of Okbra!"

My Jena was the first to get the picture. "All the crystals are gone?" she said. "Too cool. We're safe!"

Clement rushed across the room and unlocked a cabinet. I guess he'd stored a bunch of the extra antenna crystals in it. But there was nothing inside.

"The Mophones are all empty?" he demanded.

"Not empty," I said. "It's just that the antenna crystals are gone. They're still perfectly good cell phones."

"In other words we no longer have a product," said Clement. He sighed and shook his head, looking more tired than angry. He'd been playing this particular game as hard as he could, and now the game was over. "Write-off time," he added.

"How about you drop those charges against Joe?" put in Sante.

"Sure, sure," said Clement. "That was just to keep him out of this meeting. No hard feelings, Joe?"

"I wonder if I should press false arrest charges," I said. Clement looked unimpressed. No way I could beat a titan of the industry at legal saber-rattling. "How about this," I said. "Can you give Sante here a job? He'd like to be the head of Mophone Security."

"What Mophone?" said Clement. "Did you leave your brain in the jail, Joe? Without the antenna crystal, we don't have a product."

Tulip and Spazz had been whispering as we talked, and now Tulip spoke up. "What about our peer-to-peer architecture?" she said. "The Motalk operating system. That's new. So, yeah, our bandwidth's gone, but for short ranges a Mophone works without having to use a server."

"The messages can hopscotch from one Mophone to the next without using PacBell," said Spazz. "Distributed telecommunications. You buy a Mophone and, if you only use it locally, you never have to pay another cell-phone bill."

"I'm listening," said Clement Treed, straightening up in his chair.

"We've got an incredible publicity buzz," said Jena. "We could still turn this around. We come out and admit that the Mophone high-bandwidth feature is gone for now, hint that it might come back someday, offer a rebate to our customers, and keep selling the heck out of what we have. A cell phone with no cell-phone company. And of course we keep after-marketing the PacBell service as an add-on."

So that's what we did. And Sante got his job. Mophone did OK for a little while. None of us but Clement actually made a whole million out of it, but Jena and I came close enough.

We two stayed another year in California and finally we got so tight with each other that we wanted to have babies. We wanted a bigger house first, but the money from Mophone—which folded around then—wasn't enough for the Bay Area.

So we cashed in our condo for double what we paid, headed to Arizona, and bought a good house on a nice piece of land in the red rocks not too far from Sedona. Jena and I started up a public relations and ad agency business. We have some high-tech customers and we do some pro bono for the tribes. We've got a little girl now. She's great; Jena and I call her the Empress.

Jena still likes business meetings. Me, a lot of the time I watch over our Empress and work from home. I get off on the vibe from those weather-carved red rocks. The way they morph from one shape to another with the changing light—it's almost higher dimensional.

One thing about Sedona, it's a place where I can tell people about my experiences, and they'll listen. Now and then I even teach a workshop. People can't get enough of hearing about Drabk the Sharak of Okbra. And when I talk about him, I get a good feeling like Drabk hears me.

One of these days I might even write a book.